TUATH

SUSANNE CARPENTER

Tuath by Susanne Carpenter

First published in Ireland, in 2024, under the imprint of Aos Sí

ISBN: 978-1-3999-4870-8

A CIP catalogue record for this book is available from
the National Library

Typesetting, page design and layout by
DocumentsandManuscripts.com

Cover design by Karolina Smorczewska

Published with the assistance of The Manuscript Publisher, publishing solutions for the digital age – www.TheManuscriptPublisher.com

Tuath

Dedication

To my children, Toni, Chris and Beck, for your support and enthusiasm.

To my parents, May and Brendan, for your constant love and guidance.

Contents

The Legend of the Tuatha Dé Danann

In the middle years, Ireland was ruled by Eochaid Mac Eirc, the High King who reigned over the five provinces of Ireland from his palace in Tara. His queen and consort was the beloved Tailtiu.

Eochaid's people, the Fir Bolg, farmed the land and were skilled craftsmen and great athletes. Having spent centuries enslaved in Greece, the Fir Bolg resembled dwellers of the Mediterranean, short and muscular with dark eyes and hair. They were clever and artistic people, who lived in a just and fair society.

Eochaid enforced the laws of his people, and the five kingdoms of Ireland were at peace. The country was filled with music and poetry, and the people were content. He reigned for more than ten years and was known to his people as the perfect king, but Eochaid had a premonition – a dream that foretold the arrival of invaders to Ireland and the ascendance of a magical fair folk to rule the island. He was so disturbed by the dream that he prepared an army to defend the Fir Bolg from the invaders.

After ruling as High King for more than a decade, his dream came true. It is said that 300 flying ships landed on Sliabh an Iarainn (the Iron Mountain) in County Leitrim, amidst a summer storm of fire and lightning.

Hailing from the great cities of Falias, Findias, Murias and Gorias (all in the northern islands of the world) the tribe of the Goddess Anu were known as the Tuatha Dé Danann. Each city was a centre of learning, and the Tuatha Dé Danann were skilled in medicine, agriculture, warfare, technology, arts and language. They carried with them great treasures: the Claíomh Solais (the Sword of Light); Lugh's Spear, also known as the Sleg Assail; the Coire Daghda, known as Daghda's Cauldron or the Cauldron of Plenty, and the Stone of Destiny (the Lia Fail). Each treasure was magical, having great power.

Described as fallen angels, the Tuatha Dé Danann were godlike in appearance, tall, strong, blonde and red haired, fair skinned and with blue and green eyes. They were youthful, determined and fiercely loyal to their gods.

In the ancient chronicle, the *Book of Invasion*, it was said that:

The truth is not known, beneath the sky of stars,
Whether they were of Heaven or Earth.

Led by Nuada and the sister warriors – the Morrigan, Badb and Macha – the thousands strong Tuatha Dé Danann landed in what is now Leitrim, whether by fault or design. What was clear however, is that they did not intend to leave. The Tuatha Dé Danann burnt their fleet of flying vessels, and the smoke that rose caused the sky to darken for three days. It is said that the Morrigan, aided by her sisters, Badb and Macha, announced their arrival in Ireland using enchanted rain clouds and clouds of fog that rained blood and fire.

The Fir Bolg were, at first, frightened by the magical Tuatha Dé Danann and then incensed by the prospect of ceding a portion of Ireland to them. An attempt at détente was made to the Fir Bolg. Nuada choosing Bres to represent the Tuatha Dé Danann.

The Tuatha Dé Danann petitioned the King of the Fir Bolg for grant of land and a peaceful settlement. Negotiations were led by the Fir Bolg's great champion, Sreng. Despite the peaceful overtures of Nuada and Bres, Eochaid Mac Eirc was still haunted by his premonition of war. He did not want to give up part of his island kingdom to invaders, albeit magical ones. The negotiations stalled. Eochaid Mac Eirc had a stark choice – make peace or go to war. He chose to fight. He was confident that his army's skill could match or exceed those of the newcomers.

Eochaid engaged the rules of battle of the time. A period of truce allowed both sides to prepare for the great battle, the first Battle of Moytura (Cath Maighe Tuireadh). In Gaelic, Maighe Tuireadh means 'plain' and the Tuatha Dé Danann and Fir Bolg fought a great battle on the plains of Connaught, near the village of Cong in what now is Mayo (Cath Maighe Tuireadh Cunga).

The battle raged for four days and great warriors engaged in single combat. As night fell, each army retreated to their camps, to be treated by herbs and healing baths and to plan the following day's forays. Despite Eochaid's confidence, it was soon clear that his army was no match for the Tuatha Dé Danann, who were stronger, fitter and possessed superior weapons. Eochaid deemed that it was time for the champions to meet.

The Tuatha Dé Danann's leader, the High King Nuada, fought the Fir Bolg champion Sreng in single combat. The battle raged for hours, with neither champion ceding ground, but Nuada was distracted for a moment. In that moment, with one terrific blow from his sword, Sreng sliced through Nuada's shield and arm, leaving him mortally wounded but still alive. This did not bode well for the Fir Bolg. Despite disabling the High King of the Tuatha Dé Danann, their army was fresh and well equipped. Nuada's defeat spurred them on to claim victory.

The Tuatha Dé Danann warriors were overcome with battle lust, decimating the Fir Bolg, leaving a river of blood on the plain of battle. Eochaid Mac Eirc and his diminished army were exhausted, weak and in need of water. They were chased across Connaught, eventually reaching Ballysadare Bay in County Sligo where they numbered 300 warriors, their numbers diminished from the thousands that were called to battle on the plains of Mayo.

Despite pleas from the Fir Bolg to finish the fight with single combat, the Tuatha Dé Danann stopped the battle; they had no appetite for further blood loss. The Tuatha Dé Danann had never intended to go to war. When they arrived, they had hoped to live peacefully with the Fir Bolg. They ceased hostilities, and they ceded a province to the Fir Bolg, that they might live peaceably with the Tuatha Dé Danann. The Fir Bolg chose the province of Connaught, then known as Cóiced Ol nEchmacht, and it was there that the remnants of the Fir Bolg retreated.

The Tuatha Dé Danann were sovereigns of Ireland. Nuada survived the battle and Dian Cécht, the physician of the Tuatha Dé Danann, fashioned for him an arm of silver, more powerful and agile than flesh and blood.

The victory of the Tuatha Dé Danann on the rugged North Atlantic coast changed forever the history of Ireland. Peace and prosperity reigned under their protection.

The Future

Chapter 1

The Lifeboat Project

Nemed sat at the lead of the conference table, sipping a glass of tepid water. Ogma, the Chief Engineer, sat to his right side. Brigid, the Chief Medical Officer, to his left.

The room in which they sat was lit with dim bulbs and although still early in the day, the windows brought no light. Outside, the world was dark, shrouded in dense smog. The atmosphere in the room was as heavy as the air outside. The scent of the seashore drifted in from the rugged Scottish shoreline, mixing with the scents of decay and fear.

"Any news from America?" Brigid asked, over the drone of ancient air conditioning. Her blonde hair hung in a long plait over her shoulder. Her cornflower-blue eyes burned with concern.

Manannan, the Chief of Defence, shook his head grimly.

"The Canadians are on the offensive. The last we heard, they hit an enclave in Montana. There has been no word since. If even we could raise a signal, the Americans are out of battery power. The last storm destroyed their wind generators. They are in their end game. There's no food left and no means of growing it. Without power, their grow houses will have frozen. The ambient daytime temperature is about minus ten degrees centigrade."

Manannan had seen his fair share of warfare, but the situation in America was hopeless. There would be no winners. His handsome face was set in a scowl, and he looked around the room.

"How many were left?" said Nemed.

Nemed was Irish, but his allegiances lay elsewhere. Now past his prime, his skin had taken on a grey pallor, and his pale-blue eyes resembled those of a wolf. His position as leader of the Council of Europe, the de facto President of what was left of humanity, was volatile, and his attitude reflected that.

"Between the Canadians and the Americans, there were thought to be about ten thousand," Ogma murmured.

They all knew that within days, the last of the North American population would be wiped out completely. Another civilisation wiped away to join the Africans, Asians and the population of the southern hemisphere.

Aengus, the Chief Botanist, arrived late as usual, covered in dirt. He grabbed a glass of water and sat. He had spent much of the day experimenting in the horticulture labs. He pushed his fringe of curly red hair from his eyes.

"What have I missed?" he said.

"Nothing much," Nemed sighed. "No news from America."

Aengus nodded and thought for a moment.

"We'll have to write them off then. On a more practical note, is there any way to access their seed bank?"

"Have a little respect Aengus," said Brigid.

Aengus stared at her and grimaced. His green eyes burned.

"I am truly sorry that things in America have come to this, but I won't apologise for putting our people first. There are more than 30,000 people in seven communities scattered across Europe, depending on this Council to keep them alive. I'm not cruel, just blunt. Getting at the American seed bank could give us access to food crops that could significantly up our calorie intake."

Aengus had a point. Without sunlight, plants could not be grown naturally and even if sunlight were available, the ground in which to grow the plants was toxic – and had been for more than a century. The technology and power needed to grow any plant was immense. The earth needed to be sanitised and purified before it could accept seeds. Constant power was needed for lighting and to heat the grow houses. As most plant species had died out, maintaining the genetic integrity of food crops was of high importance.

Although every Council member acknowledged that Aengus was right, his bluntness sounded cold and callous. This was not representative of Aengus's personality. He normally had a sunny outlook and held the community in high regard, but constant failure was wearing him thin. Aengus had been under severe pressure to up food production, and this pressure had changed him. He had an ongoing argument with Brigid over priorities, and her presence in the room aggravated him. Ironically, their goals were the same – maintaining the health of what was left of mankind. Regardless of their shared goals and passion, they fought like cat and dog.

Manannan intervened to keep the fight from escalating. It was ironic, Manannan thought, that a soldier was the one keeping the peace. He positioned himself in the eye line of Aengus and Brigid and stared at them in turn.

Council members shuffled into the room slowly. They looked exhausted and defeated. They took their assigned places quietly, too preoccupied to waste time on greetings or small talk. When the last of the delegates took their places, Nemed banged a ceremonial gavel to bring the meeting into session. The assembled Council quieted and seemed ready to begin.

While they represented what was left of government in Europe, they did not look or act like honed politicians. Their threadbare layers of clothing were dirty and frayed. To a man, they looked malnourished and pale. They had each made the arduous journey to the edge of Scotland, by sea and foot, and the toll taken by the journey was evident. Their meeting was being held in a settlement on the Skye coast, near what was once the ancient city of Glasgow.

Seisyll sat at the end of the table, looking tired and drawn. Her black hair was shot through with grey, and her eyes looked tired. She rarely smiled: she had little to smile about.

"Can we get on with things, please? I'm ready to give the report from Camry."

Nemed nodded. As chairman of the Council, he was, in effect, the President of the European enclaves and was seated at the head of the table. Representatives from each of the seven remaining European settlements were present, as were elected ministers and specialists. The representatives from each of the seven enclaves acknowledged Nemed. Alongside Seisyll from Snowdonia in Wales, Aleric from Flensburg, Jens from Odense, Brian from Connaught, Toran from the Highlands of Scotland, Vale from Brittany and Isolde from Cornwall voiced their attendance. Originally, the Council of Europe hosted representatives from all over Europe but one by one, the settlements in Italy, Spain, Switzerland, Croatia, Finland, Poland and Serbia had withered and died.

Seisyll went first. The Welsh collective was known as Yr Wyddfa and housed 6,000 souls. Spread out over the mountainous region of Snowdonia in Wales, the community was struggling.

"The good news is that we had fourteen hours of sunlight last month. It's the highest we've had in the last five years. Unfortunately, it hasn't helped the situation. We're struggling with food production. We can grow carrots, beetroot, turnips and potatoes pretty well, but we can't seem to grow anything else. We've tried growing fruit and high protein crops, but our energy infrastructure can't generate enough power to keep the plants alive. Our seed store is empty."

Despite the genetic modifications made to the populace, humans needed vitamins and minerals that just were not available through the food chain. The lack of vitamin C and other nutrients were exacerbating other health problems. Every Welsh citizen was suffering from a form of malnutrition.

Seisyll explained that outbreaks of typhus and cholera had occurred over the last month, and there was a noted increase in the suicide rate among the older populous. Alarmingly, the birth rate continued to decline. Schools had been closed in an effort to conserve energy but in reality, there were no children to attend them.

Seisyll complained about the lack of support from other Council members – a barb directed firmly at the Irish contingent. No one commented, but Brian knew that everyone around the table was staring at him. Ogma, Manannan, Aengus and Brigid, all Irish, did their best not to make eye contact.

When Seisyll finished, Aleric, the blonde representative from the German community of Flensburg on the Baltic Coast took over.

"As Seisyll said, we're seeing much the same. We have seen a marginal increase in sunlight, and our research team found a number of fish in the Flensburg Fjord. Not edible of course: contamination levels are much too high. Our big problem is that people have given up. Our suicide rate is growing too, as is the rate of serious aggression. No babies either."

Whether as a result of too much genetic intervention or the effects of poor nutrition and a poisonous environment, the birth rate had been dropping for the past century. The slow decline had rapidly accelerated in the past decade. As colony after colony succumbed to famine, disease or war, the people that were left were in despair. The constant darkness, inability to move around outside without protective equipment and the stress of trying to survive were taking their toll.

Heads around the table nodded. Aleric nodded at Jens from Denmark to give his report. Jens gave a resigned nod to Nemed. "The same," he said.

The community in Odense was under severe pressure. The new battery system installed the previous year was working well, but food production was still low. The constant pressure to survive had worn the people down, and the easy-going Danes were fraying at the edges.

Toran, the redhead from Scotland, tried to inject some humour, letting the others know that a team from the highlands had succeeded in making alcohol from potatoes. Not to drink, but as a source of vehicle fuel. Despite his efforts to make light of the situation, the bottom line was that the society in Scotland was struggling with food, power and morale.

Vale, his dark eyes hooded, added further problems to the list. The technology used to generate heat and power in the French enclave was failing. The original design was 20th century and had a lifespan of 30 years at maximum. The equipment had been in use for over 200 years, and the community had long ago run out of replacement parts. It was a matter of time, he said, until the system failed completely. Vale looked to the Irish contingent but said nothing.

Isolde, from the enclave in Cornwall gave an equally damning report.

The room, uncomfortable at the start of the meeting, was now unbearable for Brian and for the other native Irish there. Manannan, Ogma, Brigid and Aengus made eye contact with Brian. His unspoken message was clear – don't be baited; say nothing. He understood their feelings of shame, but there was nothing that he could do to change them. The Irish men and woman kept quiet; their eyes focussed on the floor. They would not disclose information or be forced into action by the other enclaves.

The Irish settlement, unlike the others, was not only coping but thriving. This was the source of the communal shame. Geologists had found a pure source of water, putting an end to the complex filtration of polluted rain. This discovery had allowed the settlement to focus on food production to astonishing effect. Wind energy was still producing power, the strong Atlantic winds generating more than enough for the 18,000 people who called Cong their home. In the last few years, the marine biologists in Mayo had succeeded in growing freshwater mussels, first on an experimental basis but over the last year, expanding production. The same team had succeeded in breeding plankton to produce dietary Omega 3 supplements and protein. Overall, the Irish community was healthier and stronger than their European counterparts.

The Irish also had access to ancient technology sites, most of which were damaged but operating well enough for their engineers to continue research and development. Before the cataclysm, Ireland had been a global development centre for big pharma and medical devices. The technology they used had been recoverable for the most part. It was the Irish who had developed the genetic technology that the enclaves now took for granted. Without the enhancements, the tribes could not have survived the severe weather and lack of nutrition that affected survivors of the cataclysm.

Less well known was the material science and physics research undertaken at Irish universities during the 21st century. Ground-breaking research in the mid-21st century had led to the development of new technologies, using quantum electrodynamics and high-powered lasers. While the science behind the devices was known and understood in the academic community of the time, only the Irish had successfully demonstrated the application of the technology. More than a century on, the Irish were now applying the technology to the environment, creating new power storage devices, better energy distribution systems and new horticultural maturation technology. The defensive capabilities of the devices created in the Mayo labs were astonishing.

The Irish had historically had a reputation as peacemakers and humanitarians. Despite this, the settlement was reticent about sharing with its neighbours. There had been incidents in the recent past that sat badly with them, and the community felt that it had been taken advantage of. The people of Cong accepted that they needed to provide assistance to the others, but giving assistance did not mean giving away all of their resources, both in terms of materials and expertise. However, that was what they had been asked to do. Requests for help quickly became demands, and there was a high level of expectation amongst the other European sites that the Irish would fix their problems for them. While the community of Cong was willing to contribute to the enclaves, taking responsibility for their food, power and technology was a different matter. The attitude of the enclaves did little to help matters. The Irish were the subject of constant pillory and though initially the comments were accepted light-heartedly, they were now a festering thorn.

Over the past decade their stores of equipment had been rifled by the other settlements. The demands for top ups of food and medicines were too much for the Irish to bear. Medical supplies proved to be the catalyst for a change of attitude. The settlement in Cong had been forced to hand over a supply of antibiotics to the French and Welsh enclaves, despite pleas from the populace to retain them for use in Ireland. When the Irish initially refused, they were threatened with force from the Council of Europe. The medicine was handed over but not without repercussions. The Irish Council, made up of representatives of the residents of the Mayo settlement, voted to leave the Council of Europe. They justly felt that membership meant all take and no give. No one could remember an incident where membership had benefitted the settlement.

Brian, Ogma, Brigid, Aengus and Manannan had convinced the Irish Government to delay such a critical action, vowing to use their influence at the Council to Ireland's benefit. They could not, however, stop the Irish Council from taking measures to protect themselves against invasive actions threatened by their European neighbours.

Suspicious of the information available to the Council, the Irish Government was convinced that they were being spied upon. The Irish Defence Forces mounted a counter espionage programme, which had weeded out more than twenty native and foreign informers. Once they were expelled from the settlement in Cong, the settlement was closed to non-natives. Leaving the colony required permission. Fortifications had been built around the entire colony, and the walls were manned by trained soldiers, day and night.

The Council of Europe was well aware of the political climate in the west of Ireland and felt first-hand the changes to security protocols. Returning informants made it clear that there was a definite anti-European feeling amongst the residents. The Irish people felt that they should be the priority, not their European neighbours. They believed that charity begins at home. There was no problem with sharing once the Irish needs were met. As a charitable people, the surplus should go to Europe, they decided, but that was the crux of the problem. Each of the enclaves expected to supersede the needs of the local population. They felt, rightly or wrongly, that they were the most deserving of resources available and that the Irish should wait their turn.

Europe relied on the good will of Ireland for technology, food and medicine. The cut off of information and reduction in support was viewed by the Europeans as anti-social and by the British as racist attacks, meaning that the Irish were treated with further suspicion and hostility. Around the conference table, the murmurs of discontent were growing. In the decades past, when a community was in trouble, others would support it. It seemed that all of the communities, except the Irish, were in trouble, and Ireland was not backing down.

Nemed nodded at Brian to take the floor. Brian shook his head in response. He would not give a report at this session. Nemed was, at first, relieved that Brian had kept his council. Telling the others of Irish successes would be like waving a red rag to a bull, but he also knew that staying quiet would appear to the Enclave leaders as if the Irish were hiding something.

Nemed called order.

"Well, are there any additional statements," he asked.

Aleric shot his arm up and stood.

"I formally request that the Council revisit the Lifeboat project. I know that this has been raised at meetings in the past, but the situation has never been as critical as it is now. Within the next decade, the only people alive in Europe will be in Ireland. The rest of us will be forgotten memories if the Irish have their way. The only hope we have of surviving as a people is the Lifeboat plan."

Roars of support came from around the table. Nemed banged his gavel to quiet the room.

"Aleric, with respect, the Lifeboat plan was dropped more than a century ago. Even back then, the elders realised that we didn't have the resources that were needed to make it success," Nemed said.

Toran shot to his feet, his passion clearly evident.

"A hundred years ago, there were more than half a million people still alive. There were animal species alive then that are now extinct. They could afford to abandon the project. We can't."

Toran's face reddened. He was unaccustomed to public speaking.

"In ten to twenty years, we will be completely wiped out. Our birth rate is non-existent. We can't feed our people, and our power systems are unreliable at best. The Irish belittle us and hoard away what is rightfully ours. How long do you think it will be before we go the way of the Americans?"

Jens shouted his agreement, as did Vale.

Nemed dropped his head. The desperation of the Council members was clear. The Irish were being blamed for the enclaves' situation and he wished, fervently, that they had not shown up. The fate of the enclaves could very well be decided based on the reaction of Brian and the rest of the Irish representatives. All the same, Toran was correct. The colonies could not continue on like this. Very soon, Yr Wyddfa would succumb, and it would be followed by closely by Cornwall and Brittany.

Nemed hung his head and tried to make sense of the situation.

205 years ago, the world had been a different place. The surviving photographs showed a global society, rich and well fed. Although global warming was a major concern, there had been significant strides forward in environmental protection. World leaders had tackled the food supply, and malnutrition and starvation were a thing of the past. Green energy sources replaced fossil fuels, pollution was more or less eliminated in the developed world, and there was peace. For the most part, people had access to education and were content.

Then, the cataclysm happened and since then, there had been a spiral of decay. The cataclysm was a mega-colossal volcanic eruption in Iceland that caused a chain reaction in seismic activity throughout the northern hemisphere. It was followed by a deep, global volcanic winter. Millions had died during the eruptions that destroyed Iceland and decimated Europe and North America. The tsunamis and earthquakes that followed the movement of the Earth's plates had inflicted further mortal damage. Billions had died in the aftermath of the natural disaster on a global scale, as temperatures dropped and food species disappeared during that deep volcanic winter. Without sunlight plants died within weeks. Animals lasted a little longer but eventually, fauna followed flora into extinction. The soil was contaminated; the seas were poisonous; weather patterns changed and when it rained, it rained acid.

In the immediate aftermath, while the tectonic plates on which the continents stood rearranged themselves, a new reality dawned. The world had taken for granted access to good sanitation, hygiene and clean water. These basics were wiped away. Diseases like cholera, typhoid, tuberculosis and covid ran rampant through refugee camps of displaced people, killing off the old, the weak and the very young.

For the first decade after the catastrophe, food was available in the form of processed foods, dried foods and emergency rations but eventually, these ran out, along with medicines and stocks of fuel. Desperation led to war. Many of those who survived the aftermath of the cataclysm succumbed to war and genocide. Survivors formed colonies: hundreds of colonies across Europe, thousands across Russia, Asia, the Americas, Africa and Australasia. Over the two hundred years that followed, the colonies followed the plants and animals into extinction – first in Africa, then South America. The Asians, Russians, Australians and Europeans held on but the colonies dwindled away until, to the Council's knowledge, only the seven European colonies remained.

Nemed raised his head and grimaced. He personally believed that interest in the Lifeboat project was misplaced. The settlements would be better placed to focus their energies on survival rather than a pipe dream. The Lifeboat project was seen as a panacea for all of the problems the colonies faced although, in reality, it had a very low probability of success.

Nemed banged the table with his left hand.

"We'll dedicate tomorrow's session to a review of the Lifeboat project. We need to give Ogma and his team of engineers some time to prepare the data."

With that, he rose, and the Council members took their cue to return to their lodgings for another uncomfortable night.

In the years following the cataclysm, the human race began a slow recovery. In the aftermath of a global environmental disaster, countries ravaged by disease, starvation and war took stock of what was left. Governments reformed and international cooperation of a kind resumed, albeit at a much lower level than previously.

What was left of the world powers came together to form an alliance to repair the damage wrought, but it as quickly evident that no amount of science or engineering could make reparations to the earth. There was simply no way to reverse the atmospheric damage, and nothing could stop the inevitable extinction of plants and animals. The only thing to be done was to slow the decline. Even that was a massive challenge.

It was American and Russian physicists who first raised the idea of time travel, based on relativity and motion time dilation. They were ignored and ridiculed but eventually, people started to listen when they demonstrated the technology they had developed using Einstein's calculations.

30 years after the cataclysm, the Europeans, Russians and Americans had combined their resources and began building a fleet of thirteen vessels, that collectively were known as the Lifeboat project. The location for the build was contentious but a midpoint, in a neutral country, was found – on the west coast of Ireland.

The premise was simple – return to a time before the cataclysm and bring technology to mitigate some of its worst effects. The volcanic events, tsunamis and seismic activity could not be stopped, but it was potentially possible to use advanced technology to clear the volcanic winter that would follow.

The Lifeboat project was a long-term effort however and after 50 years, when the project was in its final stages, the Russian and American governments had withdrawn support. Both governments could no longer use valuable resources to complete the project when disease and starvation were threatening their existence. They could and would not divert power to semiconductor processing plants when people were freezing to death. They could not justify the data centre power usage when there was no power to fuel the vast tracts of farmland under glass. As the final assembly was being completed on the fleet, the Americans and Russians had simply left. Their accommodation and supplies were abandoned, leaving the base in Cong a ghost town.

With only the Europeans left, the project had floundered – no European government would take responsibility for it. The ships lay abandoned on the plain of Moytura, straddling the border of Mayo and Galway in the west of Ireland. The base of operations in Cong, County Mayo became home to refugees from all over Ireland, and the Cong Enclave was born.

Ogma huddled in the corner of their shared dormitory with Brian, Manannan, Aengus and Brigid.

"What the hell are we going to do?" Manannan asked.

Brian shrugged. He wrapped his cloak tightly around him.

"The colonies are desperate. Let Nemed tell them what it would take to get the fleet up and running, and they'll back down."

Manannan shrugged his powerful shoulders.

"And what if they don't back down? What then?" Ogma asked.

Brigid put her arm around his shoulder.

"We're getting ahead of ourselves. Let's just wait and see what happens," she whispered.

When Ogma had taken the position with the Council, he had not anticipated that he would have to make a choice between his own people and the people of Europe, but the Lifeboat project had changed that. He had secretly worked on the Lifeboat project for several years, painstakingly restoring the battered fleet. The hostility between the Irish and the rest of Europe had forced him to make a choice long ago. He could see things from a European standpoint, but he was Irish. He would always choose the best interests of his own people, his family, and it was in his people's interest to make their home secure and to provide the best care they could for their own community.

Now he was facing a perfect storm. The reignited interest in the Lifeboat project meant that his clandestine work on the fleet would become public. Everyone would know about the resources that had been invested in getting the fleet operational again. The people and equipment were Irish, but Ogma knew that Europe would say that resources had been used that should rightfully have gone to them. He would be branded a traitor and if things progressed and the Europeans demanded to inspect the fleet, matters would quickly unravel. Cong could not deny the fact that the sun shone through clear skies every day and that people were healthy and fertile.

He knew that Brigid was trying to comfort him, but she was not in the picture – how could she know what had happened with the fleet? Only a select few knew the real status of the thirteen ships. He felt physically sick, dreading what was about to come out. He knew that the Council would view him as a turncoat and a spy and when the truth was revealed, he would be lucky to escape Scotland with his life. Hell, any Irishman would be lucky to make it to the coast.

He could not change the fact that the meeting would happen; he could only prepare for it as best he could. He wanted to run and hide.

Nemed called the session to order, impatient to begin.

Lights in the conference room had been dimmed, but Ogma could still see Toran, Jens, Vale and the others clearly. He had all of the historic data of record to hand and had prepared material about the Lifeboat project, which did not include the current status of the fleet.

Nemed cleared his throat.

"Let's talk about the Lifeboat project then. Ogma, pull the file up on screen."

Ogma, one of the few engineers who was adept at using computer technology, shared a video file on the ancient interactive screen. The video, nearly 150 years old, showed images of the thirteen vessels of the fleet. As the statistics rolled across the screen, the Council members reminded themselves of the details of the project.

The Lifeboat was the project name for a fleet of spacecraft that had been designed to travel through time. Using relativity theory, scientists had a devised a way to bend space-time and travel backwards. Thirteen ships, representing every major technological breakthrough made in the 21st century, were designed to take a crew to the 1970s – just over 60 years before the cataclysm. In the intervening 60 years, the crews and specialists would work with the engineers of the time, to lead advances in technology that would not stop the cataclysm but would mitigate its effects soon after it happened. This would reduce the disastrous environmental impact and save animal and plant species. The effect would be to make the future habitable for generations to come.

The plan was to clean the skies of volcanic debris and gases, and reverse the global volcanic winter before it had a chance to take a firm hold. The 3,000 strong crew was to have comprised of the best and brightest scientists, electronics experts, theoretical and material physicists, ecologists, biologists and metallurgists. Arriving well before the cataclysm, the scientists would work alongside their contemporaries, accelerating advances in technology, particularly in material sciences and physics, allowing them to develop technology that could clear the deep ash clouds that would surround the Earth and allow sunlight to penetrate the blanket of volcanic debris. Genetic technology would be made available to the people of the time, to alleviate the worst health effects of the disaster, and guarantee food and water availability.

The plan was not to stop the cataclysm – because no technology could tame Mother Nature. The movement of the tectonic plates could not be stopped. Although the plan would not alleviate the suffering of the survivors and the loss of life in the immediate aftermath, it was thought that sending back a warning of what was to come, and directing society to mitigate the disaster, would guarantee the survival of future generations.

The video presentation ended and the room was once again in semi darkness. Nemed raised his head and growled.

"What you saw on the screen was made nearly 150 years ago. The ships looked pristine. The fleet has been sitting exposed to the elements, with no maintenance, for over one hundred years. It could take years just to dig it out of the morass that has grown over it. No one has opened a door of a ship in over 90 years, let alone tried to power one up."

Nemed stood and paced at the top of the room. Ogma was grateful for the darkness: no one could see the look of shame on his face.

"Do you really think that with a combined population of 30,000 souls, some starving, and without access to the original detailed designs and manufacturing equipment of the time, we could get the fleet operational? It's ridiculous," Nemed spat.

Ogma stared at the laptop screen. A part of him wanted to announce the deception. Another part of him wanted to flee in terror. He swallowed and looked shamefaced at Brian and Manannan. Manannan shook his head surreptitiously. Now was not the time to reveal what the Irish had done without the knowledge of the Council.

All eyes were on Nemed, the Council leader. He was building up a head of steam as he paced back and forward, his voice getting lower and more powerful with every word.

"And if we managed to get the fleet operational, how the hell would we man it? Each ship needs a crew of at least two hundred – that's nearly 3,000 people. That's without the experts to send back. They are all dead and buried, and their knowledge died with them."

Nemed paused to draw breath. He stared at each of the Council members in turn, his eyes lingering on Brian.

"Even back then it was understood that the likelihood of an experimental technology succeeding was tiny. They gave it a two or three per cent chance of success. Now you want to do it with no first-hand experience, no tools, no resources – you have lost you collective minds."

There was a collective murmur of dissent and then quiet. The Council was waiting for something.

Seisyll stood and walked to the top of the table. She straightened herself and took a deep breath. Vale and Toran nodded encouragement. Her earlier fatigue melted away, and she began to speak in a clear strong voice.

"You're right. It's a crazy idea, but it's the only hope left. If we send the crew and they die, then at least we will have tried. Stay or go, the crew will die anyway. Personally, if I'm going to go, I would prefer it to be fast rather than a slow death through chemical poisoning and starvation. The cataclysm opened Pandora's Box and when all of the human miseries escaped Pandora's Box, only hope was left. The hope of returning to the past and fixing this miserable existence is what keeps the settlements going. It's the hope of having real lives. Without hope, we'd be better off dead."

It was clear that the enclave representatives supported Seisyll's view. She took advantage of their cries of agreement and paused before continuing.

"Nemed, you are the chairman of this Council, but you are not a king. You don't have a right to dismiss us. This Council is ruled by a majority, and the majority have spoken. The Lifeboat project will go ahead."

Nemed took a deep breath and exhaled slowly. He smiled crookedly at her. They had been lovers in the distant past.

"And who exactly is going to manage this? You, Seisyll? Or maybe Vale or Jens? How are you going to accomplish this feat of engineering?"

Seisyll held her ground but did not reply. Isolde, the Cornish delegate, stood and walked with purpose to Seisyll's side.

"The ships are in Ireland. Ireland has the technology. They can manage it," said Isolde.

The room erupted with shouts of agreement. Brian's heart was now beating so strongly that he could feel it in his ears. He had no doubt that his friends in the room were feeling the same way. They were witnessing a coup. It was clear now that the other enclaves had planned this. His mind whirred as he tried to comprehend what this would mean to the settlement in Cong.

As he was thinking, Ogma, Manannan, Brigid and Aengus made their way to him, surrounding him like a Roman guard. Seisyll had overstepped the mark, Isolde had no right to order the Irish people to do anything.

Think Brian, his mind screamed. The Council did not have the authority to force an enclave to act, but he needed to be careful: Seisyll had widespread support. The whole meeting seemed to be baiting the Irish to say or do something that they might regret.

Brian spoke slowly and quietly. The impact of his statement was more powerful for it.

"How the hell do you expect us to get a fleet up and running? We're not magicians. This is jealousy and spite speaking. You don't have the physical or moral authority to order my people to do anything."

The reaction to Brian's statement was violent. Jens and Vale were on their feet, screaming insults at Brian. Toran was being physically being held back. Even the mild-tempered Isolde from Cornwall was visibly agitated.

Manannan brought his fist down hard on the table.

"Shut up!" he bellowed.

Manannan was a soldier and had the physique of a warrior. His size meant that when he spoke, he did so gently and quietly. When he shouted at the assembly, he projected menace. The group was startled, and silence prevailed. He had crossed the line from neutrality, and he was clearly siding with his home landers.

Anger and desperation crackled through the room like static electricity. Manannan looked at Brian and the other Irish members of the Council. It was clear that they would not back down but then, neither would their opposite numbers from the enclaves.

Nemed needed to diffuse the situation fast.

"Brian, we work together or we don't work at all."

Brian turned his head slowly towards Nemed.

"So, what you're saying is, we do what were told or we are kicked out of the Council?"

Seisyll, Toran, Vale, Jens, Aleric and Isolde were baying for blood. Before Nemed had a chance to answer, Brian answered for him.

"Fine, you already know what our answer is."

Nemed struggled to be heard over shouts of good riddance.

The spontaneous response of the other settlements had not been thought through. The leaders were reacting to the situation, rather than considering the consequences, and the consequences were severe. Even the Irish did not realise the extent to which the others depended on them. Nemed could not afford to let the Irish walk away. He banged the gavel until the room quietened.

"Brian, we don't want Ireland to leave the Council. We can work this out. As for the Lifeboat project. Ogma is our chief engineer. Ogma will evaluate the fleet and report to us next quarter."

Nemed's gaze settled on Ogma.

"When you report, we will make a decision on whether to proceed together. Then we can formulate a plan that fairly distributes the workload between each settlement."

Nemed was desperate, and the desperation spoke volumes. Brian hesitated and returned to his chair, bringing his cohort with him.

Nemed flustered on.

"In the meantime, each of you will send your three best people to Ireland. Ogma, that will give you our twenty best people to support you in your review. Lead the team, make your evaluation and report to us at the next Council meeting. Any Council member that does not support the team will lose their vote on the Council. Let me make myself clear – if full support is not given to Ogma, I will ensure the Lifeboat project is well and truly buried."

The enclave leaders looked around the table at each other. No one dared refuse.

As the meeting ended, Brian and the Irish contingent decided that a hasty retreat was needed. They had no intention of engaging in another argument, and Brian was in no mood for chit chat. Nor did they want to avail themselves of Scottish hospitality for another night. It was still early enough in the day for them to reach the coast and make the crossing back to Ireland.

Chapter 2

The Irish Enclave

Brian, Ogma, Manannan, Aengus and Brigid sat huddled in the open sailboat as it crossed the Strait of Moyle, the narrow channel linking the Irish Sea and North Atlantic. They had left from the Mull of Kintyre, the tip of the southwest Highlands of Scotland. The Irish coast would have been visible if there had been daylight, the journey was less than twenty miles to Torr Head in County Antrim.

The crew on the boat were Irish and were focussed on getting the boat safely to shore. The minister's conversations were of no interest to them.

"In two months, Nemed and the Council representatives will descend on us. How the hell are we going to explain what's happening in Cong?" Brigid whispered.

Brian pulled his long woollen cloak around his shoulders and sighed.

"We'll refuse them entry," he murmured.

Manannan growled at him.

"If they are refused entry, it will start a war. They will lose, but so will we. We'll end up with a battlefield, rather than a settlement, and to what end?"

The only sound to be heard was the slapping of the sea against the side of the boat.

"We'll keep them in a secure site and only let them see what we want them to see," Brian replied.

"It's going to be hard to hide pregnant women and children. Let alone hide the farms and workshops. Stick them in a secure site if you want to, but even in a secure site, you can't hide the fact that we have sunlight. Or are we going to stick them in a bunker? How will they inspect the fleet from there? We're screwed," Brigid replied.

Brigid's frantic diatribe brought on a fit of coughing. Despite wearing masks, the air quality was having an effect.

Aengus growled.

"We should have just walked away from the Council. Cong wants us out for good. We had the chance and didn't take it."

Manannan put his hand on Brigid's arm.

"Brigid, if they see the farms and the kids, well then they see them. As for the sunlight, what can they do? They haven't the wherewithal to attack us and if they do, we would destroy the technology we have before handing it over to them. They know that. We'll be perfectly safe. Our population is bigger than the rest of the colonies combined. We're better nourished and have weapons. We all knew that this would happen eventually. It was only a matter of time before day-long sunlight was reported back to Nemed."

Brigid was fretting.

"They'll know we lied to them."

Brian interrupted her.

"We never lied – withheld, yes but not lied. For the last 50 years, we shared everything with the colonies. It's only in the last few years that we copped ourselves on. Let's face it; they never shared anything with us in return. It's been a one-sided relationship from the get-go. We made choices years ago to prioritise research and education, and it paid off. We've only done exactly what they would have done – put our people first. And it's not exactly easy to manufacture lasers of the type needed to clear the atmosphere. We've had teams experimenting for years, and we only have three of them – and one of them is put aside for the fleet. We simply don't have enough raw materials to make more."

Brigid tried to interject, but Brian held ground.

"Anyway, the last time we reached out to help them, we had it thrown back in our faces. There is a reason we haven't shared with them, or have you forgotten? We have one working unit that clears limited sky over Mayo. We have one spare one in case the main unit breaks. That's it. There are no spare parts hidden in cupboards or on board the fleet. If we had more, then surely we would have used it by now, to double or quadruple the size of the colony?"

Ogma nodded in agreement.

"There is nothing they can do, Brigid. They can shout and swear; they can threaten us, but that's just empty words. We can survive without them, but I don't think they can survive without us. Even Seisyll is too smart to try to take sanctions against us, especially when we're keeping their grow houses powered, and we're providing them with food supplements. This is a storm in a teacup; you'll see."

Despite Brian's words, Brigid was still worried. In fact, they all were. Relations with the other enclaves had never been as fraught. This was in spite of the Irish settlement exporting nearly half of its food production to keep the people of Europe alive.

Three years previously, the research team, in what was loosely a university, called an *Ollscoil* by the Irish, developed new battery designs to better store wind energy. The Council were delighted to hear about the successful development – so happy in fact, that the Irish were tasked with replicating systems for each colony. The colonies refused to provide materials or engineers to assist and then expected the Irish team to deliver and install the systems for them. After two years of work, the team were browbeaten by the constant moans and complaints coming from the European colonies. Thing became so bad in Cong that engineers simply refused to travel overseas.

Despite complaints to the Council and directly to Nemed, the colonies were adamant that the Irish continue to provide them with resources and equipment. This was only one incident, in a string of many, that included access to water purification technology, genetic medicine and seed germination equipment. The superior attitude and sense of entitlement grated the Irish sensibilities. 800 years of servitude to the British Empire was not forgiven or forgotten by the Irish survivors, despite events. The Irish made a firm decision to keep their discoveries to themselves and prioritise their own survival. This had culminated in the closure of Cong to outsiders.

"What about the ships? What condition are they in?" Manannan asked.

Ogma panicked for a moment and then realised there was no point in keeping secrets from Manannan, Brigid and Aengus. They would find out the truth soon enough. He smiled.

"The ships are fine. We've had them powered up and running for the last eighteen months. My engineers have improved the power grid on all of the ships and have upgraded the solar arrays. It would take about six months to get them ready for launch, but the launch site is ready and so is the fuel. The big problem will be the crew."

Everyone, with the exception of Brian, was shocked.

"How the hell did you manage that?" Manannan asked. "I was in Cong and heard absolutely nothing about the fleet."

"The security we implemented is intense. Everything is compartmentalised. All information is shared on a need-to-know basis. I guess you didn't need to know."

Manannan grimaced.

"Holy shit! This will ruffle the Council's feathers."

Brigid nodded in agreement. The Council expected that the fleet would be in poor repair, damaged by the environment or simply worn down by decades of exposure to the elements. They certainly would not expect to find a pristine array of flight-ready spacecraft.

Brian, who was party to the condition of the fleet, shared more details.

"We have about one hundred engineers permanently assigned to the fleet and another 200 Ollscoil students that spend most of their time around the ships. The students are from mechanical and electrical engineering disciplines mainly, but there are some programmers, navigation specialists, metallurgists and mathematicians too. The Ollscoil has provided us with historians who specialise in 21st century culture and technology. They don't know a lot, but it's better than nothing. They have courses planned for the crew whenever we have one. We're training specialists across the board, but we would need a crew of 200 for each of the larger ships and between 100 and 120 for the smaller vessels. We've also been working on the equipment the fleet was to have brought with them. How do you think we got the lasers over Cong working in the first place?"

Aengus whistled.

"I didn't know we had that many students. I can't believe this was kept secret – not only from the Council but from our people too. What was the plan? Were we going to do this on our own?"

Ogma shook his head.

"We were waiting for an opportune moment to approach the Danes and the Germans. Even though we are the biggest settlement, we can't do this on our own. We had hoped that we would be able to work with Flensburg and Odense and bring in some of their people to crew the fleet, in exchange for environmental technology. It looks like that idea is dead now."

"Brian, we will still be expected to provide crew men though; won't we?" Brigid asked.

Brian shrugged his shoulders.

"Look, we don't know what is going to happen when the Council arrives. It might take them some time to get over the fact that we have light, food and children. It will take time for them to come to terms with what we've done with the fleet."

The others nodded in agreement.

"I really don't know what way they will want to go. They could try to take over, but the fleet is on our turf, and the real expertise is with our people, so they can't cut us out. They could walk away from the Lifeboat project, but that alienates the populations of each of the colonies. It's not in our interest for them to walk away. After all, we don't have enough skilled young people to make this happen on our own. Remember, the crew needs to be alive for at least 50 years after arrival, meaning we need to send young talented people. There's no point in sending experts over the age of 50: they'll be dead before technology is fully transferred. We also need to make sure that our population is stable. Sending everyone of breeding age will kill off the settlement. We need the enclaves to make up the crew."

Aengus, who had listened intently, interjected.

"They will be shaken by what they'll see at home. There will be repercussions. As for them providing the crew, we'll be sent novices with no experience, if they send anyone at all."

Huddled in the storm battered ship, shrouded in darkness, the ministers did their best to develop a plan to deal, firstly with the diplomatic nightmare that would surely arise when Council leaders and their best and brightest arrived in Cong; secondly, to deal with how they would ensure that they were not left to handle the project alone.

The little vessel docked at what should have been sunset. Brian led his team to a fleet of methane-powered vehicles, to begin the long trek back to the west of Ireland.

Chapter 3

The Council of Europe

Nemed paced up and down the grand hall in Cong, incandescent with rage. Ogma, Brigid, Aengus and Manannan stood before him. Each stood with straight back and a defiant air. Despite his ire, threats and warnings, the Irish had simply refused to explain why they had hidden their successes.

Nemed has singled out Aengus, Manannan, Brigid and Ogma for special treatment.

"As representatives of the Council of Europe, your first responsibility is to the people of Europe, not of this settlement. You have betrayed the Council and the enclaves. You deserve whatever punishment the Council deems fit."

Brian was elected to the Council by the people of Cong. He was not a political appointee like the others. Therefore, Nemed could not reprimand him, although Brian highly suspected that he was at the top of Nemed's hit list. Listening to the poison spewing from Nemed, Brian could not restrain himself any longer.

"You have some cheek speaking to my people like that, Nemed."

Nemed stopped pacing and stared directly at Brian.

"Your people? They are not your people Brian. They do not hold office in Ireland: they are Ministers of the Council of Europe. They have betrayed all of the people of Europe by their treasonous actions."

Brian's anger got the better of him.

"Unlike you, Nemed, they are loyal to the people that bore and raised them. They are Irish first and European second. Don't you dare accuse them of treason, because they are loyal to their country."

"Ogma has done more to help the colonies than anyone else I can think of. He has single-handedly kept their life-sustaining systems going. His team has set up a full manufacturing plant to produce spare parts, all of which are exported to Europe."

"Aengus has made sure that seed stores are maintained, even when the settlements go out of their way to not follow his advice on good horticultural management. You know that he and Brigid arrange the export of tonnes of fresh food to Europe on a daily basis, keeping the settlements fed."

"And as for Brigid, she has developed new genetic treatments, medicines and treatment protocols that are keeping people alive."

"Manannan has trained peacekeepers in every enclave and has made sure that they are properly equipped. He spends more than half of each year touring the enclaves, providing guidance on security. And now you want to punish them? You should be on your knees thanking them. And in all that, we have been supporting the enclaves. Can you name even one occasion when they helped us here in Cong?"

Brian approached Nemed and stopped when they were inches apart. Nemed was flustered and could not reply. Brian huffed and turned away from him.

"At the last meeting of the Thingmote, we struggled to name one incidence of any enclave coming to our assistance, unless it was in their interest to do so. You seem to think that you can constantly take from us without giving anything back. You're wrong, Nemed. We're done taking orders."

The screaming match had attracted attention. The noise alerted the Council members, and they quickly made their way to the Council chamber. Embassies from Scotland, Wales, Germany and Cornwall rushed to back Nemed. Seisyll and Toran, spoiling for a fight, pushed their way to the front of the melee.

"Making a few spare parts is one thing. Ogma is the Council of Europe's Head of Engineering. He knows the impact your laser devices could have on our quality of life. Why didn't he make them available to us? I demand that you provide us with lasers for Yr Wyddfa and the other enclaves," Seisyll spat.

Toran too was seething.

"Seisyll is right, Ogma was so busy fixing our antiquated power infrastructure that he failed to notice the advanced power grids operating right in front of him. Those power grids could improve our power efficiency by at least twenty per cent. They should have been deployed across all of the enclaves, not hoarded away by the Irish."

Toran took a deep breath and continued.

"And as for Brigid, she was so busy making antibiotics that she appears not to have noticed all the pregnant women wandering about and all the infants and children."

Toran pointed at Brigid, directing all the menace he possessed.

"What sort of doctor are you? You know that one of our biggest concerns is our low fertility and yet, you presided over a baby boom here. You should all be ashamed of yourselves. It's clear that the Irish have no morals and should never have been allowed into the Council in the first place."

Vale, the leader of the French settlement, went a step further.

"You do not deserve to be Council members. I vote for an immediate veto of Ireland, and I also vote to take offensive actions against the Cong settlement, in order to secure the laser technology and medical equipment necessary for our survival."

The enclave leaders, including Nemed, failed to comprehend that Brian and his colleagues were expecting this outburst. They had met with the Irish Council the night before, honouring the ancient parliament that was once held on a raised mound near Dublin Castle. It had been named the Thingmote.

The Thingmote was firm in its resolve. Unless the other enclaves stood on their own feet, no further sharing of technology was allowed. The growing settlement in Cong would no longer provide resources in the form of food, medicines or spare parts until the enclaves came to their senses. If the enclaves refused to see sense, the Thingmote would withdraw support for the Lifeboat project. While the enclaves would be given access to the fleet, the Irish would withdraw the technicians and engineers currently assigned, would do no further work on fleet maintenance and would not provide crews for the craft.

The Thingmote also issued an order for defensive measures to be taken immediately. All military personnel were placed on high alert. Defensive weapons were doubled at all access and egress points to the settlement. The military commanders were also given permission to deploy weaponised drones at strategic points on the coastline, in case of invasion.

Despite the shouts, threats and abuse directed at the Irish men and women, Brian was calm and collected.

"We have met with our own Council, the Thingmote, and their decision is final. We are not giving you the laser devices – there are no more, and we don't have the parts to make more. We are not giving you new power grids. You can have access to blueprints if and when you have the resources and personnel to make and maintain them yourselves. If you don't like it, then that's tough."

"If you fail to re-evaluate the situation, the Thingmote will withdraw from exporting food supplies until further notice."

"Nemed, you and your minions can do your worst but before you threaten the safety of our people again, be aware that any further threats will means the withdrawal of support for battery maintenance in all of the other colonies. And we will withdraw support for the Lifeboat project."

The room hushed. Brian stepped forward to face Vale, stopping within touching distance.

"Before you all leave, we would ask you to consider your threat of hostile action and your intention to steal what is rightfully ours. Look closely at the condition of our people and count them. They outnumber the rest of you combined. Look at our military personnel and their deployment. Pay close attention to the weapons they carry and the technology they use. If you still want to invade, bring it on. The Fianna are always up for a little sport."

Brian returned to his place beside Brigid. Nemed stared at him.

"You wouldn't dare go against the Council," he growled.

Brigid stepped forward.

"We have made our decision. You don't have any authority over us. Cong has been a crutch for the other colonies for too long."

Nemed did not reply. Instead, he consulted his advisors in hushed murmurs. He banged his gavel and requested that the Irish contingent leave the grand hall. Brian complied, and the Irish delegates left the room. When the door closed, the sound of screaming, cursing and smashing glass could be heard throughout the building.

"That went better than expected," Aengus whispered.

The Irish leaders headed outdoors into the bright sunshine. There was no point in standing around outside the door of the grand hall. They had the room under surveillance and if there were any startling breakthroughs, the Fianna would make sure that they were informed.

It took time for the Council of Europe to reach consensus.

The leaders of each conclave and their entourages were sequestered in the main guest house in the old town. To complete the inspection of the fleet, the delegations had to travel through the farmlands and forests surrounding the town, through clean air and sunlight. They had watched the harvesting of fruit with fascination. They were awed by the children running through the covered orchards of crimson apples. Each delegate now present in the grand hall went through the full range of emotions possible to them – anger and avarice for what had been achieved; reverence of the advances in technology that had made it possible; greed for the fruit of the labours of the people of Cong.

In the hours spent in self-inflicted isolation, the Council of Europe spoke no words of congratulation to the Irish, gave no thanks for the food and drink provided to them, showed no respect for the engineers who painstakingly explained the science behind the evident breakthroughs. The time in seclusion was spent trying to find a means to back away from the threats made without losing face. The Council needed to keep the tap of food and resources open, while showing distain for the Irish leaders.

By 10 pm, the Council adjourned and rescheduled for a further day of deliberations. The Irish were not invited to attend.

At the end of the second day, Seisyll from Snowdonia, Aleric from Flensburg, Jens from Odense, Toran from the Highlands of Scotland, Vale from Brittany and Isolde from Cornwall, with their entourages, took front row seats in the grand hall. Nemed, an Irishman by birth but a Scot by choice, was seated at a table on the small stage.

The Irish delegates were summoned to attend by Council guards.

Nemed formally made an announcement. By proclamation, the Council of Europe was in agreement over the future of the Lifeboat project.

Nemed stood, cleared his throat and read his proclamation aloud. His booming voice carried to the far corners of the grand hall. He once again implored the Irish to be forthcoming with assistance for the other colonies. He did not threaten but asked the Irish to cooperate, for the betterment of mankind. The proclamation was clearly influenced by the enclave leaders, but it was restrained. It was clear that the Council had realised that, for all that was seen by them, there were still things unseen – things that could threaten their continued existence. The Council had grudgingly accepted that they needed the Irish more than the Irish needed them.

The theme moved to the joint decision to revive the Lifeboat project. Nemed pronounced that the plan would go ahead, and each colony would support it, based on their size and resources. He was pleased to announce that the Irish would coordinate and lead the project, but the personnel to man the fleet would be provided by the enclaves.

After three uncomfortable hours in the grand hall, it was finally over. The delegations returned to their lodgings to prepare their departure.

Aengus stood at the entrance to the grand hall, the settlement's largest building that once housed a theatre, people watching. The delegations had arrived with scanty possessions but were leaving laden with food, clothing and portable technology. Their hubris did not stop them taking advantage of their hosts.

In the grand hall in Cong, the enclave leaders had signed a binding accord, leaving Nemed and Brian to sign last. Nemed read through the document for the third time. Brian stood at his shoulder. Brigid, Ogma and Manannan sat opposite him.

The decision on crew allocation had finally been made. Anu would be the fleet commander – she was not the Council's first choice, but she was a highly qualified engineer and had been instrumental in developing training materials for the crews that would be assigned in the coming months. The fact that she was Irish did not stand in her favour. However, Anu was known to be calm, measured and fair. With no other candidates coming close to her level of qualification, the Council had ratified her as mission commander. Breaking with Nemed's request to appoint a second-in-command from one of the enclaves, Anu insisted on appointing Nuada to the position. As second-in-command, he would captain the flagship of the fleet. While Anu was calm and measured, Nuada was impulsive, passionate and disrespectful. However, he was a brilliant tactician and pilot.

Responsibility for one ship had been allocated to each settlement, commensurate with the size of the settlement. That meant the six smaller vessels would be allocated to the enclaves. Each enclave, therefore, had to provide a minimum of 120 crewmen. Based on the size and capability of the Irish settlement, the balance of the fleet would be under Irish command. Ireland was crewing and provisioning seven ships, including the four largest vessels. The Irish captains were Nuada, Ogma, Morrigan and Daghda, with Manannan, Neit and Ethur (nicknamed MacCuill) taking lead on the smaller vessels.

Each colony would provide their own crews and captains, although they would be mixed across the fleet to ensure that expertise was shared. Each enclave would resource their ship as best they could. Captains and crews from each colony would report to the settlement in Ireland for intense training, prior to undertaking the mission. They would have five months in which to learn about the technology that they would bring with them to mitigate the volcanic winter, and to learn to fly the spacecraft.

Nemed went through each page of the plan, annotating here and there. When he finished, he looked around the room. He eyed Brian.

"You have six months from today to train the crews and commanders. You will be responsible for the provisioning of the ships, the fuelling of the ships and preparations for the launch. Despite the enclaves agreeing to provision their ships, they don't have any spare food or equipment and let's face it, if they did bring anything, you wouldn't want to use it anyway. The launch date is now concrete. It's in your hands."

"Remember, as part of this agreement, you will provide technical training and resources to enable the use of high-powered lasers for all of the enclaves. You will provide the training only – what they do after that is up to them."

With that, he signed the document and passed the pen to Brian.

Chapter 4

The Crews Assemble

The launch date provided the people of Cong with a reason for celebration. People consciously looked past the slim chance of success and chose to embrace the hope of a different world. The excitement was contagious and spread to the visitors who had arrived to witness the historic event. Despite more than seven hundred crewmen being supplied by the enclaves, 1400 men and women from Cong were attached to the fleet. Everyone in Cong was related to at least one crew member.

Crews from the colonies had arrived in dribs and drabs in the days after the signing of the accord and when they arrived, it took weeks to get them healthy enough to start training. The first act of the training team was to up their calorie and protein intake and then set them on a physical training regime, to build muscle tone. Their technical expertise was poor. Most had no experience of systems engineering or electronics. Programming skills were non-existent. For this reason, Ogma made had made sure that the technical training regime was strict and all encompassing.

Languages were a barrier – Goídelc was not an easy language to speak, although it was a close relation to the language of the Scots. The big difficulty was with the Welsh and Cornish crews, who refused to speak any language other than their own. It took the intervention of Nemed and the Council of Europe to make them see sense. The mission needed a common language and since the Irish were in charge of more than half the fleet, Goídelc was the natural choice.

Flight simulators worked around the clock to supplement navigation and flight training. Anu had gone as far as creating a buddy system, where crews from the enclaves partnered with their Irish equivalents, in hope to transfer expertise. The crews were brought to the point of being able to complete the basic tasks and pass simulated exercises but were still slower to respond than their Irish counterparts. In emergency simulations, their performance was mediocre. Despite the accomplishment of preparing the crew within months, Ogma was not confident in the skills of the enclave crews.

The launch site was on the plain of Moytura. The plain stretched twenty kilometres from the shore of Lough Corrib to the Cnoc Meadha fairy fort outside the derelict town of Tuam in County Galway. Days before the launch, viewing platforms had been erected, at a suitable distance, to seat the Council of Europe and local dignitaries. Areas had been cordoned off to allow the local citizens and permitted visitors from the enclaves to watch events at a safe distance.

Ogma joined the assembled crews of the *Gorias*, *Murias*, *Findias* and *Falias* – the four largest vessels of the fleet. The commanders of each ship came forward. They waited in line for the fleet commander, Anu, to address the crews.

When Anu left the makeshift podium, the crews joined their vessels. With the four largest vessels ready for departure, the remaining Irish crews boarded and prepared for launch. As the crews made their way to the launch site, the entire population of Mayo cheered. Not to be outdone, each enclave leader made a rousing speech, praising the endeavours of their countrymen. They too were cheered on their journey to their vessels.

The launches themselves were an anti-climax – the smaller vessels departing like airliners from an extended runway. The four largest vessels were launched vertically, providing the observers with an exciting display of fire and smoke and a noise so loud that it was felt rather than heard – the vibrations shaking the earth so much that standing still became nearly impossible. In an hour, it was over. All thirteen vessels had departed and were now in a synchronous orbit around the moon. From this staging point, the fleet would set formation, engage their engines and in hours, would travel back to the 1970s.

"What are the chances of success?" Nemed asked.

Brian answered calmly.

"We've done what we can and trained the colonists as best we can. We've given our best and brightest people to the project. As usual, the Council has expected us to make sacrifices over and above every other colony. There's nothing more we can do now but Nemed, after this, Cong is out of the Council. This exercise is proof of how the others think of us. We cannot continue to work with settlements who clearly despise us. It's bad enough trying to prepare for a mission like this, but we've had to deal with so many sabotage attempts, so many cases of insubordination, it's a miracle that the launch took place at all."

"We're not taking any more of this shit from the enclaves. We're quite happy to go it alone. So now that the launch is over, you and your cohort have 24 hours to get off our island. And Nemed, don't come back!"

Nemed was about to argue but looked at the steel in Brian's eyes. He nodded his head in agreement.

The Present – August 2027

Chapter 5

Ocean Harvest

Killybegs was bathed in sunlight: dappled light reflecting down the fjord that made it one of the biggest and most well-known fishing ports in Europe. The sky was cloudless, casting long shadows on the mountains that sat behind the town. Locals and tourists mixed along the quayside, the tinkle of ice-cream vans joining the cacophony of noise from traffic, machinery and the shouts of seamen. Activity was frenetic. The pelagic trawlers were in port, unloading catches of mackerel, sprat and whiting to the quayside, ready for onward transport to the local processing plants.

Despite being in the remote northwest of the country, the little town had a long history, dating back to early Christian times. The name itself meant *little cells* in Irish, a reference to an ancient monastic settlement. It was here where one of the ships of the Spanish Armada had landed, during Spain and England's Elizabethan War. *La Girona* was smiled kindly upon by a local chieftain, who repaired its storm-damaged keel and resupplied the ship, before it was lost on its way to Scotland.

Yachts and pleasure boats vied for space on the bank holiday weekend, European super trawlers reluctantly making way for pleasure craft. Holiday weekend or not, these factory ships had a schedule. Supply trucks weaved in and out along the quay, one narrowly avoiding a distinctive sculpture of an oyster shell cradling a trawler. European, Russian and even Asian consumers craved the rich oily fish from the pelagic zone of the ocean – neither close to the seabed nor the shore. Killybegs was host to vessels from all over Europe, not just the Irish fleet.

One such vessel was the *Aurora Antarctica*, a modern trawler, less than a year out of dock. She had offloaded a bumper catch of horse mackerel, locally known as skad.

The weather conditions were perfect, the sea was calm. Sean was determined to make a fast turnaround. Late July and early August was the best time of the year to reap the Atlantic Ocean's harvest. The long days in the northern hemisphere gave the crew an opportunity to harness the light to the best effect.

The skipper laid a course for Rockall, 230 nautical miles north-west from Tory Island. Of course, the British claimed it as their territorial waters, but it was closer to Ireland and the Irish had long disputed the British claim. Regardless of sovereignty, the area around Rockall, Helen's Reef, was one of the richest fishing grounds in the Atlantic.

It would be a long and arduous journey, taking days to reach the destination, but the skipper hoped to be rewarded with a haul of haddock and if he were lucky, squid. His route was plotted to take him north of the Rockall plateau, outside of the UK's 12-kilometre limit.

His computer plotted the destination on a marine map. His intended fishing ground was intentionally centre of the screen, with the island of Ireland visible in the bottom right corner and the island of Iceland in the top left. At his destination, he would be marginally closer to the southeast of Iceland than he would be to his home in Donegal.

Chapter 6

Our American Friends

The chauffeur waited patiently in his air-conditioned minibus. He wanted a cigarette but could not have one. His livery would stink of tobacco, and the Americans could be a pain in the ass – always complaining. He ran his hand through his hair and checked his chauffeur cap. The Europeans did not care if he had a uniform; it was only the American who expected the whole deal. The woollen jacket itched and despite the cool breeze from the air conditioning, he was sweating.

The sun beat down on Shannon Airport. He checked his watch. The plane from New York had landed twenty minutes ago and his passengers, twelve of them, would be travelling to Dromoland, with the obligatory golf bags and big cameras.

The driver sighed. He was paid twenty euros an hour to drive tourists and haul their luggage. With all the tax he paid and trying to keep a roof over his young family's head, he was constantly broke. His passengers earned at least twenty-thousand dollars a week. Most of them treated him like the hired help, which of course, he was, but the east coast Americans were rude with it – at least the really wealthy financial types were.

If he were lucky, there might be a bit of banter – it was sometimes like that when wives came along. More banter, more tips. He had a good line in Irish history and had loads of stories to tell if they gave him a chance. The women were often matronly and always took care of him – he had a young face after all. He wished that the group had been from Texas or California. The Texans and Californians were laid back and friendly.

He heard them before he saw them. The dozen businessmen were making their way to the pick-up point. Garishly bright clothing, enormous asses and mouths the size of the Shannon estuary. They embodied the caricature of Americans that Europeans laughed at. They could probably hear them back on Wall Street or wherever the hell they were from in the States, the chauffeur thought. Every one of them pushed an overflowing luggage cart, which would doubtlessly be abandoned beside the minivan, for him to unload while the Yanks took selfies.

He took off his cap and placed it on the driver's seat, resigned to packing the luggage compartment. He was building a sweat when he got complaints from a bear of a man with bright red hair, warning him not to scratch the Louis Vuitton luggage. He smiled politely and when the American trudged away, he slid it past a raised screw on the bodywork.

Once seated, one of the quieter members of the group informed him that the group was on a golfing trip – a corporate reward for exceeding sales targets.

The redhead interjected. Of course, it would have been better to go to St Andrews in Scotland or to where the nice young British man, Rory McElroy played – in England. The course they would play in Ireland was okay but not great. Still, it was a pity that the organisers did not know anything about golf.

As he drove through the winding roads of County Clare to Dromoland Castle, the chauffeur was seething. Rory McElroy was an Irishman, played in Portrush. The Dromoland Golf Course, like others in the county, was world famous and easily equal to St Andrews. He swallowed his resentment. It was, after all, their dime as the Americans would say. Another ten minutes and they would be someone else's problem. He was sure that the staff at the five-star Dromoland Castle would be well used to dealing with tourists like these.

The signpost to Newmarket-on-Fergus meant that he was close now, and he used the intercom on the bus to announce their arrival. As the passengers were greeted with an uilleann piper and vintage whiskey, he stood beside the minivan and tipped his hat as he received his gratuities. He helped the hotel staff unload the luggage and checked the time. He had another pickup. This time at the Trump Doonbeg resort.

This trip would be a long one – from the five-star golf resort to the historic Shelbourne Hotel on St Stephen's Green in Dublin. At least a six hour round trip. Longer in traffic. He did not hold out much hope of an easy afternoon – he would probably get a bunch of Trump supporters in the back, spouting on about making America great again, and how their Donald had been robbed of a second term by crooked Democrats. The cheek of that man, he thought, sticking out his hand for subsidies for his resort at the height of the covid pandemic. Donald was happy to flash the cash at home but expected small countries to pick up his bills. And he had the cheek to land a bill on the Scottish government too. He had driven Trump supporters on many occasions and had heard all of their rhetoric.

Most were too dumb to realise that the Irish loved the Democrats. Sure, hadn't we given America the Kennedys?

It was best just to get on with it. If he was not delayed by bank holiday traffic, he might be home in County Tipperary in time to kiss his toddlers goodnight.

Chapter 7

A Precocious Talent

"Saoirse, second year students cannot get access to the CRANN Centre. You'll just have to wait until next year," Dr Keane said, patiently trying to explain college protocols.

"Why? My project is on quantum computing and the use of molecular magnets is central to my hypothesis. I have a theorem, and I know I can prove the relationships. All I need is some time to run my experiments."

Dr Keane was Saoirse's tutor, and he had never had to deal with such a precocious teenager. Despite her attitude, she was one of the most brilliant young physicists he had encountered. At times, she could also be childish and spoilt.

"You're a second-year student. There is no way the head of department will sign off on giving you access. Maybe when you are a post grad ..."

Saoirse cut him off.

"In another six months, someone else will have found a way to stabilise the magnetic response of molecules in steady state temperature conditions at high density. I know how to take the research that's been done at CRANN and improve it. I'm not looking for credit. I just want to finish what I've started. If someone would just look at the equations ..."

Dr Keane kept his office in the old library, overlooking Library Square in the heart of Trinity's campus. The building had been completed in 1732 and was by no means the oldest building on the historic site. The college itself was founded 1592 by Queen Elizabeth I, made in the likeness of Cambridge and Oxford.

Dr Keane interrupted his student's diatribe.

"Saoirse, it's great that you're enthusiastic. Maybe you could have an informal chat with the research director. Rather than focus on your project, which by the way, your lecturer has already said will get a distinction, you should focus on some of your other elective classes. You're falling behind in some of the more mundane areas of study," the tutor said gently.

Saoirse was crestfallen. She was driven, and anything less than a straight A would be taken as a failure. Yet, it was clear that she did not consider anything other than her chosen field worthy of her academic attention. In her eyes, compulsory classes in the *History of Physics* and report writing took away time that she could use for bettering her knowledge of nanomaterials.

"I came to Trinity specifically to study this area. I could have gone anywhere, but I came here because of the research facilities. Maybe I should have gone to Cambridge – they did offer, after all!"

Saoirse ran her hand through her emerald-green hair.

Dr Keane smiled and patted her hand. He was too old for political correctness. If he were found to be sexist, they could send him out to pasture.

"Saoirse, just try. I know you think it's a waste of time but please, don't give the administrators an excuse. Get your scholarship, get your first-class degree. When you have that, you can go anywhere you want to, including Cambridge and including CRANN. Some of us know you as a great physicist, not a Goth, you know."

Dr Keane reminded Saoirse of her grandfather.

She huffed loudly, her nose ring swaying as she exhaled.

"Thanks, Dr Keane. Do what you can, okay?"

She wished him a good afternoon and grabbed her laptop bag. It was early in the afternoon and with the long holidays underway, the only people around were tourists on their way to the Book of Kells in the library.

Saoirse was still only nineteen, a wunderkind through secondary school, winner of the European Young Scientist award, well on her way to becoming a Trinity Scholar – the most prestigious scholarship in Ireland awarded to students who consistently demonstrated exceptional knowledge and understanding of their subjects. Yet, she looked nothing like the image of a Trinity student portrayed by the college. Her long hair was dyed emerald green and if anyone got close enough, they would see pale blonde roots peeping through. She wore heavy eye makeup, contrasting with her pale skin. A nose ring hooped through her nostril; another ring pierced her right eyebrow. Her clothes were uniformly black, and she wore black Doc Martins with green laces, matching her hair.

Contrary to popular belief, not all Trinity students came from money. While Saoirse's family were not poor exactly, they were definitely not wealthy. As the youngest, Saoirse watched her mother scrape by to get the three older siblings through university, relying on overtime and state grants to get them their degrees and masters. Her dad had not bothered to turn up at any of the graduations, let alone help with fees.

Saoirse trudged through the campus, making her way to the exit near the Dental Hospital. The CRANN Institute beckoned to her as she passed by. She stared at the windows, longing to be inside.

CRANN is Trinity College Dublin's largest research institute. Its Advanced Microscopy Laboratory houses some of the world's most advanced microscopes, including a Helium Ion Microscope, one of only a dozen in the world. The equipment Saoirse coveted was controlled by AMBER – Advanced Materials and Bio-engineering Research.

Saoirse was sullen. She could not understand why she had to wait. Her sisters and brother were already well established in their careers yet, she felt that she was floundering. As the youngest sibling, Saoirse had spent her whole life trying to catch up, but Saoirse did not see what everyone else saw – a shooting star ready to change the world.

Chapter 8

Recall

Sadbh left the factory on the outskirts of Westport, carrying her equipment. Although she had been assured that the factory had plenty of test equipment to hand, she had not trusted anyone's equipment but her own. She checked her equipment case and made sure her micrometers and Vernier callipers were safely packed. She placed the UV inspection torches and loupes in their pouches before placing them in a special hard case that she kept in the boot of her car. She checked again that all of the photos and videos she had taken were safely uploaded to a secure online vault. The legal team would likely need them.

The factory's management team stood at the doorway to reception, sullen faced. They were in no doubt that Sadbh would disqualify them as a supplier, halting the lucrative contract to supply metalwork to one of Europe's biggest telecoms manufacturers. Whether their company would survive the coming legal battle was a different question.

Sadbh had not expected to be in the west of Ireland at the close of the day. She had arrived for work at 7 am in Dublin and had been greeted by a flurry of activity in the test laboratory. She was making coffee when one of her junior engineers, who worked in incoming inspection, approached her. Lukas was normally bright and sunny but this morning, he was agitated. Something was off.

"I think there's a problem with the casings, Sadbh. When the batch arrived, I took a sample for inspection and when I picked up the first of the units, I noticed some staining and bubbling. I examined under 10x magnification, and I could see paint lifting and evidence of corrosion on the first unit, so I upped the magnification to 40x. Sadbh, every single sample has paint adhesion problems and evidence of rust. The plated elements of the casing are even worse than the painted parts. I could see flaking."

Sadbh left the coffee and went to the lab to look at the samples herself. While she prepared the photographic equipment and microscopes, she asked Lukas to fetch another batch of samples. It would be 8 am before the stores team arrived, but Lukas' code allowed him access to the assembly stores.

Sadbh patiently set about analysing the metalwork herself, photographing the results as she went. She could see evidence of exposure of bare metal at the welded seams of the case. Tell-tale staining was proof of corrosion. A gentle probing of the affected plated areas produced miniscule flakes of metal. Her heart sank. She did not need high magnification to see that something had clearly gone wrong during the chrome-plating process: the plated parts were covered in blisters, and she even suspected the root cause of the problem.

The housings were precision parts, designed to form an airtight seal. As a result, they needed to be machined to a tight tolerance. The machining process used lubricant oils, which needed to be cleaned before chromating. If the parts were in any way dirty, the chrome would not adhere. If any remnants of the lubricants were present, they could produce gases, which would push through to the surface of the plating and cause blistering.

The root cause was not her problem but the result of it was. She worked out all of the possible scenarios and the consequences. All of them were bad. She hoped that this was a one off – the problem affecting only a small number of casings but in her heart, she knew that it was unlikely to be an isolated issue. She needed to find out how far back the problem went and fast.

Lukas returned with a trolley of base station cases. He had barely positioned the trolley when Sadbh told his to pull all of the inspection records since the manufacturer began their supply. Each of the inspection records included detailed photographs.

It was barely 7.30 when Lukas let her know he had set up in the conference room. By that time, Sadbh had rejected and quarantined everything that had come out of the manufacturer's plant in Westport since June. Lukas called in materials and design engineers at Sadbh's instruction. Some were barely awake; others were in cars and buses on their way to work. A few objected but when Lukas explained the problem and Sadbh's request for attendance, they did as they were bid.

The last engineer arrived as Sadbh phoned the Operations Director, to inform him that she was shutting their manufacturing plant down. Her last call was to the CEO, to warn him of what was coming.

The engineering team went into crisis mode. There was evidence of problems with previous batches of casings – all of which were now either in production or shipped to global telecom customers. Dublin has a mild climate, and it was possible to see the damage to the casings after a couple of months of storage. If the casings were deployed in warm damp conditions, the deterioration of the cases would accelerate.

The company had an excellent traceability system that Sadbh had fought to implement. Every senior manager had objected to what they saw as overkill. However, the system was able to track every serial number of every unit for which suspect casings had been used, going back to the addition of the supplier to the approved vendor list.

The Operations Director pointed the finger of blame squarely at the Quality Department.

"How could you not have noticed at incoming inspection or any of the in-process inspections?" he screamed.

Sadbh patiently explained that the missing element to inspection was time – when the units were fresh, it would not be possible to identify the problems, even with high magnification. They had been lucky, or unlucky, that the metalwork plant had built up a reserve to cover a holiday shut down by upping production for the previous month. The problem had been spotted on a unit recently delivered but chromated and painted at the end of June, six weeks previously.

So much for just in time manufacturing! Sadbh swore under her breath.

The company was clearly headed into a product recall situation. Having briefed the quality engineers on the most up-to-date findings, Sadbh announced that the department was now in crisis mode.

Sadbh issued a two-word command – "Find them."

Her team understood. They started tracing and isolating every unit not shipped, including those in the loading bay. A separate team would identify the units shipped to customers and would develop a plan to inspect and possibly replace these units.

By 9 am, all of the senior management team had assembled in the CEO's office.

"How bad is it?" Gary asked.

Sadbh pulled up the photographs of the interior of the housing.

"The chrome plating is flaking, and there's corrosion around the welds and seams. Of the two issues, the chrome plating is the more urgent problem. The plated fixture sits directly above the main base station printed circuit board. As the blisters burst, they will rain down conductive confetti. It will only take one small piece of plating to short out the PCB. If it lands in the wrong place, near one of the main chips, then the damage will be catastrophic, and we lose a PCB worth tens of thousands of euros."

"It isn't a matter of if this will happen; it is a matter of when. These units are rated for outdoor use. They are rated for a temperature range of minus-40 degrees Celsius to plus-50 degrees Celsius. If the units are placed in a humid environment, at the right temperature, we could start seeing failures more or less immediately. We have a serious warranty problem."

Although the engineering managers believed Sadbh, they set off to verify her findings. The Operations Director and CEO left together, to inform their insurers and to iron out the product recall.

Sadbh left the conference room and headed back to her office. Lukas and Dom, two of her engineering team, were waiting on her. They quickly rounded up the senior test engineers and briefed them on developments. Each was assigned duties for testing, simulation and support of the product recall. Dom stepped out for a moment to take a call and quickly returned to the office.

"You're not going to believe this! There's an articulated lorry full of casings from Westport at the dock. Goods inwards want to know what to do."

Sadbh shook her head.

"We do absolutely nothing. Dom. Go down to the driver and tell him we can't receive them. He'll have to come back later, after the bank holiday, but hold him for as long as you can – give him breakfast. Whatever you do, don't tell him that there are issues with the delivery. Make up an excuse about a cock up in the stores. I don't want him warning the factory of a problem."

The engineers looked at Sadbh, she was formulating a plan.

"What are you up to, Boss?" Lukas asked.

"If the supplier has failed to adhere to the production process detailed in our contract, then they are liable for the cost of making good on our losses. We can prove that they fucked up by analysing what they shipped, but it would be better if we had some evidence from the factory itself. I'm going to do an unannounced audit of the factory and take some supporting photographs of their electroplating process. Once I have evidence, I'll let them know about the casing failures. I'm going immediately; I don't want them hiding the evidence."

With that, she tossed her car keys to Lukas.

"You know the drill. It's a four-hour drive to Westport, and I'm not doing it in a skirt and heels. Get the bag from my boot, and I'll change in the ladies room."

Sadbh emerged from the bathroom transformed from a company director to a badass. She was wearing combats, Doc Martens and a black polo shirt.

Pat, the Director of RF Test Engineering passed her in the corridor.

"Sadbh, have you joined the army or what?"

Sadbh laughed.

"No, Pat, but my daughter did."

With her test kit and camera safely stored away and after the obligatory trip to the bathroom, Sadbh set off on the long drive west. She was in Longford by 11 am and was listening to loud rock music when the phone rang.

"Mam, what restaurant did you book for tonight?"

Feck, she whispered. "I'm sorry, Brendan. There's a shit storm at work, and I have to get Mayo as soon as possible. I'm going to be there most of the day – there's no way I'll get back for half seven. Can we reschedule until tomorrow?"

Tomorrow was Brendan's birthday, and the family had planned a meal out to celebrate.

"No problem, Mam. The girls wanted to go clubbing tonight anyway. What's up? Why are you going to the arsehole of nowhere? Do you even have customers there?"

Sadbh laughed. Brendan was an RF Engineer but after graduation, made a decision not to work for the same company as Sadbh. Mammy being the Director of Quality would have caused too many complications.

"It's not a customer problem yet, Brendan. It's a supplier problem, and it's not design related. That's all I'm saying, because I don't want you running off to your boss, telling him your main competitor has a problem."

Brendan hung up and went through the call in his mind. His mother had been listening to *Out in the Fields* by Gary Moore when he rang – she only listened to rock when she was stressed. And she had sounded stressed. As he made his way back to the RF Lab, he tried to figure out if his company and hers had shared suppliers in the west of Ireland.

Sadbh smiled to herself. Despite her accountant ex-husband, she had raised two engineers, both RF and communications specialists, a GIS specialist and a physicist. Still in her prime, Sadbh had raised a family of technical experts, each with the ability to outshine their mother in their chosen specialisms. She suddenly felt more confident than she had done in years – she had created a tribe. She turned the volume up and played *Róisín Dubh* by Thin Lizzy.

Sadbh waited for nearly an hour in the reception area of the supplier's factory, for someone to collect her. The Quality Manager, Operations Manager and most of the management team were on vacation – or so she was told. The production supervisor on duty was busy holding the daily production meeting. The Marketing Manager only appeared after she threatened to pull the contract immediately if access to the production floor was not granted. The Marketing Manager agreed to bring Sadbh on a plant tour but clearly knew nothing of the process. He objected to Sadbh's use of a camera, but she ignored his complaints and produced a copy of the non-disclosure agreement, signed by both parties. He backed down.

Sadbh lingered in the pre-cleaning area of the plant. Cleaning of the base metal was essential to good hard chrome plating. The process used an alkaline electro cleaner followed by rinsing, using a dilute acid. This removed any residue of the alkaline cleaning solution. However, following a batch of parts through the process and videoing the results, Sadbh could see no evidence of thorough rinsing. The parts left the pre-cleaning process dirty. Sadbh asked to see the quality control inspection records, but there were not any. There were no records of any kind in the area. The staff on duty did not seem to understand what they were doing. They were not even wearing any protective gear.

They followed the batch of parts through to the plating baths, which were set up in a sequence – copper then nickel and finally, hard chrome. The plating was dissolved in acid baths. The parts to be plated were submerged in the baths, and an electric current passed through, to allow the metal to deposit evenly over the part. Sadbh could see no controls over the addition of chemicals to the baths. There were no timers working to control the submersion time, and the current was being manually adjusted by a technician. All of the controls to ensure good plating were bypassed.

Sadbh recorded everything on video and in still shots. The Marketing Manager tried to engage Sadbh in conversation, but she kept her answers short. He was clearly uncomfortable and avoided answering any direct questions. By mid-afternoon, Sadbh had seen enough. She demanded a meeting with the plant's senior team.

Running through the evidence collected on her plant tour, Sadbh made her case for negligence on the part of the supplier. With more than 1000 units potentially built with defective casings, her company was now looking at significant losses. The inspection of the units in the field would cost millions alone. Sadbh made it clear to the supplier that not only would she accept no further shipments of their product, but her team would also be immediately returning all metalwork they held in stock. The supplier would also be liable for the inspection, replacement and sundry costs incurred.

Finally, Sadbh got to her car. She checked her watch; it was closing on 6.30 pm. A quick call back to her office revealed that her company's manufacturing plant had gone into overdrive. They were now stripping components from finished units and were rebuilding with casings from another supplier. The factory and her team would be working over the holiday weekend, to build a stock of replacement units for field teams.

She thanked God that, despite the finance department's objections, she had insisted on qualifying a second supplier. The second, smaller supplier was Dublin-based and was a lot more expensive that their Mayo counterpart. However, they followed the rules and on request, were able to produce records validating the quality of their plating and powder coat paint. A rapid tour of their factory did not faze them, which was a really good sign. They opened their stores and had shipped their full stock to the manufacturing plant, the first batches delivered in person by the management team using their own cars.

Hanging up, Sadbh took a deep breath. There had been no failures in the field reported yet, so there was a chance that they could sort the problem out before it became a media disaster. From the following morning, field installation teams were beginning the task of inspecting installed units. Replacements were shipped by overnight express in case of need of replacement. Her own team, alongside operations and the field teams, had done a stellar job of managing the crisis. There was nothing left for her to do but get home.

Despite the picture postcard images of Westport that graces travel magazines the world over, the earlier sunshine had been replaced by a sky that looked grey and foreboding. The colourful buildings perched on the edge of the Atlantic Ocean, on Ireland's west coast, were bleached of colour – the strong Atlantic gusts threatening to topple those along the quayside.

She started the car and drove from the sleek industrial complex, past the walled estate of Westport House, heading for the town proper. The gusting wind brought waves of rain, making visibility poor. Sadbh had not eaten since breakfast, and the coffee at the meeting was bitter and strong. Her stomach ached. Sadbh hoped that she could find somewhere to eat in the town. In her haste to reach Westport, she had skipped lunch. The whole day had passed in a stressful blur.

As she drove around the Octagon and onto James Street, she was disappointed to find the shops and cafés shuttered against the storm, despite it being a bank holiday weekend. The pubs looked busy enough, but she had no wish to suffer through tipsy tourists to get a sandwich.

She drove on to Castlebar Street and followed the signposts for the N5, the main route back to Dublin. Outside of the town, she pulled over into a layby and searched the car for a bottle of water. As the wind gusted around her, she closed her eyes and rested for a while, waiting for the burning indigestion to subside.

Why the hell did I take this job, she thought? She knew why though. She was a single parent, and she needed to earn enough to pay the mortgage and pay the bills. Even though two of the kids were through college and established in their careers, one daughter was close to qualifying in GIS and one was still an undergraduate. And despite the stress, she loved her job.

Sadbh sighed and put the water aside. Her bladder control was not what it once was, and she did not want to be caught short at the side of the road during a storm. On a normal evening, it would take over four hours to get home, but this was a bank holiday weekend, and the storm would play havoc with traffic. There was no way that she would push her car to the limits. Despite the iconic brand, it only had a 1.3 litre engine. If she stopped to eat, it would add an hour to the journey. So, it was unlikely that she would be home before midnight.

Traffic was manic when she reached Castlebar over an hour later. Some idiot planned major roadworks over the holiday weekend, and it took 40 minutes to get through the endless stop-go system in the centre of town. She felt lightheaded now. The heartburn getting increasingly worse. She really needed to stop for food.

Another 40 minutes and she arrived in Charlestown, on the border of Mayo and Roscommon. It was getting dark. The storm had abated. She checked the clock; it was nearly 9 pm. Despite her dislike for fast food, she needed to eat. Her choices were limited: Chinese, fish and chips or pizza. Long queues had formed outside the local chipper, so Sadbh ruled it out. Chinese was slightly healthier that pizza, but Sadbh had never been fond of oriental cuisine, so she settled on pizza. She made her way to the counter to be told that it would take twenty minutes for a small pizza to be made. Eager to burn off her nervous energy, Sadbh paced while she waited. Eventually, the food was delivered, and she sat at a communal picnic table, near a quaint statue of farm animals. She sat and ate her pizza and drank her diet coke, eager to be back on the road.

The Past

Chapter 9

Crash Landing

Nuada banged his prosthesis down on the conference table.

"I can't keep control of the native population any longer. Have you forgotten the original mission? We weren't sent here to create a colony, we were sent here to avert a bloody disaster," he growled.

The meeting was being held aboard the *Findias*, hidden on the coast of Papa Westry in the Orkney Islands. The ship was not only the closest of the four surviving ships to Ireland but the best preserved of the fleet. The meeting had been convened in the captain's suite. Attendees had come from the settlement in Ireland and from the other ships in Iceland, Norway and Greenland.

Ireland had been selected for colonisation because of its temperate climate and equidistant position from the vessels stranded across the North Atlantic. It was beside the point that the commanders and crews of the ships saw themselves as Irish and therefore, gravitated to Ireland as home.

The establishment of a permanent base was needed, because the ships could not sustain a population indefinitely. They simply did not have the supplies or the space. They could not contain the population on board: the ships were not prisons.

Since the crash landing nearly twenty years before, the vessels had deteriorated badly, and systems were barely functioning. Although fuelled by fission cells, highly processed supplies needed to repair the craft and their systems was simply not available. If the full fleet of ships had survived, they would have had cargo enough to repair and sustain the ships. However, most of the fleet had been lost during the re-entry, and the ship that had survived did not have a large enough inventory to keep the crews clothed and fed, never mind repair and upgrade on-board systems.

It had been a simple navigation mistake made by the Danish vessel that had cascaded into a disaster, during a violent geomagnetic storm that the fleet had no way of avoiding. The Danish ship was immediately destroyed, taking with it three other enclave vessels. The smaller vessels in the fleet were not nimble or powerful enough to avoid the carnage and were destroyed by debris. Only the four largest ships of the fleet survived, but they were not unaffected. Changing telemetry had allowed them to escape destruction, but they lost control of the timeline and were at the mercy of fate. They managed to land in the northern hemisphere, their crippled vessels barely avoiding destruction in a series of crash landings. Their target had been the 1970's; they ended up in the Bronze Age.

In the interim years, survival of the crew had taken precedence and because of the high mortality rate, most of the original soldiers and scientists had passed on. Medical knowledge was an advantage, but they had no experience of dealing with the wild animals and wilder savages that they encountered when they left their stockades. They could not acclimatise to the extreme weather in Greenland, Iceland and Norway, and the dank dampness of Scotland brought with it savage infections.

The children of the survivors knew only what was passed on to them from their parents or elders. Most had no memory of Cong or the enclaves, being too young to remember the reason for their exodus or the mission that they had been entrusted with. Many of the young people were borne of mixed parentage: the crews building lasting relationships with locals, who called themselves Muintir Partholóin. Whether born from local intermarriages or relationships between crew members, the young people worried about full stomachs and freedom from attack from the marauding Fir Bolg, the dominant tribe of Bronze Age Ireland.

Anu sent envoys to the Fir Bolg settlements, to make peace and to identify the best and brightest to be brought back to the ships, for training in the arts of war and engineering. The Fir Bolg were reticent. They did not want to engage, choosing a type of guerrilla warfare rather than a civil cessation of violence.

Anu, the commander of the fleet, had aged over the twenty years since their arrival. She split her time between the four ships and the main settlement in Ireland. It had been a struggle just to keep the crew and passengers alive. Her golden hair had turned silver, and crow's feet marked the passage of time.

She sighed with a heavy heart.

She remembered the pomp and ceremony that led to the original mission. Thirteen gleaming vessels, fission powered, on a journey to the past to right the wrongs of the ancestors. She had been so proud. Thousands of physicists, engineers, doctors, mathematicians, material scientists, biologists, linguists, historians and highly trained soldiers had died to make this journey. So much work, she thought. So much hope. The hopes of every citizen of what was left of Europe. *How long did that hope last, when we never made contact*, she wondered?

Her voice was low and firm and when she spoke, all remained silent.

"Nuada, you are right of course. In another few years, we will be gone and apart from a few legends, we won't have much of a legacy. The mission seems so distant now."

She looked up from downcast eyes and sighed.

"But it is why we were sent in the first place."

She paused and looked around her.

"The ships systems are failing. We don't know if any of the technology to reverse the volcanic winter will even function and if we go ahead with the mission you propose, Nuada, there are overwhelming odds that the volunteers will die, and the mission will fail."

Morrigan, Ogma and the surviving commanders nodded in agreement. Daghda smiled sadly at Anu. They understood Anu's reluctance to endorse this suicide mission. They also understood the sacred trust that had been placed in them. Their world was dying. When this generation was gone, there would be nothing left of the story of their mission, their fleet.

Ogma, ever the engineer, explained to the assembly how the engineering team took the antimatter propulsion system from *Findias* and used it to create a portal. The portal was one way only and to date, had been tested using tamed foxes. While the animals did not die when passing through the device, there was no way to know if they survived on the other side. Technology did not fare so well. Anything bigger than a clenched fist either exploded or was vapourised during the transportation process. While it would have been prudent to continue testing to be sure of success, the engineers had a finite amount of antimatter and no means to replenish it. There was enough for one more test – and two runs by a human team.

"How many people are we talking about?" Anu asked.

Ogma suggested a team of four: someone to liaise with the locals, a soldier to act as bodyguard, a medic to deal with unforeseen illness and injury and finally, an engineer with a good understanding of laser technology. Of course, all four would receive intensive training before the mission, he explained, and what remained of the social sciences team would assist them with information about the destination.

"Obviously, we cannot send the tools they need with them. So, we will come up with a way of burying them, so that they can be retrieved by the team on arrival."

"That brings me to another point – how we communicate with the team. We had experience communicating in deep space in the 21st century, but this is deep-time communication. We are doing our best to set up systems to allow the team access to databases and linguistic programmes but all in all, access may be patchy. Let's face it, we couldn't communicate with the people who sent us here – how the hell will we communicate with the team?"

"We hope to overcome this by leaving physical clues to the technology's locations and giving each of the travellers a miniature but powerful implant for communication, and it will also hold some key geographic information. If it actually works, they may be able to talk to a support team here, but it's a big if."

Anu winced when Nuada told her they would have to select a team for the mission, and the team would be probed and prodded and given implants. They would also receive nanite injections from the ships' limited supply.

"It is really necessary, Nuada? Isn't it bad enough that we're giving them a death sentence without making them suffer at the hands of the butchers that pass for physicians?"

Nuada sighed and slumped down into his seat. He ran his silver fingers through his greying hair.

"Anu, most of the memory banks were damaged when we landed here. Our knowledge of the past or the future or whenever the 21st century is, is patchy at best. We know that there was terrorism in Europe at around the time of the cataclysm, but we don't know what form it took. We don't even know for sure what language is spoken. We struggle to keep infections at bay with a pristine environment. We have no idea what the environment at the time of the cataclysm is like. There is talk about chemical contamination. If we don't give the team the nanites, they may well die from exposure to chemicals or a rogue bacterium. And its only one implant – it's small and into the Broca's area of the left frontal lobe.

When activated with a communication device, it will allow them to understand and speak whatever language is in use. The team will need these implants, because there will be very little help we can provide. To seek out assistance, they need to be able to communicate."

Macha and Badb dropped their eyes and tried to keep out of the conversation. Working with Nuada and without the approval of the command, they had started preparations for a mission to the future. If Morrigan and Anu voiced their disapproval, both Macha and Badb would face the consequences.

"Apart from issuing a death sentence, what's to be done?" Anu asked.

Nuada had always preferred to ask for forgiveness rather than permission and in this case, he asked for forgiveness for already setting a development team to work on the equipment, which would be retrieved by the team. He outlined his plan, which was grudgingly acknowledged and accepted.

Ogma, Badb and Macha corralled teams of logisticians and engineers to put Nuada's plan into action. While Ogma explained the technical details for which the teams would be responsible, Morrigan, Anu and Nuada retired to select the team.

"Okay, so what are we looking at in terms of timeline?" Morrigan asked.

Nuada resettled himself on the conference chair.

"We need to do this fast: within the next month. By the way, in anticipation of your approval, I already have some preliminary work done with Macha and Badb."

He avoided eye contact with Anu, who was staring at him intently.

Like a naughty schoolboy, he raised his shaggy head and gave her a radiant smile.

"I swear it was only some of the basics – some weeding out if you like. I waited for your approval for the important stuff."

After twenty years of working with Nuada, Anu knew this was the closest she would get to an apology. He kept up the puppy dog eyes until she broke into a grin. Morrigan, used to Nuada's tactics, threw her eyes skyward.

"Nuada, are we aiming to send them a year before the event? A month?" Morrigan asked.

Nuada shook his head and explained that his plan was to send the team back to within days of the cataclysm. Hearing the two women closest to him object, he raised his hand.

"If you think I haven't thought this through, you're wrong. I have had a lot of time to weigh the consequences of sending the team back earlier. Whoever we pick to go will, no doubt, be excellent at their jobs, but we don't know what they are facing into. They will go in without any defensive weapons, and we don't know what will happen to them if they are captured. They will, more than likely, be incarcerated and punished – we don't know if there is capital punishment in play. There is also the possibility that the team may change their minds about pursuing the mission. We can't afford for them to get cold feet. It's best to do it fast and as close as possible to the first eruption."

Morrigan put her hand on Nuada's shoulder.

"Nuada, you could send them back during the cataclysm, and they could back out – not as a result of malice or cowardice but as a result of shock and panic. I do understand where you're coming from. Having them arrive too early means they will have months or years to mull things over, with little opportunity to discuss it with us. If you genuinely think that they can accomplish the mission if they return two or three days before, then that is the target we will set."

Anu nodded in agreement.

The threesome spent the rest of the night reviewing personnel files, hoping to identify four people to carry out the mission. Morrigan absent-mindedly glanced at a personnel file containing the picture of a chubby, smiling engineer and grimaced. She caught Anu's eye.

"You know Ogma wants to go, don't you?"

Nuada and Anu looked at each other and at the same moment, said no but for different reasons. Anu spoke first, declaring concern over the state of Ogma's health. He was approaching 70 now, and age was catching up on him. She was concerned with him withstanding the implantation of the communication device, let alone the trip itself.

Nuada had other concerns.

"We simply can't let Ogma go. I know he doesn't have a family and therefore, technically doesn't have ties here. I'm not even that worried about his health. What worries me is the loss of his technical expertise. If anything goes wrong, we may need to send a second team, and we will need him here to manage the technology if that happens."

Anu reluctantly agreed, as did Morrigan.

That left them with only two other candidates capable of managing the technology: Macha and Uiscias.

"Macha is like my sister, and I know she would go if asked. The thing is, she has three children and two foster children. I can't and won't ask her to leave them. She is brilliant and capable, and I think we need to hold on to her here for the time being," Morrigan said.

Nuada agreed.

"Then that only leaves Uiscias. He's very young and geeky. He tries to be a soldier, but it hasn't taken. Ogma loves him like a son and has taught him everything he knows. If I am to believe Ogma, he's one of the most talented engineers we have. Sending him will break Ogma's heart."

"Then we'll have to break his heart, because there is no one else," Morrigan whispered.

The trio moved on to identifying a bodyguard for the mission. All of the candidates were fine soldiers, fit and capable.

Morrigan swept the personnel files aside.

"Look, I'm the leader of the Fianna, the finest battalion we have. If you want the best of the best than we have to pick Morfessa. You all know him and how good he is."

Nuada laughed.

"That's one way to get rid of an ex!"

Morrigan blushed.

"Okay, so we had a fling a couple of years ago, and the breakup didn't go well, but that doesn't change the fact that he is the best we've got."

"Okay! Okay! We'll send Morfessa," Anu commanded.

The trio spent more than an hour debating whether to send a civilian doctor or someone from the Fianna's medical corps. Dian Cécht would want to go, but he was the best surgeon in the fleet and an expert in prosthetics, as Nuada would testify – the colony simply could not do without him. In the end, the combination of both military training and exceptional healing skills won out, and Esras was selected. The other factor was his age: at 30, he was at his physical peak.

The final candidate was that of a liaison officer for the travellers. The job description was vague – it called for charm and persuasion. Nuada nominated Bres and was answered by gales of laughter from Anu and Morrigan.

"Look what happened the last time we let Bres negotiate anything," Anu giggled, pointing at Nuada's prosthetic arm. He lost his real arm in the aftermath of a ceasefire with the Fir Bolg – Bres was chief negotiator.

"We could always send Eochaid. I'd be rid of that pain in the ass for good then," Nuada responded, referring to Eochaid Mac Eirc, the so-called King of the Fir Bolg.

The threesome erupted into laughter.

"Seriously though, we do need to send someone who is clever and adaptable. This is the least technically demanding role of all but nonetheless, critical to success. I hate to say it, but Semias is an ideal candidate. Honey drips off the man's tongue," Nuada said.

Anu shuddered.

"Did you know that you can get botulism from raw honey?"

Night had fallen and as they looked around the room, Anu, Nuada and Morrigan realised that it was long after nightfall.

"It's settled," Anu said. "Three military and one civilian on the mission. Semias will not need to meet the same physical criteria as the others. He won't be taking an active role. We will call him a liaison."

Ogma had drawn the finest technical team available to him and their brainstorming session was in full swing when Anu, Morrigan and Nuada joined them. Céthur came forward and activated a 3D imager. He was accompanied by Creidne, one of the most experienced engineers left in the fleet.

The image enlarged and took up the table's central space, slowly rotating.

"You are aware of how the engines that got us here function? The design itself was good. Unfortunately, no one expected a geomagnetic storm bigger than the Carrington Event to hit at the exact moment of travel. The solar particle event caused us to veer off course and crash land, with a little assistance from the Danish navigator."

Céthur did not mention the loss of the other nine ships – everyone knew well enough.

The Carrington Event, Céthur explained, was the strongest solar storm ever recorded. The solar storm that they had encountered was nearly twice the size and had fried the fleets complex microelectronics and communications equipment. Although shielded, the equipment could not withstand the intense magnetic disturbance, which had the same effect as a massive electromagnetic pulse. The Danish navigator, unfamiliar with manual protocols, veered off course, ramming two other vessels and causing a cascade that destroyed the smaller ships. Everyone in the room already knew this. They had all lived through the crash landing. The survivors had lost parents, wives, children and lovers.

Working with Céthur, Creidne and his team of engineers had salvaged what they could from the remnants of the fleet that had landed and had managed to create a miniature engine, capable of transporting a small number of people through time.

As Céthur continued his presentation Anu whispered to Morrigan.

"I know he's brilliant, but he's a pompous bastard. You'd think he designed all of this himself. He's standing on the shoulders of all of the engineers who built the bloody fleet in the first place."

Morrigan nudged Anu with her elbow.

"It could be worse: we could have to listen to that bitch of a wife of his, Ériu. The stupid cow only wants us to name the eastern settlement after her because of her family's standing back home. She's nearly as bad as that idiot son of hers, Bres."

Anu grinned and stifled a laugh. Her sidebar with Morrigan meant that she had lost concentration, and the room had suddenly quietened. Everyone was looking at her. Quick to recover, she sat up straight and delivered her opinion.

"It pains me to say this, but we should not transport anything other than communication and medical equipment with the ground team, and even that should be kept to a minimum. We can replace the ground team and try again, but the lasers and other equipment cannot be replaced. We simply don't have the resources to remanufacture them," Anu said.

Creidne took the floor.

"We have a finite supply of rare earth minerals and crystals and yes, I know that Ireland has a rich supply of metals and some precious stones, but they are not suitable for laser production. We have used everything we have to repair the equipment needed to clear the ash cloud before its effects are irreversible. If the equipment is destroyed, we can't remake it."

Although Creidne did not dwell on the ash cloud, they all understood. The ash cloud had created the volcanic winter that shut out the sun and led to the demise of the civilisation of the 21st century. Most of the plant and animal species had been wiped from the earth.

"With Macha and Badb's help, we have identified vaulted locations in which to place the equipment, ready for retrieval by the ground team. These locations will be reviewed by our historians using the databases we took with us on the ships and will be communicated electronically to the ground team via their handheld computer and implants. We will give them a central rallying point. In this case, we're using Tara in Mide. We hope, over the centuries to come, that the locations will be undisturbed."

"When are they travelling?" Morrigan asked.

"We are hoping, in the next few days," Nuada replied.

Morrigan shook her head.

"That's not what I meant. What I meant is, when are they travelling to? How close to the event?"

"Two days before the eruptions start, to give them time to locate the equipment before the folding."

The folding was how the Mayo people referred to the seismic event that caused the edge of the Eurasian tectonic plate to slide under the North American plate. The result had been the eruption of volcanoes all along the mid-Atlantic ridge, dormant volcanoes in mainland Europe suddenly activating, powerful earthquakes on both sides of the Atlantic. The Irish had a way of understating things. As World War II was referred to as 'The Emergency', the cataclysm was referred to as 'The Folding'.

In fairness to the people of Mayo, the folding was as good a name for the event as any. The southwest of the country – counties Cork, Kerry and parts of Limerick and Clare – had literally been folded under. The map of Ireland changed dramatically: the legs of the teddy bear were no more; the mountain ranges in Dublin and Wicklow growing significantly and taking on alpine height and appearance.

"Two days is cutting it very fine; isn't it Nuada?" Morrigan asked. "After all, we know that the travel will be debilitating. If it takes a day to recover, then it won't be enough time."

Nuada lost his temper.

"Well, how much time is enough time? A week, a month, a year? We've been through this already, Morrigan. It's a balancing act – if we give them too much time, they could be captured, and the angels only know what could happen to them."

"An extra day should be enough," she said softly.

"Fine, we'll send them three days in advance then," he said, regaining his composure.

Morrigan had more questions.

"What about their clothes? Their appearance? We'll have to make sure they fit in; that they aren't captured."

Nuada ran his hands through his hair in exasperation.

"Do you know how little information we have about that time? We've gone through everything we have, and we can't make head nor tail of their fashion and customs. It seems to have changed every day. Over the space of twenty years, they went through hundreds of fashions, and their technology is ever evolving. It seems to change every six months. We're sending them back in linen clothing and leather sandals. They're bloody soldiers. They are trained not to be caught, for angel's sake."

"But they won't have weapons," Morrigan persisted.

"But they are weapons, according to you," Nuada said, sarcastically.

Morrigan used every opportunity to praise the strength and agility of the Fianna. He hoped that she would choke on it.

Anu intervened as the conversation disintegrated into an argument. She banged the table over and over until she got their attention.

"All of you, we will support this mission and give it every resource we have available."

She glanced at Nuada.

"From the time the mission begins, the team have eight days to accomplish what they need to do: three days up to the folding and a window of five days after. Any more than that and the damage will be unrecoverable. We will put a 24-hour watch in place to support them. Either way, when the eight days are done, we mothball the equipment and prepare the ships for shut down. The ships are dying. It's time to move all personnel to Ireland. The ships will be moved to safe locations, out of reach of the folding when it happens, and those who do not want to live out their time in the settlement can go into stasis. From that point on, emergency beacons will be activated, and we wait for a rescue – if there is anyone alive in the future to execute a rescue."

Anu stood at her full height and stared down at the remainder of the fleet's command and engineering corps. They acknowledged her decision. She purposefully had not discussed sending a second team. That would only happen if they could be sure that the mission had failed. The meeting was recorded in the ship's log. Each commander knew his or her assignment.

Nuada flexed his prosthesis, the silver fingers glinting in the bright light of the ship's corridors.

"That went well," Morrigan grunted, swinging her long hair behind her.

Nuada smiled at her.

Morrigan had drawn the short straw. She needed to let Ogma know that Uiscias had been selected as part of the team.

Anu and Nuada called the chosen candidates one by one, to inform them of their selection.

Uiscias greeted the news with youthful enthusiasm, clearly excited at the prospect of going forward in time. Morfessa was stoic and focussed on the mission parameters but showed no reluctance.

Esras showed no reaction at all to the request but did ask if he could refuse. This question alone ruffled feathers within the command structure – there was talk of replacing Esras as a result. However, further discussions between Esras and Anu made it clear that Esras was willing to undertake the duty. He just wanted to confirm it as a request rather than an order.

Nuada and Anu broke the news to Semias. Unlike his colleagues, Semias took the news badly. His reaction was hysterical, and he claimed to be a victim of a conspiracy. Anu tried to calm him but only succeeded in making things worse. Semias cited his age and health as impediments to completing the mission, although he was in excellent health for a man of his age. He convinced that the commanders were plotting against him and that he would not survive the neural implantation, which was, in fact, a ruse to lobotomise him. Dian Cécht intervened at this point and walked Semias through the procedure. He also guaranteed that Semias would be able to see the others successfully come through the operation before undergoing the knife himself.

The crew and settler communities were enthusiastic about the project, and Semias found little support among them. Although he had the option to pull out of the mission, his reasons to pull out were lessening by the hour. His age, his health and his technical ability were all good. He was fully qualified to go. It was being seen by the community as a huge honour to be selected. Unlike others who had been passed over, he had no firm ties to the settlements or crew – he had no partner or family. He weighed the consequences of not going in the hours after being informed. To not go could alienate him from his power base. He would not be able to hold the moral high ground if he were thought to be a coward. Within 24 hours, he did an about face and embraced the mission.

The team dressed in silence, each wearing loose tunics of linen over trousers. They wore sandals and each was allocated a small satchel. Uiscias had a handheld computer, which doubled as a communication interface – the device would activate the neural implants once the team arrived at their destination.

The community in which they lived had no need of money. In fact, the concept was alien to them. There was nothing to buy, and precious metals and stones were seen as trinkets and baubles – they had no function. However, the historians were adamant that the travellers needed to bring something of perceived value with them, with which to barter for goods and services. After debate amongst the engineers and project team, diamonds were selected: they were easy to carry. As Morfessa and Semias did not need to carry any special equipment, it fell to them to be responsible for them. As medic, Esras carried some basic medical equipment in his satchel.

Semias tried to wear an ornate brooch on his collar, which was quickly removed. His attempts to wear a torc of beaten gold came to a quick end. He did manage to conceal a small pin on the inside of his tunic.

Anu, Morrigan and Nuada held a small reception for the team in the hours to departure. Anu was careful not to serve mead or ale, for fear that the travellers would become intoxicated. It would not have mattered: the team were too nervous to consider food or drink. Morrigan mingled with the engineering teams, historians and military commanders, carefully avoiding Ogma, who was morose, and Morfessa, who Morrigan thought might be resentful of her. Standing to one side, she tried to blend into the background.

Standing in a shaded corner, Bres did not see her.

She watched him as he was approached by a number of scientists and engaged in what looked like urgent conversation. Bres spiked Morrigan's interest. It did not take long for Semias to circle him. Morrigan was growing increasingly concerned and sneaked forward to listen in on their conversation. Semias and Bres were discussing database security – the same database that the team would rely on to find their equipment on arrival. Bres let Semias know that the virus had been activated and as a fallback, the location of the equipment had been erased. He would give Semias the new location right before departure.

Morrigan could not believe it. Semias and Bres were trying to sabotage the mission. The reception was ending. It was merely minutes to the departure. Morrigan grabbed Nuada and dragged him into a quiet office.

"Nuada, I just overheard Bres confirming to Semias that a virus he designed has been launched into the mission's database. The equipment locations have also been overwritten. I think they are trying to sabotage the team."

Nuada stared at her.

"Are you sure?" he whispered.

"I'm sure. I don't understand why though. What can either of them gain?"

Nuada thought for a moment.

"Once Semias is gone, there's no coming back. Maybe he wants to be the hero in the future. Maybe Bres sees the situation as an opportunity to curry favour: he steps in at the last minute and fixes the database when Ogma fails."

"Either way, there will be problems with the handheld computer when the team travels. They won't be able to use it effectively, which means they will be totally isolated. They won't have access to any geographic or historical information. What's worse, they won't be able to find the equipment. Shit, right now, we don't even know where it is. Whatever was in the database is gone."

Nuada cursed loudly.

"Okay! If Bres is going to give Semias the location of the equipment, we've got to let him. I'll alert the Fianna, and they will post guard. We'll get the location from Bres, and we'll make sure Morfessa has it, okay? I'll also send a team to find the historians who placed the equipment, and I'll find Macha. They've got to know exactly where it is. You stay with Semias. Watch him like a hawk."

Nuada ran to the ship's bridge and quickly found and briefed the Fianna commanders on duty. Soldiers were sent to get the locations in which each piece of equipment was buried.

Morrigan rushed to the departure point. She had missed the speeches, and Uiscias had already passed through the gateway. Esras was walking through the rippling viscous membrane as she entered the room. Only Morfessa and Semias remained. She found Ogma and begged him to halt the departure, but he told her firmly that he could not: the gateway could only remain open for only a few minutes more.

She scanned the room quickly but could see no sign of Bres. She rushed to the side of the equipment, mere feet from the gateway. With Esras through, Morfessa took a deep breath and stepped forward. Semias was looking around frantically. Morrigan felt a slight static discharge as Morfessa passed through the gateway. The situation was now critical. Semias was beginning to panic. Others in the room took his shocked expression as fear and did their best to reassure him. He kept his eyes focussed on the door while two scientists took him by the arm, to walk him to the gateway. Semias tried to shake them off, insisting that he needed to talk to Bres urgently before departure. He was ignored. As he came closer to the gateway, Semias grabbed at furniture and bystanders to halt his progress.

Nuada was suddenly at Morrigan's side.

"We can't find Bres," he said.

Morrigan screamed at the top of her lungs, and the room stood still. Everyone stopped.

"Semias says he needs to talk to Bres before he leaves. Find Bres. Now!" she shouted.

No one spoke. First one, then two more soldiers rushed to Nuada to report.

"Bres is missing. We have an all points alert, and the ship is being searched cabin by cabin."

Anu joined Nuada and Morrigan, who quickly filled her in. All three stared at Semias. Semias, realising that they knew something of his duplicity, used the confusion as an opportunity to slip through the gateway. Morrigan tried to grab him, but she was too late.

Seeing Semias go through the gateway, Ogma made to shut down the portal. Morrigan watched his movements as if in slow motion. The team that she had chosen, and who were effectively giving their lives, were betrayed at the hands of Semias. In a split-second decision, she ran forward and threw herself through the gateway before it was powered down.

The Present

Chapter 10

The Travellers

Semias struggled through the souterrain, the underground chamber stretching back under fallow fields. The earth was damp and the mud made climbing through more difficult. He was getting old, he thought to himself. He emerged into a field surrounded by stone walls, typical for this part of Roscommon.

Semias was what his contemporaries might call middle aged, but he retained his regal bearing and muscular physique. If anyone had calculated his age, they would have found his middle years were well behind him. If he had ever been measured, he would know he was tall, approaching six feet five inches but to his contemporaries, he was of average height. His upper body was covered in scars – war wounds he called them, all inflicted by knives, daggers and the odd war hammer. A Quaternary tattoo on his right bicep represented the four elements. A Celtic dragon, symbolising sovereignty and leadership, covered his left shoulder and upper arm. His complexion was fair, his eyes grey green that shone with eloquence and a hint of superiority. His fair hair was shot through with silver, cut tight at the sides and the braid in which it was worn fell to his waist.

As he crawled through the entrance to the passage, he cursed Anu for sending him here, and he cursed Bres for double crossing him. He saw Esras leaning against the stone boundary and breathing heavily. Even in the smothered moonlight, Semias could see the distress on Esras's face.

They had had no real training per se – there simply was not time. Three days of briefings had taken them through what to expect, but it was clear that the instructors were in the dark. All they really knew was that they would suffer symptoms similar to anaemia, and its onset would be sudden. They would be nauseous, tired and would suffer severe cramping. They would also be severely dehydrated.

Esras was as tall as Semias. His athletic build made him look even taller than the older man. Dirty blonde ringlets were tied back with a leather strip, falling halfway down his back. Everything about him was light, from his pale blue of his eyes to his porcelain complexion. The tree of life tattooed at his wrist identified him as a healer. Despite his leanness, there was nothing weak about Esras. He radiated determination and spirit. Unfortunately, the trip to this remote townland had taken more from him than expected. They all knew that travel of this type would take its toll on mind and body. They had been chosen because they could survive it.

Morfessa had climbed through the passage moments earlier, his white-blond hair plastered with thick mud and Roscommon muck. What could be seen of him glowed in the moonlight. Morfessa's crystalline blue eyes shone with merriment. He had the stature of a blacksmith – fit and strong. His hands were those of a craftsman, fingers long and dexterous. Like blacksmiths of old, Morfessa shared a knowledge of weaponry. Nobody would describe Morfessa as anything other than handsome. Anyone who got in his way would describe him as fearsome.

Morfessa's upper body was tattooed, but his were different from his fellow travellers – they were battle tattoos. Morfessa was a soldier and a brave one at that. His team was Uiscias and Esras. Semias was outside of the chain of command technically – a civilian on the mission, but he was a civilian with a lot of experience and a natural command authority. He was also a schemer, and Morfessa disliked him. Morfessa would feign to defer to Semias unless the mission was threatened. His orders were to let nothing get in the way of their success.

Uiscias had left the others and was exploring the surroundings. The place was barren – no animals in the fields, no crops growing, but yet, the grass was lush and damp. Somewhere in the distance, there were farms and homesteads, but no light shone through the curtain of fog. Uiscias was the youngster of the group – a teenager but an accomplished one. His background was the sea, and he was an expert swimmer and diver, but that was not why he was chosen for the mission.

His red hair was cut short at the back and sides but long on top, swept back into a ponytail. His eyes were a rich blue, and his complexion was pale and freckled. He was shorter than his compatriots but still stood well over six feet tall and had the broad shoulders and slim waist of a swimmer. Like all teenagers, Uiscias was drawn to technology and intuitively understood how to use it. It was this talent that had led to his selection. Ogma had taken the gifted teenager and honed his technical skills.

Semias stood over Esras, his breathing was still laboured.

"Where the hell are we?" he shouted.

He was not overly concerned about Esras's condition.

Uiscias bounded back from the ditch that he had been surveying. Despite the weight of the mission, he was excited, happy even. He consulted the computer device.

"Were in a place called Oweynagat – the cave of cats."

Semias made an exasperated face.

"And where exactly is that?" he roared.

Morfessa approached the others. Not here five minutes and already Semias was losing his temper. It seemed that Semias was showing his true colours early. Morfessa needed to defuse the situation.

As he was leaving the souterrain, he had noticed markings above the entrance.

"Maybe we should read the Ogham inscription at the gate. It might tell us what our next step should be."

Semias inclined his head towards the entrance to the souterrain and the cave beyond and nodded. Morfessa made his way back to examine the inscription on the stone lintel. His muffled shouts were barely audible.

"It says the pillar of Fraech, son of Medb."

The trio looked at each other and shrugged. Ancient graffiti written in Ogham.

"Well, that was helpful," Semias growled.

Morfessa ignored Semias and gave Uiscias a smile of encouragement.

"Uiscias, what do you know about Oweynagat?" Morfessa asked.

Uiscias pulled out their computer device from the leather satchel he carried across his torso.

"Okay – it says that Oweynagat is the gates of hell – the entrance to the otherworld. Its old Celtic mythology. That's probably why we ended up here – it's a location marked on the settlement's maps. We're in the midlands of Ireland, slightly to the north of the central point. Were in a place called Roscommon."

Uiscias took a breath and continued.

"The cave is part of Cruachan Aí, the ancient capital of Connacht. This is a large royal settlement. There are standing stones, burial mounds and a sanctuary ..."

They all knew that they had to find the closest way point from which to plot the route to their destination. Ancient sites were a good starting point. When planning the trip, they had made an assumption that the sites would not be disturbed in the passage of time.

"Where is the focal point of the capital?" Morfessa asked.

Uiscias consulted the device.

"There's a large ring fort called Rath Cruachan. It's about a league from here. From there, we can map a route to our target," Uiscias replied.

"Can you get us to Rath Cruachan?"

"No problem. We just follow the Slighe Assail – the ceremonial route. It will bring us right there. We should be able to mark the route with the computer."

Esras was still in no condition to travel. Rather than suggest that the team recover, which Morfessa knew would cause objections from Semias, he decided to create a diversion.

"Uiscias, let's see how well the communicator works. There should be a support team on standby. Please raise them, and let them know we have arrived safely. And then set about getting us to this settlement," Morfessa ordered.

Uiscias tried and failed to reach the support team. He adjusted the signal strength, checked the device settings and even reviewed the programming code to no avail. He checked the device functionality, and some functions appeared to be intact – the translator seemed to work. Some maps were visible. He could see their location, but the database containing information on the mission parameters and locations was corrupted. There was no way marker from Rath Cruachan to Tara, which was located in the province of Mide. Uiscias tried and failed to activate the implants and despite a review of the source code, could not get the commands to execute. He did, however, identify the tell-tale signs of a computer virus, which he could see had infected the database.

When the extent of information loss was made clear, Morfessa, Semias and Uiscias knew the mission was in in jeopardy.

"We're lost" Semias shouted.

Morfessa shook his head.

"Semias, no one is suggesting that we're lost. We all received thorough briefings, and we knew taking technology through the portal was risky. We've lost the support team and the database, but we still have what's in our heads. Finding our equipment is going to be difficult, but it's not impossible. In addition to the information on the communicator, the settlement will have left location markers, and we have a rough idea where everything is – it should be in Mide, the central province. We can find what we need to in the old-fashioned way."

"You don't understand," Semias whined. "The equipment is not where we think it is. It's been moved. Only Bres knows where, and he didn't tell me."

Semias, Uiscias and Esras stared at Semias.

"What the fuck have you done?" Uiscias demanded.

Before Semias had a chance to reply, they heard feminine shouts and foul language. Morrigan emerged from the hole cut into the earth, her raven hair plastered with muck and vegetation. She stumbled through the darkness and made straight for Semias, blue eyes blazing with anger.

"I'm going to fucking kill you," she screamed and produced a dagger from her waist.

Uiscias grabbed his commander around the waist, being careful to avoid the dagger. Morrigan struggled and cursed. Uiscias could not hold her. Morfessa grabbed both of her wrists.

"Morrigan, calm down. What the hell is going on?"

Morrigan stopped struggling, and Uiscias let her go.

"Semias has been scheming with Bres. They have introduced a computer virus into the database and erased all data regarding the artefact's location. We won't be able to find the equipment. I don't know how badly the communication functions will be affected or if we will be able to communicate with the support team, or with anyone here for that matter. Semias, what the hell have you done?"

Semias simpered.

"Bres was upset at being overlooked for the mission. He's tired of being passed over and asked for my help programming a simple virus. It's something that Ogma will be able to fix easily. Bres was going to jump in and erase it, using an antivirus programme I gave him. He also played with the data on the equipment location. He had the equipment moved from Mide to somewhere else. He promised me he would tell me the exact whereabouts before I came through, but he didn't show up. I had to come without it."

Morrigan used all her considerable strength to grab Semias by the throat.

"You've signed our death warrant. And the death warrant of every plant, animal and person in the future."

Semias struggled to breath, such was her grip.

"It wasn't me. It was Bres," he moaned.

"Bres doesn't have the intelligence to come up with a scheme like this, Semias. We all know who is capable though," Morrigan growled.

Morfessa gently placed his hand over Morrigan's.

"Killing him won't change anything Morrigan. He's a bastard, but we might need him. Let him go. He can run, but there's nowhere to run to."

Morrigan released her hold.

"Just keep him out of my sight."

Having no further reason to delay, Morfessa instructed Uiscias and Esras to prepare to leave Oweynagat.

The travellers set out to find Rath Cruachan, following the way finder on the communicator, finding the secondary road that travelled in the same direction as Slighe Assail. Signposts by the road pointed them in the direction of a visitors' centre on the site. Morfessa and Uiscias half carried Esras, still not recovered from trip. Semias led the way under Morrigan's stare. The tarmacked surface of the R392 was barely visible in the fog.

With Semias far out in front, Morfessa, Uiscias and Esras were briefed by Morrigan.

Chapter 11

Who's There?

Sadbh breathed a sigh of relief. She had made it through Frenchpark and Ballinagare and was now on the road to Tulsk. The roadworks that had plagued her for the last thirty kilometres were finally at an end. It would be well after midnight when she got home, but she was beyond caring. She just wanted the comfort of her bed.

She had not encountered a single vehicle along the way, which was good. On the other hand, the fog had gotten thicker. What had started out as a light mist in Ballaghadereen was now a pea souper. It felt solid. It had none of the swirling eddies she associated with fog. This blanket felt otherworldly.

She could see the lights of Tulsk in the distance now, a blooming light directly ahead. Could she increase the speed a little, she thought? She had kept well under the speed limit since she left Charlestown and now wanted to make up time.

The lights of the village perked her up. She would turn the radio back on, listen to Newstalk to keep herself awake. Maybe she could pick up Classic Hits and listen to some 80s music. She averted her eyes briefly to the dashboard to turn on the radio and when she looked back up at the road, she could see a moving object in her line of sight. Reacting on instinct, she hit the brakes and turned the wheel frantically to the left. The front of the car mounted the verge on the left of the road. The engine cut out, leaving her stranded with the back of the car in the path of oncoming traffic.

Sadbh was in shock, she sat for several seconds not knowing what she had seen or if she had hit it. She gingerly got out of the car, searching and calling out to no avail, narrowly avoiding falling into a drainage ditch. She realised that the car had stopped just short of it. Another few feet and the car would be submerged, completely invisible to passing traffic. She realised how close she had come to being killed.

She shakily opened the car boot and found an emergency torch. She examined the car for damage and then searched the area. She heard nothing. She could not see anyone. There was no other car there. She listened intently for the sound of loose animals, but there was no sound.

After a few minutes, she turned her attention back to her little car, surveying the damage. Luckily, her front wheel had avoided going over into the ditch, so at least she should be able to reverse back onto the road. As for scratches, she would have to wait until tomorrow to examine the paintwork in daylight. She tried to examine the front of the Audi but could not get to see properly because of the ditch. She just hoped that there was no engine damage.

She got back inside, started the engine and carefully reversed the car back into the lane. The car was not safe here. It could easily be rammed from behind. She drove carefully and parked as far off the road as she could. She pulled in on solid verge and activated her hazard warning lights. She realised that she was in shock. She turned on the interior light and grabbed the water bottle from the passenger footwall. She struggled to remember what to do next. She worked out that she needed to make the car as visible as possible. She struggled out of the car again and went to the boot. There was a warning triangle and beacon in there, as well as a Hi-Viz vest. The shaking had not subsided.

She silently blessed her father, who made her carry emergency kit in her car. With safety gear in place, she took the torch and made her way back along the road to find out what it was she had seen. As she walked, she saw nothing out of the ordinary – just the normal wild grasses, ditches and road markings. Cat's eyes gleamed in the torchlight.

One hundred meters away from the car, she thought she spotted something moving. There was no noise but then, *the fog dampens noise, didn't it?* she thought. She saw the movement again and swung the torch in the direction. Definitely something.

"Hello! Is there anyone there?" she called.

Chapter 12

Sadbh is Ainm Dom

The five travellers had been lucky: the machine had come very close to hitting them as they walked down the centre line of the road. In the immediate aftermath, they had huddled on the verge, making no noise, waiting to see if they had been discovered.

They heard the machine moving, and then there was quiet again, but it did not last. They heard a strange metallic clicking and then a human voice. Seconds later, a swinging orb of light became visible. Uiscias scanned for a weapon, but the computer failed to work.

Morrigan motioned for the others to stay back and crept forward.

She laughed. The noise came from shoes, boots similar to military boots with metal heels and toes. The woman who stood before them was wearing a tight T-shirt over fatigues, clearly a military uniform of some type. However, the woman did not look like a soldier or act like one. She smelt of roses and jasmine.

She spoke a language Morrigan could not understand yet, her face was full of concern.

She beckoned the others forward. They sagged with relief when they saw that it was only a woman.

"Uiscias, what the hell is she saying?" Semias whispered.

Uiscias consulted his device; it was not working properly. After a few seconds, he responded.

"I think she wants to know if we are hurt, but I can't be sure."

"Can you speak to her?"

Uiscias shrugged.

"I don't know, but I will try."

While Semias and Uiscias were talking, Sadbh tried to identify the language they were speaking. It was not French, German, Italian or Spanish. It did not sound Russian or Slavic, but it did sound familiar. She spoke a little Danish, and it sounded similar. A few words sounded really familiar. Could they be Irish? If they were, then this was a dialect she had never heard before but then again, the only Irish she could remember from school was 'Where is the toilet?' and the odd word for body parts and weather.

She observed them from a distance of a few meters. The young one was playing with a phone – no surprise there, just like thousands of young lads, he was a slave to technology. One of the blonde guys looked like he'd had a few too many to drink. The other blonde was holding him up and looking at her strangely. The older one, with the grey hair, was smiling at her. The woman looked like a banshee and stared at her intently.

Sadbh struggled to remember her schoolgirl Irish.

"Conas atá tú?" she said. (*How are you?* in Irish).

This got the attention of the five travellers. Could they understand her?

"Sadbh is ainm dom." (*My name is Sadbh*).

They stopped staring at her and rapidly conversed in their language.

Semias and the other travellers could not believe that Sadbh was speaking to them in broken Goídelc. How the hell could she know the language? Semias rounded on Uiscias, demanding to know what he had done. Uiscias shrugged his shoulders and said he had done nothing. The communication programmes were not fully functional. The woman was speaking Goídelc, and it was nothing to do with him.

Sadbh stared in disbelief as the banshee pointed at her boots. There was a hell of an argument going on. She focussed on trying to remember her long forgotten Irish classes. How the hell do you ask if someone is injured? She could not remember the word, but *tinn* was 'sick', wasn't it?

"An bhfuil tú tinn?" she asked. (*Are you sick?*).

Esras was semi-conscious, being tended to by Morfessa. Uiscias was trying to get his device to function as a translator, so it fell to Semias to try to talk to her while Morrigan watched like a hawk. So, he spoke slowly and clearly in Goídelc.

"Níl muid gortaithe, ach tá mo chara tinn," he said. (*We're not injured, but my friend is sick*).

Sadbh concentrated. It was definitely a form of Irish. Did he say they were dead, but his friend was sick? No, that was not right. Injured, maybe? They were not injured, but his friend was sick. She studied the blonde man lying on the verge. He definitely did not look well.

She tried to ask if they needed a doctor or an ambulance, but it was clear that these strangers could not understand her. What should she do now?

Uiscias pulled a set of wireless earpieces from his satchel and fitted them. He was grinning. He had got the translator partially working. He focussed on Sadbh's speaking. After a few seconds, the translation software processed what Sadbh was saying. The implants still were not functional, but at least he could communicate. Slowly, he began to speak.

"We are visitors to this place. We are travelling to the Lia Fail at the palace of the High King, Conn, in Mide. My friend is sick from travelling. We need water, food and weapons."

Uiscias remembered to smile after he spoke. He looked like a serial killer.

Sadbh stared open mouthed. Who the hell were these people? Looking closely, they looked like bit part actors from *Vikings* or *Game of Thrones*. They seemed to be dressed in costumes of some type, and their hairstyles certainly did not look like anything that you would see on the streets of Dublin. The redhead was speaking a form of English but with a Nordic accent. It sounded like he was repeating a script.

It was nearly midnight. What the hell were they doing in the middle of nowhere with no transport? And with no coats or proper shoes for that matter. Did they not know that they should be carrying a torch or some form of light when walking on country roads?

"Look, you've had your fun. You can stop messing now. You ran my car off the road, and I could have been killed," Sadbh said, the irritation clear in her voice.

Uiscias cleared his throat and repeated his message. This time, the smile faltered. Morrigan placed her hand over her dagger.

"We are travelling to the Lia Fail and need food, water and weapons."

"Well, the Lia Fail is a long way from here. All the shops are shut, so you're out of luck."

Sadbh turned her back on them and made her way towards her car.

The Lia Fail was the stone of destiny – the centrepiece on the Hill of Tara. Sadbh had taken her adult children there for a day trip last year and spent most of the afternoon in the visitor's centre because of torrential rain.

Semias seemed not to understand what was going on and entered into a rapid-fire conversation with Morfessa, ignoring Uiscias, who stood in the road looking like a scared rabbit. Semias realised Sadbh was leaving and moved aggressively towards her. He did not intimidate Sadbh, who heard his approach.

"I don't know who you are or what you're up to, but I can tell you that you are a long way from the Hill of Tara. Keep off the road. Traffic here moves at speed. If you don't need an ambulance, I really can't help you."

If these idiots were going to pull a fast one, she was having none of it. Sadbh turned back towards her car, hurrying to reach the safety of the vehicle and get underway.

Semias grabbed the device from Uiscias, shoved an earbud into place and hurried forward, grabbing Sadbh's arm. Before he got a chance to say anything, she shrugged him off violently. She suddenly realised how exposed she was. Thankful for self-defence classes given by her eldest daughter, Sadbh kicked him in the groin and followed up with a sharp jab to the solar plexus. Before anyone had a chance to react, she screamed.

"Who the fuck do you think you are? I stopped because I thought I hit you. Get the hell away me!"

Morrigan kept her eyes on Sadbh but smiled. It served the bastard right, she thought. She raised her hands in front of her and made her way slowly towards Sadbh, passing Semias, who was rolling around the verge in pain.

"Amadán," Morrigan murmured, as she landed another blow with her heel.

While Semias whimpered, Morrigan reefed the ear buds from him and grabbed the communicator. She fitted them and spoke directly to Sadbh.

"I'm sorry. We thought you were sent to help us. And we need help. My colleague means no disrespect to you, and you are in no danger. Frankly, he's an idiot."

Morrigan turned and stared at Semias, baiting him to say something.

Morrigan pointed to Esras.

"My young friend is suffering from dehydration and is incoherent. He needs water. I need to get him to shelter before he deteriorates. Please help us. We won't hurt you."

Sadbh stared at Morrigan and glanced at Uiscias and Morfessa. Morrigan pulled her attention back on Esras.

"I'm not lying. Look at him, please. He is ill."

"You could be carjackers or murderers. I'm not letting you in my car, and I'm not staying here with you." Sadbh replied.

"We are not murderers; we are travellers. I don't know what a carjacker is, but it sounds bad. We are not bad people. We are here to complete a mission that involves no violence. We won't hurt you. Please help us."

Sadbh took an instant dislike to Semias, who, in her opinion, was an ass. However, when she looked at Morfessa and Uiscias tending to their friend, the concern on their faces was evident. Sadbh walked forward to where Esras lay. It was clear that he was ill, his breathing was shallow and skin looked clammy. Sadbh was a trained first responder and her first aid training kicked in. She took Esras pulse and completed an assessment. His heart was beating like a piston. His pulse was rapid, and his blood pressure was off. Esras was sweating, and his face was grey. After completing her examination, Sadbh stood away from him.

The young one walked to her side and whispered, "Tá brón orm."

He was trying to say that he was sorry. In that instant he reminded her of her daughter – the same doe eyes and wounded tone.

Sadbh focussed again on Esras. He looked really ill, ill enough to need a hospital.

Sadbh bit the inside of her lip. It was a bad idea to give him anything to drink or any medicines for that matter. If she could get cell coverage, she could call an ambulance but in this weather, the ambulance would take hours to reach the roadside and even then, the ambulance might not find them. She checked Esras again, looking for signs of injury – there was definitely no blood.

The older one, who attacked her, laid back against a stone wall. He looked exhausted and was shielding his manhood, while the tall blonde trashed him in whatever language they spoke. The youngest one looked pale and frightened. The woman, covered in muck and hair like a bird's nest, was definitely frazzled. The young redhead, having taken control of what Sadbh thought of as a translation app, had explained that Esras (that was the young man's name) was not suffering from a contagious disease or injury. He was suffering from anaemia.

"Okay, I'll give you a lift but only as far as Longford."

They did not understand. Sadbh tried to explain that Longford was a large town in the midlands and that there was a hospital there.

"Get your friend and come with me," she said to Uiscias.

She made hand signals. He seemed to understand and nodded.

As they struggled to get Esras to his feet, Sadbh returned to the car. She walked around it – no damage that she could see. The tank was nearly full with petrol – well, enough to get home.

How do you fit six people into a four-seater car, Sadbh thought?

Sadbh dropped the back seats of the Audi to increase the luggage space and invited Morrigan to organise the other four in the rear. Morrigan understood and kept Semias as far away from Sadbh as possible.

Sadbh pulled her valuables into the passenger footwell. She stuffed her cigarettes and lighter into her pocket, along with her android phone and a nail file – just in case. Bottles of water rolled around the floor. She grabbed them and passed them to Morrigan. As Morrigan began to climb into the rear of the car, Sadbh stopped her and pointed to the passenger seat.

"Give the knife to your blonde friend. If you don't, I'm not moving."

Sadbh pulled away from the verge and drove slowly, mindful of her passengers. They spoke quietly to each other in their language. After 40 minutes, as they were approaching Longford, Morfessa donned the earpieces and spoke to Sadbh.

"Thank you for allowing us in your vehicle. We don't mean any disrespect to you by speaking in our language. I think you might understand some of what we say without translation. We have been discussing Esras's condition and how we should proceed. Thank you again for your help."

Sadbh said nothing. They were close to a major town now. Rather than taking the bypass around Longford, Sadbh thought it safer to go through the town. When the travellers spoke, they did so only in what they called Goídelc. She picked up odd words of what they said, but the fog was as thick as ever and the roads dangerous, so she concentrated on her driving.

The streetlights and shop signs in the town gave some respite from the fog, but the streets were deserted. The pubs and takeaways were closed. On the outskirts of the town, the McDonalds was closed too. Sadbh had a bad feeling about dropping the travellers off in the middle of the deserted town. She did not want to be responsible for making the young man's condition worse, and she doubted that anyone would come to the aid of these New Age hippy psychos. If they were unlucky, they would encounter some young bucks looking for trouble.

There was a hospital in Longford, but she did not know where or even if it was open. She drove around the town looking for signposts but could see nothing. Instead of stopping on the next loop, she kept going out of the town towards the motorway.

She had a dilemma. The next major town they would travel through was Mullingar, but they would not reach there until 1 am at the earliest, and the best that she could do was to drop them on the outskirts of town. There was a hospital in Mullingar, but she did not know its location or even if it would accept walk-in emergencies. She needed time to think. She pulled into the first layby that they came to, leaving the engine idling.

"I don't know what you are doing or where you are going, except that it involves going to the Hill of Tara. Everything between here and Dublin is closed for the night. I'm worried about your friend. The water seems to have helped a little bit, but he is in no condition to spend the night at the roadside. I can drop you off in Kildare at a motorway service station, or I can take you through to Dublin."

While Esras's condition had improved only marginally, the rest and water and the heat in the car had revived the others. Uiscias translated what Sadbh had said, and the travellers engaged in animated discussion. Morfessa, his voice surprisingly deep, took the device from Uiscias and replied.

"We do want to travel to the place of the High Kings of Ireland. We need to reach there soon, but we also need to rest. Travelling has severely depleted our strength. Can you take us to a place that is safe? We don't care where it is. We will reward you for your help."

Sadbh did not answer – not because she did not want to; she just could not think of what to say.

She weighed up the options. She could go to the Gardaí, but the travellers had not committed a crime that she knew of, except for Semias, who was guilty of being an asshole, and she would have to explain why she had picked them up.

She could drop them off at a night shelter for the homeless, but she did not think that they could survive there for long. Despite appearances, they seemed vulnerable and a bit naïve, and a homeless shelter was a rough and tumble environment to say the least. Leaving them with drunks and addicts did not seem fair.

It was pointless bringing them to a hospital. Sadbh knew that she would pass near Tallaght Hospital and St James on the way into Dublin City. The hospitals were overcrowded and the best that the travellers could hope for was a choice between a night sitting in accident and emergency, waiting to be seen, and a place in a psychiatric ward.

Dublin may be a capital city, but there were few places that were open around the clock that were safe – no all-night bars or cafés except, maybe, at the airport. And anyway, the airport was a long way out of her way.

If she took them home, would she endanger her kids? It was a possibility but then again, she had had them in the car for quite a while, and they had barely moved and despite the language barrier and strangeness of them, the soldier, the teenager and the woman were polite and respectful. The jury was still out on the older one, though she noted that the one with the deep voice, Morfessa, appeared to be keeping him in check.

Sadbh thought about the situation while she drove. There had been a lot of polite serial killers that had come to light over the past twenty years. She decided to keep driving, hoping a solution would turn up somewhere between Mullingar and Dublin. She let them know that she would be driving to the city of Dublin. From there, County Meath (what they called Mide) would be easy to reach by public transport. She would find somewhere for them to rest.

Morfessa translated, and they thanked her and tried to give her a little linen bag. She was driving and could not take it, so Morrigan put it in a cupholder. It would have to wait.

Chapter 13

Office Sanctuary

She pulled into the driveway and killed the lights. The travellers were all sleeping. She had not intended to take them home with her, but she had driven the last twenty kilometres on autopilot. She sat in the driveway of her house, an ordinary semi-detached property on a quiet avenue in Glasnevin. Sadbh had bought and paid for this house herself, and she was proud of it. It had been her home for more than twenty years.

She looked up at the windows. The bedrooms were in darkness but through the hall windows, she could see that the landing light was on. This had always been her family's way since the kids were young – it meant that they had some light coming into their bedrooms and made finding their way around easier during the night. As adults, it had not changed.

Sadbh realised that her kids were at home and was suddenly aware of the risk she was taking in bringing the travellers into her home. She needed to find somewhere to put them. Her little office was the only option. During the Covid-19 pandemic, she had a local builder convert her garage into an office so that she could work from home. With three daughters, access to the house's only bathroom was always a struggle, so she had a half bathroom installed downstairs in the office. It was plain and uncluttered, but it was private. The office had another advantage: it had its own front door. At the rear, the office was connected to the house by a short hallway, and entry to the house was via the old back door. She could lock the door from inside the kitchen, making sure that the travellers could not gain access to the house.

She quietly opened her office door, leaving it ajar. She turned on the room lights and quickly locked the door to the hallway and the kitchen, making sure that the travellers could not get into the main part of the house. Although it was early August, the office had a chill. She turned up the radiator and heard it filling. The room would heat up in minutes. She left the door ajar and returned to the car.

Grabbing her kit as best she could, she took the steps up to her hall door and opened it. The wide hallway opened out into the sitting room, dining room and galley kitchen. She had always joked that the hallway was the biggest part of the house. She made her way to the kitchen, switching on lights in her wake.

The kitchen door led into a small hallway with a door to the office, which she locked. Back in the kitchen, she filled the kettle and turned on the rings of the hob. She checked the fridge, empty except for a block of cheddar and some salami. *Damn*, she thought, *there's nothing left*.

Sadbh normally hit the shops early on Saturday, when most people were having a deserved lie in. She checked the presses – there were some beans, packet soup and a couple of tins of tuna. The bread bin had a packet of croissants and some of those bake-yourself bread rolls.

The dining room was in darkness. She stepped through the kitchen to turn on the dining room lights and when she turned, Semias was standing in hall, staring at her. After a few seconds, she regained control of herself and retrieved a paring knife from the kitchen drawer.

"I opened the door to the office. It's the white door outside. Make yourself comfortable. Do you want tea or coffee?"

Semias said nothing. He tilted his head and smiled. He did not know what she was saying.

"I have some hot chocolate, if you would prefer that?"

He remained quiet – he definitely did not understand. Sadbh cursed her stupidity at leaving the front door on the latch. She needed to get him out of her house. She grabbed her keys from the kitchen countertop. She planned to lock the door from now on.

Her heart thudded as she calmly made her way back past Semias. She walked past him, through the hall to the door and beckoned for him to follow. She went into the office, stood in the middle of the room and gestured for him to follow. She gestured to the bathroom and opened the door. She then turned to the little kitchen unit and turned on the tap. He seemed to understand. As he looked around, she checked that the radiator was warm.

When he was inside, Sadbh backed out of the room and headed back to the driveway. She walked a few paces back to the driveway and gently shook Morfessa, who woke easily. She felt safer when Morfessa was around. He, in turn, roused the others. Esras was still out of it. Uiscias and Morfessa laid him on the futon in the office and covered him with the throw that was draped over the back.

Sadbh retreated back to the house, closing the door behind her and breathed a sigh of relief. The upstairs hot press had extra pillows and blankets and thinking of Esras, she pulled some things into a laundry hamper. Out the front door and a few steps over to the office, she opened the door and presented the travellers with the laundry hamper. She took a pillow, bent her head into it and pulled a bedspread from the hamper around her shoulders, in a sort of mime.

Morfessa nodded and smiled and took the basket.

"I'll make you something to eat. I don't have much food in, but I'll find something. I'll make tea, but the machine on the counter makes coffee and hot chocolate. I can show you how."

Uiscias nodded. Sadbh pulled China mugs from the overhead press, filled the Dolce Gusto machine with water and showed Uiscias how to use it, loading a cartridge of hot chocolate. She pushed the lever over, and the hot chocolate began to flow through hisses and steam. When the cup was three-quarters full, she turned the lever back and pressed the power button to turn it off. She deftly removed the spent cartridge that went into the bin and refilled it with a fresh one from the box on the counter.

"It's ready to go if you want to make more. The cups are in the press, and you can refill the machine from the tap."

She handed the drink to Uiscias before retreating once again.

"Food will be ready in fifteen minutes," she said, flashing the fingers on her right hand three times.

Morrigan closed the door and listened for any sound outside. Satisfied that they were alone, she began to speak.

"What the hell do you make of that?" Morrigan asked.

Uiscias sniffed the contents of the cup before passing it to Morfessa. Morfessa cautiously took a sip.

"I don't know what this is, but it is delicious. I can't describe it, but it's fluffy and creamy and very sweet."

Morrigan gave him a withering look.

"This is no joking matter, Morfessa. I am asking you for your professional opinion"

Morfessa looked Semias up and down.

"My professional opinion is that Semias went out of his way to frighten that woman who, by the way, has significantly shortened our journey to the Lia Fail. If she'd had a weapon when Semias grabbed her, he'd be dead. There are two reasons that she helped us. One, she could see that Esras really was ill and two, Uiscias appealed to her motherly instincts. I think she most likely has a child or children around his age. If Uiscias hadn't intervened when he did, we'd still be at the side of the road in Roscommon. By the way, Morrigan, she doesn't like you."

Morrigan vehemently objected.

"We are not here to make friends, Morfessa."

"I am well aware of why we are here. Remember that the computer is not working. We have half a database and no support team. The translator is barely functioning. Whether you like it or not, we actually need some friends. With respect to you and Semias, we can't afford you to alienate the one friend we might have."

Uiscias had watched Sadbh make the hot chocolate and quickly made more. He intended to help Esras drink one and have one himself.

Uiscias sniffed the drink, inhaling the aroma.

"Go ahead and try it, Uiscias. It's really very good. It has lots of sugar, so it should help revive Esras."

"We didn't travel all this way for a culinary experience, Morfessa. Where the hell are we and more to the point, when the hell are we?" Semias bellowed.

Uiscias's machine beeped, and a series of lights turned from red to green.

"Okay, the computer seems to be online, for now at least. We are on the east coast, about eight leagues south of a Norse settlement called Na Sceirí. We are about two leagues from the Bay of Dyflin, pronounced Duflin, another Norse settlement. The female referred to Dublin many times – the pronunciation is similar. I think the village has become a city."

Semias, Morrigan and Morfessa breathed a sigh of relief. At last, some good news.

Uiscias continued to consult the computer.

"The good news is that I have a name for our first destination. It is called Ráith na Senad or the Rath of the Synods, and it's in a place called Tara in County Meath. Again, the woman referred to Tara several times.

Travelling in the vehicle tonight brought us within twelve leagues of the site, but I'm still having difficulty contacting the support team. The virus is still active, from what I can see."

"It will take the best part of a day, on foot, to reach the first destination but only if we are rested and have some food. As for the time, it appears we're in the right year. By my calculation, we have less than three days before the cataclysm. I can't be more accurate than that."

Morfessa, having finished his hot chocolate, butted in.

"Uiscias, we have roughly seven days to find the Claíomh Solais and get it operational. How likely is it to be in this Tara?"

Uiscias shrugged his shoulders.

"I really don't know. The notes indicate this is a very famous place and for the last century, people have scoured it clean, searching for remnants of the past. This was documented in the historic records held by the fleet. I don't think it's likely that it will be there. The best we can hope for is a signpost to another site. Look, we knew our chances would be poor before we came on this mission. Without being able to contact the support team, I have no idea where the equipment could be hidden. There's nothing in the database that can help us. The mission plan and locations are not accessible. I don't know what else to do."

Uiscias sounded tired and defeated.

Morfessa tried to encourage Uiscias.

"We know you've done your best. It's not your fault that the machine is broken. If you can, try to get the implants working – that would be a great help. In the meantime, I will try to make peace with the woman. She has been of great help so far, and we should be grateful."

Esras, still reclining on the futon but now awake, made his presence known.

"We're not here to save this place, you know. The mission is about saving our place. These are uneducated peasants. We owe them nothing. It doesn't matter if they help us or not."

Semias rounded on Esras.

"Well, I don't know about you, but I'm pretty happy to be here in one piece. While you were comatose, one of the peasants transported us across the country, gave us food and water and is giving us shelter. Don't forget, they are our family, even if it's a few generations removed. We will need their help if we have any hope of succeeding."

Morfessa and Uiscias looked on in amusement. It had not taken long for Semias to do a 360-degree turn.

"We should have had a team on the ground to help us. We should have been properly equipped for the mission," Esras replied.

Uiscias requested an update from the device, and the others could see that the news was not good. Uiscias had received a delayed transmission from the support team. He was not quite sure how it got through.

"I don't know how this was transmitted but the message says, we are on our own. The software is not functioning, and they can't isolate the virus. The anti-virus programme didn't work. The message also confirms that sections of the database have been wiped, the back-up drives are damaged, and the data cannot be restored. It looks like it's just us and whatever help we can muster locally. Something must have happened aboard the *Findias*."

Chapter 14

An Awkward Situation

While the travellers were discussion options, a car door slammed, sounding like a rifle report. The travellers stopped moving and making noise. Esras used his position to peer over the windowsill and down the driveway.

They could hear noises now, shrieks and laughter, the *click clack* of high heels on the drive and the vain effort to insert a key in the hall door. Sadbh heard it too from the kitchen. Before the key was fitted, she was opening the door.

It was two of her daughters, making their way home from a night on the tiles in Temple Bar. They were not drunk, but they were not sober either.

"Hi Ma! What are you doing up at this hour. You don't have to wait up for us, you know."

"Get in the house and be quiet. Look at the state of you!" she hissed as she bundled them into the hall.

Saoirse weaved her way into the kitchen and made for the office through the back door.

"Where are you going?" Sadbh shouted.

"The loo. I need a wee," Saoirse shouted back.

Oh shit! Sadbh thought.

"It's blocked. Use the bathroom upstairs."

Saoirse wiggled her way back out to the hall and up the stairs, while Muireann giggled at her sister's antics.

"She's going to pee herself," she said as she grinned at her mum.

The travellers waited for silence to return before they felt it safe to whisper. Morfessa put the cup down on the counter.

"Uiscias, can you make more of this stuff? I definitely feel better after drinking it."

Uiscias set about turning on the machine, while Morfessa grabbed more mugs from the press.

"Do you think this is what they call food? They have teeth, so I presume they eat solid food. I'm not complaining though – my blood sugar is definitely rising. You should try some, Semias."

Esras sat up and stretched.

"We need a plan for getting to the Rath of the Synods."

Semias raised his hand – a signal to stop.

"Let's wait until we have eaten and rested. We're in no fit state to think right now. Something is going on in the house. Maybe they are calling for help."

The girls leaned against the kitchen counter as Sadbh explained what had happened. Sadbh told them how she had nearly hit them in the fog, finding Esras delirious and told them all about their strange dress and manners.

"You picked up five weirdos on your way home from Mayo, and you brought them home! Have you lost your mind? Wait until Brendan and Etain find out – they'll go mad," Muireann chuckled.

"Hold on a second. They can't get into the house. It's my office after all, I decide who goes in there. And they seem harmless. Actually, harmless is the wrong description – more like gormless."

"They aren't Irish, are they?" Saoirse asked.

"No, I don't think so, but they all speak the same language. The really blonde one said it's called Goídelc, but some of the words sound Irish to me, so maybe they are from one of the Nordic countries. They use a translation app, so it's a bit awkward to talk to them, but they understood Irish when I spoke it."

Muireann started to giggle.

"You spoke Irish? Have you been holding out on us? All through school you told us that you couldn't speak any Irish at all and refused to help us with our homework. Now, you're suddenly a Gaelic speaker! Chance would be a fine thing."

Sadbh threw her hands in the air in resignation. She smiled at her daughters.

"Don't listen to me then, but there are a couple of fine things with long hair and tattoos in my office. They could pass for male models, even the old one. There's also a banshee that could give Etain a run for her money. If you see them, then will you believe me?"

Both girls, still tipsy, crept out the front door and peered into the office. Their attempts at spying on the travellers were comical. The clicking of stilettos on concrete was loud enough to alert Esras, who alerted the others. Both girls stood squarely in front of the windows and peered inside. Esras smiled and waved at them. The girls giggled and waved back. Morfessa came closer to the window, scowling, but even he had to smile when the young women batted their eyelashes at him. Uiscias peeped out from behind Morfessa, but when Saoirse said hello, he turned bright red and hid. Satisfied that they had the measure of the four men and strange woman, who perpetually scowled, they crept back through the front door, locking it behind them.

"The blonde looks like he stepped out from a page in *Vogue*," said Muireann, referring to Morfessa.

"Did you see the other blonde with the ringlets? He's not bad either. His hair is gorgeous – all those curls. I'd kill for his hair," Saoirse countered.

Muireann laughed.

"He's too old for you. The redhead looks about your age."

Sadbh smiled. Both girls were single and on the lookout for eligible boyfriends.

"Did you see the state of their clothes? Maybe they are film extras or something. Are they filming a new series of *Vikings*?" Saoirse asked.

Muireann shook her head.

"Not that I've heard, and everyone I know has signed up to an extras' casting site. They make a fortune when one of those shows come into town. If there was anything in the works, I'd know."

"I said I'd give them something to eat," Sadbh murmured.

"Your office is tiny. There's no way you can feed them in there. They'll have to come into the house," Muireann insisted.

Sadbh did not know if her girls just wanted to get a good look at the travellers, but they had a point – the office was built for one person.

"Just bear in mind, Mam, you're going to have to clean the bathroom after them," Saoirse said. "Can you image what state it will be in when there done?"

She made a face and held her nose. The laughter broke the tension.

"Okay. Set the dining room table," Muireann said "but make sure you keep a couple of carving knives handy, just in case!"

Chapter 15

Getting Acquainted

Etain had always been a light sleeper, and her room in the front of the house meant that she woke at the slightest noise of passing walkers or engine noise. She drifted out of a deep sleep when the taxi brought her sisters home. She would have gone back to sleep when they went to the room they shared, but they never made it up the stairs. Now she could smell cooking from the kitchen and could hear snatches of conversation. She twisted and turned in the bed. The last straw was the sound of male voices: not just one or two but a gang of men. What the hell were her sisters thinking? As the eldest daughter she had always warned her sisters about bringing home strangers. She grabbed her dressing gown, pulled it on and headed downstairs to give them a piece of her mind.

Etain was the oldest of Sadbh's daughters and the most fearsome. Her profession suited her. Etain was a commandant in the Irish Army, Communication and Information Services Corps, based in McKee Barracks on Infirmary Road, beside the Phoenix Park. Her training in engineering was put to good use, but it was her leadership skills that set her apart. Despite the corps' support role, she was a fearsome warrior. Fearsome enough to inspire terror and awe at home. Both her brother and sisters were scared of her.

Etain was full of spit and vinegar when she reached the hall. The travellers, Muireann and Saoirse had just sat down at the dining table when Etain burst in, ramrod straight with a face to sour milk.

"Just who the hell do you think you are bringing this shower of eejits home?" she demanded of her sisters, Muireann and Saoirse.

Sadbh had been busy in the kitchen but once she heard the commotion that Etain was making, she walked through to the dining room, holding a pot of tea.

"I brought them home," she said.

Etain stared at her mother. This was not right. Her mother never brought anyone home, not even work colleagues. Etain struggled to remember the last time that her mother had visitors.

"Sit down and I'll get you a plate," Sadbh said, placing the pot of tea in the middle of the table.

Etain's outburst had made her the centre of attention, and the look on her mother's face made her suddenly aware of the fact that she was wearing a flimsy nightdress and a very old and worn dressing gown. The sheer night dress left very little to the imagination. Her face turned bright red, enhancing her long auburn hair. Her embarrassment was complete when she realised that Morfessa was looking her up and down – a smile on his face and one eyebrow raised.

She immediately pulled the threadbare dressing gown over her chest, turned and ran from the room. Muireann and Saoirse giggled at their big sister. Seeing her embarrassed was a turn up for the books.

The travellers sat at the table, unsure of what to do. There was clearly an argument going on – they understood that much, even without a translator.

Sadbh caught Semias's eye.

"You better eat this lot before it goes cold," nodding at the food.

Muireann sat at the top of the table, passing fruit and yoghurt around, followed by porridge. Sadbh put a couple of packets of part-baked bread rolls in the oven, and soon the house smelt of fresh baked bread.

The family's guests clearly did not understand what was happening. Saoirse was seated beside Uiscias. She took his bowl and added some fruit topped with Greek yoghurt and handed it to him. She took a spoon to her own bowl and ate some. Uiscias understood.

"It's good, try it," he said to the others.

They followed suit. With the fruit and porridge gone, the visitors made short work of rest of the food, copying the girls who were buttering warm bread rolls and spreading jam and honey on top. Sadbh was still in the kitchen. She had not had time to eat herself. She brought another pot of tea to the table and slumped against the sideboard in the corner.

"I have been up for 24 hours straight, and I need to sleep. Girls, wake me at nine and make sure to leave some milk for Brendan. You know what he is like if he doesn't get a cup of coffee in the morning."

She snatched some bread from Etain's plate and headed up to her room in the attic. Sadbh was on the landing when a fully dressed Etain emerged from her room, wearing jeans and a long-sleeved T-shirt. Etain made herself coffee and joined the others.

The rest of the meal was spent in disjointed conversation, with a lot of gesturing and hand signals. Morrigan and Etain eyed each other like prized fighting dogs.

"God! You'd think they never invented a comb," Etain muttered, referring to the state of Morrigan's hair.

Uiscias was in deep conversation with Saoirse, and somehow they were conversing well. Morfessa tried to talk to Etain, but all he got were dirty looks, Esras yawned loudly, which set everyone off. No one had had a full night's sleep.

The remnants were cleared and the dishwasher was filled. Another pot of tea was made, and the visitors sat sipping the milky brew, stomachs full.

Etain has bided her time, waiting for a lull in the conversation – predominantly sign language.

"Well then, would you like to explain how you conned our mother into taking you home?" Etain commanded.

The interrogation had begun.

In Goídelc, the travellers discussed how best to answer the question, and their discussion was agitated.

Muireann and Saoirse were fascinated but as they built their response, Etain's agitation grew. She banged the table with force.

"You don't get to be a senior officer in the Defence Forces unless you can speak Irish. You can fool my sisters, because they barely passed ordinary Irish in the Leaving Cert, but I speak Irish every day at work. I can follow what you are saying."

She had the attention of Morfessa, Uiscias, Esras and Semias because when she spoke, it was in perfect Connacht Irish. Morrigan stood and stared straight at her.

There was no point in trying to lie. It was Semias who broke the silence. He answered her in Goídelc. There was no need for earpieces to translate.

"We are not trying to fool you. The language we are speaking is Goídelc, and it is an ancient form of Irish – a precursor to the modern language that you speak so well. And we are not Irish per se, but we are certainly of Irish descent, as you know it. Morfessa travelled from a place called Hofn in the

Eastfjord of Iceland. Uiscias is from Papa Westry, an island in the Orkneys, Scotland. Esras is from Floro on the island of Florelandet, on the Norwegian coast. I am from the coast of Greenland, near the town of Tassillaq. Morrigan is from what you call Ireland, in the West, I believe. Goídelc is the language of our society – tribe if you like. It is our native tongue."

Semias had not told the whole truth, but he had not exactly lied either. The places that he named were the landing points for the four surviving ships of the fleet. Saoirse had never heard of any of the places, despite being well travelled. Etain had worked alongside Scandinavians as part of the United Nations peacekeeping forces and had a basic knowledge of Scandinavia and its overseas protectorates. The Scots spoke Scottish Gaelic, so the redhead speaking Irish was plausible, even if his accent was wrong. However, there was no way that people from Greenland, Norway or Iceland could speak Gaelic.

"The people of Greenland speak Danish – Norwegian and Danish are also closely related. The Scots speak English, even on the Orkney Islands. And Iceland has a language of its own. How can ancient Irish be your mother tongue? It's been dead for over a thousand years."

Semias sighed.

"I'm not lying to you. It is the language that we speak on a daily basis. How else could we be so fluent?"

From Etain's perspective, Semias was clearly lying.

"There are maybe a hundred people in Ireland that can understand ancient Irish, and I'm not sure any of them could speak it with fluency. I'm sure people in the Gaeltacht could understand you well enough, given time, but that still doesn't explain how you five can speak a dead language when you are not from here."

"It's very complicated," Semias sighed.

"I'm in no hurry," Etain replied.

"We are time travellers," Uiscias blurted out.

Everyone, including the travellers, stared at him.

"So, you are time travellers now! Are you from the past or the future?" Saoirse asked.

Uiscias blushed and hung his head.

"We are from both."

"Cut the bullshit," Etain roared.

Morrigan stood from the table.

"Etain, you are understandably angry. Esras is still not fully recovered, and we are exhausted. In the morning, before we leave, we will explain everything. I just ask for a little patience."

Chapter 16

The Truth Will Sound Like a Fairy Tale

The travellers shuffled back into the office and waited for the girls to go to bed. Saoirse had forgotten to lock the connecting door to the kitchen, and Uiscias thought it better that they go into the sitting room – the office was too tiny to stretch out in.

The house was quiet and thankfully, the faded carpets deadened the sound of their feet. They sat on the sofas – Uiscias on an easy chair – and planned their next move.

Morfessa suggested resting for an hour and leaving before the family would wake. Uiscias disagreed. Esras thought it prudent to leave immediately. Semias thought it better to say nothing, considering.

Morrigan took command.

"I understand why you think leaving is a good idea, but I think it would be a mistake."

The others vehemently disagreed. Morrigan ignored their responses and ploughed on.

"Listen. If we leave now, we don't have to explain ourselves, that's true, but if we go, we are completely on our own. We have eaten, but we are still tired and still weak. We don't know our way around this place. We can barely get the computer to work. We have no resources. We have no money, and we have no transport. Before we left, it was agreed that we would have a support team to help us, and we don't. Right now, this family is the closest thing we have to a support team."

Morfessa interrupted.

"If you were in their position, would you believe us? More importantly, would you help us?"

Uiscias shook his head.

"In their position, I would think we were crazy or worse. If we are to stay here, we need to make them believe us. Should we invent an excuse?"

"There is no excuse," Esras said. "The girls are clever. They will see through a lie. We will have to tell them the truth. And remember, there is a son that we have yet to meet. It's likely he will be as astute as his sisters."

"The truth will sound like a fairy tale," Uiscias whispered.

"Uiscias, the youngest one, with the ring in her nose, is a mathematician. Sweet-talk her. If you could show her the maths, maybe she could convince Etain. If we win Etain over, the rest will follow."

"I doubt anyone could win Etain over," Morfessa said gruffly.

"So, what am I supposed to do?" Uiscias asked innocently.

Esras glanced and Morfessa and broke into a broad grin.

"Chat her up, just like you chat up girls at home. You have had a girlfriend, haven't you?"

Uiscias shook his head and blushed.

Chapter 17

Diamonds in the Rough

Muireann woke early, checked her sisters and her mother and hastily dressed. There was no need to check on her brother: she could hear him snoring gently from the landing. Today was his birthday. When she woke first, she thought that the previous night had been a dream but then, she found herself remembering the discussion in the dining room and bolted upright in a panic.

She went downstairs, as quietly as she could and noticed the sitting room door was ajar. She gently nudged the door open and saw the travellers asleep. She pulled the door closed and began to hyperventilate. *It's best to leave them*, she thought.

She wanted her sisters and brother awake before the travellers were approached. She tiptoed into the kitchen, avoiding the creaky floorboard in the hall. In the kitchen, she noticed her mother's car keys on the counter and realised that her mother's jacket and laptop were still in the car. Knowing that her mother would panic, Muireann thought it best to bring them inside and take them up to the bedroom for her.

She made her way out to the Audi and opened the boot, making sure nothing important was left in it. As an afterthought, she checked the interior. She checked the glove compartment for reading glasses. Her mother often put them there, and she panicked when she could not find them. It was then that she noticed the small felt bag tucked into the cupholder between the front seats. It did not look to be anything special and when she picked it up, it felt like it was full of pebbles. She took it into the house, along with her mother's possessions and quietly closed the front door.

Sadbh was still asleep when Muireann left the laptop, handbag and glasses on the dressing table up in the eaves of the house. She nearly tripped on a large box from Thomann, her brother's birthday present. Wide wake now, Muireann went downstairs and into the large room that she shared with Saoirse. Making sure the door was locked, she sat cross legged on her single bed. She tipped the contents of the bag on the duvet and began to examine the little rocks.

Sunlight streamed through the window, and she picked a stone randomly. She looked at the first and gently put it aside, selecting a larger, pale-blue one to examine. Then it was a yellow one and one that looked like a piece of quartz. The smallest was the size of the nail on her little finger. The largest stone was the size of a quail's egg. She examined them again using a little magnifier and then, a jeweller's loupe.

When she had first seen the stones, she thought that her mother must have picked them up in a New Age shop in Westport. All of the tourist destinations had shops that sold sun catchers and crystals but after an initial examination, she was not so sure. The hairs on the back of her neck pricked. She carefully climbed off her bed and went to wake her younger sister.

"Saoirse, do you have those crystals I gave you at Easter?"

Saoirse, still asleep, told her sister to get lost and tried to push her away.

Muireann shook her sister hard.

"Saoirse, this is important. Do you still have the corundum crystals I gave you?"

It was not what Muireann said; it was the urgency in her voice that made Saoirse sit up, hair like a bird's nest. *What are corundum crystals?* she thought for a moment.

"Oh! The bag of crystals you brought home after your last field trip. They're in the drawer of the dresser in the little gift bag. Why do you need crystals at this hour? I'm going back to sleep."

Muireann shook Saoirse roughly until Saoirse swung her feet out of the bed. Saoirse yawned and asked her why the hell she needed crystals at stupid o'clock in the morning.

"Because the weirdos gave Mam a bag of rough diamonds and I need corundum crystals to test them."

Suddenly, Saoirse was wide awake.

"What the hell are you talking about?"

"I found a bag of pebbles in Mam's car, in the front seat where they must have been sitting, and I examined them. I studied geography you know. That included two semesters of geology. I know what a diamond looks like. These are huge – they must be worth a fortune."

Both sisters sat on the edge of Muireann's bed and examined the little pile of coloured crystals. Saoirse had no idea of what she was looking at.

"How did that lot get their hands on diamonds?" Saoirse asked.

Saoirse lifted each stone in turn and gently examined them. They looked like pieces of weathered glass with an oily sheen. If they really were diamonds, the travellers needed to supply some answers and quickly.

Saoirse was still tired and despite the treasure on her sister's bed, could not resist the urge to close her eyes. She could hear Muireann babbling on about Mohs Hardness Scales as she rifled through Saoirse's belongings in search of corundum. Seemingly, corundum was a nine and diamonds were a ten. Only diamonds could scratch corundum.

Muireann did not notice Saoirse nodding off, and she scraped one of the yellow stones against one of the crystals that she had given her sister. Without a magnifier, she could see the scratch it made. The stones from the felt bag left a trail of scars across the pristine corundum crystals. It seemed that these really were coloured diamonds. They needed to be tested, of course, but they could not be tested at 6 am on a Saturday morning, particularly when it was a bank holiday weekend. She repacked the stones and put them in her locker drawer.

"We'll sort it out in the morning," she yawned.

She let her head fall to the pillow and dozed off.

Chapter 18

Family Meeting

It was after 9 am when the Saoirse woke. Muireann was still asleep, and there was no sound from her mother's room or Brendan's.

Saoirse tiptoed into Brendan's room and shook him roughly. She hastily explained all that had happened and at first, Brendan laughed, thinking it was a joke. When Saoirse told him that the travellers were still downstairs, he got angry. He admonished his little sister for not wakening him immediately. As an afterthought, Saoirse wished him a happy birthday.

Saoirse was thrown out of the room while Brendan dressed, and she used the time to quietly waken Etain, Muireann and her mother. The family congregated in Sadbh's bedroom, sitting on the edge of her bed, while Muireann explained what she had found in whispers. The family decided that it was best to give the travellers some breakfast and send them on their way, stones or no stones. They would diplomatically ask them to leave if they showed any sign of dawdling and if worse came to worst, Etain and Brendan would strong arm them from the house.

Before her children left the room, Sadbh asked Muireann to bring over the large box with a red bow that was at the end of her bed.

The girls were excited. Muireann presented it to Brendan.

"Happy Birthday Brendan. Its from all of us," Etain said.

Brendan laughed and shook his head, and ripped the box asunder. Inside was a Suhr electric guitar, a sleek take on a 60's design, with a roasted maple fingerboard and cherry finish.

Brendan was shocked. "I can't take this, it cost thousands."

Sadbh put her arms around her son.

"We know you were saving to buy one. And that you used your savings to build Saoirse a laptop with the speed she needed. So, you'll take it and play it and make us happy."

The sun poured through the windows of the semi-detached house, but it was still early enough for the avenue on which they lived to be quiet. They tiptoed downstairs and Sadbh led the way into the kitchen. Etain made coffee and mugs were passed around. No one spoke. They were waiting for movement from the sitting room. The smell of coffee worked. In a few minutes, Morrigan knocked on the kitchen door. She greeted Sadbh, who offered her a cup of coffee, which she refused, but she did take some apple juice from the carton on the counter. She left the kitchen to wake the others.

Although the house was big by Dublin standards, it was not big enough for everyone to congregate in the galley kitchen. The dining table sat eight, so they adjourned there, Brendan fetching a chair from the kitchen for his mother.

Muireann eyed her mother. She looked worn out and somehow, she looked a lot older. Muireann suddenly felt an ache in her chest and wanted to throw her arms around her. The thought of someone taking advantage of her mother was too much to bear. It seemed to Muireann that Sadbh has struggled since they were children, and she deserved to rest and take things easy. Etain looked at Muireann and instantly understood what she felt. Etain made her mother sit down and brought her a fresh cup of coffee. She whispered quietly that they would take care of everything. There would be no trouble.

As the travellers seated themselves, Sadbh asked Saoirse to bring them some fruit juice. Saoirse tried to object, but Etain stayed her with a glance. She meant it when she said no trouble.

Etain cleared her throat and spoke quietly but firmly.

"My mother agreed to get you to Dublin, which she has done. It's time that you left. We'll gladly give you directions to get wherever it is you need to get to. I'll give you change for the buses, or I can pay for tickets with my credit card, but you need to leave."

Uiscias looked bewildered. Morfessa was crestfallen. It was not what they had expected or hoped for.

Esras replied in an even tone.

"We thank you for your help and we will comply with your wishes but before we go, there are some things that we need help with."

He looked at Semias, who was also taken aback with the request to leave. It was not what he had anticipated. Semias nodded at Esras, a sign to continue.

"We also need to pass on some information. You probably won't believe us, but there is a disaster coming. It will start elsewhere but within hours, Ireland will be affected. Within days everything will change for the worse. If you can, leave this place. Don't go to the coast. Stay somewhere inland and on high ground. Make sure you have provisions and fuel. It will get cold and dark fast."

Esras shrugged his shoulders and stood. Morfessa stood with him. They shuffled out of the room and began to make ready for their journey ahead. While Semias, Esras and Morfessa collected their belongings, Uiscias approached Saoirse.

Uiscias smiled at her – a sad smile.

"We're not joking you know. The warning is real. There really is a disaster on its way. There's a very old book from Iceland called *Edda*. It foretells the end of the gods."

Saoirse nodded.

"I know, I watched the TV show on Netflix."

Uiscias grinned.

"What is TV and what is Netflix?"

Even though it was summer, Sadbh worried that the travellers' light linen clothes would not be suitable for Irish weather, but Semias refused her offer of windbreakers and sweaters and socks.

"We'll be fine," he said.

He did take the coins and notes that she offered, when she explained that they would be needed to board buses and trains.

Esras and Morfessa took the opportunity to have long hot showers while Semias prepared to leave. Now dressed and ready to go, Morfessa and

Esras joined Semias, and they called out to Uiscias to join them. The found him wrapping the distraught Saoirse in a tight embrace. Morrigan showered after Esras and Morfessa and was the last to join the others.

Taking advantage of the predominantly female household, she had used shampoo and conditioner to remove all the muck from her hair, and the woman that emerged from the bathroom bore little resemblance to the woman who had entered it. Her raven hair was in a plait that dropped past her waist. Etain had given her an old field uniform to wear and although a little short, the trousers fitted perfectly at the waist, worn with a green army T-shirt and vest. Morrigan's dagger was secured on the webbed belt that she wore. An old pair of army boots completed her ensemble.

Etain was herself in uniform, wearing a Norwegian pattern combat shirt, disruptive pattern material trousers and military tactical jacket, her name tag on the right breast pocket and Óglaigh na hÉireann (Irish Defence Forces) patch on the left breast pocket. Her long auburn hair was tightly rolled and pinned in place to allow her uniform cap to sit correctly.

Both women entered the dining room at the same time. Seeing the two women stand beside each other was a shock. The likeness was uncanny. Both had the same brow and chin and the colour of their eye were identical – vivid blue.

Morrigan was perhaps an inch taller than Etain, but both had the stature and bearing associated with soldiers and as they moved, they mirrored each other. Even in uniform it was possible to see their lithe figures and muscled forearms. The only significant difference was Etain's lack of Celtic tattoos.

Everyone, including Sadbh, was dumbstruck. Esras elbowed Morfessa.

"They're definitely related. You thought you had problems dealing with one Morrigan. Now you have Morrigan and her twin sister to deal with. Good luck with that."

Uiscias was flustered. He clearly did not understand Saoirse's explanation of television. Saoirse giggled.

"It doesn't matter, and I know the story of the Edda. The world is consumed by water, the sky turns black, and there's something about fire. Gods and giants do battle and the Gods are killed."

Uiscias was pleased, Saoirse knew the basics.

"Good, you know a little then. The poem isn't a folk tale. It's a warning. It's not a coincidence that it is Icelandic. The story survived in Iceland, because that's where it will happen."

Saoirse grinned and shook her head, her emerald-green hair falling into her eyes.

"How could an ancient story foretell a disaster in the 21st Century? You're having me on!"

The computer in Uiscias's hand beeped and vibrated.

Uiscias looked down and smiled. The software menu to activate their implants was now accessible and wasting no time, he set about turning on the devices. Uiscias had not expected the pain – he doubled over from an ear-piercing, high-pitched whistle. Morfessa, Morrigan, Esras and Semias experienced it too. Screaming, they all fell to their knees.

Uiscias grimaced and shook his head. The pain was short-lived. When he had recovered enough, he tried to explain how the Edda had been written.

"This is hard to explain, so please let me get through this, and then I can help you make sense of it. Imagine that the catastrophe happens, and there are massive volcanoes and earthquakes that radiate out from Iceland and destroy Europe and North America in a domino effect."

"Now, let's say that people survive it, so the memory of it is vivid. They pass the story down through generations."

"Now, two hundred years later, the descendants of the survivors try to travel back in time to before the volcanic eruptions. They want to stop the worst effects on the environment, but it goes wrong, and they end up travelling back much further in time than they planned. They end up stranded in the Bronze Age. Their ships are damaged, so they can't move forward in time. So, they create a memoir of the events that are in their past but in reality, are thousands of years in the future."

"For the story to be passed on through the generations, they tell the story of the catastrophe through the Edda, and they use the vernacular language of the time. In the time travellers' story, they are not gods, but the people describe them as gods as time passes. The Edda poem wasn't created for hundreds of years, and the story that survives now was shaped by a people that didn't understand the science that was involved, but it did survive."

Uiscias focussed his blue eyes on her, and she blushed.

"I know you don't believe me, and I wish I had a way to prove it, but it's the truth."

"The equipment we have with us won't demonstrate what will happen, but I have seen the aftermath. I was born in the 23rd century."

"The loss of life in the northern hemisphere will be nearly total – not just people, animals and plants too. There will be a volcanic winter, unlike anything that has gone before. The countries and places that you know will either be submerged or displaced. There is no map that won't change, even in the southern world."

Saoirse looked at Uiscias from under her eyelashes.

"What do you mean, Uiscias?"

"I mean, volcanic eruptions will completely destroy Iceland and waves so big and powerful that whole countries will be submerged. The plates supporting the continents will move. The ash clouds and gasses released into the atmosphere will cause temperatures to plummet. The air quality will be destroyed, and acid rain will fall. Society will crumble."

"If you know so much, why don't you stop it? If you had the technology to travel through time, surely a volcano is a simple challenge."

Uiscias sat down on the corner of the sofa. Saoirse sat beside him. He smiled at her and took her hand.

"We have some technology, but nothing we have is powerful enough to stop nature. We can't stop Ragnarok. All we can do is try to lessen what comes after."

Muireann stood at the door, observing her sister and the redhead. *Jesus, they look like an Irish flag*, she thought – *green, white and orange*.

Saoirse and Uiscias were in a world of their own, oblivious to her presence.

"Aww, this is so sweet. She can't stand redheads you know," Muireann said loudly.

Uiscias dropped Saoirse's hand and jumped away in panic.

Saoirse, trying to hide her embarrassment, hung her head.

"What are you two up to?" Muireann inquired.

Saoirse walked up to her sister's side.

"Muireann, can I talk to you for a second please?"

The sisters took a walk into the front garden.

"Are you angry at me for disturbing you? He seems like a nice enough guy …"

Saoirse interrupted Muireann mid flow.

"Muireann, what do you know about Iceland?"

"I know that swimming in the Blue Lagoon is magical, and I can't afford to get drunk there – it's too bloody expensive. The glaciers and volcanoes are amazing."

"You've been to the volcano, right?"

Muireann had taken a summer trip to Iceland in her third year in college to study volcanoes. She had studied Eyjafjallajökull near Reykjavík and then had travelled south-east to study Katla, one of the largest stratovolcanoes in Iceland.

"I didn't go to *a volcano*. I studied several volcanoes. Do you have any idea how active Iceland is? There are hundreds of volcanoes there."

"But none of them are exploding, right?" Saoirse asked.

Muireann decided to play the part of teacher.

"At any given time, there are lots of active volcanoes, Saoirse. There are eruptions all the time, but the level of activity is normal for Iceland."

Saoirse breathed a sigh of relief.

"That's okay then. Uiscias kept going on about how Iceland is going to explode, and there's going to be a tsunami that will hit the Atlantic Coast. It sounded like the apocalypse."

Muireann could see that Saoirse was genuinely worried. Her time in Iceland had been one of the most exciting in her life, up close and personal with volcanoes on the glaciers around the towns of Vic í Mýrdal and Skógar. Volcanic activity there was as normal as rain in Ireland. She needed to ease her sister's mind.

"Look, if you are really worried, I can show you some live feeds of volcanoes from Iceland that will put your mind at ease. I have them saved in my favourites on my laptop. Then you can see that there is nothing to worry about. You can even sit beside the redhead when you watch," Muireann teased.

Saoirse went back to the sitting room, first sitting beside Uiscias, then jumping up and pacing, wringing her hands.

Muireann returned with her laptop and plopped down on the sofa.

"Did you know that Iceland tourism authority shows live feeds of volcanoes on its website? Look, I'm pulling it up now."

Muireann brought up the Visit Iceland website and instantly, they could see Fagradalsfjall, just outside of the capital. From experience, Muireann knew that what she should be seeing was stream rising from the ground and possibly some minor fissures. What was being streamed was a violent eruption, lava spewing across the uneven barren glacial surface, rocks and molten orange starburst shooting into a smoke-filled sky.

Saoirse whispered, "Muireann, does this look right?"

Muireann shook her head but did not answer.

She rapidly typed into the search engine and opened a website known to volcanologists globally. She focussed on the Reykjanes peninsula, and what she saw shook her. The volcanic activity was not elevated; it was off the scale. Strong volcanic tremors were being reported, indicating that magma movements underneath the area were likely causing a seismic swarm.

Muireann was getting anxious: looking at live feeds was supposed to reassure her sister. Saoirse and Uiscias looked terrified. Muireann knew that the eruption in Reykjanes was a problem, but her fear was Katla. She remembered the website for the local newspaper in Reykjavík from her trip – mbl.is – and pulled it up. They also carried a livestream, but their cameras were in a different part of the country, near the Katla Volcano.

The livestream was active, but all that could be seen was an orange and black blur. Muireann took a deep breath. This was very bad. She motioned for Saoirse to move closer to her. Muireann checked volcanology blogs, which were full of chatter about the sudden rise in activity. When she had checked and double checked every live reference site she could find, she pulled her sister into a hug.

"Saoirse, let me explain about Iceland."

"Iceland sits on top of the mid-Atlantic ridge. This ridge marks the boundary between adjacent tectonic plates. These volcanoes form a chain of mountains that reach from Iceland right the way down the Atlantic Ocean, past the Azores."

"Now, the actual place where the plates move against each other is in a rift valley that sits beside the ridge. This is where magma from the mantle reaches the seafloor, erupting as lava and producing basaltic volcanoes. Its' like a big crack along the ocean floor and the crack in the ocean floor pushes up the magma – that makes the volcanoes. All of this volcanic activity is what made Iceland over millions of years. Look, it's been volcanically active for twenty-five million years. There's always volcanic activity, but I have never seen it as active as it is now. I'm amazed this isn't all over the TV and radio."

"You saw some of the eruptions on the livestreams. The last one was Katla. It's one of the most powerful volcanoes in the world and from what I could see, it's active. Öræfajökull and its neighbour, Bárðarbunga – they sit in the same glacier – are both erupting. Fagradalsfjall, Eyjafjallajökull – the one that caused the big ash cloud over Europe – and its really scary neighbour, Katla are erupting."

"One is kind of normal, two is a cause for concern but if all of these become active at the same time, we could be in for a rough time, even here."

"Is a tsunami possible, Muireann?"

"It depends. If the level of activity of any or all of these volcanoes increases, there is no telling what could happen. I can't say that anything is impossible."

"And what would happen if they all erupted?"

"The worst case – if all of the big volcanoes in Iceland have violent eruptions – a seven or eight on the Volcanic Explosivity Index, then the ash cloud that stopped air travel is going to look like small potatoes. Iceland could literally be blown to pieces. We could be heading for a volcanic winter."

Saoirse whispered, "Fire, ice and darkness – Ragnarok."

Muireann replied, "Fire from the eruptions, followed by ice and darkness from the volcanic winter. Yes, Ragnarok."

Muireann pulled Saoirse into a hug. She was sobbing gently. Muireann made eye contact with Uiscias, who looked fraught. She dropped her eyes to the top of Saoirse's head and nodded at Uiscias. He gently pulled Saoirse to him and held her tight, making soothing noises and stroking her hair.

While Uiscias was taking care of Saoirse, Muireann grabbed Brendan and Etain. She quickly explained what Uiscias had warned Saoirse about and walked them through she had found online, site by site and blog by blog. No matter what the travellers had told them, the live cameras did not lie. Muireann was clearly rattled.

"Etain, can you talk to Morfessa and see if you can get them to hold on. I know some researchers in Iceland. I want to see if I can get some idea of the scale of this thing from them. I don't believe a word that Semias says, but I think Uiscias is telling the truth. He seems reluctant to tell me any more. It's like he's under instructions not to say anything to us. Semias is an asshole, and I don't want to ask him, but Morfessa seems like a straight arrow, and he likes you. He might just do as you ask. Please, will you talk to him, for me?"

Brendan and Etain could clearly see how worried Muireann looked, and Saoirse was scared. It was decided that Brendan would divert Uiscias by talking tech with him, while Muireann would divert Esras, leaving Morfessa and Morrigan to Etain.

Chapter 19

History Lesson

Morfessa was uncomfortable being in such close proximity to Etain. There was something about her that put him on edge. It was probably because they were both soldiers, albeit from different armies. Etain was not beautiful in the traditional sense. She was built like a big cat, strong and lithe, but Etain's eyes were focussed and commanding. She had the air and presence of a military leader. The thought of being attracted to Etain briefly crossed his mind. He did not have time for romantic entanglements, and he needed to focus on the mission, but being so close to Etain and having her focus on him made his heart beat a little faster.

"Morfessa, before you go, we really need to talk to you. Semias gave us that warning earlier. Uiscias put the fear of God into Saoirse and Saoirse asked Muireann to do some research on volcanoes in Iceland. She's in a panic. Seemingly, there are signs of big eruptions all over the country. It's not on any news report yet, but I believe my sister when she says something is wrong."

Morfessa could feel Etain's breath as she spoke. He shook his head to focus himself.

"Etain, you are a military officer and so am I. I don't lie, at least about important things. I'm not lying now. What we said is the truth. What Uiscias said is the truth."

"Then tell me what you know," Etain implored.

"I don't have the time or authority to explain it, Etain. You'll have to trust me."

"But Morrigan does, doesn't she?"

Morfessa nodded.

"Then how do we get her to tell us what is really going on?"

Sadbh could see trouble coming when all of her children asked her to sit outside in the garden with them. Sadbh was immediately on alert. It was clear from Saoirse's face that she had been crying. Muireann looked like a frightened child. Etain looked like she had swallowed a lemon, and Brendan was following his sisters like a bewildered toddler.

In the blazing morning sunshine, Muireann carefully stepped her mother through the websites and data from Iceland and asked her mother to sit in on a call to Muireann's researcher friends in Vik. After a debate on the best course of action, Sadbh agreed to ask the travellers to stay and explain.

"I'm going to sound like an eejit. First we tell them to go; now, we ask them to stay. You're all going to stay with me though, aren't you?"

Her children nodded in agreement.

Etain took her mother's hand and explained the situation with Morrigan.

"Mam, you're going to have to pander to her. Imagine you're dealing with Etain. According to Morfessa, she's the only one not bound by orders from the top brass at home, and she is the commanding officer."

Etain hugged her mother, and each of her children followed suit. Sadbh stood and took a deep breath.

"Let's get this over with."

Sadbh approached Morrigan in the kitchen and offered to make her something to eat before she left. She declined politely but firmly. Surely, a cold drink on a hot summer's morning was permissible. Sadbh pored chilled juice into a tall glass and beckoned Morrigan into the garden. They sat around the picnic table, shaded by a parasol.

Sadbh asked if they could spare an half an hour to really talk. Morrigan declined at first – they really needed to leave, because they did not know how long it would take to reach their destination. Sadbh admonished her. The travellers had, after all, dropped a bombshell on the family, announcing a global disaster of biblical proportions. Surely she could spare her the time to explain exactly what would happen. Morrigan agreed but only if Sadbh would drive them to their destination.

Sadbh immediately assured her that a quick trip to Tara was not a problem. In the hour that followed Morrigan told her everything that had led to the mission; told her the issues that they had encountered thus far and explained the steps they needed to complete, to ensure the mission's success.

Sadbh took charge.

"We need to get everything out in the open with my family. We need a meeting with all of us together. I'm not sure if I trust you, but I do trust Muireann, and she thinks that there is something to worry about. My family is a collection of the best engineers and scientists in the country, and I'm not saying that because they are my children. If you need help, then these are the people you need around you. Anyway, you don't have time to go looking elsewhere, do you?"

Morrigan nodded in acknowledgement.

"You're right, we don't have much choice. It will begin in the next two days, so time is of the essence. I'll call the team together – and your family."

They sat on the patio in the morning sunshine. They waited for Sadbh to begin.

"Muireann checked out some of your story. It appears you may be right about Iceland. We need to know what's going on. Tell us everything."

"We have figured out that you're not from here or at least from this time," Etain said.

"Your language and clothing make us think you are from the past, but your technology and knowledge of what's going on is futuristic. We don't think you're aliens or anything, but it would help to understand how you know what you know."

The travellers reverted to Goídelc and had a rapid discussion. They all appeared to agree. Uiscias took up their story.

"We are not from this time; that is true but as for past and future, it's complicated. We are from both. The four of us served on the crews of what you would call star ships. Morrigan was the captain. Before you ask, we do come from Earth, but we come from a future Earth, which is very different. When we come from, this garden would be a miracle. The Earth is heavily polluted. There are only pockets of animal and plant life. There are only a few thousand people left alive. Most species are extinct. We're dying."

"But your technology is advanced. How can that be if you're dying?" Muireann asked.

"Despite the environment, technology flourished, and that was partly because the people who survived what will happen shortly were scientists. We pushed the boundaries of genetics and power generation because we had to, but we reached a tipping point, and our leaders decided that the best way to resolve our problems was to send a fleet back in time, to help guide technological development and give your people the tools to deal with the disaster that is coming and lessen its impact."

"If you can fix what's going to happen here, why not just do it in your time?" Etain interrupted.

"There's no point. We can't recover extinct plants and animals, no matter how advanced the technology we have is. We don't have the time or the resources to wait. There simply are not enough people to carry the weight of a task that big," Semias explained.

"The plan had been a simple one: take leading experts in physics, biology, medicine and sociology and bring them to the 1970s. Then, accelerate the breakthroughs that would be needed to reach a point where your society would have the means to mitigate the disaster. Of course, the actual plan was more complex and nuanced. We were taking the best engineers, doctors, metallurgists, physicists – the best people we had – and we would assign them to universities all over Europe and some further afield. It was all about building capacity."

"What went wrong?" Brendan asked.

"In theory, we understood how to time travel, but we'd never done it before and not with a fleet carrying over 2,000 people. There were thirteen ships in all, and everything went well until we encountered solar flares. Bad luck and poor navigation did the rest."

With most of the confidential information now out in the open, the travellers relaxed. Morfessa took up the story.

"The science never accounted for the impact of solar flares on our power systems. Nine ships were destroyed, and the balance had damage to critical on-board systems. We couldn't control the ships, and we couldn't control the timeline."

Saoirse had a myriad of questions but sensed it better to wait.

"We weren't as good as we thought we were. Instead of arriving at the end of the 20th century, we miscalculated and ended up in northern Europe during the early Celtic period. The four ships that were left had severe damage. We lost communications. We lost power, and we had no navigation systems. Our craft were scattered over the northern Atlantic, luckily each reached land."

"Stop please," Etain commanded. Looking at her sister she said, "Muireann, do you have a pen and paper?"

Muireann searched through her handbag looking for something to write on.

"Before you go on, I think I know where this is heading. Your commander was Anu, right?"

Semias nodded his head. *How did Etain know that?*

Muireann handed Etain a notebook and pencil – all that she could find. On the paper, Etain drew a grid – North, South, East and West. In the North, she wrote Falias; in the South, Findias; in the West, Murias and in the East, Gorias. In the grid she added the names of Uiscias, Morfessa, Semias and Esras. She then added, Coire Daghda, Lia Fail, Claíomh Solais and Sleg Assail.

"Go on now. Repeat to me your names and the names of the places you come from."

"Do you mean where we came from before we left, or where we landed? We landed in what you call Iceland, Greenland, Scotland and Norway," Morfessa responded.

Etain thought for a few minutes, tapping the pencil against her front teeth. She shook her head and whispered to herself. Etain placed the notebook on the bench and asked Saoirse to pick it up.

"What are your names, and what were the names of your ships?" Etain asked again.

Uiscias repeated their names and the names of the four ships: *Gorias*, *Murias*, *Findias* and *Falias*.

Saoirse looked dumbfounded when she read what was on the page and stared at the travellers. She passed it to Muireann, who read what her sister had written and looked equally as shocked.

"Before they said anything, I wrote down the names of four mythical cities of the Tuatha Dé Danann, and Uiscias here has just recited them."

"Etain, how the hell did you know that?" said Muireann.

"I took a course in Irish military history. It's part of the story of the Tuatha Dé Danann. They came from four mythical cities. Each city represented a compass point. Falias in the north, Findias in the south, Gorias in the east and Murias in the west."

"The Tuatha Dé Danann had four teachers. Funnily enough their names were Morfessa, Esras, Semias and Uiscias."

"The cities were the sources of the treasures of the Tuatha Dé Danann: from Murias in the west, the Coire Daghda or the Cauldron of Daghda; from the south, the Sword of Light (Claíomh Solais); from the North came the Lia Fail or the Stone of Destiny and from the east, Lugh's Spear (Sleg Assail)."

"When they arrived here, the Tuatha Dé Danann landed their floating ships on the summit of Sliabh an Iarainn (the iron mountain) in County Leitrim. It's not really a mountain – more of a big hill near a lake. Do you want me to keep going?"

The travellers were shocked that Etain seemed to know so much about their history. Semias, in particular, was impressed by Etain. His response was expected.

"It seems that we became a part of legend. I suppose that makes some sense. After all, our crews numbered more than the entire populations of the areas we landed in. I could understand that over time, our ships were called cities. They were the hubs of our society. We did land in the North Atlantic – again giving some credence to the legend of the four compass points. And it's not a coincidence that our names are listed as teachers. We were instructors in what you would call our army and by taking part in this mission, we became legends in our own right. The floating ships were what you would call a pinnace – a small landing craft."

Semias explained that the locations in which the ships had landed were hostile, and the survivors needed a place where they could establish a settlement. Ireland had little or no population, and the land was fertile. The temperate weather meant that they could farm, and there was an abundance of other resources: like iron, aluminium, gold and diamonds. It was also a median for the landing sites, easily accessible using the landing craft or makeshift, seagoing vessels.

As for the treasures of the Tuatha Dé Danann, it was their equipment. The indigenous population treated the survivors and all of their equipment as magical. And for them, it probably was magic.

The indigenous people were Neolithic – short and dark. The survivors were tall and fair, predominantly with blue and green eyes. The survivors were well nourished, healthy and in comparison to the Neolithic men and women who struggled to survive, they appeared youthful.

The survivors had access to a form of internet and used devices similar to mobile phones to communicate. They had advanced weapons that they used for defence and hunting. They understood construction and built homesteads with fortifications. They knew how to preserve food, how to harness energy and they had a structured society – much more so than the tribes that roamed the heavily forested interior of Ireland. The tribes fought them at first but then learned to fear them. They were treated as gods.

"You weren't one of the settlers were you?" Saoirse asked Uiscias.

"No. Each of us," he said, pointing to the others "had a supporting role for the settlement of Ireland – technical experts who were called upon when needed. Esras was and is a healer. I am a communications and maritime expert. Morfessa, a metallurgist and Semias ... manages things."

"The three of us," Uiscias said, pointing to Morfessa and Esras, are part of our army. We call it Na Fianna. Morrigan is our commanding officer."

"Why didn't you just go home when you arrived in the wrong time?" Saoirse asked again.

Semias held his hands up.

"We couldn't go home. We couldn't even communicate with home. We can only assume that they thought everyone was lost. Even if they thought there may be survivors, they had no way of knowing what time we ended up in or, geographically, where we were. We had put everything into building the fleet. Even if they wanted to send a search party, there were no more ships."

"So, why are you here now?" Sadbh asked Morrigan.

"Some of the survivors were content to settle in Ireland. A core of our people stayed with the ships, maintaining what we could and trying to find a way to complete our mission. Our surviving scientists found a way to create a portal – not a stable one; one that would last for minutes. It was decided to send a few people back – just people, no equipment – and let them try to ease the effects of Ragnarok. The four treasures of the Tuatha Dé Danann are tools to help us in that mission. You have given them names as part of the legend that has grown up – the legend of the Tuatha Dé Danann. Just before we left, these four pieces of equipment were left in locations that we can access."

Uiscias interrupted Morrigan.

"We don't need to find all four pieces of equipment immediately; we really only need one – the Claíomh Solais."

Saoirse was listening intently.

"What will the Claíomh Solais do?"

"We'll use it to clear the ash cloud. It will only be temporary and will operate in a small window, but it will buy time," Uiscias replied, looking into her blue eyes.

Birds chirped and flitted from tree to tree around the walled garden. The sun shone, and the voices of children could be heard in the distance.

"These volcanoes will spew a mixture of rock, gas, minerals and glass particles," Uiscias continued. "The particles are measured in nanometres. The cloud will reach the stratosphere and within days, will be thousands of miles wide. If the eruptions will be as strong as we think they will be, there is nothing that can stop it."

"How can one piece of equipment stop an ash cloud?" Saoirse replied.

"You are right," Semias said. "We cannot disperse the ash cloud, but we can make holes in it by vaporising it, using a laser."

Brendan spoke up for the first time.

"There is no laser strong enough to vaporise an ash cloud that size. You would need a laser more powerful that anything ever built to do that. You're talking about petawatts of power. The only ones like this have been built in laboratories in China and Eastern Europe, and I think there's a little one in Texas, but they are in massive containment structures."

"That's why we need to find the artefact you refer to as Claíomh Solais. It is a portable 100-petawatt laser, made from a cylinder of titanium-doped sapphire. That is why you know it as the sword of light. If we can find it and make it operational, it could vaporise the ash in area up to 1,000 square kilometres," Morrigan explained.

Brendan, an electronics engineer, was not going to stand down.

"Grand. So, we make a big hole, and then the wind blows more ash in to replace it. Then what do we do? And how the hell do you charge a device like that? Do we have anything that can generate enough power?"

Morrigan sighed.

"I'm not giving a physics lesson. The power is stored in an electric, double-layer supercapacitor. It doesn't matter how it works. You don't have the materials to create one, so there's no point in explaining it. It creates a highly effective solar battery that retains its charge with infinitesimal losses. It was charged when it was passed over to the settlement team and unless they discharged it – which I know they didn't – it will retain 99.9999% of its charge."

"Each discharge will dissipate 97.2% of ash in the targeted area, right up to the stratosphere. It will destroy any particle with a radius of more than one nanometre. We set it to these parameters so we don't disturb any gaseous components and burn the atmosphere. It gets rid of the ash and leaves everything else behind. We have enough power for two discharges and perhaps a third low-power discharge. So, if the wind blows more ash into the cleared area, we recharge the damn device using solar energy and keep going until we find the rest of the equipment to clear the ash permanently."

"So, you vaporise the ash without vaporising the atmosphere? Just a little bit risky, huh?" said Brendan.

"If anyone has a better idea, speak up now. We're on a countdown." Semias's voice was thick with sarcasm.

Saoirse ran her hands through her emerald-green hair and asked if Uiscias could walk her through the physics. Morfessa offered to, but Morrigan stopped him.

"We don't have a lot of time, and we really need to get on with the operation. Now I have a question. Are you going to help us, or are you going to run?"

Sadbh spoke up. She needed to talk things through with her children.

"Stay here. We won't be long," she said.

The McNamara family left the tranquillity of the walled garden and headed indoors.

They had choices. They could ignore everything that had happened in the last eighteen hours – because it might be a lie. They could run away, but where could they run to, and was there any point in running? Would they or should they help the travellers?

As the debate came to an end, Morrigan entered the living room.

"Time is passing. We need an answer."

Etain stood.

"You never asked how you were remembered Morrigan. According to legend, you are The Morrigan – the Phantom Queen, the Goddess of War. You appear as a crow on the battlefield, foretelling death, but you are also the Goddess of Victory. You could inspire fear or courage in the warriors of Na Fianna. Well, inspire some courage. We're going to need it if all you say is true."

Chapter 20

A Move to the Country

The family had decided that leaving Dublin was a good idea. Before Sadbh's parents had passed away, they had moved from Dublin to a little cottage outside of Ardee, on the border of County Louth. The children had spent their summers and holidays at the cottage in the townlands of Collon and knew the area well. The cottage was surrounded by verdant fields, had its own well and outhouse. As an only child, the little stone-built labourers' cottage had passed to Sadbh and although not falling into neglect, it was infrequently used, especially as the children grew to adulthood. It was inland, though near a main route to Northern Ireland. If and when things got bad, the cottage would be safer than the house in Dublin.

The plan was simple. Brendan would take his car and travel there. He would prepare the cottage for the rest of them, making sure that basic supplies were available, including power. He would also take responsibility for setting up a communications network. He would take equipment with him and use the old outhouse as a base of operations.

Sadbh's car was not big enough to take the remaining team. The travellers and Sadbh's family would split into two groups: one to find the Claíomh Solais and the rest to pack up supplies and take them to the cottage. As Etain had access to army vehicles, she took responsibility for securing a suitable four-by-four, powerful enough to take on any terrain they might encounter in the search for the Claíomh Solais. Etain immediately made her way to McKee Barracks to borrow an army landrover.

"We're going to need help with directions and logistics, Muireann. We need to pinpoint the exact location of our target, and we will need a route. We may also need help to identify secondary locations. Can you work with Esras on that, please?" asked Morrigan.

Muireann noted Morrigan taking the lead and asserted herself.

"We need a way of communicating in case the phone network goes out of action. Brendan would be able to do that, but I need to tell him now, while he's still at the house," Muireann said.

Morrigan nodded.

"Muireann, can we get Uiscias to Brendan? It would be better if they worked together."

Morfessa gave Uiscias the all-clear to leave, and the youngster rushed out find Brendan.

"Sadbh, we cannot escape what is coming. Within 48 hours, the southwest of Ireland will effectively cease to exist. Volcanoes in the north will become active, and the remainder of the country will experience seismic activity. We will need food, extreme weather clothing, fuel, medical supplies and water. I don't know how long for," said Morrigan.

"I'll work with Saoirse and put together a list of what we might need. We can take what's in the house and pick up anything else we might need on my credit card."

Morrigan took control.

"We need to get busy. Morfessa and Muireann, work on directions and locations. We need to get to the first coordinates as soon as possible. Esras, make a list of what medical and other supplies we might need."

Morrigan stared at Esras.

"You know what I mean, don't you?"

Esras nodded.

An hour flew past as each person tackled their individual tasks.

Morrigan called the travellers together while the family were busy.

"They are smart; aren't they?" Uiscias whispered, referring to Sadbh's family.

Esras and Morfessa nodded in agreement.

"Brendan made some good points – the Claíomh Solais will only work for a short period. If there isn't enough light, it won't recharge, and it will gradually weaken," Uiscias whispered.

"Look, this was only ever meant to be a stop gap. You know what the long-term plan is – find the rest of the equipment, duplicate the technology and hope we're not too late," Semias replied.

Esras spoke up.

"What is the plan to find the rest?"

Morrigan shook her head.

"I really don't know. The original plan is unworkable now – we're going to have to wing it. We have to hope for the best but unless we find the Claíomh Solais, there is no hope."

"Would we be better doing this on our own? It may be kinder to leave the family alone," said Uiscias.

"If you had asked me before we came here, I would have said we work alone," whispered Morfessa "but we'd never have gotten this far without them. They each have skills and the dark one, Etain, is quite a warrior. She reminds me of you, Morrigan – the same temper."

"Morrigan is a bitch," Semias growled.

"Yes, she is, but she is our bitch!" Morfessa laughed.

Uiscias, preoccupied with technology, as always, added, "Don't underestimate Brendan. He seems to be a good engineer, and we may well need one before this is through. The blonde one understands the geography and geology of the country. Saoirse is a brilliant physicist."

Morfessa gave Uiscias a friendly nudge.

"Of course, you think Saoirse is wonderful. You know, we saw you kissing and cuddling."

Uiscias blushed bright red.

"I was just comforting her. And even if I wasn't, I'm not exactly alone. We all know what you think about Etain. We're never really sure whether you are going to attack each other or ravage each other. It's very hard to watch."

Esras was leaning against the counter but could not resist joining in the action. He whooped it up when Morfessa blushed.

"Have you noticed their eyes? It's strange that they all have the same eyes. I swear I've seen those eyes before," Semias said.

"I have seen eyes that colour of blue only once – they are Nuada's eyes. He was badly injured after we crash landed. He very nearly died and as it was, he lost his right arm at the shoulder in a fight. It took months and a lot of effort to get a prosthetic limb to work."

Morfessa laughed.

"Come on now, Semias. Nuada had working prosthetics. He just kept destroying them."

"How?" Uiscias asked innocently.

Morfessa patted Uiscias on his back.

"He kept fighting the natives."

Morrigan looked at her team. The light-hearted banter was what they needed right now.

"It's a pity the mother doesn't seem to have any special skills," Uiscias added.

Semias roared with laughter.

"Uiscias, don't underestimate an Irish mammy."

Saoirse was packing tinned food, packets of soup, rice and pasta into a cardboard box. Uiscias offered to help.

"Check the press under the sink. I think there are packets of tea lights, some candles and matches in there."

Uiscias rummaged through the press, not exactly sure what he was looking for but Saoirse seemed satisfied with what he presented.

"Where are we going?" he enquired.

"My grandad had a little cottage just outside Branigan's Hill in Collon. It's on the border of Meath and Louth. The cottage is on its own land about a mile from the main road. It's easy to access Slane, Dublin and the M1 motorway. It has its own well for water and even has a small generator. Nana and grandad lived there before they died. It's ours now, and we only use it at weekends, so it's not in the best of order, but it's a solid place. Its one story, so it should be less risky, and it has an old granary building that Brendan will probably commandeer."

Saoirse used Google Maps to pull up the location and showed it to Esras and Uiscias, who looked at the area on the map that Saoirse had pulled up on her phone. They both agreed that it would be a good move.

Saoirse and Sadbh worked with Esras and Uiscias to list the supplies they needed. Some they had, some were easy to get, and other items would require collection or delivery to the cottage. Sadbh made a mental note to pick up a birthday cake along the way.

Brendan was busy modifying Motorola SL4000Es to increase their range. The radios were dismantled and aligned under the magnifier on Brendan's soldering station. Despite the fact that the whole family had mobile phones, Brendan was aware that the networks would crash once the tsunamis started. It was best to be prepared. Spare batteries and a vehicle charging pack were added to the two identical comms packs that he was preparing: one for the group travelling directly to Collon and one for the team that would locate the device. He rubbed his hand absentmindedly through his short dark hair. *What have I forgotten*, he thought.

He left his desk and made his way to the shed that doubled as his workroom. He found the components that he needed and an old base station, stuffed them into a holdall with a power supply and cables, a soldering iron and a component kit. From the shelf, he pulled front-end modules and a couple of spare GPS cards. If he had to, he could configure a private communication system in Branigan's Hill.

Etain rolled her long auburn hair into a bun and secured it with a biro. She had managed to requisition an old landrover, painted a drab green like all army vehicles. The motor pool objected at first and getting someone to sign off on the paperwork was not easy, but she managed it. The landrover four-by-four was filled with diesel, and everything was in perfect working order. Although not a particularly large vehicle, it was solid and well maintained. It would comfortably seat five but if push came to shove, it had been known to hold more.

Etain pulled out onto Infirmary Road and negotiated the light traffic on the North Circular Road. In a few minutes, she would be in Finglas, travelling over the railway bridge in Cabra. Then, it was a straight run through Finglas Village, down Glasnevin Avenue and home.

Muireann took little time in locating a detailed map of the Hill of Tara. Finding Ráith na Senad (the hill of the synods) in the ancient complex had taken only a few minutes.

"Look, we can access the site through the old church, St Patrick's. The access should be easy enough" Morfessa looked over her shoulder at the screen and nodded in agreement.

"How will you find out if something is there?" she asked.

"There are inbuilt beacons in all of the artefacts that were left for us. When we get close, our communicator should be able to latch on," Morfessa explained "and if the communicator doesn't work, we dig."

Muireann plotted a route from Glasnevin to the site on Tara.

"We'll take the motorway to Navan, and it's only a short distance from there. If Etain can get us a vehicle we could be there in an hour."

Almost instantly they heard the roar of a powerful engine outside.

"I'd say she's made it," Muireann said smiling.

Chapter 21

Circles Inside of Circles

It was decided – Morrigan was leader, Etain the driver, Muireann the navigator and Morfessa would handle recovery. Sadbh threw a backpack at them as they ran to the idling jeep.

Despite traffic jams caused by the West End Retail Park and Blanchardstown Centre, once Etain got passed hoards of weekend shoppers, the Motorway was clear.

The Hill of Tara was pretty well signposted and even if it had not been, it would have been easy to find – just follow the tour buses to the site.

Tara was after all one of the most famous places in the country. For more than 5000 years, Tara had been the seat of the High Kings of Ireland. In terms of archaeology, the oldest section of the site dated to 3000 BC, Dumha na nGiall, the mound of the hostages, but the complex was more than just archaeology. Tara evoked a mysticism that fascinated the Irish. It spoke of another time, when Ireland was united and was a focal point of the known world.

Tara was the royal centre of Mide, the middle kingdom and fifth province of ancient Ireland, but the heart of the complex was the Forrad or the royal seat.

In its centre was a standing stone known as the Lia Fail or Stone of Destiny. In legend, the Lia Fail cried out when a true king of Ireland put a foot on it. The legend began with the High King Conn of a hundred battles. When defending Tara from the otherworld, the stone had cried out, and the cries were heard by the god, Lugh. Lugh granted Tara to Conn, the Goddess of Sovereignty Maebh served Conn ale from her magical vat, a tradition that continued with Conn's descendants.

The stone in the centre was not the original stone. It was said that it had been taken by the Scots, at a time when Ireland and Scotland were a united kingdom called Dalriada. The stone, renamed to Stone of Scone, was captured by the English and had sat under the coronation throne of the British for centuries, before finally being returned to Scotland.

It was nearing lunchtime when they pulled up outside the old church of St Patricks. The traffic was heavy, and there was no parking, so Morfessa, Morrigan and Muireann got out and made their way to the churchyard. They could see that the wall separating Synod Hill – or Ráith na Senad – was low and would be easy to cross. Within minutes, they were on the historic site.

Morfessa walked the site, holding the handheld computer. It took several laps before a quiet ping was heard. As they moved closer, the sound intensified. They got a hold on the beacon, but it was clear that they would need to dig. Not only had they come without tools, but the tourists wandering around the site would make any excavation difficult.

Muireann rang Etain, who had parked the landrover. Etain laughed, and her blue eyes danced merrily as her sister told her that they would need some shovels. Etain had loaded a set of tools in the rear of the landrover before she left the barracks. She hoisted the tool bag on her shoulder and marched to the church. Wearing her uniform, the guard on the site and the tourists assumed that she was undertaking official duties.

They waited until late afternoon when most of the tourists were packing up to begin digging. Etain, in uniform, informed a passing security guard that she was getting a soil sample. He waved her on, not really interested.

The rest of the team were waiting. Not one to hold back, she took a shovel and dug where the communicator's signal was strongest. She was careful: she did not want to damage the artefact. The hole that she was digging was getting deeper, and the palms of her hands were blistering. The signal was not getting stronger – it seemed weaker if anything.

Morrigan called a halt to the digging.

"Whatever's here, it's not the Claíomh Solais. We need to look through the spoils and see if there's anything there."

Muireann kicked the mound of dirt and for an instant, she saw a silver glint. She scrambled to her knees, too excited to tell the others and began clawing through the heavy clay until she found what she was looking for. It was a silver coin, showing circles inside of circles, with what looked like an Ogham inscription. Muireann ran her hands through her golden blonde hair in a gesture of defeat.

"I have no idea what this is."

Morrigan examined the coin. As she brought it near the computer, it was clear that it was the source of the beacon signal.

"It's a marker for the true location of the Claíomh Solais. We need to find out what it means," she said.

While Morfessa was examining the coin, Etain pulled up an ogham translator on her phone.

Within seconds. she had a translation – *Aileach*.

The moment Etain spoke the word, Muireann knew exactly what it referred to. It was a stone fort on the Inishowen peninsula at the northern tip of the island of Ireland. The silver coin made sense. Muireann pulled up an aerial view of the site on her phone. From the stone fort, set 250 metres above the sea, Lough Foyle and Lough Swilly were visible, but what interested them was the shape of the fort. It was built with concentric circular walls, creating an outline mirrored by the coin.

"It looks like we're off to Donegal then," Muireann said.

Morrigan was concerned but did not voice her opinions. Why the hell would the settlers leave the Claíomh Solais in such an exposed location? Was it an accident, or was it Semias and Bres ensuring that the mission would fail?

Etain checked the time – it was nearly 5 pm. She did a quick estimate of the journey time. This was not going to be a quick spin. While the others planned what to do next, Etain tried to figure out how she was going to get an Irish Army vehicle over the border into Northern Ireland. They did not have time to drive around the border; they would have to drive through it. They would follow the road to Derry – or Londonderry, as the Unionists called it. Then, they would re-cross the border into the Republic and make the final part of the journey through Donegal.

Etain loaded her passengers into the army jeep and headed to a petrol station outside of Navan. She filled the tank to the brim and filled the jerry cans, fitted in the rear, with fuel. She did not know how quickly the jeep would use the diesel, but it was heavy. While she was filling the tank, she told the others to freshen up. She did not want to stop every few miles for them to answer calls of nature. On the way to the cash register, she filled a basket with sandwiches, chocolate and caffeinated drinks. She made herself a cup of coffee. This would be a long journey and as driver, she needed the caffeine.

Chapter 22

The Evening Darkens

By 5 pm, Sadbh had unloaded the third and last load of supplies from her little car and drove back to the petrol station in Collon, to fill up some petrol cans. She had found a birthday cake for Brendan – chocolate fudge, his favourite, and carried the box carefully into the kitchen.

Saoirse was busy stowing extra clothes and linens into the cottage's two bedrooms. Brendan was setting up a Wi-Fi router to the granary building, which would become the communications hub. On Morfessa advice, the old wood burning stove had been cleaned and the flue checked. If things got as bad as they thought, they would need the heat source.

Esras was busy too, taking inventory of medical supplies. With Sadbh's help, he had purchased a supply of splints, bandages and surgical equipment in small pharmacies along the route. Without her knowing, he had also helped himself to a range of painkillers and antibiotics while the elderly pharmacist was preoccupied, helping Saoirse load the car with filter masks and other paraphernalia that they would need over the coming days.

Medical supplies were stored in the bath, food went to the pantry. Sadbh had loaded up on five litre jugs of water and water purification tablets, just in case. In the local hardware shop, she had picked up boxes of candles, batteries in all sizes and paraffin oil. Her parents had kept a paraffin lamp for decoration – now it would be used for a more practical purpose. The wood-fired range in the kitchen, which sat beside an electric stove, was cleaned out and ready for use. Semias had earlier stacked seasoned wood from the granary in a basket at its feet.

The August evening was darkening.

It is too early to be dark, Sadbh thought, *it should be bright until at least 9 pm*.

She checked the clock. It was 6.15 pm. She found the TV remote control and switched on the RTÉ News.

"Of the thirty active volcanoes in Iceland, Hekla in South Iceland is one of the most active and potentially, the most dangerous. Since the last Hekla eruption in 2000, the Icelandic government has increased monitoring. To the west of the Hekla volcano, Katla is one of the largest volcanoes in Iceland. Government sources in Reykjavík are implementing a disaster plan to evacuate the region. The European Union and the UK have offered assistance."

Sadbh stared at the screen.

"Holy shit!"

Saoirse, Esras, Uiscias, Semias and Brendan sat around the TV, watching live coverage of the activity in Iceland on Euronews after the end of the broadcast on RTÉ.

"It's too soon. We should have had more time," Uiscias whispered.

Esras gripped his shoulder.

"It's out of our hands now. Let's just pray to the angels that it doesn't reach the peak just yet."

Sadbh was getting worried. Neither Muireann nor Etain had called, and they should have been back to the cottage by now. Navan was only a short drive cross country. She left another voicemail and busied herself preparing a meal that would go uneaten.

Chapter 23

A Stony Place

The weather had worsened as Etain drove the landrover through Strabane. They had a close call in Enniskillen, the locals noting the registration and army insignia.

They probably thought I was a one-woman invasion, she mused.

Still, she had not been stopped, just followed for about fifteen minutes. Thank God it had been a private car that followed and not a police vehicle.

Just let me get to Lifford on the right side of the border, she prayed.

The Grianan of Aileach location was raw and desolate. The gale force winds blowing from Lough Foyle, the dark sky and thunder added to the sense of foreboding. It was after 7.30 pm, but it felt like the middle of the night. Etain had broken every speed limit, on both sides of the border, on the way to the deserted mountainside.

Despite her uniform, Etain shivered once the engine turned off, and the heater stopped working. Muireann was wearing a T-shirt and was visibly shaking from cold. Luckily, army vehicles are well equipped and have a small locker of bad weather gear. Muireann and Etain pulled on the odds and ends of foul weather clothing stored in the boot of the four-by-four and followed Morfessa and Morrigan. Although they had been offered a share of the extra clothing, both had refused.

Maybe they don't feel the cold like we do, Muireann thought. *It's probably genetic*.

After the steep climb over the rocky terrain, the force of the wind took their breath away when they reached the crest of the hill.

The Grianan of Aileach was a hillfort with a stone cashel within its ramparts. Cashel is an anglicised version of *caisheal*, a Gaelic word for stone fort. *Aileach* means stony place in Irish and because of the geology of this area of Northern Ireland, the area became known as Aileach. And the area lived up to its name: the ground was rock strewn bog with tufts of heather and rough grass. The fort was built by a descendant of Niall of the Nine Hostages, a legendary High King of Ireland and ancestor of the O'Neill clan and was royal centre for centuries.

The fort lay within eyeline of Lough Swilly and Lough Foyle. Lough Swilly being a glacial fjord between the Inishowen peninsula and Fanad to the west and Lough Foyle, the estuary of the River Foyle that flowed through Derry, to the East. Although situated on a low hill, the fort held a dominant position over counties Derry, Donegal and Tyrone.

The walls of the fort were fifteen-feet thick and twenty-feet high. Inside were three terraces, linked by steps and containing two long passages. Although buildings had once stood in the central ring, the passage of time had erased any traces of them. If the visibility had been better, Sadbh and Muireann might have seen the outlines of the old well that served the fort and the tumulus mound marking a Neolithic grave site.

Outside of the fort, large earth banks had been raised for defence, making access in the dark even more difficult. Thankfully, the torches they had were powerful, and the backpack that Sadbh had handed them had spare batteries in the front pocket. They walked every concentric circle of the ring fort, on each level, but found nothing. The heavy rain and gale force winds made it difficult to see, let alone search. The communicator was quiet – no pings. They switched formation, checked the walls inside and out but still drew a blank.

Totally sodden, the sisters were sent back to the landrover, while Morfessa and Morrigan searched the inner courtyard, again in grid formation.

Chapter 24

The View from Dublin Bay

The last tour left at 8.30 pm to take in late sunset. The pier in little fishing village of Howth was crowded. It was a holiday weekend, and the weather was perfect for late summer. Despite the crisis in Iceland, tourists and sightseers flocked to the harbour, some to people watch at the yacht club, some to enjoy the live music from the many bars around the harbour. The street food festival added to the occasion, and the smell of barbecue and shrimp scented the air.

The island ferries boat was small, taking only 30 passengers but for those lucky enough to get a ticket, it would be worth the lack of facilities. The boat was heading out into Dublin Bay and circling the islands there, timed so that the sunset over Dublin Bay could be captured by cameras and phones. As the diesel engine chugged out of the harbour, the passengers caught a glimpse of the seals that made the harbour their home. The passengers were eagle eyed, watching for a pod of dolphins that were reported to be in the Irish sea, not far from the city.

Andy snuggled up to Jennifer as the wind picked up. Andy was 19, Jennifer was 18, and this was their first date – a day trip to Howth. Andy booked the tickets at the last minute, hoping to impress Jennifer. So far, the day had been magical, Jennifer posted over twenty pictures to Instagram, including a lovely shot of a baby seal. There were selfies of both of them smiling too. Andy took this as a good sign: Jennifer would not post pictures of them both if she were not interested, would she?

As they approached the bird sanctuary on Lambay Island, the tour guide gave a potted history of the island, but it was difficult to hear over the roar of the engine and gust of winds. The sky was changing colour, from the rich blue of earlier in the day to purples, greys and pinks. Jennifer shrugged away Andy's embrace. She wanted to get a shot of all the birds flying towards land. Her phone had an excellent camera, and she used the zoom function to focus on Lambay Castle. It was then that she noticed the plume of smoke rising from the hill on the island.

"Someone must have lit a fire over there," she shouted.

Andy could not hear her over all the noise, so he nodded and reached out to hold her hand.

Jennifer stared at the screen in front of her. It looked like an orange river was oozing out from the top of the hill, flowing down the side towards the castle, steaming and spurting as it went. She did not bother with Andy and went straight to the purser on the boat. She gesticulated wildly at the island, but he did not take her seriously.

Two middle aged men were busy taking photographs of the birds, and she accosted them, showing them her phone. Their attitude towards the mini-skirted teenager changed when they saw the photograph she had taken. Their camera equipment was more sophisticated than Jennifer's and in seconds, they had confirmed what she had seen. Their screams and demands to turn the boat around immediately caused a chain reaction among the passengers. Seeing the panic, the captain turned the boat back to shore.

As the engine revved, the activity on the island became more pronounced, great geysers of lava were thrown into the air, resembling fireworks. Ash and pumice were thrown out into the bay, hitting the boat like a heavy shower of hail stones. However, hail stones are not hot. The debris was molten.

A mother, taking her small children out for a day trip, had the presence to call the emergency services. The operator clearly did not believe that there was an active volcano in Dublin Bay. When the call ended, she rang a friend who was a reporter for an RTÉ radio show. She shared live footage with the news team and from that point on, there was no doubt that an emergency was unfolding. The live feed was picked up by TV channels and internet feeds in seconds.

The boat careened into the harbour and moored haphazardly. The passengers clambered over each other to get back on land and once their feet hit concrete, they ran from the pier, not stopping to look back at the island. Their sole intent was to get to their vehicles and get as far away from the coast as possible. There had been no official warning at this point, so no evacuation. The faster they got away, the more likely they were to make it out of Fingal before the roads were jammed.

Chapter 25

Aurora Antarctica

The skipper of the *Aurora Antarctica* was happy, although the seas were unseasonably rough. The ship had never had a catch so large. The refrigerated holds were full to the brim with haddock, hake and a surprisingly large number of monkfish. The monkfish were ugly as hell. The skin was mottled and the body flat and an oversized head full of razor-sharp teeth, but it was a delicacy and commanded a high price in Europe.

The crew had planned to be at sea for at last another week, but there was no point in continuing to trawl: with the holds full, there was nowhere to put the catch. The first mate was plotting a course back to Killybegs, trying to avoid the worst of the weather. It felt like a January gale, not summer weather for the North Atlantic. Still, both the skipper and crew were happy. They would get a few days holidays with their families and if they were lucky, they would catch the end of the bank holiday at home.

As the hours passed, the wave height increased, and the wind was off the Beaufort scale. His instruments had registered an 11 and now were stuck on 12 – twelve was reserved for hurricanes. The crew struggled to keep the trawler upright. Excess equipment had become a liability and had long since been jettisoned, along with the catch.

The skipper tried the radio again, but all he got was the hiss of static. It was possible that the mast had been damaged. They had definitely lost the trawl winch. He frantically looked around the bridge. He could not see any of his crew mates. He came to the realisation that anyone who had been on deck was now gone, at the mercy of an angry sea.

As he looked out at the black ocean, the ship was overwhelmed by a thick, rushing cloud that seemed to suck the oxygen from the air. The smell was foul, sulphurous and acidic. He watched as his remaining crew succumbed and fell to the cabin floor. He was on his knees and having difficulty breathing when he felt the trawler rising. Used, as he was, to high seas, he knew the boat was in serious trouble.

As the seconds passed, he began to pray for his wife and children in Donegal, and he screamed apologies to his crew. After the ascent, the boat seemed to pause and was suspended in the air. Seconds later, it plummeted straight down and was swallowed by a wall of water higher than any skyscraper in New York.

Chapter 26

Absent Without Leave

Water dripped from Etain's head and shoulders. Muireann's blonde hair was a sodden mess stuck to her face and neck. Neither felt the cold, which was not a good sign. They stripped off some of their wet clothes and turned on the landrover's heater, steaming the windows in the process. Muireann's face and hands were bright red, and she had pins and needles. Etain's feet felt like blocks of ice, and she considered removing her uniform boots but decided against that – at least her feet were dry.

Barely seated in the car, Etain's work phone rang. She answered with a sinking feeling.

"What the fuck are you up to?"

It was Etain's commanding officer, Lieutenant Colonel Jack Kelly.

"Sorry, sir. Family emergency."

Etain crossed her fingers when she lied.

"I've had the PSNI on the phone from Derry. You nearly got yourself killed with your little trek through the North. You are officially on report. Now get your ass back to Dublin on the double."

"Sir, I have something I need to deal with and will leave for Dublin by …"

She checked the clock; it was nearly 11 pm.

"I should be able to report in the morning."

"Are you deaf?"

"No, sir."

"I need you back here to head up logistics an hour ago."

"Sir, I'm off duty. Can you not bring in someone else?"

Lieutenant Colonel Kelly was breathing heavily. Etain thought he was having a heart attack. Jack Kelly was a great commanding officer. He was calm and balanced and might even have been described as easy going. This was not like him but then again, it was not normal for someone to drive an Irish Army vehicle across the border into British territory, in full uniform and then claim to be on leave.

"Etain, if you are off duty, why did you take a landrover from the motor pool? You gave them a cock-and-bull story about an urgent assignment – from me. We can discuss this when you get back, but I don't have time to waste on it now. Do you not know what's going on?"

"No, sir. I've been really preoccupied, and I haven't been near a radio or seen the news all day. I honestly have no idea."

Jack breathed heavily on the other end of the line.

"Apart from the two volcanoes that took out parts of Antrim, Slieve Gullion and Slemish Mountain, we've had a teeny-weeny, little problem with the volcano on Lambay Island."

"Sir, there is no volcano on Lambay Island."

"Oh, yes there is. I know, because it's just bloody erupted. And Portmarnock, Malahide, Rush, Lusk and just about everywhere else, from Howth northward along the Dublin coast, is being hit with whatever the hell comes out of a volcano. I need you here to help execute an evacuation plan. We've half a million people on the northside to move. That's on top of the Iceland thing."

Etain cursed under her breath. This thing was moving faster than anyone had anticipated. They should have had at least another day. She was afraid to ask her CO what the Iceland thing was – whatever had happened, it was sure to be bad news.

"Sir, it's a four-hour drive back and that's cutting through the North. I'm not going to make it back until at least 5 am if I go around."

"Don't make excuses, Etain."

"I'm not making excuses. I'm a communications expert, not a logistics expert," Etain spat.

"Do whatever the hell you need to do to get back. No one else here has a clue about how to deploy the emergency 4G LTE network, and we need to start requisitioning vehicles now."

The LTE network he referred to was wireless broadband communication network for mobile devices, accessible only by emergency responders.

Etain tried to placate her boss and eventually, he mellowed.

"I'll call the PSNI back, and they can arrange an escort for you. Wait for them at the border. Do not attempt to enter the North without them."

In the background, Etain could hear her CO being called. He hurriedly said goodbye and hung up.

Muireann heard every part of the conversation.

"We're out of time," she said.

Muireann and Etain re-dressed in the raingear and rushed back to Morfessa and Morrigan. The gale threatened to push them over as the girls screamed at them to get back to the landrover. Morfessa shook his head and tried to continue on, but Etain grabbed his arm. She manoeuvred her head close to his ear and screamed at him.

"Just turn the damn thing on."

She took a deep breath and screamed again.

"If you turn it on, it might guide us to where it is. We need to do it now. Iceland has erupted and three volcanoes here have too. If the tsunami hits like you said it will, this whole area will be wiped from the map. We'll all be killed in the process."

Morrigan struggled over to Morfessa and Etain. She had just about heard Etain's plea.

"We can't do that," Morrigan shouted. "We'll lose too much energy."

"If we can't find it, it won't matter. We'll be dead," Etain screamed.

Etain tried to grab the computer from Morrigan, but she pushed her away. She slammed into Muireann, and they both lost their balance. They fell and rolled down the slope over the rough and barren terrain.

Morfessa and Morrigan closed in on each other.

Morrigan tried to walk away, but Morfessa grabbed her arm and screamed at her.

"She's right. We're out of time. If we don't turn it on, we will never find it in time. The volcanoes have erupted, and the shockwave will be on the way. In less than an hour, this whole peninsula will be under a tsunami."

Grabbing the device from Morrigan, Morfessa struggled to find the correct settings on the computer. It was difficult to see the tiny screen in the driving rain. He persisted and adjusted the controls and hit the on switch.

Muireann and Etain's descent was stopped by a cairn of rough stone ensconced in bog. Somewhere on the way down the hill, Etain had lost the keys to the landrover. Muireann's face was scratched by gravel, and her jacket was torn under the shoulder. Etain managed to tell her that the keys were missing. They scrambled around on all fours, searching for the key ring. Etain hoped that the light from the next lightning strike might reflect from the keys' surface.

As Muireann foraged through the undergrowth beside a large boulder, she felt something. Her fingers were fizzing. It felt like a mild electric shock. She pulled away moss and lichen and through a fissure, she thought she saw a very faint emerald light.

"What colour is it?" she shouted to Etain.

"What colour is what?" Etain responded.

"The Claíomh Solais. What colour is the light? Is it green?"

Etain shook her head.

"I don't know. What have you found?"

"There's a green light coming from under the boulder. It's very faint, but my hands feel all tingly when I put them near the rock. I can't think of anything that could produce a green light in the middle of nowhere. It has to be it."

Etain left Muireann kneeling at the side of the boulder, desperately trying to pull away grass, mud and gravel. She tried jumping up and down, but Morfessa and Morrigan could not see her. They were intently searching at the base of the fort.

She stumbled up the hill towards them, falling more than once. When she finally reached them, she pulled Morfessa down the hill and pointed at Muireann. She repeatedly screamed about the green light. He instantly understood. Morfessa grabbed Morrigan, and she followed close behind. The trio struggled against the gale force winds and driving rain to reach Muireann.

First Morfessa and then Morrigan lay on the sodden ground and peered into the hole that Muireann had excavated. They briefly examined the light and agreed that it was the Claíomh Solais. Morrigan stood, muttered and then rushed towards the car, suddenly realising that she had no keys. While Morfessa and Muireann worked on the boulder, Morrigan and Etain found the keys in a small clump of heather, halfway down the hill.

It took Morfessa and Morrigan nearly twenty minutes to work the boulder loose, using tools from the car and a tyre iron. They reverently removed the soil and plant matter from the depression under the rock and gently removed the artefact.

The Claíomh Solais was about three feet long, a perfect cylinder of opaque crystal, glimmering in the light of their torches. The hilt was of polished gold, engraved swirling Celtic symbols, complex Dara knots vying with stylised animals and fish. The pommel was set with a cabochon of amethyst, the size of a gull's egg. Morfessa and Morrigan were in awe and needed to be pulled back to reality. Etain shook them and told them they needed to get away from the coast immediately.

They carefully wrapped the artefact in an old blanket retrieved from the landrover. The gale force wind was reaching hurricane strength as they were dragged back to the vehicle. The white wave tops were cresting both sides of the peninsula, and the wind exceeded known hurricane strength. Despite the weight of the landrover, it felt like it was going to be lifted clear from the parking spot. Inside, it felt like they were inside a shaking coffee can.

Etain pulled off the raingear and wiped her face. She turned the ignition key, pressed the accelerator hard and headed inland.

Chapter 27

Ominous Warnings

The dashboard clock said 11.40 pm. The landrover rocked with the force of each gust of wind, the noise of which drowned out any hope of conversation.

The old road from Grianan an Aileach was waterlogged and treacherous. Rivulets ran down the hills and quickly became streams and rivers. Along with the water, loose stones and rocks hurtled down on them. It was as if the fort knew they had taken its most precious possession. They were on a peninsula and could not help but see the angry waves in Lough Swilly and Lough Foyle. In the darkness, lightning lit the angry waves hurtling up and over the beaches.

The rough tracks back to the main road were treacherous. Etain struggled to keep control as the vehicle slewed over the slippery surface. It took all of Etain's concentration to get them back to Derry. There was no fear of the vehicle being recognised now – it was covered in debris and mud. The roads were deserted, only a fool would drive in conditions like these.

When they got to the border, the Police Service of Northern Ireland squad car was waiting, blue lighting them through Strabane. They were left to their own devices outside of the town, their escort pulled away to deal with an emergency up the coast. Etain tried to tell the Police Service of Northern Ireland's young officers to keep away from the coast, but they did not listen.

Etain followed the A5 into Omagh and then turned towards Enniskillen, fighting the wind and rain for the entire journey. As they approached the town, the damage inflicted by the hurricane force winds was everywhere. Roof slates, road signs and loose garden furniture flew at them like missiles. Alarms blared all around them as they approached the war memorial, the site of the infamous Enniskillen bombing that had devastated the local community during the troubles. Etain knew she had to keep going, but a part of her wanted to stop and let the raging storm pass. Morfessa, sensing her thoughts, urged her to increase speed and get outside of the town as fast as possible. They would be safer in open country.

They followed the road through Derrylin and the townlands of Teemore and Belturbet and eventually saw the signs for Cavan town. Buffeted by the winds, Etain pulled over onto the verge on a dual carriageway and let the engine idle.

"I need to know where to go," she said.

Muireann said the quickest route south would be the M1 motorway, but she discounted it, as it would take them down the east coast. Not only would they be affected by debris from the Antrim volcanoes, but they would also drive straight into the volcano in Dublin Bay. Although the road was not as good, the N3 was part motorway and would be the fastest route to Navan. From there, they could cut across country to the cottage. Etain could drop off her passengers and return the landrover to the barracks before reporting for duty.

On their journey back, they had been updated by the radio news on the situation in Iceland, which seemed to get progressively worse as the minutes passed. The attempts to rescue people from the towns and villages around the volcanoes had been abandoned, and the loss of life was considerable. In the last hour, the newscaster announced that there would be no more attempts to airlift the citizens from Reykjavík airport. The Reykjanes peninsula, with all its volcanic activity, had simply blown itself apart. The airport had ceased to exist, along with most of the capital.

Closer to home, Slieve Gullion and Slemish Mountain, both extinct volcanoes in County Antrim, had erupted. Seismic activity in the region was the strongest ever seen in Ireland. Lambay Island in Dublin Bay, once a prisoner of war camp and now owned by a descendant of the founder of Baring's Bank (the bank that was famed for its rogue trader that led to its collapse) had also erupted, leaving most of the north side of Dublin in a state of turmoil, and whole sections of the city near the coast were being evacuated. Parts of Sutton, Howth and Donabate were on fire.

The roads out of the city were jammed solid and the emergency services could not keep up with the calls that they were receiving. Beaumont Hospital had received the first round of injured residents and had now closed its doors, because they simply did not have the capacity to triage and treat that many patients, diverting people away to James Connolly Memorial Hospital in Blanchardstown to the west and to the Mater Hospital in the city centre.

RTÉ News could not keep up with the reports that were coming in. Despite its state of penury, there were no advertisement breaks – just constant news. Throughout it all, the newscasters appealed to the listeners to keep off their phones, lest the networks collapse.

News was now arriving of natural disasters across Europe, with Mount Etna in Sicily and Nea Kameni in Santorini the latest to erupt. Edinburgh had been partially destroyed by the eruption of Arthur's Seat on the outskirts of the city. The super volcano that no one had ever heard of, Glen Coe, had cleared its throat and had left the inhabitants of Argyll in the Scottish Highlands in a state of emergency. As far away as Russia, Klyuchevskaya Volcano in Kamchatka was erupting. Seismic activity was being reported from across the continent.

Unusually, there were no politicians having their say and no analysts brought in to give their opinion. No one really gave a shit what the politicians thought, and there was no time to listen to analysts. The sparse interviews that were given airtime were with the emergency services, advising citizens how to survive, and how to give Emergency First Aid. The army was interviewed. They laid out the evacuation plan, and how to get the old and vulnerable to evacuation points. What people wanted to know was what would happen next.

It was the interview with the Dublin Institute of Advanced Studies that had the nation rapt. The obscure institute was a national institution and used the historic Dunsink Observatory as its base. The observatory, located between Finglas and Castleknock on the north side of Dublin City, had been a research centre since 1785 and in its time, had been responsible for numerous scientific breakthroughs, including those of William Rowan Hamilton, the famous mathematician and physicist. Known for astrophysics, the institute also investigated natural phenomena, including the physics of volcanoes.

The doctoral candidate explained, in layman's terms, exactly what had happened in Iceland and the knock-on effects that the movement of tectonic plates was having on Ireland. Being near the edge of the plate, Ireland's geology was under unbelievable pressure, causing earthquakes and volcanic activity. She was the first to raise the subject of a tsunami, stating that math indicated that tidal waves would hit both sides of the Atlantic.

Realising for the first time that a tsunami was imminent, alarms were sounded across the country, giving scant warning to those near the north and west coasts. Almost simultaneously, warnings were issued from Scandinavia to Iberia and across the east coast of the USA and Caribbean.

The interview had barely finished when the sombre reporter announced that maritime agencies from the Scotland and other parts of the United Kingdom were reporting sightings of a massive wall of water, heading south-east from Iceland. A similar wall of water was heading southwest and would hit landfall between Boston and New York. Reports were limited, the newscaster said, as the ships' transmissions were abruptly cut off. All thoughts were now with the Irish and international fishing fleets who were at sea. The expected landfall would be within fifteen minutes. That was the last report that was issued.

The news team advised listeners to evacuate the Atlantic coast and make their way inland away from the coastline. For those inland, they were to shut off gas mains, disconnect electrical equipment and fill containers with drinkable water. Anyone who lived in a high-rise building was to leave it now and find a place of shelter. No one could predict what would happen next.

The newscaster signed off with a prayer, and all radio stations switched to emergency transmissions. His prayers were joined by countless hundreds of thousands of Irish men and women who, when they had woken on the holiday Saturday morning, thought only of sunshine and fun. Understanding now that this was a life and death situation, people rushed to their phones to contact loved ones across the country, particularly those enjoying a bank holiday weekend by the sea. As predicted, the phone system collapsed under the volume of calls.

Despite the ominous warnings issued by the national broadcaster, the N3 was eerily quiet. The normally busy road was empty, and Etain could see no headlights in either direction. She managed to get the landrover up to 60 kilometres an hour. She dared not go any faster. She and her passengers had felt the vehicle rocking as wave after wave of tremors hit. Etain has nearly lost control more than once.

The outskirts of Virginia were in sight. She had thought that the roads would be busy with people evacuating from the town, but she realised that people were staying put. They would be safer in their homes, well inland and anyway, where was there to run to? West and north were in the path of a tsunami. To the north-east and east, volcanoes were erupting. This was the safest place to be.

Chapter 28

Life's Been Good So Far

It has been a busy day in the rolling hills of County Clare. The Dromoland estate had occupied its guests with clay pigeon shooting and archery. Fishermen had teased the trout with flies, and a bumper catch had made its way to the Michelin-starred kitchen, to be added to the dinner menu.

After an activity packed day of falconry, tennis and exploring the 450-acre estate, guests had cooled off in the swimming pool or relaxed in the sauna or spa. Of course, for some, the highlight of the day was a round golf on the 18-hole golf course – one of the best in Europe.

Michael Parker relaxed in the Brian Boru suite, bedecked in duck-egg blue and gold. Earlier in the day, the suite had glorious views out over the lough and estate. Now, the windows rattled in the high winds. Michael sipped on the aged Powers whiskey in its Waterford Crystal glass. Later, he would slip into the bedroom of the suite and enjoy the four-poster luxury of a firm mattress, Egyptian cotton sheets and silk covered duvet. He might even have the staff light the open fire in the sitting room.

He had met his buddies in the Earl of Thomond restaurant for dinner earlier that night. They had booked the last sitting and boy, it had been some night. The meal was an eight-course extravaganza, accompanied by some of the finest wines and port that the five-star resort had to offer – a feast as advertised.

It was a little after midnight, and his hunger was sated. He had dined on roast West Coast scallops and confit of Clare Island salmon, steamed wild turbot with langoustines, herbed rump of Burren lamb and elderflower sorbet with pink gin, a chocolate mouse with oak-aged, single-grain Irish whiskey and to finish, a crème brulée with rhubarb and strawberries and cheese board, washed down with vintage red.

Life was good. This was exactly what he needed. He had fought tooth and nail to be the top salesman in the New Jersey office, and this was his reward. He was mixing with the company elite from Manhattan. That was where he wanted to be – in the Manhattan Office, where the action was.

He was going places and after the golf round, it was clear that a promotion was coming his way.

He laughed when he thought of his ex-wife, leaving him to move inland to some hick town in Iowa. He wondered if she would regret leaving him when he moved into a fancy apartment and upgraded his car to a BMW. He wondered if there were any BMWs in Mount Pleasant, Iowa. The farm boy schoolteacher that his wife ran off with probably drove a truck or an electric car. Well, she could shove her cornfields up her ass. At least the kids had plenty of room to run around, and the schools in Iowa were some of the best in the country. He shook his head. He tried not to think about the kids, and it made him maudlin.

The roaring outside the window sounded like a low flying jet, Michael rose from the sofa and went to the window. He scanned the sky for the tell-tale lights of a plane. They were close to Shannon Airport, so aircraft noise was no surprise, but the sky was empty.

Had he listened to the radio or watched an Irish TV station, he would have heard or seen the flash warning for the west coast. Had he been on the other side of the hotel, he might have seen the stream of vehicles speeding inland. Had he been in the lobby, he might have been lucky enough to be a passenger in one of them. The phone is his room had rung earlier. He had dismissed it as a room service call. Now, he wondered whether he should have answered.

As he looked over the estate, he saw flashes of white above the tree line. He could not quite make out what it was. He stood at the floor-to-ceiling window and stared out. Whatever it was, it was coming straight for him. The trees in the distance disappeared from view, and it was then he realised that the white he saw was foam lashing from a wave – a gigantic wave.

He dropped his glass on the Persian rug and stumbled backwards, disturbing the coffee table and its floral display. He backed out of the suite, not bothering to close the door and ran with all his strength down the long corridor. At the junction, he did not know whether to turn left or right. He chose right and kept running until he reached the lifts. He bypassed them and charged down the stairs, stumbling and nearly falling. He was out of breath when he reached the lobby and ran towards the main door. It was only when he reached the door that he realised he had run in the wrong direction. The wave was directly in front of him.

His last thoughts were of his estranged wife and of their children, who he knew that he would never see again.

Chapter 29

Not Normal Circumstances

Morrigan, Muireann, Morfessa and Etain were on the road to Virginia, the picturesque, rural County Cavan town. The town had been founded during the Plantation of Ulster in the early 17th century and had been named for Queen Elizabeth I, the Virgin Queen. The town had a remarkable history: a Protestant enclave in Catholic Ireland. Still, the people maintained much of the original architecture and ambience of the town. As Ireland's economy grew, it became a dormer town for Dublin City, people making the two-hour commute to the industrial estates all around the metropolis.

They felt the earthquake before they could see its effects. The ground beneath the vehicle began to quiver, then shake. Around them, they could see the roadside verge disappear, and the road began to undulate violently, swinging the car from side to side and up and down.

"Hold on," Etain screamed.

She fought the urge to brake – instead, hitting the accelerator to power the heavy vehicle forward. The streetlights in the near distant town blinked out, leaving Etain with only her headlights to navigate by.

Muireann screamed as she fell into Morfessa, who was desperately holding on to the door. Even Morrigan, sitting in the front passenger seat, looked ashen.

"We've got to get to the bridge before it collapses," Etain screamed.

Muireann instantly understood.

The old Lee Bridge lay on the outskirts of the town on the Dublin Road, beside the Victorian mill that straddled the river flowing into Lough Ramor. The road on which the bridge lay was the main route out of town. This was their only way back to the cottage. There was no way that the side roads would be passable.

Etain sped through the nightmare that was the centre of Virginia town. The old Victorian and Edwardian buildings that lined Main Street had fallen. Sections of town were ablaze from ruptured gas mains and house fires, and sparks flew from fallen streetlights and traffic signals. They could hear car alarms blaring. They passed a row of cars that had been flattened. Another row of cars was alight, and the threat of ruptured petrol tanks was imminent.

Dazed Virginians wandered through the rubble of what was once their homes. The injured lay on the streets and in doorways. There would be no help coming. Cities, towns and villages all over the country were in a similar situation.

Muireann thought of her mother, brother and sister in the cottage and prayed that they would be okay. She did not realise that they were praying for her and Etain.

Etain drove the engine remorselessly; the street scape, a serpentine chicane designed by an angry mother nature. As each second passed, new obstacles were thrown in their way as a result of secondary quakes and strong tremors. The old buildings simply could not take the strain of the earth's movement and gave way in their path.

As they passed the Ramor Lodge on the outskirts of town, all noise suddenly stopped. Etain stood on the brakes. There was no further seismic activity – everything was paused. Etain had managed to get through the town unscathed, despite fires and debris along Main Street. She paused briefly to make sure her passengers were all right and then, she hung a sharp right to take her out the Lee Bridge.

She had barely made the turn before screeching to a halt. What was left of the bridge was right in front of them. Two arches of the bridge, on the Dublin side of the river, were intact but near the mill race, part of the stonework had collapsed.

Etain jumped from the landrover and ran to bridge to examine it in more detail. The bridge itself had been built alongside the mill in the late 1890s. Although it was of solid construction and parts had been refurbished in the 1980s, Etain could not see the extent of the damage from the landrover. Part of the surface, at the Virginia side of the bridge, was still intact, but was it wide enough to get the heavy landrover through? In normal circumstances, she would not have taken the risk, but these were not normal circumstances. She ran back to her sister, Morfessa and Morrigan.

"Get out," she yelled, banging on the doors.

The others jumped out onto the road and stared at the collapsed section of the bridge. Muireann pulled on Etain's sleeve. She told her sister that they would have to find another route. Etain rounded on her. There was no other way.

"Muireann, check all the maps you want. We can't go back. You've seen that for yourself. The only other road leads to Lough Ramor, which is useless – it's a dead end. To get to the Bailieborough Road and the Dublin Road, we have to get over the bridge."

Etain ran to the back of the landrover and thrust the backpack from the boot at Muireann.

"You've got to get over the bridge. I'm going to take the landrover over on my own. I don't know how stable the bridge is or if it's wide enough. It's a 30-foot drop to the riverbed, and there's no one to rescue us if we fall. The walkie-talkie is in there. If you get close enough to home, then Brendan will hear you. Now go."

Morrigan looked at Etain and saw the determination on her face. There was no point in arguing. She grabbed Muireann by the arm and dragged her towards the bridge – the Claíomh Solais in her other hand.

Morfessa held his ground. He was not going to run away and leave her alone.

"Are you sure there is no other way, Etain? Maybe there is another side road we could take."

Etain shook her head.

"You felt the power of that tremor, Morfessa. Do you really think that a side road would be passable, even if there was one? Anyway, one way or another, we have to get across the river. Look at the stonework on the bridge – it was built to last. A modern bridge would have been completely destroyed. If you look at the ramparts on the intact section of the bridge, they are solid; they won't fall. I'm going to take the landrover over on that side if I can."

Morfessa did not agree with Etain, but he could understand her decision. Now was not the time for an argument.

"Do you have rope in the back?"

"Yes. There should be some bungee cords in the boot."

He opened the back of the landrover and found them.

"I want you to tie these around your waist. I'm going to take one end and walk ahead of you, to give directions. If you get into trouble, then jump. I'll get you out."

Etain wanted to explain that there was no way to get over the bridge with the driver's door open, without tangling the makeshift rope, but she decided not to. He meant well.

Morfessa did a good job of getting the car into position to cross the remains of the bridge, but it was clear that the front driver's side would never make it – the surface was just too narrow. Morfessa tried to get Etain to abandon the landrover, but she would not.

Etain walked around the landrover, inspecting the bodywork as she went.

"Get the tyre iron and hold on to it. We'll need it in a minute," she said.

Morfessa did not know what a tyre iron was, but he assumed that it was metal and heavy and knew instantly that he had made the right choice when she nodded grimly.

Etain got into the landrover and fitted her seatbelt tightly. Starting the engine, she reversed the landrover and instead of aiming for the centre of the remaining road surface, she aimed the landrover into the stone wall that ran along the length of the bridge.

Morrigan saw her and screamed.

"What the hell is she doing?"

Muireann watched her sister reverse and drive forward again at a slightly deeper angle. She placed her hand on Morrigan's arm and said softly, "She's taking out the front-passenger side wing and doors. She's trying to make the landrover narrow enough to make it over."

They watched in fascination while Etain smashed the front and side of the army vehicle into the unyielding stonework. The steel of the landrover's frame screamed as it contacted the granite blocks.

Etain reversed, turned off the engine and climbed out. She surveyed her work. Taking the tyre iron, she hit the side of the car with all her might, finishing the work that the stone had started. Glass from the windows and plastic from the sidelights cascaded across the tar-covered road. Changing her stance, she used the tyre iron to smooth the wheelhouse of jagged edges. The last thing that she needed was a shredded tyre. Grabbing a torch, she ran the light over the full side of the landrover, finally satisfied with her work. She checked the passenger doors. Despite the battering they had sustained, they still opened and closed smoothly.

"Morfessa, get over the bridge now. I'm coming through."

Morfessa was going to argue with her but realised that there was no point. She had made her mind up. Before she crossed the remnant of the bridge, he secured the elastic rope around her waist and held the other end tightly. When he was positioned on the other side, he gave her a signal to go ahead.

Rather than take it slowly, Etain reversed the battered vehicle back as far as she dared and aimed it so the passenger side would make full contact with the capstones. She hit the accelerator and ploughed forward, holding her breath for what felt like an eternity as the landrover became airborne. With a thud, she landed and skidded onto the undamaged section of the bridge. She braked hard.

There was no sound. Etain exhaled. She did not care about the reprimand that might come from writing off the landrover or the damage that she had caused. She just felt relief. She opened the door and stood shakily on the tarmac. She felt her legs go out from under her, only to be caught by powerful arms.

Morfessa held her up, grinning wildly. She put her head against his shoulder and closed her eyes. There were no tears: she was still in uniform.

Morrigan and Muireann ran forward to Etain. Muireann embraced her sister and kissed her cheek. Etain waved her away. They wasted no time climbing back into the vehicle that was still idling. Before they departed, Morrigan placed her hand on Etain's arm.

"You are lucky you don't report to me. That was the stupidest, most irresponsible move I have ever seen a soldier make. You could have been killed. It was bloody brilliant. Thank you, Etain."

Muireann threw the backpack between her and Morrigan, who was now a back-seat passenger.

When Muireann was settled, Etain powered away, full headlights illuminating the crumpled road ahead.

While Etain negotiated her way through fallen trees, downed power lines and massive potholes, Muireann rummaged through the backpack looking for the walkie-talkie that Brendan had readied. Etain insisted that they try to contact Brendan as soon as they were within range. She knew that her mother, brother and sister would be frantic with worry by now.

As the landrover rumbled on, Muireann pulled the contents of the backpack out onto the back seat. The walkie-talkie was there, but they were not yet in range. Muireann put everything back, expect for two things.

"Guess what I found?" she shouted.

Etain kept her eyes on the road, but Morfessa and Morrigan turned to her.

She held up a flask and a Tupperware container.

Chapter 30

Put the Kettle On!

Sadbh paced back and forth in front of the cottage. She could not call Etain – the networks were down. Tremors and aftershocks rattled the little homestead but thankfully, the thick stone walls were solid, even if the dishes were not. The water was not affected – yet. Sadbh had filled containers with the sweet well water, just in case.

She had busied herself to occupy her mind lest she dwell on the fact that her daughters were out there on their own. She could not watch TV or listen to the radio anymore. It was bad news after bad news. Anyway, they were both transmitting a loop of emergency announcements for the past hour, interspersed with disaster updates. She checked again with Brendan. Etain and Muireann still were not in range of the walkie-talkies, wherever they were.

When the kids were small, she would take them to the coast at Portmarnock or out to the beach at the seaside town of Donabate. Once or twice, they took a little boat out to Lambay Island, to see the bird sanctuary there. She remembered a big hill in the centre and an old castle belonging to some English lord. Who knew that the whole island was a volcano?

Good luck going back to that family seat, she thought ruefully.

A little over an hour ago, a tsunami had hit the north and west of the country. Places that she knew growing up – Bundoran in Donegal and the walled city of Derry – had ceased to exist. Westport in Mayo and Enniscrone in Sligo were gone. Parts of Castlebar were completely destroyed, as was Sligo town. Galway took the full force of the wave – the commentators were expecting few survivors. Every little village and town along the coast in Clare, Galway, Mayo, Sligo, Leitrim, Limerick, Donegal, and Kerry were gone. The scale of the disaster was incomprehensible. She could not think about the loss of people she worked with, friends she went to college with. She could not think about her ex-husband in his seaside love nest near Ballina. She did not mention her ex to Saoirse and Brendan, but she knew they were aware of what had probably happened to their father. Despite everything that had happened in the past, she felt sorry for him. A part of her mourned him.

There were some lucky ones. Although the warnings gave short notice, some people had managed to get away from the coast. They were now heading inland. There had been no announcements on where to go, no directions from the government and emergency services. She felt another tremor and thought about what was happening in Dublin and other towns and cities. The force of the earlier earthquake made her think about collapsing buildings, fires and destruction. The emergency services had never had to deal with a disaster on this scale.

They were probably trying to put together a plan on the fly, she thought.

Sadbh realised that the survivors were on their own, just like Etain and Muireann were on their own. She had spent her whole adult like scrimping and saving and making do to keep the house in Dublin, and there were many times that she honestly thought that she would lose it to over-eager banks looking for repossessions, but she had held on, and now the house was hers. It was old and faded, but it was her pride and joy, along with her kids. Now she did not give a damn if the house fell down or burned down. All that she cared about now were her daughters and them getting home alive.

Her mind kept wandering. Was the worst over now? What more was to come? According to Semias, this was just the beginning. She paced back and forth across the kitchen to try to burn off some nervous energy. It was Saoirse who finally told her mother to go and have a smoke. Brendan was out in the granary. She could check in on him while she was outside.

She smoked a cigarette outside of the granary and as she stooped to put it out on the flagstones, she heard voices coming over the radio. She pulled the door open to hear Brendan talking animatedly with Muireann. Brendan grabbed her hand.

"They're okay, Mam. They're just outside of Ardee. You can put the kettle on. They're nearly home."

Sadbh burst into tears.

Chapter 31

Fumbled

Etain was exhausted. The drive was taking every ounce of concentration that she had. Despite constant tremors, total darkness and heavy rain, they were on the final stretch of road leading home. With less than five miles to go, they had avoided countless mains ruptures, fires and sink holes. Muireann had offered to take over, but she had never driven an army vehicle and was unfamiliar with the power of it. The last part of the trip would be on one of the worst stretches of road in the country. Etain thought it safer that she should keep going.

Ironically, she had loved this section of road when she was a kid. They had all called it the rollercoaster. They had loved nothing more that jumping into grandad's old handcart – the one that he used to carry dry turf from the bog to the house. He would drag it part way up the hill, and the kids would roll down. When their grandmother found out, she put a stop to it. Sadbh would never have forgiven her father if anything happened to her kids.

For several miles, the road had been laid up and over a series of steep hills, meaning steep climbs and steeper descents. Even in good weather and bright sunshine, the road was notorious for accidents – you never knew was coming at you. Etain crested the top of the first hill, giving just enough acceleration to push the four-by-four over the brim, being careful not to go to fast. She started the descent, keeping her foot on the brakes despite the roaring of the engine. Speed would not have mattered though. Etain had no way of seeing the sink hole that swallowed the road until just before they hit it.

She swerved wildly, as soon as it became visible, pushing the landrover into a skid and saving the back-seat passengers from serious injury. She was not so lucky. The front, driver side of the landrover took the full force of the impact with the remnants of underground water pipes and ducting as it landed. Despite the heavy bodywork, the steel door was impaled by an iron girder and Etain's side was pierced. Glass was embedded deep in the muscle of her shoulder. These injuries were survivable. It was the impact to her temple that was life threatening. Air bags could not protect her from the rock that smashed through the driver's window and hit her just above her hairline.

The passenger side of the landrover hung precariously over a steep drop but was unscathed. The back of the vehicle rocked wildly but was undamaged. The landrover was balanced on its chassis, like a seesaw over a deep chasm. No one moved. No one breathed, and they all understood that they were unlikely to walk away from the situation. In the silence, the bodywork creaked and moaned, and the wind caused the landrover to swing like a pendulum.

"Muireann, can you open your door?" Morfessa yelled from the passenger seat.

"Just about," she said.

Muireann gingerly opened the door and let it swing wide open. She found her torch on the back seat, lifting it carefully to minimise movement. She shone the torch outside.

"I think I can reach what's left of the road from here."

Morfessa judged that she was the lightest passenger. It was safest to get her out first.

"Get out really slowly and when you do, go around to the rear, and put your weight down on back."

Morfessa hoped that the added weight to the back of the vehicle would stabilise it enough to stop the rocking.

Muireann was frightened – so scared that she could not move. Morfessa sensed her panic and told her that she had to move. Otherwise, they would go over, and her sister would be lost. Muireann's fear of losing Etain was greater than her fear for herself, so she jumped and landed roughly on her side. She lay still for a few seconds, hardly believing that she was on solid ground and then got to her feet and ran to the back of the landrover. She pressed directly down on the bumper and felt the wheels connect on what was left of the pavement.

"Morrigan, I need you to pull Etain back to you once I get the seatbelt undone," Morfessa shouted.

For once, Morrigan did not object.

Minimising his movements, Morfessa manged to untangle Etain from the seat belt, and she slumped forward, causing the landrover to shift its position. Muireann screamed but pushed down hard on the bumper. When the vehicle stabilised, he gently but firmly gripped her upper body and pulled back, dragging her torso closer to Morrigan and the rear seat. The four-by-four oscillated wildly, and Muireann pushed the back down with all her strength, hoping to keep it stable while Etain was moved. For an age, both travellers struggled to gently pull Etain into the back seat. Each movement set the landrover swinging but moving the weight back helped.

Morfessa ordered Morrigan to move near the door that Muireann had exited.

"I'm going to move into the back, but I need you to get out and try to hold us, stop us from going over."

Morrigan carefully pulled herself free and rushed to help Muireann, who was, by now, exhausted. Muireann still had some of the cord that they had used earlier. Morrigan quickly opened the back of the landrover and retrieved tools and rope that she hoped would help save then. Muireann and Morrigan tied the bungee cords and rope on to the trailer hitch. Morrigan took the weight and walked backwards, trying to pull the heavy load with her. Muireann did what she could to help her.

In the panic of trying to get out, no one had thought of getting the Claíomh Solais. It rolled around in the footwell of the passenger seat. Morfessa saw it and cursed. He would have to go forward again. Trying not make sudden movements, he crawled forward and grabbed it. His carefully manoeuvred himself over beside Etain, who was resting on the back seat.

"Muireann, the Claíomh Solais is still here. I'm going to have to get you to come level with the door and try to catch it when I throw it."

Morfessa realised the Claíomh Solais was unwrapped. He struggled out of his tunic and wrapped the Claíomh Solais in it, hoping that the padding would at least partially shield it if it fell.

Muireann objected, screaming that she could not catch it. She begged Morrigan to come back and get the Claíomh Solais from Morfessa.

Morrigan, understanding that moving back towards the vehicle would be a death sentence for Morfessa and Etain, calmly tried to talk a hysterical Muireann around.

"Baby steps to the side, Muireann. Remember, you can't do anything wrong. If you don't catch it then you don't catch it, okay. This is not your fault."

Morrigan nodded at Muireann, and she walked slowly to come level with the door, mindful that a further section of the road could collapse at any second. Without Muireann's help, Morrigan struggled to maintain her foothold and felt her hands slip on the cord.

Morfessa threw the artefact and Muireann tried to catch it but at the last moment, she fumbled and could not hold it. It landed and rolled forward, towards the abyss. She jumped forward and grabbed it up from the ground, nearly falling to the foot of the chasm. She teetered on the brink then, deftly turned and ran to Morrigan, swapping the Claíomh Solais for the rope. She took it from her without examining it and pushed it into the folds of her robe. She immediately grabbed the elastic cord and pulled with all her might.

"Muireann, is there a tree or a rock that we can anchor the cord on?" Morrigan shouted.

Muireann looked around her and spotted the entrance to a field a few yards down from them.

"I think there's a farm gate a few feet down. If it's solid, we could wrap the cord around it, and it could help take the weight."

Morrigan shooed her over to check it out. She prayed that she'd hurry. Her arms were aching, the muscles twitching from exertion. Her legs were cramped. She did not know how much longer she could hold out.

Muireann ran back and grabbed the cord, easing the pressure on Morrigan.

"It's a heavy steel gate – the type used to keep cattle in. It's anchored into concrete pillars that don't seem to be damaged. These bungee cords are designed to hold things down. We can use the claws on the end to secure the cord to the gate. We just have to get there."

Morrigan screamed at Morfessa to hold on and then, she and Muireann crab walked to the gate with superhuman effort, pulling the back of landrover with them. It took their last reserves of strength to pull the cord between the steel laths of the gate, but the steel barb on the end of the cord did its job. It hooked into the steel structure and gave Muireann a chance to wrap the cord tightly around the gate latch.

Running back to the landrover they shouted to Morfessa that they had the vehicle anchored. Morfessa called back to Muireann.

"Muireann, I'm going to try to get Etain out. I'm going to manoeuvre her to the door, and I want you to pull her arms with everything you've got. Morrigan should stay at the back with the cord just in case the gate won't hold the weight. Morrigan, I need you to pull with everything you've got."

Muireann saw that Etain's uniform tunic was covered in blood, and she whimpered. A section of the pathway at the edge of the chasm fell away.

"We'll kill her if we move her," she cried.

Morfessa shouted back at her, understanding her distress.

"Morrigan is strong, but she can't hold this thing forever. If the cord fails and were inside, we'll both die, and Morrigan will likely get pulled in after us. We have to move her to give her a chance of surviving this."

Muireann sobbed as she lay down on the damp road and grabbed her sister's arms. Etain's head lolled at a strange angle. She was like a rag doll.

On Morfessa's mark, Muireann pulled with all her might. Etain did not budge.

Morfessa shouted again, "On my mark!"

Muireann rearranged her grip and threw herself backwards. In a jerking motion, her torso freed. Etain's head and shoulders were on solid ground. As Muireann struggled to pull her sister away from the landrover, Morfessa did his best to push her waist and legs free. For an instant, Muireann thought that they would both fall but with a strength that she did not know she had, she got her sister's hips and legs over the ledge and onto the road. Etain's breathing was ragged and knowing that her sister was dying, Muireann dragged her as far from the vehicle as she could.

Morrigan was sweating, her muscles straining as she held the weight of the landrover, which now rocked violently. She could feel the fibres of the rope giving way. The steel claw holding the rope in place at the trailer hitch was opening. They had seconds before the landrover dropped into the chasm.

"Morfessa, I can't hold it any longer."

Morfessa grunted and threw himself forward, kicking his legs off the door frame. In the instant that he hit the ground, Morrigan's muscles gave out. The claw holding the cord in place gave way, and the landrover plunged over the edge, falling for what seemed like an eternity before bursting into flames.

Morfessa and Morrigan were both breathing heavily as they stumbled towards Muireann, who was cradling her sister in her arms, sobbing quietly.

Morfessa pulled Morrigan aside.

"Thank you. You saved us both by holding on as long as you did."

Morrigan grunted an acknowledgement to Morfessa.

"I don't know where we are, or where we're going," he said.

"Etain's injuries are severe. She probably won't make it. Is the artefact intact?"

Morrigan pulled it from her robe and examined it. She shook her head sadly. Even in the dim light, she could see a crack in the shaft.

"It's not going to work," she whispered.

She looked over at the fallen warrior.

"The least we can do is take Etain home to die."

Chapter 32

Óglaigh na hÉireann

Lieutenant Colonel Kelly rested his head in his hands.

Dún Uí Mhaoilíosa Barracks in Renmore, Housing D Company had been wiped out by the wave. Sarsfield Barracks in Limerick was gone. Finner Camp in Donegal had been wiped out. Collins Barracks in Cork had lost a fair percentage of men and equipment. Haulbowline, the Naval Defence headquarters, had been hit too and any vessels out at sea, which was most of the fleet, were deemed missing.

Casement Aerodrome had no loss of life, but the runway was beyond repair, as was every civilian runway in the country.

Soldiers on leave in the west of Ireland were classed as casualties, adding to an estimated death toll of more than 800,000 in the Republic alone, God only knew what was happening in the north.

The Curragh Camp was still there, but he could not reach them, so he had no idea what condition they were in. He could not get through to Army Headquarters in the Phoenix Park, nor Garda Headquarters, which sat next to it. There had been no contact from the office of emergency planning, housed in the Department of Defence headquarters in Newbridge, County Kildare – close, ironically, to the Curragh.

Emergency services all around the country were in chaos. The phones lines were dead, the roads were unpassable, and the hospitals that were accepting emergencies were doing so by torchlight.

Parts of Cork, the coast of Kerry, Mayo, parts of Sligo, all of Clare, most of Donegal and sections of Limerick were completely wiped out. The north of Ireland was beyond hope. The northern coastline had taken the full brunt of the tsunami and two volcanoes, Slieve Gullion and Slemish Mountain, were literally blowing themselves apart.

The remainder of the country was experiencing earthquakes unheard of in Ireland, and there were at least three active volcanos erupting.

Dún Laoghaire port has sustained significant damage. Dublin Port was in flames. The earthquake had ruptured liquid petroleum gas tanks and aviation fuel tanks and when ignited, they set off a chain reaction through the North and East Wall. Firefighters could not reach the area. The roads were jammed and the Port Tunnel had collapsed. There were widespread reports of building collapses, including the much-publicised high rises in Donnybrook and Santry, and Intel's plant in Leixlip was venting hydrogen fluoride and toxic gases over Leixlip, Lucan and the west of County Dublin. All national airports, including Shannon and Dublin airports, were on fire. Any remaining air strip in the country was buckled beyond use.

A runner came in to let him know that the Chief of the Defence Forces and the Garda Commissioner were on their way in, but it would take a while, and there was nothing yet from the Office of Emergency Planning. Lieutenant Colonel Kelly doubted that he would hear from them. The office was not manned on a 24-hour basis. The chances were that any that assigned personnel were caught up in the disaster.

Jack Kelly screamed at one of the sergeants, who dropped what he was doing and ran over to him.

"Get the Electricity Supply Board and the electricity networks teams on the phone, and ask them to get their senior people down here. We need an update on power. See if the Met Office knows what's going on. They might still have access to satellites. And while you're at it, get a report from Irish Water. We need to see if the reservoirs and water treatment plants are still functional. Is there any update from the national ambulance service? Their offices in Tallaght shouldn't be too badly affected. Oh, and ask someone to get on to the mobile phone services and see what's happening."

The sergeant left, assuring his commanding officer that he would return immediately with any news.

Jack surveyed the frantic activity going on around him, in the makeshift command centre that he had established in the barracks' conference centre. He had commandeered the biggest conference room and breakout areas when the situation had kicked off in the early hours of the morning. He had some men and was in the process of bringing more in. He had about 40 vehicles and a meagre supply of fuel for the trucks in McKee Barracks. Cathal Brugha Barracks was better serviced. They had a large fleet that included ambulances and emergency vehicles, but they did not have the manpower to take them out on the roads. Even if the First and Second Battalions could evacuate people, where could the army take them?

"Where the hell is Etain?" he muttered.

His only hope lay with the Engineering Corp and his team in Communications and Information Services.

Think, he willed himself.

He walked and paced the room and came to a stop in front of the map of Ireland on the wall – the largest map of the country, produced especially for Óglaigh na hÉireann by Ordnance Survey Ireland.

He ran to the main conference room and swept the table clean. He laid the map in the centre of the table and shouted for his aides. They needed to find an evacuation point. It needed to be away from the coast and outside of Dublin. It needed to be on high ground but accessible, with not too much seismic activity, if that was possible. It needed to be reached on what was left of the road network. There needed to be a water supply in the area. There needed to be room enough to house the evacuees – at a rough estimate, several hundred thousand men women and children.

A runner was sent, literally, to Cathal Brugha Barracks in Rathmines and within an hour, representatives of the First and Second Battalions and the seven support corps had joined him. No one stood on ceremony and rank no longer mattered. Generals and sergeants shared cups of steaming tea. The smoking ban was permanently lifted. No one cared if cigarettes were smoked indoors. The pollution outside was worse.

Jack Kelly took a baton of wood and a black whiteboard marker and drew a diagonal line across the map from Donegal to Cork.

"Everything west of that line is or was underwater, or close enough!" he shouted.

The military team looking on agreed.

He moved the baton and drew a second line through Dublin, Louth and Wicklow, along the coast.

"The volcano on Lambay is showing no signs of slowing down," he said.

"The greater Dublin region needs to be evacuated. So, for our purposes, everything east of this line is gone."

Once again, he had total agreement from the room. East of the line was Dublin Bay.

Finally, he drew a line from the north to the north-east.

"This area is affected by the two volcanoes in Antrim. I know, from talking to our counterparts in the British Army, that the infrastructure there is destroyed and the air is heavily polluted. Everything north of this line is out of bounds."

With the north, west and east effectively no-go zones, what was left of Ireland looked very small indeed.

"We need to focus on what's left. We need to find a place that's high, stable and easy to access. And it's got to be big. Okay, suggestions please?"

Jack Kelly left his colleagues to examine the map as he spied a commotion at the door.

The Garda Commissioner arrived with Peter Clancy, the Chief of the Defence Forces. The Garda Commissioner immediately requested that the inter-agency emergency plan be consulted. It was Peter Clancy who told him that while there was a plan in place, it was regional and not national and certainly did not take earthquakes, tsunamis and volcanoes into consideration. The Office of Emergency planning was not contactable. They appeared to be on their own.

The Garda Commissioner, not one to give up, immediately got on his mobile and used his personal contact list to get the Health Service Executive's Head of National Emergency Management on the line, taking advantage of the emergency phone system that had been rigged up by Jack's CIS Team – the Communication and Information Service.

Mr Kennedy, a consultant in emergency medicine and interim lead for the National Emergency Management function, was relieved to finally speak to someone in authority. He too had been trying to contact government agencies but could not get through. He had copies of Area Major Emergency plans for each region in the country with him, in both hard and soft copy, but needed to coordinate their implementation with the principal response agencies – namely, the Gardaí. He also had contact lists for every county and city council in the country, the details of contacts for transport, infrastructure, power and just about everything else.

After spending several hours on his phone and getting only a dialling tone or out-of-office message, the network had died. Not knowing what else to do, he loaded his BMW off-roader with survival gear, strapped in his family and dog and headed out of Dublin. Mr Kennedy was currently sitting in traffic on the Quays, trying to reach the N4. His plan was to head for the midlands. The Garda Commissioner told him to divert to McKee Barracks immediately. It did not matter that his wife, children and dog were in the car with him.

Commissioner Hardy made his way to Jack Kelly and told him the good news. The information that they needed would be available in minutes. Jack Kelly asked the Commissioner and the Chief of the Defence Forces who was in charge nationally. They looked at each other and made faces. Peter turned to Jack and told him that until someone in authority said otherwise, he was.

Chapter 33

Grandad's Old Handcart

Muireann had finally let go of Etain long enough for Morfessa to give her a cursory examination. After checking her pulse and her pain response, he was now more convinced of the severity of her head injury. They knew that they needed to get Etain to shelter, but they needed a moment to figure out what to do next. He made a pillow from Muireann's jacket and gently laid Etain down, covering her with his tunic.

The radio cracked to life. Muireann had forgotten that she had it in her pocket. It was Brendan, wanting to know where they were. Muireann grabbed the radio.

"Brendan, we're at the big hills in Collon. Etain is badly injured, and I don't know what to do," she sobbed.

The panic in Muireann's voice was evident. Whatever had happened, it was serious. Uiscias was in the granary with Brendan and ran to find Esras. Brendan tried to calm his sister enough for her to tell him what had happened. Esras rushed from the cottage to the granary building. He calmly took the radio from Brendan and spoke gently to Muireann, asking her to describe Etain's injury.

He muted the radio, addressing Brendan directly.

"She has glass in her shoulder and a bad laceration on her side, but I don't think any major organs are damaged by the sound of things, but the head injury sounds severe. She could have a fractured skull. We need to get to her fast. I'm going to get my pack and when I come back, we'll leave. We might be able to find them."

Brendan took the radio back and told Muireann that he would take Esras in his car and would find them. The line went dead for a moment, and the voice changed. Morrigan was very clear when she took the radio from Muireann.

"Do not take the car. It is just too dangerous to attempt to drive. Look what happened to Etain. You need to come on foot. Muireann knows the way back to the cottage. We'll start walking and meet you along the way. Bring torches and medical supplies."

Brendan reluctantly agreed. He stood and turned and found his mother standing stony faced in the doorway.

"Were you going to tell me?" she asked.

He shook his head.

Sadbh eyes were full of tears, but she did not reprimand Brendan. Instead, she asked him for help.

Sadbh walked steadily to an old, wooden outhouse on the edge of the property and threw open the doors.

"Do you remember what's in here? You just loved it when you were a kid, and your granda took you up and down the road on it."

"Grandad's old handcart! Is it still here?"

Sadbh's father had put together the handcart over twenty years ago. The homestead came with a bog, which her father cut annually. When the bog was wet, it was too risky to bring a car, and he did not have a tractor, so the handcart became his way of taking cut turf from the bog. When the kids were small, they rode in the handcart, pretending that their grandad was a horse. Sadbh and her father had nearly come to blows over the kids riding downhill in it.

Sadbh rubbed her hand along the worn arms of the cart and thought of her father. She missed him with an intensity that took her breath away.

Brendan looked at her sceptically.

"It won't be a problem to take it. It's light and if we clip on some of the torches from the house, we should be okay. We can lay Etain out on the back. It will be better than trying to carry her."

With Esras's help, they pulled the old contraption out onto the road. As Sadbh had said, once out of the shed, it was light and easy to manoeuvre. A first aid kit, some cushions and blankets were thrown into the bed. Esras took his bag, containing his medical kit. Sadbh was relieved that Esras was there. At least there would be proper medical help. After a few minutes walking at a fast pace, they got into a rhythm and focussed on meeting the others.

After a few minutes rest, it was time to move. Muireann had been hysterical, but she calmed down a little when she heard Brendan's voice.

Knowing that her big brother was on his way gave her a little confidence. She knew the way back to the cottage and was able to direct Morfessa and Morrigan. Morfessa noticed Morrigan limping and asked if she needed help. Morrigan brushed it off as a small sprain and told Morfessa and Muireann not to worry.

Morfessa carried Etain in his arms, gently resting her head against his shoulder. After a kilometre, Morrigan offered to take over, but he refused. He did not complain – just kept going with grim determination.

Morrigan walked with her arm around Muireann's waist. She was still sobbing, clearly in shock. Morrigan was limping, resting her weight on her left side. In the distance, Morrigan saw a wobbling light but could not make out what it was. She called to Muireann, and she just stared ahead. Grabbing the radio, she hit the transmit button and called to anyone who could hear her.

Sadbh, pushing the rear of the cart, could make out movement in the distance.

"It's them," she whispered.

Esras and Brendan heard her and broke into a run towards Morfessa.

Within minutes, they could see each other. Muireann and Morrigan shouted and waved. Morfessa was relieved when he saw his comrade, Esras. Sadbh and Brendan ran the remaining distance to Morfessa, who could barely carry Etain any further. With help from Brendan, Morfessa laid Etain into the cart, laying her on a duvet snatched from the double bed in haste. Esras pulled his medical equipment from his satchel and began his examination of Etain.

Sadbh could not see what he was doing clearly, but she knew that the equipment he used bore no resemblance to anything she had ever seen in an emergency room. It looked like something from *Star Trek*. Esras was systematic, starting at her legs and working up her body.

"Okay, her arm is broken quite badly," Esras explained. He checked her torso and shoulders before continuing, "She has debris in the shoulder wound and the wound in her side. Both need debriding. I'm going to look at her head and neck now. That's what I'm most concerned about."

Sadbh, Saoirse, Brendan and Muireann stood by as Esras gently probed Etain's neck and the back of her head. He ran his hands gently over her eyes and nose before checking her ocular response, using a pin light.

"She has a fracture to her eye socket and a fractured skull. She's unconscious, but I'm going to give her a sedative and some medication to keep her blood pressure stable. I think there's bleeding inside her skull. We need to get her back to shelter as quickly and gently as we can."

Esras did not need to tell Etain's family that her condition was life threatening – they already knew. Brendan brought the old cart around to face home in a wide circle. Sadbh folded blankets to hold her daughter steady. Each movement of the cart jostled Etain, her head moving from side to side.

It was Brendan who said it.

"We can't leave her like this. If she falls or bangs against the side, it will kill her."

Sadbh pushed forward, but Morrigan held her back.

"Sadbh, you're not strong enough to hold her steady. Let Morfessa do it. Please."

Morfessa climbed into the back and lifted Etain's head. He rested it gently on the makeshift pillow on his lap and put his arms around her protectively.

"I'll take care of her. Esras can walk beside and monitor her."

Muireann pushed Esras out of the way and grabbed an arm of the cart. Saoirse ran to her side and grabbed the arm too. She looked at Muireann and Brendan. Brendan nodded and grabbed the other arm, and the siblings drew the little handcart towards home.

Sadbh tried to run behind them but was restrained.

"Let them go. They are young and strong, and they are smart. Esras is a talented healer. If anyone can fix Etain, it's Esras. And Morfessa clearly won't let anything happen to her. He has the strength to hold her steady. Let's just follow them. Okay?"

As they walked on, Sadbh realised that Morrigan was trying to distract her. Right now, she was not needed. In fact, she was getting in the way. Mile after mile they walked in companionable silence. They had long since lost sight of the cart. As Sadbh began to recognise familiar landmarks, she sobbed. Morrigan took her hand in both of hers and patted it. She nodded encouragingly, and they kept walking.

Uiscias had lit the fire in the stove, and the old living room glowed with warmth. Saoirse told him to set pots and kettles of water on the range to boil as she was leaving. He lit all the lamps and candles he could find to make sure that the cottage was bright. Not knowing what else to do, he fixed the bed in the main bedroom and lit a fire in the little grate. He grabbed a medical kit from the bathroom and added bandages, surgical instruments, sutures, disinfectant and gauze and placed them in a kidney dish on the dressing table. He found a large enamel basin – he would fill it with hot water as soon as the rescue party arrived.

Uiscias checked outside to see if there was any sign of them. There was nothing yet. From the doorway, he looked around the room. In a blur of activity, he cleared the furniture to give a clear path to the bedroom, for once getting help from an unbidden Semias. He rifled through the kitchen drawers and found a pair of scissors. Esras would need that to cut away Etain's clothes. Still full of nervous energy, he copied what Saoirse had done and made soup from packets that he found in the pantry and brewed tea, in anticipation of the rescue teams' arrival. It would be another ten minutes before they arrived.

Brendan kicked the door open, while Morfessa took Etain through to the living room. He stared straight at Uiscias, who pointed at the bedroom door. He did not wait, just ran to the room. Esras was close at his heel, his hands on Etain's neck. Saoirse half carried Muireann inside. Uiscias wanted to ask Saoirse what had happened, but she shook her head, sadly.

Morrigan and Sadbh followed minutes later. Sadbh tried to go to her daughter, but Brendan guarded the door.

"Mam, the room's too small to have anyone else in there. They know what they are doing. We've got to trust them."

He guided his mother to a kitchen chair near the stove and sat her down. Sadbh broke down and sobbed.

Muireann's face was grey and her eyes vacant. Saoirse sat her down on the sofa.

Morrigan, although limping, seemed in better condition than Muireann and Sadbh.

"Give your mother something hot to drink," she said.

Saoirse brought a cup of black coffee to her mam and sat at her feet, gently rubbing her hand. Uiscias found an old tartan rug in the dresser and draped it over Muireann, who was shaking. Uiscias took a ladle to the bubbling pot of soup and poured some into a mug, which he handed to Morrigan. Morrigan took it gratefully.

"It's going to be a long night," Uiscias said.

"You have no idea how long," Morrigan whispered.

When things had calmed down, Brendan went outside to put away the little cart. He did it out of respect for the little wheeled buggy that had got his sister home safely. Without it, they would still be carrying her along the road. As the adrenaline bled away, it was replaced by a fury that Brendan had never experienced before. He needed to speak to the travellers.

Brendan slammed the door to the cottage behind him. The sight of Semias smiling to himself while being warmed by the fire was too much for him.

"My sister would be fine if it wasn't for you," he shouted.

He slammed past Uiscias and threw himself at Semias. The cup of soup he was holding smashed on the flagstone floor.

Uiscias grabbed Brendan's arm and dragged him away. Brendan went to his knees and sobbed.

Uiscias quieted Brendan while Semias was bodily dragged from the cottage by Morrigan.

Throwing Semias to the ground, Morrigan screamed at him.

"Are you happy now? She's going to die because you messed with the coordinates of the artefacts. If we had known where the Claíomh Solais was, this wouldn't have happened. Her blood is on your hands. By the way, the Claíomh Solais is damaged beyond repair. So, the mission has failed."

Semias, scared beyond belief, did not respond.

Uiscias went to his commander's side, ready to restrain her if she attacked Semias.

"How did Brendan know Semias was responsible?"

Morrigan slumped down against the granary wall and rested her head in her hands.

"I don't know how he knows. I certainly haven't told him, but they will have to know, especially if Etain doesn't pull through."

She slowly stood, leaving Semias where he had fallen.

As she walked past, she murmured, "If you believe in God, start praying that she lives. If she dies, I will be the least of your worries."

Chapter 34

Hope Floats

Morfessa paced back and forward at the end of the bed, his shoulders hunched and his arms crossed across his body, almost hugging himself.

"There has to be something you can do."

Esras shook his head. He walked over to the head of the bed and turned up the oil lamp as high as it would go.

"Morfessa, there is nothing else. If we were aboard one of the ships and had access to an operating theatre, then maybe we could relieve the pressure, but here ..."

Esras shrugged his shoulders in defeat.

Morfessa was not going to give up.

"You have scanners and theatre equipment though. You could operate if you had to," he growled.

"Morfessa, I know you are fond of her, but there really isn't anything I can do. I'll kill her if I try to operate. All I have is a scalpel. It might as well be a sledgehammer."

Morfessa stared at Etain. Her face was grey, her lips blue. Her hair lay limp across the pillow. Her temple was deformed, an angry bloated bruise adding the only colour to her skin. Under the pristine white sheet, her chest barely moved, her breathing was so shallow. She was no longer the fierce Etain. She looked like a fragile porcelain doll.

Esras put his hand on his friend's shoulder.

"It won't be long now."

Morfessa shrugged him off.

"Esras, you didn't see her out there; what she did. She got us through Hell and in the end, she swerved so Muireann and Morrigan would be saved. She sacrificed herself for us."

"Is there any medicine that would help?" Morfessa begged.

Esras grimaced and shook his head. Esras knew from experience that it was pointless to give hope in circumstances like these, only to have those hopes dashed. It was better to be cruel now than add to the hurt later.

Morfessa slid to the floor and leaned back against the bedstead.

"If you were on board the *Gorias* right now, what would you be doing?"

"If I were on board the *Gorias* and one of the infantrymen had an injury like this, I would probably programme genetically compatible nanites and inject them locally, but I don't have nanites. I don't have her DNA sequence and even if I had them, I couldn't inject them – I don't have the equipment."

Morfessa raged about the small room but soon realised that his angry outburst was not helping. He sighed, opened the door and headed out the cottage door towards the granary. He stood outside in the rain, not caring that he was cold or soaked through. He did not know how long he stood there. He did not know how he ended up in front of the stove in the granary.

"How bad is it?" Brendan whispered.

"There's no hope. She has a fractured skull, and the pressure inside her head is just too much," Morfessa burst into tears.

"Does my mam know?" Brendan asked.

Morfessa shook his head.

Brendan wiped tears from his own eyes.

"I better tell her then," Brendan said, knowing he was about to break his mother's heart.

Morfessa knew what was coming and could not face being there when Sadbh was told. He did not have to wait long. He heard the high-pitched keen from the granary. It sounded like a banshee.

Sadbh had never smoked in the house. She lit a cigarette in the granary and although Brendan hated the smell, he said nothing. Sadbh's eyes were red and raw. She had cried herself out. Her expression had hardened. The grief had been replaced by rage.

"You said you had nanobots."

Morrigan ran her hands through her hair.

"No, we didn't say we had nanobots. We have nanites inside of us. We are given them at birth to help us cope with the environment. They are engineered to match our genetic makeup. We don't carry around bottles of nanites just in case we need them. They can only be administered under controlled conditions, in a specialised hospital laboratory."

"If they are in your blood, take them out. Do a lumbar puncture or extract them in plasma or do a blood transfusion. I don't care. I want you to do it and give the nanites to Etain."

The voice that emanated from Sadbh was not hers. It was much deeper, and the words were slow and enunciated.

"The nanites will kill her," Semias whispered.

"No, Semias, the nanites won't kill her. The fractured skull will kill her, and she has that because of you lot. Esras has told me that she might as well be dead, so what's the problem. There's no point in getting high and mighty now."

Morfessa has listened closely to what Sadbh had said. If there was even a slight chance that the nanites would work, then he had to take the risk.

He strode purposely back to the bedroom where Esras was on death watch.

"Tell me how to get the nanites out of my system and into hers," Morfessa demanded, pointing at Etain.

"There's no point. Your DNA ..."

Esras did not get to finish the sentence. Morfessa grabbed him by the neck of his tunic and lifted him off the ground. Esras had never seen Morfessa react like this before.

"Do whatever tests you need to do. If there's a chance that one of us is a match, then we're taking it. She could be a descendant or she could be a forbearer, take your pick."

He threw Esras away from him.

Esras was not angry. The compassion that Morfessa had for Etain made Esras respect him all the more. He nodded his head.

"I'll scan her, and then you and I will scan each other. If were not a match, we'll call Uiscias and ask him. Okay? Semias, we'll leave out of it for now. Morrigan will help. I know that she would gladly give her blood to save her."

Morfessa nodded and watched while Esras ran his medical scanner over Etain's wrist. Esras inhaled deeply and repeated the scan on himself. There was no match.

"Are you ready? It will feel like your skin is being pricked by needles, but please don't move."

Morfessa felt the scan and waited while the machine did its analysis. Esras stared at the screen.

"Did you know?"

"Did I know what? Morfessa whispered.

"Did you know that you're related?"

Morfessa interpreted the question as a threat.

"She's not exactly my sister, is she?" he shouted.

Esras put his hand on Morfessa's shoulder.

"You share a paternal lineage."

"Does it mean that it will work?"

"No, it doesn't, but the chance it might has improved," Esras whispered.

They decided not to tell anyone what they were doing. Morrigan would object, and the McNamara's would build their hopes up. If they said nothing and Etain died, they would never need to know.

Esras ran through the options for transfer but without a lab, there was nothing that he could really do except a blood transfusion. He had never done a live donor transfusion, and it scared him. Before doing anything else, he took a tiny sample of blood from Etain to check her blood type.

"Etain is B group rhesus positive. Morfessa, I need to check your blood type."

Morfessa thought he was blood group O.

"Morfessa, I need to analyse a blood sample. If you really are blood group O, then you are a universal donor but if your blood group is not compatible with Etain, then we're not going ahead."

Esras used the scalpel that Uiscias had laid out in the kidney tray and cleaned his finger with an alcohol wipe before he pricked the tip of Morfessa's finger. The analysis verified that Morfessa was group O rhesus positive.

Esras fitted a catheter into Etain's hand. She did not react to the line being fitted. He then cleaned Morfessa's arm with alcohol. He slowly and firmly pushed the needle into Morfessa's forearm. Esras connected the needle to a line filled with saline. Morfessa watched with fascination as the blood flushed through the clear liquid and reached Etain. Now, all they could do was wait.

40 minutes later, Esras removed the transfusion line. Morfessa flexed his arm. The injection site was already mottled and bruised. There was no change in Etain's condition.

Morfessa was thirsty and hungry and tired but could not eat or sleep. He was having second thoughts about the transfusion, and he knew that he would have to take responsibility. He had never felt so guilty. He went to the stove in the kitchen. Saoirse handed him a cup of soup, but he brushed it away.

"We can't afford to waste food right now, Morfessa. Drink it please."

He took a sip and his taste buds went crazy. He drank the soup quickly and went to the pot to refill his cup.

Morfessa and Saoirse had just sat down at the kitchen table when they heard a commotion from the bedroom. They could hear the sounds made by glass breaking and the thuds of furniture. Everyone in the room heard Esras screaming for help. Morfessa and Brendan sprinted to the bedroom door.

"Hold her down! She's fitting," Esras roared.

Morfessa tried to position himself behind Etain and pushed down on her shoulders. Brendan ran into the room behind him and held his sister down at her hips. Etain's blue eyes were wide open. Her whole body jerked in response to a force that her brother could not understand. Suddenly, she flopped back onto the bed and vomited violently over Morfessa. A guttural noise passed her lips, and she lapsed back into unconsciousness.

They were all stunned. The bed where she lay was covered with blood, faeces and urine.

"What's happening to her?" Brendan asked.

Esras could not answer. He did not know.

Chapter 35

The Claíomh Solais

When Morfessa returned wearing Brendan's jeans and an old sweatshirt, Sadbh and Saoirse were in the bedroom. The linen was changed, and Etain had been washed from head to toe. Saoirse gently brushed her sister's long auburn hair and wept. Sadbh swallowed hard, on the verge of tears herself, and announced that she was going to find some of Etain's body lotion.

Etain had not moved since she had the seizure. As Saoirse moved her hand, the brush tangled. She tugged, but the knot would not move.

"Stop pulling my hair!"

Saoirse was afraid to move, afraid to breathe.

"Did you hear that?" she asked Morfessa.

Morfessa's face broke out into a glowing smile. He nodded.

Saoirse whispered in Etain's ear.

"How are you doing?"

"My head hurts ..." then, after a few seconds, "I want a diet coke ..."

Saoirse ran to kitchen and grabbed a can of coke and a straw.

"Can she sit up a bit? I don't want her to choke."

Esras scanned Etain's temple.

"She's okay, Saoirse. She has a concussion. We need to watch her for a while, but we should be able to prop her up just a little bit."

Etain took a long drink, burped and closed her eyes, this time to sleep.

With Etain resting, Morfessa and Esras came clean to the others about the live donor transfusion. They had been incredibly lucky not to have killed her. The nanites from Morfessa's blood had taken some time to adjust to Etain's body, causing her system to purge itself, but they had done their job, reducing the swelling on her brain and knitting the bones of her skull back together at their weakest point. Her broken arm had knitted itself back together perfectly. The lacerations to her side had healed, now barely a scratch. As to side effects, they had no idea how Etain would be affected and if the effects would be temporary or permanent. All they could say for sure was that the nanites would not be passed through normal bodily functions. They were designed to stay put. What was there was there to stay.

The family drew up a rota to keep watch on Etain, while Esras, Morfessa, Uiscias and Semias bedded down for some rest. Esras was reluctant to leave Etain, in case she had another seizure, but Sadbh promised him that he would be woken if he were needed. Morrigan hovered in the background, refusing offers of food or rest.

Sadbh sat alone with her daughter, the lights in the room dimmed. She barely saw Morfessa enter. He gently kissed Etain on the forehead and whispered something to her that Sadbh could not hear. Morfessa was incredibly gentle with Etain, brushing a loose strand of auburn hair from her cheek.

"You care about her, don't you?" Sadbh whispered.

Morfessa jumped when he heard her, turned to her and smiled. He nodded in response and made his way quietly from the room, leaving mother and daughter alone.

Morfessa laid out his sleeping bag near the stove, next to Uiscias. As he was removing his sandals, Morrigan caught his eye. The kitchen was lit with an oil lamp and candles and for the first time, he could see Morrigan's legs clearly. Her trousers were bloodstained. Morfessa called Esras, who persuaded Morrigan to let him look at her injury.

Morrigan had a deep gash running from the top of her ankle to her knee. The damage to her lower leg was severe. Esras admonished her for not speaking up earlier. Morrigan shook it off, saying that Esras had better things to do, and his priority was Etain. Uiscias and Morfessa were not surprised by Morrigan's selflessness. She had always been that sort of leader, putting her team's needs before her own. Esras spent an hour cleaning, stitching and dressing the deep wound before helping Morrigan to lay down.

Despite all that has happened that day, the travellers were asleep in minutes.

Morfessa was the first to wake. When he woke, he could not remember where he was, but the memory of the night before soon surfaced. He dressed quickly and peeped into Etain's room, mother and daughter were both asleep. He cleaned out the range in the kitchen, lit it with some sticks and old newspaper and fed it with turf until the fire burned ferociously. The kettle was filled and set to heat. Uiscias was asleep in the corner, so Morfessa crept out the front door into twilight. *It must be before dawn*, he thought. He heard a sharp crack from the granary and went to investigate.

Brendan was stringing a cable across the ceiling. He nodded at Morfessa when he entered and told him that he was trying to rig an antenna up for shortwave radio. He climbed down from the ladder that he was perched on.

"I didn't want to wake anyone. It was a rough night," he said. "I figured if you didn't wake in another hour, I would make some lunch and get everyone up."

Morfessa was confused.

"Lunch? It's not even time for breakfast."

Brendan smiled.

"It's half past twelve."

Morfessa looked outside at the twilight.

"This is the brightest it's been today," Brendan said.

Morfessa shook his head and sighed. He went back into the cottage and woke the other travellers. The noise that they made in the kitchen roused Sadbh and Saoirse. Saoirse in turn woke Muireann, who was sleeping in the cottage's second bedroom.

While the women were dressing, the travellers went outside and walked to the boundary of the homestead. The darkened skies were evidence of the beginning of the volcanic winter. In five days, the amount of pollutant pumped into the atmosphere would be irreversible. In weeks, plants and animals would begin to die. It was clear that they were running out of time, and they had no idea as to the condition of the Claíomh Solais. Uiscias was carrying it in an old satchel. He took it out and examined it in the dim light, looking at the tell-tale signs of cracking.

Brendan watched them curiously. They acknowledged him when he approached, explaining what had happened and how their effort to identify the extent of the damage was futile.

"I have a Mantis," he said.

Uiscias scrambled to translate what he said.

"That's an insect?" he asked.

"No, it a 3D stereo microscope," Brendan replied.

Brendan's work involved designing communications products and when they were built by specialist assembly houses, the PCB assemblies (or boards, as he called them) needed to be examined under a microscope. When the company he worked for upgraded his equipment, he took the old Mantis home. It still worked, and he used it for personal projects. It meant that he could solder using both hands.

For the travellers, this was a godsend. It would give them an opportunity to examine the Claíomh Solais under a bright inspection lamp, at 40 times magnification. They could twist and turn the Claíomh Solais to any angle to inspect it thoroughly.

Uiscias joined Brendan in the granary. Brendan brought the diesel generator just outside the granary door and pull-started it. It started with a dense plume of black smoke and then settled into a gentle chugging. The old Mantis was manhandled onto a work bench and powered up. Brendan turned on the Mantis's powerful light and quickly showed Uiscias how to use it, letting him get familiar with device by inspecting an old PCB. When Uiscias was confident enough, the PCB was replaced by the artefact. For twenty minutes, Uiscias examined the Claíomh Solais and when he was through, he gently placed it on the workbench, turned off the microscope and stretched like a cat.

"The bad news is, there is definitely a crack, but it's not as bad as it could be. By rights, it should have shattered on impact. It's one fine fault running about a third of the length through. It's what's causing the problem."

Morfessa, Uiscias and Semias nodded their understanding. Morrigan insisted on using the Mantis herself to examine the Claíomh Solais, to be sure that she understood what Uiscias was talking about.

"If we were on the ship, I could repair it but here, I really don't know. I need a really powerful laser to make the repair. I don't know if that technology exists here, or where we might find it."

Saoirse pushed the door of the granary and said hello, interrupting Uiscias. He gave her a brief overview of what he had found. She asked if she could help.

Chapter 36

Lasers and Physics

When Saoirse offered her help, the travellers were sceptical. Only Brendan seemed to take her seriously.

"I'm working on molecular magnets for applications in nanotechnology," Saoirse said.

Brendan laughed at everyone's blank expressions.

"She gets this effect every time she opens her mouth," he laughed.

Saoirse pushed him away good naturedly and made a huffing sound.

"The point is that single molecular magnets can operate more than one hundred times faster than traditional materials used for data storage, with significantly reduced energy consumption and lower storage space requirements. This will have a massive impact on cloud computing."

Uiscias nodded in agreement, clearly understanding what she was talking about. Morfessa, Esras, Morrigan and Semias did not have a clue.

"Historically, research done in this field led to the McNamara theorem, it is widely studied by our engineers," Uiscias interjected.

Saoirse made a face.

"There is no McNamara Theorem," she said.

Brendan poked at her.

"Maybe you haven't come up with it yet," he whispered.

Saoirse blushed.

Semias busied himself adding logs to the small stove in the granary, where a kettle of water sat heating. He pretended not to listen to Saoirse.

"Anyway, to make the magnets, you need lasers. There's a research laboratory in Trinity that has a laser lab suitable for the creation of molecular magnets. It's in the CRANN building near the Dental Hospital, just off Pearse Street. The lasers may not be what you need, but it's the only place in the country that will come close."

The discussion raged for over an hour, but it was clear that they would need to travel to Dublin City Centre, to determine if they could get access to the lasers in the CRANN building. Then, they could see if the lasers were, indeed, suitable for carrying out the repair and finally, to investigate getting the complex equipment operational. They had no idea if the roads would be passable and what condition the city would be in.

It was nearing dinner time, and the chicken stew cooking on the kitchen range was ready. Not wanting the food to spoil, Sadbh wandered over to the granary to call everyone for a late lunch. She watched Uiscias and Saoirse deep in animated conversation. Although Semias and Brendan were there, they were ignored by the teenagers. Despite the disparate appearances, they looked incredibly at ease in each other's company, and they understood each other. Even Brendan, who was cynical about love and romance, seemed to be looking on fondly. Sadbh caught her son's eye, and Brendan smiled at her. Leaving Uiscias with Saoirse, he made his way to the door.

"Young love, eh? They are completely oblivious to everything except lasers and physics equations."

Sadbh smiled.

"There seems to be a lot of it about these days."

Brendan was not quite sure what his mother was talking about and shook his head.

"Mam, you're not going to like what I'm going to tell you but here goes ..."

The stew was left to boil as Brendan laid out the plan to repair the Claíomh Solais, using the CRANN lasers in Trinity. As an engineer, Sadbh understood that it was a reasonably sound proposition. Her problem was not the lasers; it was getting there.

"You're not taking the car," Sadbh insisted.

After Etain's near fatal injury, she could not reconcile the thoughts of Brendan taking his old car out on what was left of the country's roads.

"Mam, we can't walk to Dublin. If I don't drive, then how can we get there?"

Sadbh answered with a question.

"Who's we?"

Brendan had dreaded this moment.

"Morfessa, Uiscias obviously, me ... and Saoirse."

Morrigan made her way to Brendan's side, ready to defend him. Brendan was a grown man but in Sadbh's eyes, Saoirse was still a kid. Sadbh rounded on Morrigan as leader of the travellers.

"You nearly killed Muireann. Etain nearly died only twelve hours ago, and now you want to take Saoirse and Brendan! Forget it."

Morrigan was going to try to talk to Sadbh but realised that it would be a vain attempt to placate her. She recognised that she had stepped into a family argument.

The normally mild-mannered Brendan got into his mother's face.

"Mam, I know you're upset, but this isn't Morrigan's fault. She knows nothing about this. Saoirse came up with this plan and if it were anyone other than Saoirse who came up with it, you would think it was genius. We're not children – we are all experts in our fields. For God's sake, let us do what were good at without interfering."

Neither Brendan nor Sadbh was about to back down.

Saoirse gave her mother a hug and whispered in her ear.

"They don't know where the equipment is, Mam. I know the building. I know you're worried, but we'll go slowly, and we'll be careful."

The house was empty when Etain woke. She remembered the accident but had no recollection of how she ended up in the cottage. She felt achy and groggy but otherwise fine. She was a little dizzy when she stepped out of bed, but it passed quickly. She searched the room for her uniform but could not find it. She found an old dressing gown in the wardrobe and quickly put it on. When she moved her arm, it was sore, but she could not see anything wrong when she looked – it was probably a muscle strain.

She used the bathroom, cleaned her teeth and brushed out her hair, tying it back with scrunchie. She looked at her face in the mirror. She stepped back and stood on a splinter of glass. She screeched loudly, cursed and then put her foot up on the bath to pull it out of her heel. She caught sight of herself in the mirror, and her eyes looked funny. After applying a plaster and disposing of the glass in the little waste basket under the sink, she examined her eyes in the mirror. She could see flecks of gold around the edges, but they seemed to fade after a few seconds. It was probably a trick of the light.

Etain found a T-shirt and a pair of jeans in the other bedroom. She did not know if they were Saoirse's or Muireann's, but she knew that they would not mind.

Etain had limped into the kitchen. The chicken stew smelt delicious, and so too did the bread rolls on the table. The kitchen though, was deserted. She heard voices coming from the granary and went outside to investigate. She caught the tail end of the row.

"There will be checkpoints along the route. I should go with them to get them through. I may be about to be court-martialled, but the patrols won't know that," she said.

It was clear the Etain was still weak, her normally bright eyes were dulled, encased in dark circles. Her voice sounded tired, but Etain was up, dressed and mobile and was clearly in control of her faculties. Not eight hours before, she had been in a coma with severe head injuries. Everyone stared at her.

"What?" she said indignantly.

Sadbh held her arm and guided her back into the cottage, making her sit down. Sadbh gently explained what had happened and how near she had come to being killed. Sadbh also explained what Esras and Morfessa had done to save her. Etain did not believe her at first but after Esras and Morfessa confirmed the story, she sat dumbfounded.

Etain had enough of everyone fussing around her.

"Okay. I get I'm not one hundred per cent, but my brain still works. I'm just saying that you're not thinking your plan through. I know you need to get to the laser thing in Dublin but getting there is not going to be straightforward, and you might need my help. After all, I'm superhuman now, aren't I?" Etain said.

Sadbh had had enough.

"Hold on a second. The four of you," Sadbh said – pointing at Morfessa, Uiscias, Saoirse and Brendan – "want to take off to Dublin on roads that have been hit by a magnitude 7.4 earthquake, with an epicentre somewhere off the coast of Wexford. There's been a tsunami that wiped out most of the west of the country. There's a volcano erupting off Howth and an ash cloud to boot, and you think I'm going to make you sandwiches and pat you on the heads before you go. Think again."

Morfessa looked at Uiscias and shrugged his shoulders. He could understand why she was angry.

Morfessa knew that he could not beat emotion with diplomacy.

"Sadbh, everything we told you about has come true, hasn't it?"

Sadbh nodded.

"Then you have to believe me when I tell you what comes next is worse. We have a sliver of a chance to stop it, but we're running out of time. We have two days left, three at the most to deploy the Claíomh Solais. It's Sunday. We only have until Thursday at the latest. We need Brendan to get the equipment working. We need Saoirse to help us find the place and to help Uiscias effect the repair. One way or another, they are coming."

Sadbh felt tears of anger roll down her checks.

"I let my kids go without me once and nearly lost them. If they go," she said – pointing at Brendan and Saoirse – "then we all go, and we go at first light in the morning. And from this point on, Etain rests. Is that clear?"

Morfessa nodded in agreement.

"And one other thing," Sadbh said, "I know you're not telling us everything. So, before we make a move, I want the truth – all of it – from you Morrigan."

Morrigan paced up and down outside the granary. Semias was slumped in the corner in silence.

"Ideas anyone?" she asked.

Esras kicked a rock away from the old doorway.

"Sadbh knows there is something were not telling her. She will be enraged when she finds out, but its best to tell her and get it out of the way."

Esras stared at Semias.

"Although, I wouldn't like to be him when she finds out her daughter nearly died because of his stupidity."

Morfessa agreed. Uiscias did too, although he was more worried about Brendan's reaction than Sadbh's.

"Like it or not, we are stuck with him. He might be of some use at some point," Morrigan said, "though right now, I'd like nothing better than to cut him loose. If the family want him gone, then I'm okay with that. Do you understand what I mean?"

Semias sat up.

"Can I at least explain why I did what I did? You know it wasn't meant to turn out this way. It was just to help a friend win some favour. There was no malice in it. I swear."

Morfessa dragged Semias to a standing position.

"Semias, you are an arrogant son of a bitch. You have no conscience. You value your own intelligence too highly. You thought we were stupid grunts. You were going to hail yourself a hero when we couldn't find the artefacts and claim all the glory for yourself. Semias, saviour of the world! Well, newsflash! Your heroics nearly killed someone that I care about. You've put the lives of millions more at risk and lost the most valuable piece of technology known since humankind picked up a stick. Explain that away. I dare you."

"There's no need to explain anything more," Sadbh said.

Sadbh, Brendan and Etain were standing at the cottage door. They had overheard everything.

"Keep him away from me. I won't be responsible for what happens if you don't," Brendan roared.

It was four o'clock, and there was a lot to do. Since the decision for everyone to travel was made, there was discussion about using the cars after all.

It was Muireann that suggested taking a walk into Nobber. On the outskirts of the town, there was a quad bike dealership. Muireann had been out on all-terrain quads and was confident that they would be safer than the cars. Saoirse, Brendan and Muireann all had driving licences and would teach rudimentary skills to Esras, Morfessa and Uiscias.

Etain insisted on going, but Brendan held her off. If they needed to, they would tow a quad for her. Brendan knew his mother had reached her limit, and Etain stepping foot outside the cottage would push her over the edge.

Etain, Semias, Morrigan and Sadbh watched them set off on the two-hour walk. Morrigan was true to her word – she watched Semias closely and kept him well away from Etain and Sadbh. Etain served dinner for the four of them and took the stew off the heat. The others would be hungry when they got back. Semias ate in the granary.

Etain was persuaded to go back to bed. While she succumbed to the enforced rest, Morrigan joined her and sat at the edge of the bed.

"He's a good man, Etain."

Etain turned and stared at her.

"I don't know what you're talking about."

Morrigan laughed.

"Yes you do. Morfessa carried you for miles you know, and held your head steady while we wheeled you back her in that rickety old cart. He's a typical soldier. He doesn't say much. His actions speak for him. When things calm down, give him a chance."

Etain sat up on her elbow and stared at Morrigan.

"You didn't give him a chance, why should I?"

"Ah, you picked up on that ... It was a very long time ago, and the circumstances were not good. I was his commanding officer, and the relationship caused ... complications. Let's just say, it didn't end well but looking back, it was my fault and not his. Anyway, he's loyal, he's kind, and he's good in bed. That's about the best recommendation I can give."

With that, Morrigan stood up and left the room, closing the door behind her.

"That is not a conversation I ever want to have again," she muttered to herself.

While the others were out, Morrigan and Sadbh found backpacks and saddle bags and filled each with an emergency kit – two bottles of water, torches, basic first aid kits, charged power banks, air-filter masks (the medical kind), the walkie-talkies and extra batteries for them, protein bars and high energy snacks. Into her own backpack, Sadbh added a couple of bars of chocolate, paracetamol, heavy woollen socks and gloves and a thin fleece blanket. On impulse, she added a small soldering kit, a snips and pliers. Into Morrigan's, she added a small tool kit and mini drill from Ikea, on her insistence.

She pulled out old maps, neon light sticks and rain jackets to have to hand. She would not tell anyone what to pack. They could decide for themselves.

This was the first opportunity that Morrigan had had to talk to Sadbh.

"When do you stop being a mother?" she asked.

Sadbh stopped and smiled at Morrigan.

"What do you mean?"

"I mean, you're tough and obviously very capable, but you spend all your time and energy running after people who clearly don't want you to. So, I'm being blunt and asking, when do you stop?"

For the first time in her life, Sadbh stopped what she was doing and thought about the question.

"For the last twenty years, I needed to take control, because our lives were out of control. I needed to do things alone that most couples do together. I guess I'm so used to taking control, I've forgotten how to let go. If I treated my staff the way I treat my kids, they probably would have walked a long time ago. I suppose I'm scared that I'm not needed anymore."

Morrigan smiled at Sadbh, who was on the verge of tears.

"I very much doubt that you're not needed. You raised a strong family. Let them take the strain for a while. Trust them. They might surprise you."

It was dark outside when they heard the triumphant tooting of horns. Brendan was first, with headlights blazing. His Polaris Ranger had a small cargo bed. The back was loosely filled with fuel cans. Muireann was next, driving a John Deere Gator XUV, its diesel engine growling. Saoirse had mastered a Corvus Terrain DX4. Morfessa looked proud as punch as he pushed the Kawasaki's petrol engine. Uiscias and Esras led up the rear in a pair of Polaris Ranger RZR 900s. They laughed and smiled as they dismounted, removing the helmets that the dealer had insisted they took with them.

Brendan jogged over to his mother, helmet in hand.

"What do you think, Mam?" he said "They're all brand new. We found the dealer no problem and when we said we needed utility vehicles to get to Dublin, he gave us the keys to the showroom. He said we could take whatever we wanted. He even showed us where the helmets and fuel tanks were. We couldn't believe it."

He brought his mother and Morrigan over to show them the vehicles.

"They had loads of electric vehicles, but we thought it better to go with diesel and petrol. The dealership has its own filling station, so we filled them to the brim, and we got extra fuel. We picked up extra helmets, just in case."

It was clear they had made good choices. Not only were they all four-wheel drives, the roll cages and seat belts were sturdy, and each vehicle was a two-seater.

As Sadbh served dinner, the chatter was optimistic, it had taken only thirty-five minutes to get back from Nobber. The UTVs handled the cracked and twisted roads with ease, and they had been able to avoid most of the destruction along the way. As they ate, they decided who would drive and who would be passengers.

Morrigan insisted that everyone had an early night, and an alarm was set for 6 am.

Chapter 37

Evacuation

Jack Kelly felt like he was losing his mind. He had the combined brains of the Irish Army, the Gardaí, Civil Defence and the Health Service Executive at his disposal and so far, every suggestion that had been made for an evacuation point had been shot down. Either the sites had been hit by the tsunami, were in the path of a volcano or were just plain inaccessible.

It had taken all his strength not to physically assault one captain, who suggested the Phoenix Park as a base camp for refugees. The famous deer park on the banks of the Liffey in Dublin City was covered in a heavy coat of volcanic ash – a refuge it was not.

He had thought that he had hit the jackpot when the Curragh had been suggested. The flat open plains of the Curragh covered a massive area – over 5,000 acres. It was easily accessible from all points in the country. More importantly, it was the home of an army camp and military college, meaning that there were resources already in place to cope with the influx of bewildered and frightened men women and children, who would be coming from all points in the country.

It had taken nearly an hour to get through to the Curragh, and his hopes were dashed when the General Officer Commanding told him out straight that it was a no go. The base and college were evacuating due to liquefaction. The ground beneath had lost its strength and was acting like a liquid, swallowing anyone or anything that came in contact with it into a morass. That included roads, buildings and a few unfortunates who had been too brave or too stupid to run in the opposite direction.

Jack had cursed loudly when he hung up the phone. He grabbed the nearest thing to hand (a cup of cold tea) and threw it at the wall. He did not need to tell his team that the Curragh was a no go. They had figured it out for themselves.

He fervently wished Etain was there. She knew how to get things organised. She would already have a site by now and would have convoys underway. He wondered if she was still alive. The last time that he had spoken to her, she was near the coast in Donegal.

Chapter 38

Cracks and Buckles

They were on the road by 7 am, Etain seated beside Morfessa and wrapped up against the cold despite her protests. Sadbh was seated in the four-by-four driven by Saoirse. The travellers drew straws to carry Semias, who ended up as Esras's passenger. Muireann and Morrigan travelled together, Morrigan observing Muireann's driving, so that she could take a spell at the wheel.

They set off in convoy and began hitting obstacles within twenty minutes. There were no other vehicles on the road, but cattle and other livestock were loose and the effects of the earthquakes on the country roads meant that they had to divert around sink holes and deep fissures in the road. On more than one occasion, they were forced to travel across pastures and fields of autumn crops to avoid obstacles.

Conditions got worse as they approached Slane. As they left the countryside and approached suburbia, they could see and feel the effects of the disaster on the town. Whole sections of Main Street were still blazing, smoking cars and trucks lay abandoned. While sections of the town seemed to be without power, down lines cracked and hissed and poured blue sparks across the concrete pavements. The town was eerily quiet as the convoy tried to make its way through.

The great bridge beside the castle had taken a beating, and the drivers made the choice to take it at slow speed and in single file. The rushing waters of the Boyne far below them made them cautious. Closer to sea level, the air was more viscous, thick with abrasive dust and smut. Breathing, even wearing medical-grade masks, was difficult, and the grit scoured their eyes.

After crossing the Boyne, Esras made everyone stop and rinse their eyes with water. He also ordered everyone to change their masks, as he could see the levels of pollutants built up on the pristine white of the masks' outer surface.

They were doggedly determined and kept going, even when rain began to pour. While the rain temporarily cleared the dust from the air, it burned their skin. They were in open country and had no choice but to keep going. There were cracks and buckles along the way but when they reached dual carriageways at Ashbourne, they had a straight run for several miles.

As they got closer to the city, the roads became impassable again. Not only was the motorway congested with abandoned cars, but the road surfaces were also cracked and buckled. They detoured around numerous fires caused by broken gas mains. The air quality had also deteriorated notably on the journey into to the city. Whether this was as a result of the volcano by the coast or the effect of the Icelandic volcanoes, they were not sure, but it was bad enough for everyone to replace their masks again, and they pulled at scarves and collars to protect their eyes from the swirling grit.

It was just after 11 am when they arrived in Finglas, and the normally thriving suburb was deserted. Once again, abandoned vehicles littered the streets, buildings stood ablaze, and debris and rubble blocked the suburban arteries. There was a smell of decay, whether as a result of open sewers or something else, no one was sure.

Breathing was laboured, and Morrigan made a call to look for shelter, so that they could clean themselves up. Charlestown Shopping Centre's underground car park was open. Sadbh suggested that since the building seemed to be unaffected, it might be a good place to shelter. Brendan nodded in agreement and went to inspect the entrance. He entered the underground car park and a few moments later, re-emerged at the top of the ramp and called them.

The underground space was empty except for a few abandoned vehicles, but it was dry, and the air was clearer. They stood and stretched and grabbed water from their backpacks. Leading the way, Muireann escorted the travellers to the bathrooms upstairs in the main centre, using a concealed stairwell. The escalators had stopped working long ago. They were amazed to find the main supermarket and department store open, emergency lights blazing. They used the opportunity to discard their grubby clothing, which was full of dust. Despite searching, the only eye protection that they could find was sunglasses. Muireann went scavenging and returned with bottles of eye wash, which they dutifully used to rinse their eyes.

"Well, nothing's changed in Finglas," Saoirse said. "The drinks aisle has been cleared of alcohol, and the cigarette cabinet has been forced open. Looks like someone's having a party."

"We should have thought of goggles," Brendan said. "I can hardly keep my eyes open; it feels like I have half the Sahara in them."

"There's a hardware store not far away beside the old Dunnes Stores supermarket in Finglas West," Etain said. "There's a chance the Defence Forces opened it to get access to tools and equipment. We should try there. They have a big paint section, and I saw DIY goggles on a display the last time I bought varnish. Anyway, the roads towards town from Finglas West are wide and straight – the access would be better than going through housing estates."

Before leaving, they grabbed gloves, extra water and supplies and packed newly acquired backpacks. Etain wanted to leave money to pay for it, but there was nowhere to leave it. Brendan lingered in the homeware section, picking up extra screwdrivers, fuses and cabling from the display. Sadbh was relieved that the route through Finglas West was decided. She dreaded going past the family home – she was afraid of what she might find.

They drove the convoy over the dual carriageway and headed for the police station in Finglas. The station itself had no signs of life. In fact, there were no signs of life at all, and even the wandering horses associated with the area were missing. As they approached the old shopping centre, they spotted the first signs of activity.

Etain was right. An army truck sat idling outside the hardware store in the otherwise deserted car park. They parked in the far corner and dismounted. Etain felt it best that she approached the army truck alone. She had insisted on wearing her army jacket, even though she wore jeans on the bottom. Semias dismounted from his four-by-four and tried to issue orders. Etain roared at him, and he backed down.

"Jeasus, would you look at what the cat dragged in," the army driver shouted. It was one of Etain's crew – a corporal whose name was on the tip of her tongue. His face was disguised by a heavy mask.

"The boss has been going mad looking for you. We thought you were dead."

Etain smiled.

"I thought I was too, for a while."

"Weren't you supposed to be in Donegal when the tsunami hit on Sunday morning?"

Etain nodded and explained that it had taken quite a while for her to make her way back. In fact, she was not even sure what day it was.

She nodded towards the open shop front.

"Can I go inside. I need to get a few things."

"Help yourself. You won't be arrested, because there are no gardaí at the station up the road. They are all in town or out at the coast."

Etain really did not want her colleagues to see the travellers – there would be too many questions. She called Brendan and Saoirse, and they went inside.

It did not take long – they emerged with a bag of safety goggles, batteries, hand tools and a couple of torches. They had also found machine oil, a paraffin lamp with oil and some reels of rope and twine.

"Jeasus! Some looters you are. If you were in LA or New York, you'd be taking tellies and jewellery. In Finglas, all you get is DIY shite," the corporal shouted.

The rest of the soldiers laughed heartily. Etain smiled, kept her eyes on the four-by-fours and gave them the finger. That encouraged more laughter.

As Etain reached her vehicle. She heard a scuffling behind her. The corporal was shuffling over with a large black bag.

"Boss, I don't know what you're up to and all, but I think you might need these."

He thrust the bag at her.

"They're proper respirator masks, like the emergency services wear. They're not comfortable, but they sure as hell beat the shit out of what you're wearing. And they seal around your face, so your eyes will be protected. There should be enough of them for all of you here."

Etain smiled and thanked him. As promised, there were enough full-face respirators for everyone. Before donning their masks, each took a drink of water, it might be their last chance to hydrate for a while.

Brendan led the way, and they headed down the Ballyboggin Road and out onto the Finglas Road, passing Glasnevin Cemetery and crossing the canal at Phibsborough. The closer they got to the city, the more destruction they came across. Whole swathes of the city were collapsed, and what was left standing was clearly unstable. Roads were completely blocked, leading to detours down side lanes and in some cases, through private gardens. Even wearing the face masks, they could detect the sickly-sweet smell of decay. Moving in twilight exacerbated their problems – the dust and grit swirled through the atmosphere and on more than one occasion, they stopped to clear the engine filters.

Although it was slow going, they reached the Liffey by afternoon. The problem was that there was no way to get across. The bridges, from Heuston Station in the west to O'Connell Street in the heart of the city, were either collapsed or barricaded. Emergency services advised Brendan that they were simply too unstable to cross. They had no choice but to continue down to the docklands, in the hope of finding a way to the south side of the city.

It took another 30 minutes to reach the docklands and the harp-shaped Samuel Beckett Bridge. The cable-stayed bridge, a relatively recent landmark in Dublin, joined North Wall Quay on the north side of the city to Sir John Rogerson's Quay on the south. At the mouth of the River Liffey, the bridge opened daily to allow traffic up and down the river. The bridge was open during the worst of the tremors and quakes, meaning that it had been protected from the worst of the seismic activity. Like the rest of the city, there was no power to the bridge.

With no route between the north and south of the city, emergency services could not reach casualties or move urgently needed equipment. The army engineering corps had taken control since early morning and had cranked the bridge into place manually – allowing restricted access across the river for smaller vehicles. Despite the movement caused by the seismic activity, the bridge closed in position, more or less.

Leaving the quad bikes parked on the quays, the group set out across the bridge, only to be stopped by military guards. The city centre was restricted. Etain pulled rank and admonished the junior officer in charge. The barricade was lifted, and they went through but not before Etain issued instructions for the guards, to make sure that the next shift knew that they would be returning in a few hours. Donning their backpacks, the group set off to make their way to Trinity College on the south banks of the river, Saoirse and Uiscias leading the way. Despite the haste, they did not get far ahead – they roads were virtually unpassable.

The city was deserted. On Pearse Street, they tried to take a short cut through to the CRANN building, but the roads were strewn with masonry, and the buildings surrounding the area in Westland Row were unstable. They had no choice but to aim for the main college entrance at College Green and take an alternative route.

Despite the age of the buildings making up the Trinity campus, they seemed to have fared better than the newer offices and shops that surrounded them. In the midst of the disaster, the Bank of Ireland and college campus were standing proud. They stopped and rested for a few minutes beneath the college entrance. The sky had darkened further. There was barely enough light to see where they were going.

"What time is it?" Etain shouted.

Brendan checked his watch.

"It's barely three in the afternoon."

Making their way through library square, they headed past the college park, with Saoirse leading the way. Within minutes, the CRANN building was in sight.

The group paused outside the glass structure, staring at the tangled mass of steel and shattered glass. Saoirse was unperturbed.

"It's not as bad as it looks. The building is a hell of a lot sounder that the outer shell. It was built to be thermally stable and vibration proof, so there's way more structural engineering gone into it than you would think."

Brendan put his arm on her shoulder.

"It wasn't built to withstand an earthquake, Saoirse. God only knows what it's like inside."

Saoirse pushed his arm away.

"The labs are in the basement," she said.

She readjusted her backpack and headed for the entrance. Morrigan called her back and ordered her to stay outside. It was, after all, the travellers' mission and as such, should not be undertaken by civilians.

Brendan laughed at her.

"Morrigan, you guys can't do this without Saoirse. She knows where the equipment is and how to use it. I need to go, because I will be needed to get the power on, so they can do what they need to do. Uiscias is your technical expert when it comes to the laser. He needs to go inside, but going inside just because you are a traveller is stupid. You'd be a liability and a major risk to everyone else. We had this conversation yesterday; or are you going senile?"

Morfessa stepped forward.

"Brendan is right, Morrigan. We have communications gear and if they need us, they will call, and we'll be waiting. Let's just let them get on with it, shall we?"

The building was pitch dark inside, and it took an age to locate the emergency stairs to the basement level. Uiscias, Brendan and Saoirse returned to the main group. They advised the others to find shelter while they tried to locate the lasers downstairs – this would take at least a couple of hours. Morfessa reverently handed the Claíomh Solais over to Uiscias, who carried it carefully.

As the threesome descended in the darkness, Brendan expressed his concerns about power. Saoirse explained that all of the main systems have state of the art UPSs – uninterruptable power supplies. Once the main power was cut, these would kick in to take their place.

Outside, the rest of the group were now feeling the effects of the ash in the air and were finding it increasingly difficult to breathe. Etain took command.

"We need to get indoors while Saoirse, Brendan and Uiscias do their thing," she said. "The older buildings seem to be more stable – most of them are solid stone. We need to head back towards the campanile and the main quadrangle."

Morfessa used a walkie-talkie to contact Brendan and let him know what they were doing.

Etain led the way back through the campus, reaching the post-graduate reading room. This had always been Etain's favourite place on the Trinity campus, and she knew the building well – it would serve their purpose.

The door was locked, but Esras and Morfessa got the heavy oak door open. Once inside, the group sagged into the chairs by the reading tables. Despite everything that had happened, the glass in the octagonal skylight was intact. The air in the room was remarkably clear. In an anteroom, Sadbh found a water dispenser and rinsed her mouth, before drinking several small glasses. Etain and Muireann followed suit, using the downtime to take a bathroom break.

The ceiling in the basement of the CRANN building had collapsed. Damaged equipment lay where it had fallen, under mounds of twisted steel and a tangle of cables, which had once been neatly routed above the suspended ceiling.

The UPS was not working, and Brendan was forced to crawl around the debris to find the UPS system. With just a handful of screwdrivers and a torch, he tried to jerry-rig a power source for the laser and support equipment. He isolated the problem to a damaged PCB. There was only one way to fix it, and he needed a soldering iron and some wire to jump the damaged tracks.

Brendan got on the walkie-talkie. He was answered by Morfessa.

"Morfessa, I need to speak to my mother. Can you get her for me?"

Sadbh grabbed the radio.

"What's wrong, Brendan?"

"Mam, I know you took some gear with you. What's in your bag of tricks?"

"Jesus, Brendan. I just threw in some stuff from my toolbox in the car. I didn't really look."

She grabbed her backpack and emptied the contents onto a nearby table.

"Okay. There's a couple of precision snips, two rolls of wire, a roll of solder, a soldering clamp – you know the little one with the magnifying glass, a gas soldering iron, a couple of probes, a lope, a multimeter and a box of random bits and pieces."

Sadbh barely got to finish the sentence. Saoirse and Uiscias were whopping in the background.

"Mam, I need you to get all of the soldering kit and bring it to me. The UPS's PCB is busted, and I need to fix it. Can you drop the bag at the door for me?"

"No, I bloody well can't, Brendan. You may be really good at design, but you can't solder for shit. I know more about PCBs than anyone else here. I'm coming in."

Sadbh threw down the walkie-talkie and quickly repacked her backpack. She carefully redressed and replaced her mask and headed back to the CRANN building.

Saoirse was panicking.

"Brendan, you've got to stop her. She'll get herself killed trying to climb down."

Brendan grabbed Saoirse by the arms.

"Listen to me. There is no one alive that knows PCBs better than Mam. She's a bloody legend when it comes to fixing them. I'm good, but she's way better. If it can be fixed, then she'll fix it. Stop thinking of her as our mother and think of her as an engineer. Right now, if you want to be able to power up the lasers, you need her here."

Sadbh gingerly made her way to the basement, surprising herself at her agility more than once. It took more than twenty minutes, but she eventually found the others.

"Okay Brendan, show me what you've got," she ordered.

Sadbh cleared a space to work in and set up her meagre kit. Using a small magnifier, she examined the PCB, using every bit of light available to the team in the form of torches.

"Brendan, it looks like the power circuitry took a wallop from a sledgehammer. The main track is pulled away from the board, but there is still continuity, so the circuit might be operational. I'm going to solder in a jumper wire to bypass the broken area. I need you to keep as much light as you can on the board for me. Saoirse, I need you to hold the soldering iron for me and pass it over when I ask."

Sadbh worked in the confined space with the dexterity of a surgeon. She prepped the jumper wire and with a deft touch, soldered it securely into place. Using the multimeter, she verified that the circuit was intact. As an afterthought, she checked the trip fuses. The outer fuse was blown and luckily, she had a replacement that fitted neatly into the socket. She moved aside and allowed Brendan to take her place. He examined her work and nodded.

"Right then. The only way to know if it will work is to power it up. It's all yours, Brendan."

Brendan grabbed the board and set about reassembly of the power supply. It was difficult but eventually, he was satisfied.

"Right. Keep everything crossed. I'm turning it on."

The UPS system hummed into life; its LEDs casting an eerie green glow over the space. Saoirse climbed over upturned desks and office chairs and reached the laser control panel. Turning one switch started the initiation sequence. Once powered up the laser, with its computer control, displays and viewing systems, was fully operational. The machines hummed quietly and Uiscias stared at the heart of the system, fascinated by the complex start up routine.

Saoirse and Uiscias took control of the delicate laser set up. Miraculously, it was completely undamaged. Brendan could hear them arguing from the server room. When he got back to the lab, they were hunched over the keyboard. Saoirse set about calibrating the laser using the machine's calibration kit. Once done, Uiscias suggested a trial run, using silica blocks that they found in an adjacent storeroom. Satisfied that the set up was working, Uiscias carefully aligned the Claíomh Solais in the machine's chamber and returned to the control terminal. Saoirse and Uiscias checked the settings again and then a third time, before activating the laser. In a flash that illuminated the room for less than a millisecond, it was done.

Neither Saoirse nor Uiscias wanted to be the one to inspect the shaft, so Brendan volunteered. Using the high-powered microscope attached to the laser, he focussed on the shaft and found no evidence of damage.

Uiscias was nervous.

"Just because we can't see any damage, doesn't mean that we fixed it."

Saoirse put her hands out to take the Claíomh Solais.

"The only way to check if it works is to activate it, Uiscias. Turn it on."

Uiscias nodded stoically.

"Outside," he said.

Uiscias was terrified that the Claíomh Solais would be damaged during their transit from the building. He feared that if the Claíomh Solais took another knock, the device would die. Brendan and Saoirse understood his concern and swung their torches around the lab, looking for something to protect the delicate instrument.

Sadbh was searching in an ante room when she tripped over something on the floor. It was a hard-shelled instrument case, designed to protect sensitive equipment from shock during transport. She shone her torch down and found the latches. Inside was some sort of sensor and a tablet. The sensor was about 20 centimetres wide and 120 centimetres long, and sat in an antistatic foam bed. It could have been made for the Claíomh Solais.

Sadbh dragged the case back to the others. Brendan quickly removed the equipment and handed the empty case out to Uiscias.

"Will this work?" he asked.

Uiscias tried it for size; it was nearly perfect. The foam cut-outs were a little long and the pommel of the Claíomh Solais would not fit, but that was soon remedied with the aid of Sadbh's tools. The latches on the case had a double-locking mechanism. The case would not open unintentionally. It even had sturdy handles on each side, making lifting and manoeuvring the Claíomh Solais easy.

They scrambled out of the building and stumbled back towards the heart of Trinity College. The direction of the wind had changed, and the air was thick with volcanic and noxious fumes. The masks that they were wearing did little to protect them.

"Uiscias, can you turn it on, and then try it at its lowest setting?" Saoirse asked. Uiscias nodded.

"I'm going to set it down over there," he said, pointing to the quadrangle.

He lifted the instrument from the case and mounted it carefully, using tripod legs concealed in the handle. He spent a few moments reviewing the set up and programming the device using his handheld computer. He repositioned the device with the shaft pointing directly skyward. He waved Saoirse, Sadbh and Brendan back.

"I can handle it when it on. It's a bit uncomfortable but quite safe, but we can't be near it when it triggers," he shouted. "Go back as far as you can, and shield your eyes."

When he was satisfied, he ran back to Saoirse, Sadbh and Brendan.

"I'm going to set it to the lowest setting and one single pulse. We should see a really short, bright light. Whatever you do, don't look at it. Turn around and cover your faces. If it works, the sky above us should clear. Okay?"

Brendan, Sadbh and Saoirse nodded and turned away.

Despite covering their heads and facing the other direction, the brief pulse blinded them. The heat they felt on their backs was incredible.

After spending days in semi- darkness, the bright sunlight that fell on the Trinity quad was painful. Their breathing eased. The air tasted fresh and clear, like a sea breeze.

Saoirse broke out into a grin and high-fived her brother.

"Can you smell the ozone?" she said, amazed.

Brendan laughed and nodded.

Uiscias was too preoccupied to celebrate. He was on his knees, lovingly examining the portable laser. When he had checked it for a second time, he shut it down and fitted it into the recess of the hard-shelled instrument case that they had found in the lab. Only when it was securely packed did he look upwards at the clear, blue sky.

"How much did it clear, do you think?" Saoirse asked.

Brendan looked around.

"It's hard to tell, surrounded by buildings, but the sky is clear as far as I can see, so it must be a few kilometres at least."

He called Uiscias and asked him what the power setting had been.

"I set it to one per cent," he said. "I couldn't go any lower."

Brendan did not need to call Etain or Muireann on the radio. They came running from the reading room.

"How did you know?" Brendan asked.

"There's a skylight in the middle of the room in there. We were nearly blinded by a flash and then, seconds later, the sun lit up the room. We came straight outside and we couldn't miss you," Etain said.

Morfessa, Esras and Semias joined Muireann in congratulating the four heroes. Morrigan called a halt to the happy chatter and said that it was time to leave. They hurried back to riverside, carefully carrying their prize. As they walked down the quays, people began appearing from apartment blocks and the small, terraced houses off Pearse Street. Everyone was looking at the sky and celebrating. The group could hear people shouting questions. *Did you see the flash? Do you know what happened?*

The group said nothing, kept their heads down and hurried past. They did not stop to talk to the guards manning the bridge. They focussed on getting back to their vehicles.

Etain went around the group, whispering directions to a rendezvous point. Uiscias decided that he would feel better holding the case and gave his four-by-four to Sadbh. He would travel with Saoirse. Etain had told everyone that the rendezvous was at the Hungry Tree. Although the travellers had no ideas what it was, the Dubliners understood. It took more than an hour to get to King's Inn Park. They threaded the vehicles through the open gates and stopped near the famous Hungry Tree. Morfessa looked curiously at it.

"It's just a tree," he said. "Why do you call it the Hungry Tree?"

"Look at the bench," she said.

Morfessa and Esras guffawed.

"The tree ate the bench," Esras roared.

"That's why they call it the Hungry Tree," Muireann shouted.

They felt the stress of the last few days bleed away as they rested in the sunshine. Looking over the city of Dublin from the elevated position of the park's entrance on Constitution Hill, the skies were clear for as far as they could see.

"It must have cleared most of the city," Sadbh said.

Semias shook his head.

"It just seems that way. Enjoy the respite. In a few hours, the air will be as poisonous as it was before, if not worse."

Morfessa and Uiscias, with Saoirse's help, positioned the Claíomh Solais in the sun to charge. Even though the discharge had been slight, they wanted to make sure to keep the battery as full as possible.

Morfessa returned to the others and sat beside Etain.

"It will take an hour to bring the Claíomh Solais up to full power again. It's best to do it here, as close as we can be to the discharge point. This is where the sky will be cleared fully and therefore, the sunlight most intense. If we go further or wait, we can't guarantee the sunlight. So please, rest and take a drink. Saoirse and Uiscias are keeping watch."

In minutes, Etain was asleep, resting her head on Morfessa's chest. Muireann and Esras were dozing, leant against the Hungry Tree. Sadbh rested her head on her backpack and closed her eyes, disturbed only by Semias's loud snores. Brendan laid himself out on the grass and dozed. Morrigan refused to rest and prowled through the park, alert for intruders.

When they woke, they could feel the difference in the air, and the brightness of the sun had dimmed.

"How long were we asleep?" Morfessa asked.

"About two hours," Saoirse replied.

Chapter 39

What About Leitrim?

Lieutenant Colonel Kelly was on a roller coaster. He was devastated when the Curragh camp was ruled out as a refugee holding area and had been struggling to find a location to move the hundreds of thousands of displaced people.

He went from despair to elation when suddenly, the skies over Dublin miraculously cleared. He tried to find out how and who was responsible, but no one knew. Although raised a Catholic, he was never much for religion but like many, had wondered if it was divine intervention. Perhaps it was a miracle.

The elation did not last. After a few hours, the darkness and foul air was returning.

It was early evening when he took an opportunity – possibly his last, he thought – to take a walk outside in the barracks. The fear in the conference room was palpable, and everyone was feeling the pressure, including him. He needed some respite and time to think.

Corporal Mick O'Connor was unloading a truck and waved at the lieutenant colonel. Not in the mood for chit chat, the corporal was waved off by the senior officer.

"Sir, I thought it was all hands on deck, all leave cancelled?"

"It is Mick. It's a national emergency," Jack Kelly responded jadedly.

"Then how come yer wan, the commandant, was wandering around Finglas with a crowd of hippy weirdos then?"

Jack Kelly had walked past the hood of the truck but upon hearing the corporal, turned back.

"Explain yourself, Mick."

"Commandant McNamara was in uniform, driving a quad bike and drove up to us when we were getting supplies in Finglas. She wanted to get into the hardware store we had seconded. There were at least half a dozen of them quads. Now, I think there were some girls and an older woman but Jeasus, the fellas with her looked odd."

"Are you sure it was her?" Jack asked.

The corporal grinned.

"Of course it was her. Sure, didn't she put me on report two weeks ago. I'd know her anywhere and sure, if I didn't know her face, I'd know that ass anywhere. She was wearing skin-tight jeans with her tunic over the top."

In normal circumstances, Kelly would have reprimanded the corporal for speaking in that way about a senior female officer, but these were not normal circumstances. Jack Kelly, hurried back to the conference room.

"When I get my hands on Etain, I'm going to string her up," he mumbled to himself.

Jack Kelly wasted no time in ordering his team to find Etain. As he went to walk away, one of them asked to speak with him privately. Jack motioned him to the corridor outside and the private followed.

"What's up, son?"

"Sir, I know you're looking for a place to set up an evacuation centre. Have you thought about Leitrim?"

Leitrim has a reputation for being a rural backwater.

"What about Leitrim?"

"Sir, I know it's on the edge of the grid that you set up, but there are places there that are definitely suitable."

"Tell me your name and explain yourself," the senior officer ordered.

"Private O'Connor, sir. I'm from outside of Carrick on Shannon in Leitrim. As you know, Carrick is on the N4, so it's a straight run from Dublin, and it's easy to get through, from the west and south, using main roads. The thing is, about twenty kilometres from Carrick on Shannon, you have two major tourist destinations – Lough Key Forest Park and Lough Allen. Now, Lough Allen is a source of clean water – it feeds directly into the Shannon. The ground around there is pure rock, and the rock is laced with iron. Sure, Sliabh an Iarainn, means the Iron Mountain. The ground around there is stable. What happened on the Curragh won't happen there."

The private clearly had more to say but was waiting on permission from his boss.

Jack Kelly nodded at the private.

"Tell me more."

"The place is full of camping sites – plenty of flat ground at the base of the mountains. Drumshanbo is right on the lakeside. There a big visitor centre on the lake. We could use it as a headquarters. There's plenty of vacant buildings and farms around the place. We could make them into medical centres easily. As for shelter, we can set up a tented city – there's plenty of space around Carrick for that. And sir, CIS could set up a communication centre there and put their gear up on the Breifne Mountains – they could get really good coverage."

Jack Kelly nodded.

"What about Lough Key?"

"Now, if you go the other side of Carrick towards Roscommon, there's Lough Key Forest Park. Again, lots of flat ground, clean water and again, you get there from the N4. Lough Key Forest Park has camping and caravanning facilities, so there's some infrastructure we could take advantage of."

"How many people could they hold?"

"I don't know, sir," the private answered truthfully.

Jack thought for a minute. Leitrim was not huge, and the location was a little off. Leitrim is in the northern half of Ireland, bordering Donegal to the north, Fermanagh to the northeast, Roscommon to the west and Cavan to the east. To the south of the county lay Longford in the midlands. The county has the smallest population of counties in the Republic. The sparse population and abandonment of rural communities that had started 50 years ago, now meant that there was a lot of space and many abandoned buildings that could be repurposed. Access to the county was good, particularly cross-border access.

Although the six Ulster counties that comprise Northern Ireland came under the jurisdiction of the United Kingdom, they were always considered as being part of Ireland. Reunification had always been on the cards. After Brexit, more than half of the population of the North held Irish passports and considered themselves Irish citizens. They could not be abandoned. They could easily access Leitrim.

Jack knew there were probably a lot of better locations, but he did not have time to continue the search for somewhere more suitable. He needed to get a plan and act on it.

"Get over to the emergency team and tell them what you told me. Unless there is a major reason why the Lough Allen site is unsuitable, I want a preliminary plan within the next 30 minutes. Tell logistics to requisition every tent and portable structure they can – that includes the boy scouts and private companies. I want the names and details of an advanced party and a plan to set up shelters, field hospitals and communications infrastructure. They are going to need your help."

Private O'Connor nodded.

"And Corporal O'Connor, report back with them. I need someone with local knowledge with me. You are now on my staff."

O'Connor stared at the senior officer.

"Sir, I'm a private."

"You're a corporal now, son. It's a field commission."

Finally feeling like he was moving forward, Kelly headed indoors to find Etain. Kelly grabbed the first team he could find. They had one job – locate Etain and get her into barracks as soon as possible.

Chapter 40

So Long Ago

After three hours of clear skies, the volcanic ash and debris was winning the battle. The convoy at once pulled out their masks; they would need them soon. It was now approaching evening, and they needed to find shelter while the laser still provided some respite. With little choice, they set off towards Glasnevin on the north side of the city, to Sadbh's family home. Brendan reassured his mother that he would be able to rig up battery power in the house, and he could get some limited communications working – if there was anyone to communicate with.

Etain fretted about reporting to her Commanding Officer. It was clear that the Defence Forces needed everyone on the front line. Seeing the soldiers on duty had pricked her conscience. She was torn between helping the travellers and doing her duty. Morfessa did his best to reassure her as he rode alongside. Morrigan was more forthright. Etain was doing her duty. Simply working with the others to briefly activate the Claíomh Solais had done more for the people than anything else she could have done.

The air was acrid by the time they reached home. The avenue was buckled, trees felled and the rooves of the houses on Sadbh's side of the street were sagging gracelessly. Her own house still stood, but she could see where part of the roof had given way in the rear. The gable wall was deeply cracked, and Sadbh wondered how much force it would take to pull it down completely.

Once inside, it was clear that the house was more or less uninhabitable. Ceilings had collapsed upstairs, and there was a hole where the Velux windows used to be in Sadbh's bedroom. The stairs were rickety at best.

Brendan and Muireann risked going to the hot press for laundry and rifled through the bedrooms for clean clothes and shoes.

The power was out – it did not bother Sadbh. She had wanted power so she could prepare a hot meal but looking at her kitchen, it was clear that she would not be cooking today.

Esras somehow found fuel and lit the ornamental stove in the sitting room.

Saoirse rummaged through the press under the kitchen sink and found the packs of vanilla and strawberry scented tea lights, which were always part of the haul of goodies bought in Ikea. She dropped them into holders and lit them. The scent was sickly sweet when combined with the sulphurous air, but no one seemed to mind.

Between them all, they made the sitting room habitable – the stove giving light, supplemented by the tea lights.

Muireann found a steel pot and used two litre bottles of water to cover the base. She placed it on the stove top.

"It won't be much, but we can make some soup or noodles," she said.

Sadbh busied herself searching the cupboards for anything edible that could be rehydrated with hot water. She had a sixth sense of someone coming up behind her and spun around. Semias was standing in the doorway.

"I'm glad to catch you alone. I need you to do something about your daughters."

"What do you mean?"

"I mean you need to control their hormones. I have a mission to accomplish, and your daughters are a distraction to the team. I need the team focussed, not lovesick."

Sadbh stopped her rummaging and stood up. She could not believe the cheek of the man. She slammed her hands down on the countertop.

"Hold on a second, you bastard! You sabotaged your own mission. It would be in the toilet if it wasn't for my kids. Etain nearly died to get your laser; Muireann helped you find it; Saoirse and Brendan fixed it, and you have the cheek to tell me to get my daughters to behave. They have done nothing wrong. Who the hell do you think you are?"

Semias face flushed.

"I am a leader of this mission, and I am in control. You will respect my orders," he shouted.

"No, she won't. You're not in command of my family or anyone else for that matter. You should have been left for dead at the side of the road if there was any justice."

Brendan did not lose his cool. His voice was strong and firm.

Semias had not realised that Brendan has been standing in the dining room, with a full view of the conversation.

Morfessa stepped into the kitchen and stood nose to nose with Semias. He was joined by Morrigan.

"She won't do anything. Not because her daughters have nothing to answer for – they haven't done a damn thing. She won't do it, because you're not the commander of this mission, and you don't get to issue orders to anyone anymore."

Morfessa paused and turned towards Sadbh.

"Sadbh, I'm sorry you had to hear this. Esras, Uiscias and I have the greatest of respect for your family. We acknowledge the sacrifices you have all made to help us."

Morrigan turned to Semias.

"I'm in charge, and I always have been. Your position here was only ever meant as an excuse to get you away from the settlement, or hadn't you figured that out? You have been watched for years, Semias. I know all about what you did for the Council of Europe, how you acted as Nemed's lackey and gave away all of Cong's secrets. It was why you were designated as a crew member – it was to remove you from causing further trouble. And it didn't end there; did it Semias? You tried the same tricks on board ship and again in the colony. You tricked and lied and finagled your way into positions of power. Did you really think that we were all that stupid?"

Sadbh was eager to take Semias on but for the moment, said nothing. It was hard to stop herself grinning.

Semias was enraged.

"Morrigan, you will respect my position. If you don't ..."

He did not get to finish the sentence.

"If I don't what? What will you do? Run to the Council like you always do? Call on a few friends to have the team quietly removed? Do what comes naturally – bribe, threaten or manipulate? Sorry, that's not going to happen this time. You sabotaged the mission. You were responsible for the erasure of the artefact's coordinates. You're the one that risked our lives, our friend's lives and the lives of every future generation. And you have done fuck all to help us fix it. You wanted a legacy, well you've got one – you will forever be remembered as a liar, a murderer and a traitor to your people. Hell, you make Hitler, Stalin and Caligula look downright nice."

Morfessa pressed his forefinger in Semias's chest.

"You have a choice, either help us or go. We have the full measure of you. We are more than capable of dealing with things here without you. After all, you have no technical skills, no mission experience and frankly, you rub people up the wrong way. So, keep your mouth shut and keep out of my way. Next time, I won't be so polite."

Morfessa took a step back and turned to go back to the living room.

He looked over his shoulder.

"Don't bother talking to the rest of the team. It won't do you any good – it will just make them angry."

With the threat of reprisal hanging over Semias, Morfessa slammed the kitchen door as he left. Sadbh, not knowing what to do, followed him into the sitting room. The house was not large, and everyone in the sitting room had heard most if not all of the exchange. Uiscias and Esras looked relieved.

"Thank the Angels it's finally done. Semias was driving me crazy," Uiscias said.

Brendan found his and Muireann's guitars in a corner of the dining room, still snugly seated in their stands. While the rest of the room was in disarray, they were undisturbed. Brendan's birthday gift was pristine. Brendan took his guitar and went out into the back garden. The air was still clear enough for it to be comfortable. He sat on the iron bench and began to strum.

The blues melody took shape and as he played, Brendan broke into a strain of *Still Got the Blues (For You)* by Gary Moore. He did not hear Morrigan approach and when he did feel her presence, he did not stop playing until she took a seat beside him.

"I have never heard anything like that before. It's beautiful ... and so sad."

Brendan sighed and put the guitar down.

"I grew up listening to Gary Moore and Thin Lizzy. They were my grandad's favourites. The song is called *Still Got the Blues for You*. It was written before my mother was born."

"You make the instrument sing," Morrigan whispered.

"It doesn't sound that great without an amplifier. When I was a kid, Muireann and Etain and I would all play together. We were good too. All classic Irish rock songs. I guess we haven't done that in a while. Sometimes, I play when I'm down, and I guess tonight is a bit of an anti-climax, after what we did today. I was in the mood to play."

Morrigan nodded.

"I don't want to disturb you. I just wanted to thank you for what you did. If you hadn't stepped in and fixed the power supply, we would never have fixed the Claíomh Solais."

Brendan interrupted her.

"Before you go any further, my mam fixed the PCB and Saoirse and Uiscias got the laser working. It was a team effort. I just did one little piece."

"Even so, thank you. If I stay will you stop playing?"

Brendan smiled and shook his head. Morrigan sat back and waited. Brendan looked at her and laughed. He broke into the distinctive riff of *Oh Pretty Woman*, another Moore classic. As the song ended Brendan put down the guitar and ran his hand through his short dark hair.

"Why are you encouraging Etain to go after Morfessa, Morrigan? I'd say you're still interested in him, looking at it as an outsider?"

Morrigan sighed deeply.

"I won't deny that there was something between us. It got complicated. I was his CO and nearly got us both court-martialled, because I made some very bad choices. Afterwards, we agreed to go our separate ways. He's a good guy and she reminds me of me. I think we're alike. I mean, just because I'm alone doesn't mean they have to be, does it?"

"It does if you're still carrying a torch for him," Brendan whispered. "It's not fair on him or on Etain or on you."

Morrigan gave Brendan a lop-sided grin.

"I'm over him, I swear. Anyway, I need someone who can stand up to a strong woman."

Brendan laughed heartily.

"Sweetheart, you don't even begin to understand what that means. Try living in the witches' coven that I live in, and you might begin to get an idea what strong women are like"

Brendan stood, holding his guitar in his left hand and reached out his right hand to Morrigan. She took it, and they went indoors to see what the others had been up to.

Etain found some instant soup in a kitchen cupboard and set about preparing it for whoever wanted it. Morfessa took a cup from Etain. Morrigan joined them.

The women entered into an urgent discussion about what to do next. Morrigan called everyone together.

"We need a plan to get to high ground. Somewhere fairly central. When the Claíomh Solais is fully powered, it should clear a radius of between 600 and 1000 kilometres. If it works as well as it did in the test, then it should be able to recharge itself enough to keep functioning for several days. Etain, we can't do this alone, we need your help."

Etain nodded in agreement.

Morrigan took the lead.

"Uiscias, Saoirse, figuring out how to keep the Claíomh Solais operating will be up to you once the initial pulse is done."

Morfessa sat and warmed himself in front of the stove. The temperature had dropped as the sky had clouded over again.

"Muireann, I need to you help us figure out how to get to a suitable place. You know the country best. Brendan, Sadbh and Etain – we need your help in getting us to this location. We need to be able to move fast, and I don't think the quad bikes will be an option. I'll leave it up to you. We'll come up with a plan and leave early in the morning. We need to make sure that we time the operation to take advantage of as much sunlight as possible."

As the others worked on their tasks, Esras approached Morfessa.

"What do we do with Semias?"

Morfessa looked up to the ceiling.

"Unfortunately, have no choice. We have to take him with us."

"There is another choice," Esras growled. "It's within our mission parameters."

Morfessa smiled lopsidedly at his comrade.

"Apart from being a pain in the ass and a know-it-all, there's nothing more he can do to jeopardise the mission. Let's hold on a while longer before we make that decision."

Chapter 41

Epiphany

Semias was shaken to the core.

Semias had not known the extent to which his contacts with dissidents had been exposed. His double dealing, both before the Lifeboat project and after, had been laid bare.

Semias had fervently believed in sharing all of the Irish technology with the enclaves, not for his own benefit but for the benefit of humanity. Yes, he had shared what data he could with Nemed and had passed on blueprints that had crossed his desk for the betterment of mankind. He knew in his heart that this was not a betrayal of Cong. Nemed and the other Council members had pushed him forward and coerced him onto the Irish Council, had manoeuvred him into the inner circle, and he had enjoyed the power and notoriety that it gave him.

During all of the years he shared information, the Europeans had never given anything in return, he realised. Nemed had used him. The Council of Europe had stroked his ego, using the technical information he provided against the Cong settlement. That's why he ended up as an advisor to the fleet and from there, a crew member. There were others that followed that had done exactly the same thing after the fleet had crash landed. Bres was the last in a long line that played him for a fool.

Morfessa was right. He was seen as a traitor to his own people. He felt his body fold under him and ended up on the floor, his back to the countertops. He hung his head in his hands and wept.

Uiscias roused him.

"Stop feeling sorry for yourself and get back inside. You need to make yourself useful," he said, kicking the older man's boots.

Semias took a deep breath, wiped his face and stood. Whatever his failings, Semias needed to make this mission work. He understood the consequences for the future of mankind if it failed. It did not matter what had gone before. His only loyalty now was to humanity. He needed to redeem himself. He accepted that Morrigan was in charge, and he accepted that he did not have any input into the team's decision making. All he wanted to do now was prove himself to be worthy of his place beside them.

Chapter 42

Bunkered Down

The call was taken by an officer from Cathal Brugha Barracks. He looked concerned when he found Jack Kelly.

"The Department of the Taoiseach is looking for you urgently," he said.

So, the government has finally emerged from its hiding place, he thought. How long had it been? Two days or maybe three? The Lieutenant Colonel had not slept since the kick off with the volcano in Dublin Bay and had lost track of time.

Jack nodded and rushed back to the Comms Centre. He listened for twenty minutes without the opportunity to get a word in. Firstly, the Taoiseach and senior ministers in the Dáil were unhappy with the choice of Drumshanbo as a rallying point and refugee centre. Several ministers had suggestions for evacuation centres in their home constituencies in the west of Ireland, in Kilkenny and in Louth. Surely, there were better places than Leitrim, for God's sake?

The Taoiseach, who hailed from Limerick, wanted to know why a rescue mission had not been immediately instated for his constituents. Jack tried to tell the Taoiseach's secretary that Limerick was gone, along with large segments of Clare, Cork and Kerry, but he cut no ice.

The Minister for the Environment, who hailed from Wicklow, wanted an urgent and immediate review of the activities of the emergency services and expected Jack to rally the various agencies and appear before the Dáil within hours.

Secondly, the Taoiseach was receiving disturbing demands from the embassies of the USA, Germany, the UK and most of the rest of the world.

It was obvious that the Irish had staged a military intervention to clear the ash cloud over Dublin, and the embassies wanted to know what had been done and if the system that had been activated was a weapon. They were concerned that the Irish were about to use a weapon of mass destruction against them. The British and Americans, in the interest of world peace, demanded that the weapon or weapons be handed over to them immediately. The government was considering this proposal.

The Minister for Defence wanted a full technical report immediately. He also wanted to know why the system had not been activated in the border region – he was the elected representative for Cavan/Monaghan, both counties sitting on the border with Northern Ireland.

As a military man, Jack had no political affiliations or preferences. He thought all politicians were idiots. Despite reaching national government, the ministers were clearly still stuck in parish politics. He knew damn well that going to the Dáil would be a waste of time. The Dáil was not in session, and it was in the heart of the city that had been hit with wild tremors, causing major power outages and fires. The streets were unsafe and volcanic ash and gases were blowing into the city, from the volcano in Dublin Bay and the ash cloud caused by the destruction of Iceland. The one place where he knew the government would not be was in the Dáil, in Leinster House. This was not the States. Leinster House did not have the emergency bunkers that were under the White House to protect its elected representatives. And Jack knew that these gombeens would never put themselves in danger to attend a meeting.

He sat glumly at his desk, not knowing what to make of the ministers' requests. Lieutenant General Peter Clancy saw him and dropped by to see how things were going. Peter Clancy was the Chief of Staff of the Defence Forces of Ireland. Jack explained the Taoiseach's demands to his old friend. When he got to the ministers' requests, the Chief of Staff was doubled over in laughter.

"Peter, what the fuck do I do?"

Clancy wiped the tears from his eyes.

"Jack, we can't ignore them and frankly, since we had nothing to do with whatever cleared the skies over Dublin, there is nothing we can tell the government. Now it seems to me that they want the Army to take the lead. Well, you've done that, and you have my full support and the support of every other service that has assembled here."

"So, what happens next?" Jack pleaded.

"I'm going to make a phone call to the Dáil and ask for a time for this meeting," Clancy responded.

"We both know that the reception team aren't there, and it's unlikely that the phone will be answered. Since it's the Taoiseach's office that made the request, not the Taoiseach himself or a minister, I will ask to speak to the Taoiseach directly if the phone is answered. Again, I doubt that I will be put through to the Taoiseach or one of his aides."

"Why don't you just ring the Taoiseach on his mobile?" Jack asked.

Peter Clancy grinned at his old comrade.

"You know Jack, I lost my mobile phone what with the earthquakes, volcanoes and tsunamis. Anyway, there's no cell coverage. No, I think, under the circumstances, its better that we use an old-fashioned landline that may or may not work. The call will be logged on my end, so if there is still a government when all this is over, we will have plausible deniability. When I can't contact the government, I will have no choice but to go to the Áras."

Jack laughed out loud. He could not believe Peter's audacity.

"You're going to bypass those eejits and go straight to the President in Áras an Uachtaráin?"

"Yes. I'm going straight to the President, and I'm going to ask him to authorise the evacuation of survivors to Leitrim. Despite his artistic background, President Brosnin has a good head on his shoulders, and you've made a good case for Leitrim. What we need now is to roll out the evacuation – not dither and play politics. At the end of the day, the man is a realist. He is just as aware of what's going on as we are."

Jack grabbed his commanding officer's hand and shook it.

"Thanks, Peter. I'll get everyone moving immediately."

Peter raised his hands and motioned Jack back. He became serious.

"We have to be realists Jack. There's a very good chance that getting people away from danger along the coast or from the volcanoes will be of little use. The air quality is dropping quickly. The blast over the city helped for a few hours, but the rest of the country is covered by a dense pall of volcanic dust, and God only knows what's in it. From everything I have been told by our top people, it's only going to get worse. We're already seeing deaths in people with respiratory illnesses, like asthma. It won't be long before the healthy are affected. Which brings me to the other subject."

Peter Clancy paused for breath and pulled a chair over to Jack to sit beside him.

"Now, I don't know any more than you do about what happened in Dublin. I've heard the same reports as you – a blinding flash followed by clear skies. Whether it was an act of God or a mad scientist, I really don't have a clue. When you have the evacuation under control, you need to find out, Jack. If it was done once, it can be done again. You know it, I know it and thanks to the Diplomatic Corps, every country with an embassy in Dublin knows it. These countries are as ravaged as Ireland is. Scandinavia, Spain, Portugal and Italy are destroyed and countries with huge populations – like Germany, France, Poland and the United Kingdom – will do whatever it takes to preserve their society. The thing is, we don't have the military prowess that they do. They will want whatever it was that cleared the skies, Jack. We need to get this sorted before the British Army, EUFOR, NATO or someone worse comes calling. Our lads can't stop them but no doubt, they would die trying."

"Jack, foreign governments, even within the EU, won't take no for an answer. We can't protect the people who caused that flash of light that cleared the skies from them if a foreign power decides to take matters into their own hands. If they really want the technology that cleared Dublin, they'll invade us and take it. And no amount of complaints to the United Nations will stop them. So, find out who is responsible. Help them if you can. This is about saving lives."

Jack nodded, heavy hearted with the weight of responsibility placed upon him.

"I'm going to delegate the evacuation once I find Commandant McNamara. She's well able to handle it. I'll get a team together, and we'll try to track down whoever it was. If we find them, you have my word that we'll do everything we can to help them."

Chapter 43

Iron Mountain

Muireann spread the map of Ireland across the floor, in front of the stove and used candles and an old oil lamp to provide illumination.

"Okay, so all of the largest mountains in the country are out of bounds," she said, pointing to the map.

"Carrauntoohil in Kerry was the highest but from what I can tell, Cork, Kerry and Limerick either no longer exist or would be impossible to reach. For that reason, Cnoc na Péiste and Mount Brandon are also discounted, as are all of the other mountains in the region. Sliabh Donard in County Down, up north, is out too because of what's going on in Antrim. We'd never make it across the border. And remember, we'd have to pass through North Dublin to reach the six counties."

As she spoke, Muireann indicated the locations on the map, so that the others could follow. As she outlined the reasons for discounting each mountain, the others nodded in agreement.

"Now, we could reach the Dublin and Wicklow Mountains, but what news bulletins have aired are talking about major seismic activity in the area. We could try to reach the foothills, but there is little chance that we could actually get to the top of Lugnaquilla or Three Rock. If it's as bad as the reports suggest, we'd probably be killed long before we could make the climb."

Again, the team agreed with her rationale.

"That leaves us with the lower mountains. Mweelrea is on the coast of Mayo, so that's out of the question – the region is most likely under water. We're left with Mount Leinster in Carlow, Blackstairs, also in Carlow or the Breifne Mountains in Leitrim, in particular, Sliabh an Iarainn. We have a choice – we can go south to the Blackstairs or north-east, to Leitrim."

Semias had positioned himself in the far corner of the room, not wanting to draw attention to himself since his dressing down by Morfessa and Morrigan and the epiphany that had followed. His estrangement did not stop him listening intently. Muireann had struck a nerve when she outlined their choices. Semias was trying to remember why.

Semias coughed politely and the others focussed on him.

"I'm sorry. I know I have no right to interfere. The name Iron Mountain sounds so familiar. When we first settled in Ireland, Morrigan led a landing party to the north-east of the county. Badb and Macha were squadron leaders. Macha made quite an impression if my memory serves me – she established quite a large settlement to the north of the mountain. The mountain site was chosen because of an abundance of iron deposits, along with other minerals. We set up an iron mine to replenish our supplies once the base camp was established."

Morrigan stared at him and nodded.

"Yes, the name Iron Mountain is familiar now that Semias mentions it. I wasn't there for long, just a couple of weeks when we were setting up the settlement. We had an ongoing guerrilla war with the Fir Bolg. We spent most of our time trying not to kill them. They came at us with spears and clubs. After seeing what our rifles and guns could do, they retreated, calling us Hells Angels. Morfessa, were you part of that too?"

Morfessa shook his head.

"Before my time, Morrigan."

Muireann and the others could see the map clearly but Semias, standing in the corner, was too far away from the map to see any detail.

"Macha's settlement became the city of Armagh, in Goídelc that would be Ard Mhacha – Macha's Height. The people thought she was a goddess," Etain said.

Semias smiled.

"Macha would like that. She likes to be obeyed."

He was beckoned forward into the inner fold near the stove, where he could get a proper look at the map.

"I was with the landing party when they first arrived – they scared the hell out of the natives. The little runabouts we used were tiny by our standards, but the natives thought they were magical – descending from the skies. It was the first time that the crew had been able to swim. The remnants of the fleet were marooned in areas too cold to enter the water. It was in early summertime, and it was so hot for the time of year. The water of the lake near the mountain was glorious. The water fed out of the lake into a great river, and it tasted so fresh. We fished for trout and salmon and then didn't know how to prepare it."

Semias remembered it as if it were yesterday.

Morfessa looked at him.

"Do you know the area, Semias?"

"I was there for a few months on and off, helping with planning and operations. I must have walked those meadows around the lake a thousand times, completing mineral surveys. Oh, I didn't do much – I just held the equipment. The devices did all the work. They just needed to be carried. It's a wonderful place."

"How much metal was in the mountains, Semias?"

"A great deal of iron back then. Goibniu was the chief geologist and was quite excited by the find. There was coal too, if I remember correctly, which we used in a smelter near our settlement. Goibniu was an expert in metallurgy, we called him the smith."

Morfessa looked at Uiscias, who nodded at him.

"I think fate has made the decision for us. We are in favour of going to Sliabh an Iarainn."

Sadbh, Muireann, Saoirse and Brendan nodded in agreement.

Morrigan put her hand on Semias's shoulder.

"We need you to remember every detail of the mountain, the meadows and the lake, old man. This is your only shot at redemption."

Etain bit her lip. Per her training, her mind had jumped ahead to the logistical challenge of getting to Leitrim.

"We don't have any way of getting there on our own. We will need all terrain vehicles, there's absolutely no other way."

She began pacing back and forward.

"I'll have to report into McKee Barracks and ask for help from the army. I will most likely be treated as a deserter and court-martialled, but it's the only way. I'll do whatever I can to help get you to Drumshanbo, but you'll have to finish this without me," she whispered.

Morfessa hugged her and whispered, "In the morning, Etain. There's nothing else we can do tonight."

Sadbh and Muireann tried to dissuade Etain but in their hearts, they knew she was right. They spent most of the night talking it through over and over again. They needed help, and they needed it urgently. There was nowhere else to turn.

Brendan set up a comms link with a heavy heart. He was frightened for his sister, especially after her brush with death only days before. As soon as the LTE network that Brendan had rigged went live, she dialled into her commanding officer. Jack Kelly answered on the first ring.

"That was fast, sir," Etain said, trying to make light of the situation.

"I recognised the number. We've been searching for you for the last couple of days. I thought you were dead after what happened in the North, only to have one of the support team tell me you were with a bunch of wankers in Finglas, robbing a hardware shop. Really Etain, in fucking fancy dress? The last they saw of you was yesterday, riding into the sunset on quadbikes. Care to elaborate?"

Etain cleared her throat.

"The story is so fantastic that you wouldn't believe me. I need to come in, sir."

"Yes you bloody well do, Commandant."

Jack Kelly paused for a moment.

"Get your ass in here and take over the evacuation. I don't have time to deal with the other shit right now, so we'll pretend it never happened. The evacuation site is being set up in Leitrim, but we need someone to handle comms and logistics. We've pulled a decent joint task force together, but I have another mission I need to complete."

"So, get in here chop-chop, and get that site prepared to take refugees."

"You'll need to liaise with the hospitals, blood bank, Irish Water, the Electricity Supply Board and the Gardaí. Oh, and talk to Bus Éireann – they may have useable buses for transport. The Irish Prison Service needs to evacuate from Mountjoy, Wheatfield and Cloverhill prisons in Dublin.

Their own vans won't have capacity, so you'll need to set up a special transport for them, and make sure we have a high security area for sex offenders from Arbor Hill prison. They can't be allowed anywhere near civilians."

Etain's family and the travellers were all listening to the call. The relief was palpable when Etain's commanding officer mentioned Leitrim.

"Sir, you don't understand. I also have another mission I need to complete. It's really important, sir."

"More important than saving the lives of the people you swore to serve?" her CO asked.

"Sir, my mission is all about protecting the people I swore to serve."

The phone line went quiet.

"Get your ass in here and meet me in the main conference centre. And bring your merry men with you. I can't wait to get a look at them."

Etain tried to ask her boss how he knew about the travellers.

"The army has eyes and ears everywhere, Etain. You should know that."

Chapter 44

Clear Skies

It had not been easy to get the message through to GCHQ in Cheltenham, but the British embassy had persevered. The consular staff and diplomats had been eyewitnesses to the bright flash that had illuminated the dark ash-filled skies of Dublin. They had also experienced the aftermath – bright sunlight and clear air that tasted of a sea breeze.

The embassy was not clear on what had happened but from speaking to allied embassies (namely, the American Embassy in Ballsbridge), it appeared that a weapon of some kind had been discharged. Since Ireland was a peaceful country and had limited offensive or defensive capabilities, it had to be something experimental. As a hub for innovation, it was quite possible that the Irish were developing equipment for a foreign power unknown. China had made significant investments in Irish technology companies, so it was possible that the device used was of Chinese origin.

By the time the message had been relayed and the embassy had received confirmation of its receipt in Great Britain, the skies had clouded over again and if anything, the ash pollution was heavier and more noxious. Of course, the British embassy was not the only embassy reporting the strange and miraculous event. The American chain of command had been informed but rather than going to the State Department in Washington, the information had been sent to the President, at a location undisclosed. Washington and the whole east coast of the USA had suffered a mortal blow when the tsunami had hit.

The European Union had received flash traffic from its delegations in Dublin City, and member states verified the information with confirmation from their own embassies. The European consensus was that the technology used was American, due to the close friendly relations between the Irish President and the President of the United States, who was, coincidentally, of Irish descent. The level of US investment in Ireland was astounding, particularly in the technology sector.

Chinese and Russian diplomats also reported the event to their beleaguered governments and their suspicions of US involvement.

Around the world, satellites were repositioned and focussed on the Emerald Isle. Satellite photographs and video recorded at the time that the skies were cleared were scoured for information.

The diplomatic corps based in Ireland all received the same instruction: Find out what caused the skies to clear and find out where it is. Report back as soon as you can. Locate it. Figure out how it works. Secure it and get it back home at all costs.

Agents, official and unofficial, were activated and left their embassies like vipers leaving their nest.

Chapter 45

Na Fianna

In the end, Sadbh's family and the travellers used the last of their jerry cans to fill the quad bikes, knowing that they were likely to run out of fuel within a few kilometres. As it happened, the quad bikes made it to the North Circular Road before finally giving out. The motley crew made the last part of the journey on foot to McKee Barracks.

The soldiers on guard duty hardly recognised Etain, but they had been expecting her. She and her entourage were escorted to the conference centre by six armed guards, who refused to make eye contact with her.

They were led to a meeting room, where Jack Kelly was waiting. Before Jack started issuing commands, Morfessa made an executive decision to get in first. He began by explaining what the Claíomh Solais was, and what the travellers intended to do with it. Despite their ridiculous clothing and avant-garde hairstyles, the foreigners, as Jack thought of them, did have a military bearing. This was the only reason he let Morfessa speak.

When Morfessa finished, Etain outlined her plan to get the Claíomh Solais to Sliabh an Iarainn.

Jack Kelly refused to believe a word of Etain's and Morfessa's explanation, despite Morfessa explaining the origins of the device and how it worked. Uiscias provided a step-by-step account of events in Trinity College.

"The Claíomh Solais doesn't exist," Kelly said.

"That's why it appears on your rank insignia then?" Esras observed.

"Enough of your cheek young man. Now I've heard enough. Etain, get to work. As for the rest of you, I would advise heading inland."

Saoirse opened the hard-shelled case and gently removed the Claíomh Solais.

"Sir, this isn't a figment of our imagination. It's very real."

This was a make-or-break opportunity, and Saoirse decided to go out on a limb.

"How about a demonstration?"

Jack stared at the device and could not help but reach out to touch it. It was a work of art.

"The gold for the chasing was mined in Mayo, near the coast. The amethyst was mined on Achill Island also in County Mayo – there is a very large seam of amethyst on the island on the mountainside above Keem. Some of our best artisans worked on this and on the other equipment that was left for us," Semias explained.

Jack had not believed the travellers explanation but looking at the Claíomh Solais, he had second thoughts. Maybe a demonstration would not be a bad idea. He was thinking, weighing up the options.

Morrigan had enough.

"I am commander in chief of Na Fianna. I demand to speak to someone of equivalent rank immediately."

Jack stood up.

"Now hang on a sec ..."

Morrigan got up in his face and screamed, "I am Morrigan, of Na Fianna. Get someone in here who can make a bloody decision. Now!"

Jack left them alone in the conference room and ran to his office. He called Peter Clancy immediately. He was breathless.

"Peter, you're not going to believe this. Etain has brought the damn thing in. I've seen it. She's with Na Fianna, the whole bloody lot of them. Get everyone over here as soon as you can."

Peter Clancy did not have time to respond to Jack Kelly – Jack had shouted down the phone and hung up. The Lieutenant General was with President Brosnin in Áras an Uachtaráin, the President's residence, located minutes away from the barracks in Grangegorman.

"That sounded interesting," the President laughed.

"I swear that Jack Kelly said that Na Fianna brought it in. He'll be talking about Oisín and the Children of Lir next. If what he says is true, the device is in McKee. I better get over there. God only knows what's going on."

The President shook his hand.

"This is the first bit of good news we've had in days. And if you think you're going to have all the fun, think again. I'm coming with you. I really want to get a good look at Na Fianna or whoever the hell they are."

The presidential motorcade consisted of one all-terrain vehicle – the Aide de Camp seated beside the driver, the President and Lieutenant General in the back. Nevertheless, the guards at the barracks reacted with all due ceremony. The President and Lieutenant General Clancy were quickly ushered into the conference centre. They were met by a flustered Jack Kelly.

"There in here, sirs," he said, opening the conference room door.

The President took one look at the ten assembled men and women and burst out laughing.

Etain immediately came to attention and saluted.

Morrigan did not take the laughter well. Her eyes bore straight through the President, and her face grimaced. Sadbh, Muireann and Saoirse looked at each other and smiled.

"Well, you're sure as hell not what I expected. I was expecting mythical monsters. The only thing you have in common with Na Fianna is a GAA club in Drumcondra. So, what the hell is going on?" President Brosnin asked, his eyes alive with merriment.

Morrigan stepped forward and cleared her throat.

"Morrigan is my name –"

She got no further.

"As in The Morrigan?" the President joked.

"Yes, as in the goddess of war and victory and leader of Na Fianna, of the Tuatha Dé Danann. That Morrigan," she replied.

"That Morrigan, sir, I believe is the phrase."

The President was enjoying himself.

"You are not my superior. I bow down before no man." Morrigan was losing her temper, not realising that the President was playing with her.

Morfessa stifled a grin and gently put his hand on Morrigan's arm. He got her attention and nodded at her.

"Sirs, my name is Morfessa, also of Na Fianna. I don't think it's us you are interested in. I think it's a piece of technology that we have retrieved and repaired with the help of Etain and the McNamara family. From what I understand, you are aware of its effect on the ash cloud that has engulfed Ireland. With your permission, I am inviting my colleague, Uiscias and Saoirse, a gifted physicist, to explain the device to you and let you examine it. When they are done, we can discuss a demonstration."

The President and Lieutenant General were seated, and they were hastily joined by engineers from CIS and other army corps. Uiscias opened proceedings by giving an overview of the petawatt laser and its capabilities. He also explained the history of the device, confusing the audience with the complex timeline on more than one occasion.

When he was done, Saoirse took over, explaining the material science behind the laser, its power, charging capability and general precautions for use. She was careful to emphasise the targeted particle size, although this went over the heads of all those present.

Finally, when questions were answered, the device itself was carefully taken from its case and passed to the President for inspection. Brosnin marvelled at the exquisite workmanship and flawless execution. "It belongs in the National Museum," he mused.

"Sir," Sadbh ventured, "we can put it in a museum when its work is done. Do you want to see it working?"

The polo ground had been in existence since the 1870s and was now home to the All-Ireland Polo Club. The flat expanse of grass, surrounded by mature woodland, with an open viewing stand, made it an ideal location. The members of the Defence Forces' task force, along with Etain, her family and the travellers made their way there in a fleet of landrovers. Uiscias and Morfessa were in charge of the Claíomh Solais, bedded securely in its case. The President and his entourage were waiting for them when they arrived. They wore rebreathing apparatuses due to the contamination in the air.

Morfessa introduced himself and his team. There were considerably more people in the stands than had been in the conference room. Looking around her, Saoirse thought she recognised a few from the physics community.

Uiscias provided an overview of the Claíomh Solais and warned each observer not to look directly at the device during discharge. When the observers took their seats in the stand, Saoirse and Uiscias walked to the centre of the polo pitch and carefully set the device up.

"How high should we set it?" Saoirse asked.

"I think no more than five per cent. It's higher than our initial test, but I don't want to drain the power source. If it works, we'll need to recharge it in the sunlight, before setting out to Leitrim. It's still only 9 am. We should be recharged by early afternoon and should arrive at our destination by tonight. It will give us time to scout a location and have the device set up to fully discharge in the morning."

Uiscias set the device to five per cent, and they made their way back to the cover of the stand. Again, Uiscias issued a warning about looking at the beam. Shouting a countdown, he activated the Claíomh Solais from the control panel on the computer.

The power of the laser was intense, even with shielded eyes. Unlike the previous test, the discharge was accompanied by a powerful electrical field that was felt by anyone within a kilometre radius. The observers were blasted by a gale force superheated gust, as the air pushed away from the beam of light. The blast was strong enough to threaten the stand on which the observers were seated. It was an experience that the observers were not likely to forget. It took minutes for their sight and hearing to return.

When the leaders could open their eyes and focus, they saw clear, blue, cloudless skies and even without looking, they could taste the clear, ozone-tainted air. The intense sunlight made colours appear sharper and more radiant. From their vantage point on the stand, the assembled dignitaries could see clear skies over the whole of the city, reaching towards County Kildare.

The President, Chief of Staff and the core team were rushed from the Polo Ground to the platform of the papal cross, a memorial to Pope John Paul II's visit in 1979. Saoirse and Uiscias would not leave the Claíomh Solais, so were left behind at their insistence.

The simple white cross stood 116 feet high, the platform offering views across the city and county of Dublin. There were clear skies as far as they could see, which was straight over the city. Using binoculars, the Dublin Mountains were bathed in sunlight. The River Liffey was a sparking ribbon running through the suburban landscape. The joy of the President was palpable. The senior army officers beamed, congratulating the travellers, Etain and her family.

Morfessa and Morrigan approached Jack, Peter and the President.

"Thank you for the opportunity to give the demonstration, but we really need to get to our destination as fast as possible. We need to be in place and ready to activate the device as soon as the sun has risen fully tomorrow morning. Even if we left now, we couldn't reach Leitrim before nightfall, and it's too dangerous to make the ascent of the mountain with the Claíomh Solais at night. Mr President, we really need to activate the device on full power tomorrow at sunrise. If we leave it any longer, the damage done will be irreversible."

The President and the head of the Defence Forces had a myriad of questions that they needed answers for. Senior scientific advisors and the army engineering corps had a slew of questions about how the device worked. Morfessa stayed them.

"We will do our best to answer your questions but please, can we do it en route? Time is of the essence."

"Hold on just a minute," Peter shouted. "Your young friends said they needed time to get the device charged. We have about two hours to get you a convoy, get you kitted out properly and make arrangements in Leitrim. Give the engineers half an hour. You never know; there may be something they can do to help."

Morfessa and Brendan went with the engineers and did their best to answer their questions. Brendan, thinking on his feet, gave preliminary instructions for the communications equipment they would need for their ascent of the mountain. Morfessa gave instructions for kit and equipment.

Morrigan stayed to one side, eager to get some time alone with someone senior. The President, watching her, made his way to her side.

"Something is bothering you. Spit it out, Morrigan."

"Sir, I'm really worried about security. We only have one device and no way of replicating it. If the device is stolen or damaged, then Ireland is finished. Looking at the army, I don't think you have the defensive capability to protect the Claíomh Solais."

Brosnin nodded sagely.

"Well, it's clear that we are in agreement. I feel exactly the same as you do. The first time the device was activated, there was a sharp peak in consular traffic. Every major power in the word focussed on Ireland. By now, half an hour after its second outing, you can be sure that one or more of them has a plan underway to secure the device. The ash cloud and volcanoes may slow them, but they won't be stopped easily. We'll give you the best protection we can – everyone we can spare."

Morrigan looked at him squarely.

"You know it doesn't end with tomorrow's discharge? This is just the first step, and the most critical. There are other devices that we need to locate. The Sleg Assail will stop the invaders in their tracks. We just need time to find it. If we work together, we can fight off anything that comes at us."

"You have my word of honour," President Brosnin said, shaking her hand.

"And you have the word of Na Fianna."

Jack sent a runner back to the barracks to arrange secure transport for the travellers, Etain, Saoirse, Brendan, Muireann and Sadbh. He also made sure that a spare uniform was secured for Etain.

The President stayed with them and requested that they join him in the Irish White House, a few hundred meters from the papal cross, directly across Chesterfield Avenue from the American Ambassador's residence. As they walked, the Morrigan and Etain kept step with President Brosnin. The Irish President wanted to know what would happen next.

"So, you will start in Leitrim, but where to next? Do you have a route that you plan to take around the country?"

Morrigan did not understand. The President rephrased the question when he saw the puzzled look on Morrigan's face.

"Will you move from location to location? The discharge cleared a radius of at least twenty kilometres, if not more. To clear the country, you'll need to move around and zap the cloud in different places, is that not so?"

In their haste, the travellers had not explained that the Claíomh Solais was operating at a low power setting.

"Sir, what you saw in the demonstration was a power setting of five per cent. Uiscias didn't want to run down the power and wanted a minimal recharge time, so we felt it best to use a low setting. We expect a full discharge to clear at least a 600-kilometre radius. It will be one discharge to clear the whole country, tomorrow morning, in Leitrim."

The President and his entourage were awestruck.

"My God!" the President said, "It is the most powerful device in the northern hemisphere, Peter. No wonder Morrigan was worried. For God's sake, take whatever resources you need to keep the Claíomh Solais safe."

The President had not spoken directly to Etain at any point and as they reached the main gate of the presidential compound, he approached her.

"I'm being evacuated to Leitrim along with the government and senior officials. I'll be there in the morning to watch the fireworks. Let's keep this a secret for now. I've already told Jack and Peter the same. Once you're done tomorrow, come and find me. I need to know everything. Then we can find a way forward. And Etain, we are all very proud of you. Don't let those foreigners out of your sight for a minute."

He handed her a secure phone, and the Aide De Camp materialised at his side, with a full weapons kit for her.

Chapter 46

Refuge

It was just after 8 pm when they finally reached Drumshanbo. They had been travelling for more than seven hours. Despite the relative comfort of the army jeeps, the journey was full of stops and starts, diversions and delays as the engineer corps deployed temporary bridges along stretches of the motorway damaged by seismic activity.

The Irish Army and the Gardaí had thrown a protective ring around the area, which started at Carrick on Shannon and extended to the northwest, to Manorhamilton, to Blacklion in the northeast and to Mohill in the south. All connecting roads were manned with sentries and were closed to unauthorised personnel.

In the town proper, the primary and secondary schools were in the process of being converted into a field hospital. Medical equipment was being ferried into emptied classrooms. Spare hospital beds and trollies were brought in from local medical offices and nursing homes. The engineers, with the support of the local Electricity Supply Board office, set up a makeshift grid for the town and surrounding area. Where power could not be restored, local farmers volunteered diesel generators.

The Drumshanbo Mart, the local animal auction site, with its many sheds and outhouses, was handed over to the warehousing and distribution team.

The chefs from the Irish Army drew in all local restauranteurs and café owners and set up food service areas throughout the town, knowing that the refugees would be tired and hungry when they arrived. The nuns from the local convent went to work in the industrial kitchens of the Shed Distillery's visitors centre, starting to prepare simple wholesome food, ingredients sourced from local supermarkets, while awaiting deliveries from army central stores. The local pharmacists arrived with infant formula and took it upon themselves to make up and refrigerate hundreds of bottles of baby milk. Families opened their homes, offices and farm buildings to offer shelter to refugees, understanding that the army's hospitality could not extend to all of the arrivals.

Tented cities were erected by the lakeshore in the Lough Allen campsite, in farms and on common land. True to their word, the boy scouts had arranged for hundreds of tents to supplement the emergency supply. Event and marquee hire companies had surrendered their stocks to help in the effort. The people of Leitrim provided bedding, spare clothes and other necessities, standing at the roadside and handing supplies to passing convoys.

The tented cities were being filled as fast as they could be erected. Even without publicity, thousands of ordinary people had made the pilgrimage to Drumshanbo, arriving in clapped out cars, on bicycles and on foot. The people were tired, hungry and many were in respiratory distress.

In the twilight, the travellers and Sadbh's family commandeered a local café, with permission from military command. The place resembled a barn, with a small stage set at one end, complete with a sound desk, speakers and microphones.

No sooner were they seated at a long refectory table, than a team of local nuns appeared, with hot meals for each of them. They had not eaten since early morning and suddenly realised that they were ravenous. Silent and gracious, the local sisters brought second and, in some cases, third helpings, along with soft drinks and water.

As soon as the meal was finished, the team were brought to a makeshift kit area. A lieutenant from CIS, known to Etain, was there to greet them.

"Commandant, as instructed, we have filled five kit bags to your exact specification. We have a range of hiking boots, clothing and rations available. You can take whatever you need. I have also been instructed to have a number of weapons available to your team, in addition to flare guns. There are rifles, revolvers and a selection of bows, and a practice area if you need it."

He swiftly returned Etain's salute and withdrew.

Sadbh cornered Etain.

"Why are there only five kit bags? There are ten of us."

Morrigan stepped forward and stood by Etain.

"Etain and I made a decision about who should climb the mountain. Obviously, we need Uiscias and Saoirse. They will activate the Claíomh Solais. The rest of the team are there to support them and protect them. We can't afford to lose time with dragging extra people up there. Esras will stay here with Brendan. Muireann, you and Semias will also stay behind and act as a support team. Etain and I, along with Morfessa, will help them get the Claíomh Solais up there."

Brendan was angry to be left behind. Morrigan spoke to him at length to get him to calm down. Muireann was not at all surprised that she would not be making the final journey but took responsibility for providing the team with whatever they would need to get them to the summit with relish. Seeing her daughter accept the decision readily, Sadbh swallowed her pride and weighed in to help.

Brendan and Esras left to view the communications systems.

Morrigan briefed the climbing team.

"So, to the crew. I need Uiscias and Saoirse to operate the Claíomh Solais. If either is injured or can't make the summit, the other will take over full responsibility. I need Etain, as she is our liaison with the Irish Army, and because she is a trained soldier. If anything goes wrong on the mountain, I need Etain to defend Saoirse and Uiscias, along with Morfessa. Now before anyone objects, I have already spoken with Etain, and she feels that she is well recovered to take on this responsibility. As commander of this mission, I will be carrying the Claíomh Solais up the mountain, and I will also provide defensive cover, if it is needed. Now we need to find the best way up the mountain. Muireann will be working on this with Uiscias and Saoirse. The three of us – that is, Etain, Morfessa and I – need some weapons practice."

Morfessa tried using a rifle and revolver, but his aim was consistently off. Going old school, he picked up a crossbow and his aim improved. The model that he selected was lightweight and easy to carry. Morrigan and Etain both excelled with all of the firepower placed before them. Morrigan selected a Heckler and Koch MP7, while Etain felt at home with Irish Army standard issue – a Steyr AUG assault rifle with an Advanced Combat Optical Gunsight. Both women cleaned and prepped their weapons and stowed ammunition with their kits.

Muireann had left during the start of the planning phase and missed most of the discussion. Before the group were through with weapons selection, she returned, accompanied by a wiry elderly man. She introduced him to Saoirse and Uiscias as Sean Óg, a local hill walker.

"I met Sean Óg when I was in the local hardware store. He climbs the mountain every day during the summer, guiding tourists. He might be able to help."

While Sean Óg introduced himself, Muireann found the rest of the ascent team.

Uiscias, Morfessa, Saoirse, Morrigan and Etain stepped outside with the spry local, and they viewed the mountain through the hazy twilight. Sean Óg brought them to a large noticeboard containing a map of the mountain. He told them that it would be easier to view the route using the map.

"The first part of the climb is the toughest. To get access to the western side of the mountain, we need to start at the forest that you can see to the left and cross over a stretch of bogland. There's a temporary bridge over the river there. The ground is treacherous. It's very easy to break an ankle or worse between pits and loose rocks. There's a rough track up the western edge – and I mean rough. The route itself is well marked, and it's hard to get lost. Whatever you do, don't try to take the route over the ridge – it'll get you killed. Go the long way around. You'll see a lot of new posts and stiles along the way. If you follow them, you'll be grand."

Etain and Saoirse were relieved. The local man's knowledge was invaluable.

"Now the thing is, once you get past the track, you'll be exposed on the side of the mountain. It looks calm enough up there now, but we're having problems breathing on the ground, without any exertion. You'll have to make the climb wearing a mask. And it's going to be very cold up there. Even without the muck in the air, it's always cold at the top."

Sean Óg pointed to just below the mountain summit, barely visible in the dim light.

"That whole open area you can see is bogland, which is dangerous. If you can stick to the peat hafts – that's where the peat is firmest."

To illustrate what he was talking about, he walked with them the short distance to the edge of bogland. He pointed to the hafts, so that they knew what to look for.

"You need to be vigilant and keep to the paths up there. You know you are on the right track when you pass the stone alter – there's a white marker beside it. The good news is that if you get to the bogland, the rest of the climb is easy. Now the summit itself is flat but again, 'tis wet, boggy and exposed. The trig point, or triangulation pillar, that marks the mountaintop is at ground level, so it's easy to miss."

"Is there any firm ground up there?" Saoirse inquired.

"Why do you need firm ground?" Sean Óg asked.

"We want to set up equipment. We need about a square meter that's solid and stable."

Sean Óg nodded his head.

"The trig point is set-in three-foot square of concrete, and it's flat. Will that do?"

Saoirse nodded, satisfied that she and Uiscias had a place from which to deploy the Claíomh Solais safely.

"How long will it take to climb?" Etain asked.

"On a good summer's day, about two hours, depending on how fit you are. On the outside, maybe an extra hour for groups, but you won't be climbing in the sun; you'll be climbing in the dark. You'll be masked for the whole trip, and you'll be carrying a bit more gear than hill walkers. It could take three-to-four hours up and the same coming down, under the circumstances. A word of advice – make sure you have good boots, good cold weather gear and decent gloves. Take a warm drink with you. Take breaks regularly. Use walking poles and have someone take the lead to check the ground before you commit yourselves. I know you're young and fit and well trained by the look of you, but that mountain is fickle. You'll need to look after yourselves up there."

Sean Óg turned to leave and as an afterthought added, "If you need a guide, I can take you part or all of the way up. What you do up there is your own business. The pub painted pale blue is mine. Just knock on the door if you need me. Going up there tonight is suicide. Wait until morning and take your time. Sure, I'll probably see you later at the wake."

Muireann was standing on the sidelines, and when Sean Óg left to return to his home above his pub, Muireann produced laminated maps of their route. She had obviously spent more time with Sean Óg that the team had at first realised. Muireann had cleverly attached small, push-button LEDs to the corner of each map and had fitted them with lanyards.

"I've sorted out your gear. I have trousers and waterproof overtrousers for each of you. Thermal underwear, breathable shirts and water and wind proof jackets. They came courtesy of the local adventure centre, so it's the best gear available – even better than army issue, I've been told. I know Saoirse and Etain's shoe size, so I've gotten them strong waterproof boots and thick socks – good for ankle protection. Uiscias, Morfessa and Morrigan – I got boots in several sizes for you, so hopefully you'll each find a pair that's the right size. Don't even think about going up there in sandals. I've gotten rucksacks with liners for each of you. I've put in emergency rations: a flask, torches, walkie-talkies with spare batteries from Brendan and basic first aid kits. I've also taken the liberty of stowing your weapons and ammunition and flare guns. Morfessa, your crossbow wouldn't fit, so you'll have to sling it over your shoulder. You need to tell me what else you'll need."

Morfessa smiled at Muireann, who was out of breath.

"You've done a great job. Sean Óg was right. We can't go up tonight to look around. We'll prepare our packs tonight and get some rest. We'll head off in the morning. By the way, what was the old man talking about? What's a wake?"

Etain laughed.

"A wake is a party to celebrate the dead. Either someone has died or someone is going to die. I just hope the wake isn't for us. Muireann, did he say where it was?"

Muireann smiled and shrugged her shoulders.

Chapter 47

Covert Operation

Palace Barracks in Holywood, County Down was the regimental headquarters of the Royal Irish Regiment of the British Army. It was also base to the Royal Scots Highlanders, an infantry regiment experienced in disaster relief, having previously been deployed in deployed to Sierra Leone on Operation Gritrock. Their mission: to fight an Ebola outbreak.

The barracks was no stranger to violence. It was a flash point during the troubles, and both the barracks itself and regiments that cycled through it were the targets for bombings. Palace Barracks was well known as an army base but less well known as a base for MI5, the British Intelligence Service, who used it as a headquarters during their terrorism investigations in the six counties of Northern Ireland.

The 152 Logistic Regiment had been deployed at the start of the emergency and as part of the royal logistics corps, the part-time regiment had their hands full evacuating County Antrim. Since the Northern Ireland ceasefire, the British Army had not been deployed on the streets of Belfast but under the circumstances, the Royal Scots Highlanders were once again on the streets of the capital, assisting the emergency services and providing peacekeeping services.

Reports from the Republic had been sketchy at first but this morning, the rumours of a weapon that could clear the atmosphere of carbon dioxide, sulphur dioxide and high concentrations of hydrogen sulphide, all of which were directly linked to the destruction of Iceland, were confirmed. The description of the device was clear – it was a portable laser, highly ornate casing, over a meter in length. It appeared to be remotely controlled from a handheld phone like device.

The results yielded over Dublin were spectacular according to eyewitness reports filtered through GCHQ. These reports were pored over by COBRA. COBRA was an acronym for the Civil Contingencies Committee, made up of government representatives and emergency services, intelligence agencies and military representatives, convened to handle matters of national emergency or major disruption. The thick acrid cloud of volcanic debris that had settled over the United Kingdom, the earthquakes that had decimated England and Scotland's infrastructure, and the volcanic activity in the highlands of Scotland and along the Pennine Ridge, made this the biggest single emergency that COBRA had ever confronted.

MI5's mission was to protect the United Kingdom from terrorism, espionage, cyber threats and the proliferation of weapons of mass destruction. From their perspective, although not a weapon of mass destruction, the device represented an essential asset to clear the skies over England. Instructions from COBRA had been clear. Obtaining the device was of critical importance. Already, hospitals all over the country were inundated with patients suffering from respiratory illnesses. People literally could not breathe, and it was getting worse by the second.

Although loath to invade another sovereign state, COBRA deemed that it was in the national interest to covertly enter the Republic of Ireland and retrieve the device, and time was of the essence. While attempts to enter Ireland by sea or by air were discussed, it was clear that no port of entry on the north, west or south coast was accessible. To get to the east coast, a military unit would have to travel through the Irish Sea, where the volcanic activity made the situation unpredictable. Travel by air was completely out of the question. They would have to use feet on the ground: namely, resources available in Northern Ireland.

MI5's Centre for the Protection of National Infrastructure made the mission objectives clear to the ranking security officer, Martin Turner, the most senior security officer assigned to Northern Ireland. Secure the device and get it to the UK for deployment as soon as possible. The MI5 team needed information, and Martin turned to his contacts in Irish Military Intelligence and the Gardaí – relationships painstakingly built during the troubles. They needed to find out what the device was capable of and more importantly, how they could get to it.

Getting to sources was difficult, but Turner's persistence was repaid when a ranking member of the Gardaí told him that the laser was being transported, with its handlers, to a place called Drumshanbo in County Leitrim. Luckily, County Leitrim bordered Fermanagh in Northern Ireland. Access from there to Lough Allen was easy enough. The quickest route to cut over the border passed through County Cavan, south of Enniskillen and the town was just a few miles farther on national roads.

With only hours to plan and implement the mission, Martin Turner called upon the men of the Royal Scots Highlanders. These highly trained infantrymen were no strangers to foreign infiltration. The patrol of 24 men assigned plotted a route that was thought to be clear of the worst obstructions and gathered their gear together. By late afternoon, their convoy of mismarked vehicles was on the road, heading for the border.

When the ascent team arrived back at the café with Muireann, they were escorted upstairs to an open plan mezzanine that had been repurposed into a makeshift dormitory. The nuns had been busy making up beds for each of them. Their kit bags were neatly stowed beside their lockers, and the nuns had left some chocolate and a Miraculous Medal for each of them, looped with pale-blue string.

Muireann smiled. She had not seen one of those since she made her First Communion. She explained to the travellers what they were and to her surprise, they put them on.

"We need all the help we can get," Morfessa muttered.

The rest of the team returned, with the exception of Brendan. Muireann and Saoirse were worried about their brother, thinking he might be disappointed about not being part of the team to deploy the Claíomh Solais. Esras laughed and said no; he was downstairs on the stage, playing a guitar.

Etain was too wound up to sleep and decided to join Brendan. Not to be left behind, her sisters and Sadbh followed. The lights were out downstairs, with the exception of a single spotlight, which was fixed on a drum kit older than all of them. The well-worn pedal glinted in the glare.

Brendan was playing a melancholy riff. Muireann gave him a playful punch. Brendan smiled and pointed to the corner. A second guitar and bass were propped up behind ancient speakers. Saoirse grabbed the bass guitar and began to tune it, while Muireann did the same to the second guitar. All three began to play but without amplification. Etain watched their playful antics on stage and clapped her hands loudly to get their attention.

"Are there any sticks up there?" she shouted. The others laughed.

Martin Turner and his team of elite soldiers arrived at the outskirts of Drumshanbo nearing midnight, in a convoy disguised as Irish Army vehicles. They had been waved through every checkpoint. He had been assured by his handlers that a local informant would be available to him and would make contact but with a patchy phone network, contact was near impossible. Turner hoped that control would be able to get a message through for him to rendezvous on the outskirts of town. In the meantime, the soldiers had commandeered an abandoned barn two kilometres from the town.

Martin had a total of 24 men at his disposal, all combat veterans, all Scots and experts in the guerrilla warfare that was common during the troubles in the North. All had lost friends and comrades in Northern Ireland and had little love for the Irish. In saying that, he was not sure how they felt about operating in a friendly country. They were, after all, an invasion force.

While he waited, he pored over the information he had been given. The snipers cleaned and prepared their rifles for deployment. The NCOs reviewed a detailed map of the area, and recon patrols made their way to the edge of the refugee camp and out across the lakeshore. From eyewitness reports in the Phoenix Park, he knew what the travellers looked like. From all accounts, they were totally unlike their Irish friends – they were taller, with long fair hair and covered in tattoos. There were Irish with the travellers – four women and a man – but there appeared to be nothing special about them.

His mission was to disable the party by whatever means necessary but to capture the devices operators – two teenagers. One, an Irish girl, distinctive in that her hair was dyed green. The other, a tall, red-headed boy, easily identifiable by his distinctive hairstyle. One or both of them needed to be taken alive, along with the device and its control pad. Everyone else, including the Scots Highlanders, were expendable.

Once the mission was accomplished, two vehicles would make a run back across the border into Northern Ireland and would head towards what was left of Derry and Lough Foyle. An astute class submarine would be on standby to get them aboard and away from Irish waters and back to the UK within hours. The rest of the team could make their way back to Northern Ireland under their own steam. The border was completely unmanned. Martin Turner just needed to find the team and stop them from using the device. He had been warned that under no circumstances must it be allowed to discharge.

At 3 am, the recon teams returned and reported. The Irish Army were deployed in force but were poorly armed. Sniper positions had been documented and marked on the map. They would be easy to avoid and anyway, the team was wearing authentic Irish Army uniforms and the snipers were unlikely to fire on their own. All information pointed to another discharge tomorrow morning – the reports from the Phoenix Park were clear. The travellers were operating on a strict timeline.

The boffins at GCHQ were convinced that the discharge would be staged on high ground, and the highest point around was the mountain in the near distance. Despite not knowing where the travellers and their device were, he deployed three fire teams, a full squad, to the mountain. Two fire teams would cover the most obvious approaches. The final fire team would deploy at the summit itself.

By 3.30 am, the comms check had been completed, and the fire teams had begun their march to Sliabh an Iarainn. Martin arranged for the balance of the Scotsmen to set up surveillance on the town.

The travellers each lay on their cots, not sleeping. Each was occupied by thoughts of the mission, what could go wrong and what they would do in the event of failure. They did not speak. Instead, they willed the time away. From below, a baleful Celtic melody drifted upwards. Morrigan had an idea what it was. Uiscias was entranced, as was Esras.

"What is that sound?" Esras asked quietly.

"It's Brendan," Morrigan answered.

Moments later, the drums responded, and Brendan's guitar was joined by another and the deep thrumming of a base guitar. The volume and tempo increased to produce a wall of sound.

The travellers dressed and made their way back downstairs. Brendan, Muireann, Saoirse and Etain were all on stage. The lights were bright and the old amplifier was cranked up to its highest. As the travellers walked into the café, Brendan began to sing Thin Lizzy's arrangement of *Whiskey in the Jar*.

The nuns, cleaning in the kitchen, made their way into the café and clapped and danced to the music. It did not take long for soldiers on guard duty to join them. By the second chorus, there were at least 50 people in the audience, clapping and singing along. By the end of the song, the café was full. *Whiskey in the Jar* was followed quickly by a succession of Gary Moore, Horslips and other Thin Lizzy hits. People from the camp were drawn to the music and danced and sang and laughed, despite the muggy air.

Sadbh spotted Sean Óg pushing his way through the throng. He carried half a dozen bottles of Guinness in his arms. He dumped them on the table beside Morfessa and Morrigan.

"You didn't know what a wake was when I spoke to you earlier. Well, this is as good a wake as you'll find anywhere in the country."

He handed each of them a small glass of Guinness, reserving a pint for himself.

"To success," he said.

The travellers woke at 5 am. It was not intentional, but their internal body clocks seemed to be aware of the urgency this morning. When they went downstairs. The nuns were there again, pouring hot tea from a gigantic teapot and placing hot food on the table. While the others got something to eat, Sadbh filled the ascent team's flasks with hot sweet tea and made each of them carry a high carb snack. She pushed protein bars into each backpack.

Etain said nothing, she arranged her weapon, which she wore in a sling across her chest. Morrigan carried the Claíomh Solais diagonally across in chest in a harness. Overnight, a local leather worker and his team had fashioned a leather harness for the Claíomh Solais, based on photographs and measurements supplied by Jack Kelly. Somehow, they had replicated the Celtic motifs on the device exactly. The harness was a work of art. The modern survival gear changed how Morfessa looked. He could easily have passed for an elite ranger; such was his bearing. He rapidly checked each pack to make sure that they had their essentials.

Uiscias and Saoirse looked like children playing dress up. Their clothes looked at least a few sizes too big, and their young faces shone out from under heavy woollen caps. They each donned full-face respirator masks before leaving the building and setting out to the edge of the mountain, in transport provided by their army escort. They left the building via a secluded side entrance and were watched over by an armed guard.

Despite consuming a vat of Guinness, Sean Óg was leaning against the lead landrover, smoking a pipe.

"Great day for it," he shouted in greeting.

To maintain security, each landrover, with blacked-out windows, left the shrouded laneway individually and took a different route through the town. By 6.30 am, the convoy had re-established itself and was heading to Sliabh an Iarainn.

Chapter 48

The Early Birds

Muireann, Brendan, Esras, Sadbh and Semias watched them leave. Sadbh silently whispered a decade of the Rosary for their safe return.

"What do we do now?" Sadbh asked.

Brendan replied, "Esras and I need to go down to the comms centre by the lake. We'll be in contact with them once they set off on the climb. We need to be close in case anything goes wrong, and they need our help. You three should get some rest."

Sadbh shrugged.

"I'm too wound up to rest, Brendan. I won't go with you, because I'd get in the way."

She looked at Semias and Muireann.

"Maybe we should help with the refugees – you know, get them settled. The reception centre is undermanned, and the children will be very upset. It would take our minds off things. It's nearly seven. The nuns might need some help with breakfast."

Semias nodded and gave a resigned sigh.

Muireann and Sadbh spent the next hour dealing with lost children, fetching bottles for screaming babies and finding places for the elderly to rest. Semias handed out blankets, carried drums of water and even cleaned the bathrooms.

By 7 am there was still no sighting of the travellers or of an army convoy to transport them. If the travellers had left the town under cover, Turner needed to find out where they went.

Martin Turner had missed the departure of Etain, Saoirse, Morfessa, Morrigan and Uiscias – that much was clear. He cursed silently. He knew from his briefing that there were others involved with the device. He stayed in the undergrowth of the café's car park until he saw Brendan and Esras emerge. They were surrounded by an Irish Army squad and were ushered into a fleet of waiting vehicles.

The British soldiers would be unable to overpower that many armed Irishmen, so Martin kept his cover in place. It was ten minutes later that Sadbh, Semias and Muireann emerged from the building and set off towards the centre of town on foot, wearing heavy clothing and breathing equipment. This was Martin's opportunity to find out where Morfessa and Uiscias had headed with the Claíomh Solais. He could not take them: there were too many people around, and he did not want to alert the Irish Army to his intent.

The British spy and his cohort of men followed the walkers and watched them enter the refugee centre. Using binoculars, the British observed them for nearly an hour before Turner gave the order. There was no gunfire, just some shouting and a bit of a kerfuffle. There were a few army privates in the local church that served as the reception centre, but they had not been armed. They were easily overcome by the soldiers of the Royal Scots Highlanders, who used chemicals to knock them out. Their faces were masked with rebreathers, but their Edinburgh accents gave them away. Despite their menacing looks, the armed men did their best to reassure the refugees that their intent was peaceful.

"We just came to collect a few people, and we'll be on our way," their leader said, in a broad Lothian accent.

Sadbh, Muireann and Semias knew that the soldiers were there for them.

"Etain and the others should be halfway up the mountain," Sadbh whispered. "We need to buy them some time."

Sadbh and Muireann stepped forward, flanking Semias.

Sadbh said gently, "It's us you have come for. Let's take this outside."

The soldiers did not try to move towards them but rather, motioned to the church porch. Once outside, the soldiers held their accuracy international rifles at their sides. There was no need to hide them. They were, after all, the same model that the Irish Army used.

Sadbh, Semias and Muireann were directed towards a Mercedes Benz troop carrier that carried Irish registration plates and the insignia of an Irish regiment. Once on board, the troops positioned themselves near the back of the carrier blocking their exit. There had been no time to raise an alarm, and no one would notice another group of armed men when Irish soldiers were milling about the town.

Sadbh hoped that the Irish soldiers recovered quickly and were able to raise the alarm. Her thoughts were with Esras and Brendan in the comms centre by the lake. If the British soldiers got to them, then the location of Saoirse, Etain, Morfessa, Morrigan and Uiscias – and with them, the Claíomh Solais – would be given away.

Semias, Muireann and Sadbh huddled closely on a bench behind the cab. Their guards were several feet away and the canvas sides provided no sound insulation from road noise. Their whispered conversation could not be overheard.

Semias whispered, "They've come for the Claíomh Solais. If they get it now, Ireland won't have a chance. It will be taken to wherever they have come from. Morrigan, Etain and Morfessa will kill to defend it and will, more than likely, die in the process. We've got to do something."

Sadbh reached out, touched his arm and shook her head.

"No Semias, we'd be foolish to try. These men may be restrained at the moment, but they have a mission too. They won't hesitate to pull the trigger if we force them to. We're going to buy our side some time. Hopefully, enough time for the Irish Army to realise that we're under attack and enough time for Uiscias and Saoirse to power up the Claíomh Solais. We need to send the Brits on a wild goose chase."

Sadbh thought for a few minutes, desperately trying to recall her college engineering classes.

"Do you know anything about reflection and refraction?"

Semias made a face.

"I know what refraction is, and I know what reflection is. I know some of the basic science. Why?"

"It doesn't matter Semias, just follow my lead."

They were taken outside of the town to a spot on the lakeshore. The troop carrier drove into the parking lot of the remote Cormongan Pier, on the shore of Lough Allen.

Martin Turner was waiting for them. He smiled politely.

"Thank You for coming here to meet me. I think you know what we are here for. We would like your laser and the team that operate it. Time is of the essence, and there are a lot of lives at stake, so I won't beat about the bush – where are they?"

With prodding from the barrel of a gun, Sadbh answered him.

"You said there are a lot of British lives at stake. There are a lot of Irish lives at stake right here, including yours. Why should I tell you anything?"

Martin motioned to his team, who grabbed Muireann.

"Perhaps you won't be so flippant if we go to work on your daughter."

Despite being held by two burly soldiers, Muireann held her head high. She refused to be afraid.

Sadbh shouted at Turner with all the spite that she could muster.

"And maybe you wouldn't be so cocky if you had any idea of what the people on this side of the border will do to you when you're caught. You do realise this is an invasion of a peaceful country?"

The slap that Sadbh received knocked her to the ground, and she landed at Turner's feet.

"You bloody Irish are always so melodramatic. I spent years in the North during the troubles. I'm going to use the same tricks on your comrades here that you lot used on us. I'm not going to start with kneecapping. I'm going to go for stigmata. The IRA would shoot people through the hands and feet, mirroring the injuries of Christ on the Cross – very Catholic. Feet first as they say."

The report of the rifle was loud and Muireann screamed. Turner let the rifle drop to his side. Sadbh's instincts were to howl in pain, but she somehow kept quiet as the pain radiated up her left leg.

She looked up at Martin and said quietly, "It's fashionable to have a matching pair."

As Martin raised the gun, Semias pulled himself free from the guard holding him. He headrushed Martin and took a bullet to the gut. He fell where he was shot and dragged himself over to Sadbh. He pulled himself up and sat with his back resting against a bolder.

Understanding that Sadbh would not talk, a second shot directed at her rang out. Sadbh looked down at the blood pooling at her feet.

Turner waited for her to open up.

"They are my kids," she said simply.

One of the soldiers holding Muireann looked away from the scene in disgust. One of the others guarding the car park threw his gun down and cursed. Sadbh reminded him of his own mother.

"The next shot will shatter your kneecap. I'm not going to hurt your children – I just want the device," Turner shouted.

Sadbh looked at Muireann, who was sobbing.

"They went to the north side of the lake to check the reflective and refractive index of the water. They need to find a perfect location near water or the device won't work," Sadbh gasped.

The air quality and pain made it difficult for her to speak.

"Bullshit – where are they?"

Turner focussed on Sadbh's left knee.

"I'm not lying. Look, I work in an office. What would an old woman like me know about technology. I'm just repeating what I was told. They need a flat-water surface for the laser to work properly. They have to find the correct location to discharge the device."

"For fuck sake! It worked in the middle of the Phoenix Park." Turner screamed.

Semias took this as his cue to take over and weave a web of mistruths.

"That's not true. The device was set off at the edge of the park, near the wall that encloses it. On the far side of the wall is the River Liffey. It flows parallel to the park. The discharge was elevated, and the water was used to reflect the beam."

"That's crap! We have a first-hand report from an eyewitness," Martin countered.

"It's not crap," Semias shouted, the effort to speak through his pain clear. "I am the commander of this mission and have a team of highly trained scientists working with me. Forty per cent of the laser power is radiated downwards, reducing the effectiveness of the discharge immensely. To counteract this, we raise the laser near a body of water and when conditions cause the water surface to be mirror-like, we discharge. We must achieve specular reflection – that is when the light is reflected at the same angle as it hit the water. This is how we maximise power upwards, towards the volcanic ash cloud. Now the test conditions were not ideal, but it was only a test, with the power setting at twenty per cent. If we tried to operate the laser without a body of water to reflect the power, the ground around the site would superheat, causing the destruction of the laser and since it's the only one we have, we need it working."

Martin and the soldiers went into a huddle and could be heard arguing over Semias's explanation. The debate raged for several minutes.

"Explain it again," Turner demanded.

Semias asked for a pen and paper and drew a series of diagrams to illustrate specular reflection. Since Martin and his platoon had not seen the discharge in the park and had nothing to compare the explanation to, they were left in a quandary.

Semias went through his explanation a second time, adding flourishes.

"Again, the body of water acts like a mirror. That is what specular reflection is – mirror-like reflection. This only works with clear water. If the water is polluted, the effect won't work. That's why this body of water is so important – the water here is perfectly clean. The flat surface of the water reflects the laser's energy upwards, rather than absorbing it. Irregular shapes, such as the mountains and bogs around here, absorb light. The water however, when calm, acts like a perfect surface. The angle of beam radiation is the same as incident light radiation emitted by the laser. The laser's wavelength is unchanged when it bounces off the water's surface, and its energy is not diminished."

Martin Turner went back to his vehicle and contacted headquarters. Nearly half an hour passed before he returned. The guards, unsure of what to do next, gave Semias, Muireann and Sadbh space. Released from the soldier's grip, Muireann ran to her mother.

Turner wasted no time in contacting the British authorities. Once through to his handlers, he sent through a recording of the interrogation of Semias and images of the drawings that he made. MI5 accessed technical boffins from the Defence Science and Technology Laboratory (to be exact the team from Command, Control, Communication and Computers, Intelligence, Surveillance and Reconnaissance, known as C4ISR).

Amazingly, the experts understood the phenomena that Semias had described and did not disagree with him. The experts put information gaps and anomalies in data down to the fact that a non-scientist had completed the interview. It was understandable as Semias was, in fact, the project leader, not part of the engineering team controlling the device. Without knowing how the device operated, its radiation pattern and power, they could not make a full assessment of the device, but it was plausible that specular reflection could be used to enhance the weapons focus.

It was now possible that Semias, Muireann and Sadbh were telling the truth. Turner would have to base his next move on the data from his captives.

Martin stood over Sadbh with his gun aimed at her head.

"Where did they go to carry out the tests?"

"One of the locals took them to a place on the northwest side of the lake. It's called Spenser Harbour. There's a small man-made island off the shore, a crannog. That's where their doing the testing," Sadbh whispered.

Sadbh prayed that she remembered the name of the little island correctly. She had seen it last night on a tourist map of the lake.

Martin tilted his chin to the transport and ordered the driver to plot a route. Two soldiers remained behind, guns trained on Sadbh, Muireann and Semias.

"If you've lied, we'll be back. You won't get far," Martin shouted as he sprinted towards an Irish-flagged Toyota Land Cruiser.

Muireann, Sadbh and Semias watched the vehicle pull away and stayed perfectly still until the engine was out of earshot.

"Have we bought them enough time?" Sadbh whispered.

Chapter 49

The Ascent

The first part of the ascent of Sliabh an Iarainn went fairly smoothly. Sean Óg, despite himself, had been waiting for them. He said that he would take them to the base of the mountain but in actual fact, he guided them halfway to the top, over the worst of the ground. He shook hands with them and wished them luck before starting his descent.

Saoirse held Uiscias's hand.

"Do you think that old man will be okay alone. It's so hard to see where you're going?"

Uiscias gave her a hug.

"That man is like a mountain goat. He could find his way down blindfolded," he laughed.

Despite the fact that the sun rose early in August, the sky was dark and the air swilled around them, pregnant with ash. Sean Óg had been correct about the cold. In the last half hour, the temperature had plummeted.

Etain called everyone together.

"It's time to take a break before we make the final push up the mountain."

Morrigan found the perfect resting place, a crack in the cliff face that protected them from the strong winds. Their hands were numb and no one had feeling in their faces or feet. Saoirse was shivering, both from excitement and from cold.

They were all wearing head torches and removed them before settling down into the natural alcove. Morfessa was the last to join the huddle, carefully taking the harness from Morrigan and resting the Claíomh Solais on a rocky outcrop. Etain broke some light sticks that bathed the rock fissure in green light. They each retrieved their flasks and let the hot liquid revive them. They were grateful for the energy bars that Sadbh had made them take.

Saoirse pulled the radio from her backpack and set the channel. Brendan answered her call immediately.

"We're approaching the summit now. We're less than an hour away. We're just taking a short break for something hot to drink. It's freezing up here."

Brendan's reply was broken by static, but they caught parts of the transmission – enemies, kidnapping and search. Morfessa, Uiscias, Morrigan and Etain huddled closer to the radio.

"Brendan, you're breaking up. Can you repeat please?"

"They took Semias, Muireann and Mam, and they're trying to find you. For God's sake be careful – we don't know how many of them there are. We're sending a team up the mountain to protect you, but they will be nearly two hours behind you."

Saoirse signed off on behalf of the team.

Etain was the first to speak.

"We can't worry about anyone down below right now. We need to focus on the mission, okay? Mam and Muireann are resourceful, and they have the whole of the Irish Army looking for them."

They nodded in agreement. Morfessa pulled Etain close to him and hugged her. Saoirse sobbed quietly into Uiscias's shoulder.

Etain composed herself quickly. She did not feel vulnerable. She was angry. Who the hell were these people, kidnapping innocents? She understood that they were after the Claíomh Solais and was going to do her best to make sure they did not get it. Her adrenaline spiked and suddenly, she was injected with a surge of strength. She no longer felt cold. An internal heater kicked in.

Morfessa noticed the change in Etain immediately. He peered into her face and in the dim green light of the glow stick, he was sure he could see golden swirls in her blue eyes.

Before Morfessa could say anything, Etain jumped to her feet.

"They won't be able to see us up here, with the air being so hazy, so unless they are within twenty feet, we're safe for the moment. Take off anything brightly coloured. We need to camouflage ourselves. Leave everything we don't need right here – we're not carrying excess weight. Morrigan, you and I both know what we would do if we were them. We'd plant snipers and assault teams on the routes to the summit and on the summit itself. I will take the lead. One of us on the left, one on the right. Morfessa, guard Uiscias and Saoirse. Don't move until we clear a path for you."

Luckily, most of their clothing was of army issue, but hats and gloves had fluorescent panels. Etain had taken a folding knife with her and cut away the bright strips on the clothing, not caring if she cut into the fabric. She buried the scraps in a hole burrowed in the gravel.

Morfessa made his way to the edge of the cliff and surveyed their surroundings. On his return, he crouched beside the rest of the team and drank the warm tea that was left in his flask.

"There is nothing moving out there that I can see. There could be snipers in position, but they won't shoot if there are. It's too risky – they could hit the Claíomh Solais. If there's anyone out there, we need to make as little noise as possible and stay low. Are you ready?"

They nodded in agreement.

Morrigan moved to the right, Etain to the left. The going was slower but steady. Morrigan used hand signals to alert the team if she spotted something. Etain moved like a wild animal, low and stealthy. In minutes, she was at Morrigan's side.

"There are four of them: two burrowed down in the heather, one hidden by the peat ridge and one sniper on top of the rocky outcrop."

Etain saw them instantly. She gestured to Morrigan and then, the sniper and the ranger hidden by the ridge. She pointed at herself and then, the two gunmen in the heather. Morrigan understood and nodded.

As soon as Morrigan had confirmed, Etain took off at speed. Although fast, her footwork was light, bounding between culverts and over morass. Etain judged her position well. On her last jump, she planted her right foot on the first gunman's neck, breaking it instantly. She rolled and brought a straight forearm down on the second gunman's trachea, leaving him to suffocate. He had no time to shout a warning. She never broke stride. From the roll, she flexed and was running again.

Morrigan was as stealthy as Etain, although her preferred weapon was a knife. She left the soldier bleeding out on the peat ridge.

Both women reached the sniper's nest at the same moment, both calm and breathing normally. The sniper was viewing a target through his scope and never registered the kick under his chin that immobilised him.

Morrigan grabbed him by the hair and whispered in his ear, "How many?"

He could barely reply.

"Four on the summit; four more on the other side."

Morrigan wrenched his neck, severing his spinal cord.

Morrigan and Etain made their way back to Uiscias, Morfessa and Saoirse.

"We've taken care of four of them. There are eight more: four on the summit and four on the other side of the mountain. They covered both routes," Morrigan whispered.

"What's more, they're in contact with each other," Etain added. "Get Brendan on the radio now."

Saoirse fumbled with the radio but managed to raise her brother. Etain grabbed the handset.

"Brendan, it's time for the hummingbirds to sing."

"Gotcha, five minutes," Brendan responded.

Etain took the radio and removed the battery. She flung it to the side.

"Brendan is going to block their radio signal. From here on out, it's radio silence."

Brendan dropped the microphone and roared for Esras. Both men sped from the comms centre to their commandeered landrover. Brendan dragged a heavy case from the rear and began undoing the catches.

"What do you need?" Esras asked.

"You know that base station that we modified as a jammer? Get it for me, and grab the heatsink it's sitting on. We're going to make that baby fly!"

Esras rushed back to Brendan, who was assembling a professional drone. Quickly, Esras mounted the heatsink onto the base of the drone, while Brendan was jerry-rigging a power supply for the base station. In minutes, the drone, with operational jamming device, was ready for launch. On launch, it would immediately disrupt all radio signals in its vicinity. Any two-way radio on the mountain would cease to function.

While Esras prepared a launch site, Brendan sent word to command – the ascent team were under attack.

The drone hovered like an angry wasp and using the joystick and camera, Brendan moved it deftly towards the summit. When it was in position, he handed it over to a soldier to control.

"Keep it moving over the area. Make sure the snipers can't shoot it down," he roared.

A light drizzle had descended as they approached the summit, the gentle rain stinging their faces due to its chemical content. Before they were in sight of the pinnacle, Morrigan halted everyone.

"The rain is acidic. It's absorbed chemicals from the volcanic dust. Get your goggles on," Etain shouted.

As Saoirse rummaged through her pack, she shot a look at Uiscias.

"Will the device work in the rain?" she asked.

"It survived that hole in the ground in Donegal just fine. A little rain won't kill it," he said, smiling.

Saoirse smiled back at him.

Chapter 50

Fool's Errand

Turner and the Royal Scots were on the move. After abandoning Sadbh, Muireann and Semias at the side of the lake, they set out on a route to Spenser Harbour. They had no choice but to follow the lakeshore in a clockwise direction, and this lost them valuable time. It took them more than an hour to make the journey. Luckily, the area was well signposted.

From the little pier, they could see the crannog, but there were no visible signs of activity. Turner ordered two men into the water, and they swam to the man-made island, built on wooden foundations piled into the lakebed during the Neolithic age. The soldiers emerged into the dense foliage that engulfed the crannog. In minutes, they gave the all-clear. The island was deserted. Turner and his men lost further time searching up and down the shoreline.

"When the fuck are they?" Turner shouted.

If they were not on the lake, Turner realised that they must be on the mountain. Rushing back to their vehicles, he radioed the fire teams. All he could hear was static – the radio did not work.

Turner flung the microphone at the steering wheel and screamed at the comms specialist. He confirmed that the radio had worked only hours before.

"We've been played for fools," he screamed.

Chapter 51

The Hunters and the Hunted

As Turner was reaching the crannog, Morrigan was stealthily approaching the fire team on the other side of the mountain. While the soldiers were expecting movement from below, they neglected to monitor the ground above their position. Using her dagger, Morrigan immobilised the sniper first and then, the remaining three soldiers, all without a making a noise.

Etain crawled through the bog leading to the summit. Despite the rain and poor visibility, the plateau was visible. There were no high vantage points from which a sniper could base himself. The men were dug into the bog and rock. Etain could hear a buzzing noise above her and searched the sky. She could see Brendan's drone barely. It was whizzing back and forth in a random pattern over the mountaintop. She needed to change her location to get a better view and primed herself to move forward. As she raised her torso, the ground beneath her gave way and she screamed involuntarily. She had no choice but to throw herself to safety.

In that split second, the fire team had her in their sights. Despite their instruction not to open fire on the travellers, Etain felt first one and then, a second bullet graze her face and neck. She felt no pain, just a surge of adrenaline unlike anything she had ever felt before. Time slowed. She observed a third bullet heading directly for her and gently dropped her shoulder and head. She could see the trajectory and looked directly at the face of the man who had made the shot, more than 200 yards away. The third bullet was still in the air as she vaulted from her position and charged over the boggy landscape, at a speed that she knew was impossible. Using a gun seemed irrelevant. She did not need one: she had her hands.

She snapped the sniper's neck before he had a chance to pull the trigger for the fourth time. Waiting no more than a heartbeat, she ducked and rolled to cover. Her hearing was now so acute that she could hear hares running over the heather. Locating the next target was easy, she focussed on his breathing, which was amplified by his mask. A punch to the sternum literally stopped his heart. She exhaled slowly and cocked her head. Number three was mere feet away, unaware of what had become of his comrades. Etain crushed his temple under her boot.

Etain could hear her heart beating. It was steady. So was her breathing. She scanned the summit for the final Scot and saw movement in the corner of her eye – and then, a streak of red. It was followed by a high-pitched keening, which was loud enough to be painful. Not knowing if this presented a danger to Saoirse and Uiscias, she leapt like a wolf through the uneven surface and found the source of the noise. It was Morrigan, and she was holding the severed head of the final member of the fire team. She was grinning like a maniac and howling like a banshee. Morrigan threw the head that she was holding. It landed in marshland and quickly sank from view.

"Nice going," Morrigan said.

"I could say the same to you," Etain replied. "What about the other team?"

Morrigan smiled at Etain.

"Met their maker in the same was as these guys."

Etain made to shake hands but instead, Morrigan grabbed her into a sisterly embrace. They made their way back to where Morfessa, Saoirse and Uiscias waited.

Within twenty minutes, Etain, Morrigan, Uiscias, Saoirse and Morfessa reached the edge of the summit. They switched from walking to a crouched shamble, to minimise their profiles, just in case there were further enemies on the mountain. They reached the plateau of Sliabh an Iarainn, a relatively flat, boggy surface. Visibility was poor, and they set about searching for the low concrete plinth that held the trig point.

Etain spotted it and rather than shouting, she made her way to each member of the team and used hand signals to point the way. She led the team forward, but she missed her footing and tripped. She used backward momentum to stop herself falling and stood erect for only a moment. Immediately, a shot rang out from her left. She felt the pressure from the bullet on her shoulder. She had been lucky again. If she had not tilted her torso, it would have been a perfect kill shot. On instinct, Etain dropped to the ground, using hand signals to tell the others to follow suit. She prayed that the others had done the same. Etain's heart was beating wildly. Her adrenalin levels spiked. Her body was ready for fight or flight. For the third time that day, she felt an energy fizz up inside her, only this time, it was much more powerful.

Saoirse, Uiscias and Morfessa had all dropped down when they heard the gunshot. Uiscias and Saoirse were to the right of Etain; Morfessa, a few hundred meters directly behind her and Morrigan, to her left. Morfessa scanned the area looking for the source of the bullet. Another shot rang out, aimed in the other direction. They heard a loud crash.

"The drone is down, Morrigan. Their radios are now working," Morfessa screamed.

Etain quickly calculated the trajectory of the shot. Crawling over the boggy surface, she reoriented herself. Her eyesight had always been good, but it seemed more acute now, and she spotted the sniper, partially camouflaged by a peat mound.

In a lupine movement, Etain bounded over the heather on all fours, circling the snipper. She placed her hands on his head and neck before he registered her presence. She twisted sharply, severing his spine.

She stayed crouched, not moving. In the stillness of the mountaintop, she could faintly hear a voice – it was coming from the headset that the sniper had been wearing. She pulled the headset from the soldier and put it on. It was another enemy gunman. He had heard the shot fired and was asking for an update. He reported no activity near the sheep track. Etain waited to hear if there was anyone else on the channel, but there was no activity. She pressed the transmit button twice to acknowledge the message, hoping that the remaining assailant would take this as a sign that everything was under control. During combat, a sniper would not talk, for fear of giving away his or her location. Not responding by voice would not be viewed suspiciously.

Etain still had the little map Muireann had given her, secured on its lanyard. She could see the sheep track on the map and knew it trailed downward off the mountain. Without thinking, Etain sprinted across the mountain, out of range of the other gunman, her ears acutely listening for sound of movement. Her instincts took over. She sniffed the air for the sniper's scent. A mountain hare ran across her path, giving her vision a new target. And then she had him. He had readjusted his position when the hare ran past.

Etain approached him from behind, using her stealth to inflict a jarring blow to the temple using her fist. The soldier struggled with her, but Etain's strength was supernatural. She hit him repeatedly in the chest, breaking ribs and sternum. She only stopped when she could no longer hear him breathing.

She stood and looked down at her hands – she was bleeding but felt no pain. She wiped them on her jacket. She felt perfectly calm as she made her way back to Morfessa, Morrigan, Uiscias and Saoirse. Morrigan was on the prowl, searching the mountain for further threats. They were still crouching low when she called out to them, her voice several octaves deeper than it had been minutes before.

"The threat is neutralised. We're safe," she shouted.

As they approached her, each of them stared at her face. Her eyes glowed. As they looked closely, they could see a radiant ring of gold in each iris, surrounding the deep blue of her eyes. Morfessa asked her if she was okay and Etain waved him off. He was concerned that this was the effect of the nanites in her system, but he also understood that this was not the time or place to ask questions.

Once again, they located the trig point in the rock-strewn mire. Uiscias carefully removed the Claíomh Solais from the harness and handed it to Saoirse, who unwrapped it reverently. Etain, Morrigan and Morfessa's part of the mission was over. The fate of Ireland now rested on two nerdy teenagers.

Saoirse and Uiscias carefully positioned the Claíomh Solais on the concrete plinth. They checked that the device was perfectly vertical before setting the power level to maximum.

Before they retreated, Esras and Morfessa had agreed that people on the ground should be given a warning before the discharge.

Saoirse and Uiscias waited while Morfessa, Morrigan and Etain radioed the communications centre with a 30-second warning. A few seconds after ending the report, all four could hear the plaintive wail of an air-raid siren in the distance.

They all backed away from the concrete plinth and found shelter a few hundred meters away in a deep crevasse. With a nod from Morfessa, they turned away from the Claíomh Solais and Uiscias and Saoirse activated it.

The beam of light was searing. A shockwave followed immediately, knocking them from their feet and throwing them like ragdolls. It radiated down the side of the mountain; its ferocity and strength growing as it descended. The sonic boom that accompanied it burst the ascent teams eardrums; such was the loudness. They all lapsed into unconsciousness.

Chapter 52

Tomorrow Is a New Day

In Drumshanbo, the refugees and locals had been warned of what was to come with seconds to spare. Everyone had found shelter but even a few kilometres away, the power of the blast could be felt. The shockwave tumbled cars, lifted rooves and flattened outhouses for kilometres around. The tented city, so painstakingly erected, collapsed in flurry of support struts and canvas. Despite protection, people were dazed, blinded and deafened. However, there were no reports of serious injury. The skies were the clearest they had ever been – bright and pristine. The device had worked.

The discharge of the Claíomh Solais had taken Muireann, Sadbh and Semias's guards by surprise. They were on their feet in the open when the shockwave hit, violently throwing them into ragged boulders. While not dead, they were close to it. Semias, Sadbh and Muireann were prepared when they heard the sirens in the distance. They lay flat on the ground and covered their heads and ears. When it was over, they made their escape. Muireann helped her mother to stand and then gently got Semias to his feet. They hobbled slowly in the direction of Sliabh an Iarainn.

Minutes after the discharge, once senses had returned, the Irish Army launched a search mission for Etain, Saoirse, Morrigan, Morfessa and Uiscias. Soldiers, accompanied by local guides, including Sean Óg, who now regretted leaving the young people alone on the mountain, headed out to the base of Sliabh an Iarainn, taking the road to Cormongan. They had nearly reached the staging point for the ascent when the convoy abruptly stopped.

The lead vehicle had spotted Semias, Muireann and Sadbh stumbling down the road. Brendan and Esras left the jeep they were travelling in and walked up to see what was going on. When they reached the top of the column, they saw the trio stumbling towards them.

They ran to Sadbh and literally carried her back to the lead vehicle. Muireann and Semias followed, supported by Irish soldiers. After hugging his mother and sister, Brendan stood aside to allow Esras to administer aid to the gunshot wounds that his mother had suffered, while the army medical corps tended to Semias.

With Semias, Sadbh and Muireann on board, there was no room for Esras and Brendan. The medics in the landrover assured them that their patients would be well cared for.

Once safely loaded into an army jeep, Muireann could not help herself.

"Where the hell did all that stuff about light reflection come from?" she asked.

Sadbh and Semias laughed.

"Your mother prompted me, and I have spent years around scientists, so maybe something rubbed off after all," Semias laughed.

"But was it real? I mean, is the science real?" she implored.

"I have no idea. I used bits that I knew were true and weaved them into a lie. It's what politicians do," he answered.

Brendan and Esras ran to Sadbh's jeep once the convoy came to a halt. Brendan told his mother that he was going up with the rescue party to find his sisters.

"Don't worry Mam, I'll bring them back in one piece."

But Sadbh did worry. She had felt the effect of the discharge from kilometres away. Her daughters had been in close proximity. With a force that strong, it was likely that they were injured or worse.

It took less than an hour to reach the summit, the bright sunlight making the ascent seem like a pleasant ramble. A snaking line of mountain rescue personnel, local guides, armed soldiers and medics made their way up the mountain, replete with stretchers, radios and medical equipment.

It took another ten minutes for Brendan, accompanied by Esras, to find Morfessa, Morrigan, Etain, Saoirse and Uiscias. Esras knelt beside them in turn and brought them around.

Although groggy, Morfessa was keen to know if the device had succeeded.

"You can rest easy. Clear skies from coast to coast. Military communications have confirmed that the ash cloud has been cleared completely. This is the first time in history that Ireland has absolutely no cloud cover," he laughed.

Morfessa laid back on the heather and breathed a sigh of relief.

The army medics were happy to report to Saoirse that Muireann, Sadbh and Semias were located and were in good spirits. The news quickly spread across the mountain.

Saoirse and Uiscias had both suffered damage to their eardrums but apart from deafness suffered, no further ill effects. They would have bad headaches for quite some time. Both of them were in high spirits, hugging and laughing. Neither answered questions: partly because they could not hear them and partly, because they were preoccupied.

Morfessa stood in front of a reclined Etain and held out his hand. She took it and pulled herself up. He stared into her eyes. The golden halo was still visible but had faded.

"What happened to you?" he asked.

"I don't know. I think something else took over. I have never been faster or stronger or calmer for that matter. Everything seemed to be moving in slow motion. It felt like I had supernatural powers. I know that sounds silly, but that's what it felt like."

Morfessa nodded.

"I think it might be because of the blood transfusion. The nanites we gave you activate when your body is under stress, and the snipers may have been a trigger. I'm sorry, but I can't tell you what effect they will have, as we simply don't know."

Etain sighed.

"It doesn't matter, Morfessa. Without the infusion, we'd all be dead and so would all of the people down there," she said, pointing down the mountain.

"I know I'll have to deal with what I did to those soldiers but right now, I don't regret it, and I'd do it again."

Morfessa put his arms around her and held her close to him.

"They were invaders in your country, and they started this war. The war isn't over, but we definitely won this battle."

Morfessa and Etain's moment did not last long. Seconds later, they heard Morrigan bellowing.

"For God's sake! How many Brits were there? We've accounted for fourteen – three teams of four and those two, but there could be hundreds. The Claíomh Solais is not safe," she screamed.

Morrigan was, of course, correct.

A message was quickly relayed to the command centre, and troops were deployed to find the British base of operations. The answer came before the ascent team were evacuated from the mountain.

The British base had been found and following a fire fight with Irish Army Rangers, six Scots Highlanders had surrendered. The captives made full disclosure about their mission and the make-up of the team. There were four commandos still at large, led by Martin Turner from M15.

Before descending the mountain, Uiscias and Saoirse made sure that a protective detail was deployed around the Claíomh Solais, which was charging in the sunshine. Hundreds of troops had ascended the mountain and formed protective inner and outer rings around the device. Further troops were deployed on the access routes and around the base of the mountain. All were heavily armed.

Dismissing the rescue team and offers of support, Etain, Saoirse, Morrigan, Morfessa and Uiscias descended the mountain under their own steam, the only support accepted was the use of some walking poles. They could have made it down quicker but decided that it was best to take it slow, until their hearing improved.

As they made their way through the staging area, they were swamped by soldiers and civilians offering their congratulations and thanks. By the time they reached the heart of Drumshanbo, refugees were clamouring to see them and cheered them into town. At the comms centre, the crowd was so thick that the jeeps that they were travelling in had difficulty getting through.

The ascent team had an emotional reunion with Sadbh, Semias and Muireann, each relieved that the others were safe. Brendan and Esras were there to support them and were, in turn, congratulated for their work in jamming the British radios – which had proved to be critical to the success of the mission. The command centre updated them on the status of the missing MI5 agent and his crew of commandos, which dampened spirits. Capturing the invaders was now the single biggest priority for both Gardaí and the Irish Army.

All ten of them were exhausted and too tired to debrief the military and government liaisons, so it was decided that they should get some rest. Instead of heading for the meagre comforts of the café, they were taken instead to the Lough Allen Hotel, just outside of the town. Jack Kelly let Etain know that it was on the orders of the President.

The rooms had been allocated to government ministers, who were now dispersed to various campsites around the town. On arrival, each was given a key to an executive suite. With power restored to the building, the showers were operating. The rooms were supplied with extra towels and robes. Food was presented by the room service team, who included a bottle of champagne and a glass of local whiskey on each tray. The travellers were informed that clean clothes and footwear would be delivered to them and left outside their door, ready for them to collect whenever they wanted.

Etain stared out of the window of her suite at the pristine lake below. She caught her reflection in the mirror. Her hair was plastered to her head by muck and dirt. Her face and hands were smeared with peat and the odd bits of heather. She could see blood spatter on her clothes and skin. She caught hold of herself. She acknowledged the fact that she had killed but refused to be guilty. She had nothing to be guilty for. She grabbed the little bottles of shampoo and body wash from the counter in the bathroom and turned on the waterfall shower. Before she slept, she wanted to be clean.

In the adjacent room, Morfessa listened to happy voices from along the corridor. Shrieks and laughs were followed by the popping of a champagne cork. He smiled to himself, hoping that Uiscias and Saoirse would not get themselves into too much trouble, but what if they did? As long as they did not hurt each other or anyone else, they had a right to celebrate. Morfessa suddenly felt old. He checked the clock; it was not yet noon. He showered quickly and used every bottle of soap that had been laid out. Even with scrubbing, it took an age to remove the layer of grime that had accumulated on the mountaintop. When he put on the robe, he closed the curtains and sat down on the side of the bed. In seconds, he was in a deep sleep.

For the next few hours, the travellers and the McNamara family were free to rest and recuperate. Mostly, they spent the afternoon sleeping. The sun was dimming, but the sky was still bright when they were roused.

At 7 pm, they were all requested to join guests in the function room of the hotel. The remnants of the Government were there – the Irish Prime Minister or Taoiseach; the Tánaiste, his second of command; the Ministers of Defence, Foreign Affairs and Finance and a rag tag bunch of junior ministers and public representatives. The Garda Commissioner, senior judges and the heads of emergency services filled the room.

The travellers quickly spotted Jack and asked him for an update on the Claíomh Solais. Jack brought them outside, where the summit of Sliabh an Iarainn was brightly floodlit. Even from a distance, the military presence on the mountain was clear.

He reassured them that there had been no further incursions, and the Claíomh Solais was perfectly safe. The guards would be in place on the mountain for the foreseeable future.

He also let them know that the army had found an army jeep containing foreign soldiers at the lakeside. Evidently, it had been caught up in the shockwave after the activation of the Claíomh Solais. With nothing standing in the way of the wave, the jeep had apparently been thrown violently over rough terrain. All of the passengers were dead. The passengers had been identified as British soldiers from their dog tags. A civilian was also found with them and it was assumed, from his description, that he was Martin Turner, a senior MI5 agent. Before Jack could say anything else, a junior officer summoned them inside the function room.

It was President Brosnin who stepped forward to congratulate the travellers, followed closely by Jack Kelly and Peter Clancy from the Irish Army. Floating around the edges of the room, a couple of journalists and a reporter from RTÉ News covered the event, which would be the main feature on tonight's news. RTÉ was using a mobile studio rigged to a makeshift transmitter to provide a limited local service.

The room was hushed and the Taoiseach stood at a makeshift podium to make a speech. Within seconds, his speech sounded like a party-political broadcast, telling the nation about the sacrifices made by the government to get the people through this crisis. The politician made no mention of the sacrifices made by the men and women wearing the uniforms of medics, ambulance personnel, civil defence, armed services or police. The trojan work undertaken by civilian services also went unmentioned.

President Brosnin had enough. He approached the stage and physically pushed the Taoiseach away from the microphone. When the room quieted, the President took the floor.

"Before anyone suggests a speech by any government representative, let me remind you that you all did absolutely nothing to avert this crisis. It was left to the emergency services, Gardaí and the Army to put their own plan together, and they've been very successful under the circumstances. They were supported by civilians, thousands of transport workers, engineers and aid givers."

"We currently estimate that over 1 million people are dead on the island of Ireland. Another million are missing, presumed dead. The estimated death toll will rise, and it will take time to reach any survivors that there might be."

"We have no way of accessing imports – and that means that essential items such as medicines, fuel and food will become critically important and will need to be secured."

"As many of you know, we are only here speaking freely because of the Claíomh Solais, a gift brought to us by strangers, whose actions will become part of Irish folklore. They were ably assisted by a Dublin family, who despite the disaster, overcame adversity and helped the travellers complete their mission. That mission has culminated in clearing the skies over Ireland."

"As a result of their actions, we are now free to begin our recovery, but we face an imminent threat of invasion from forces unknown. Today, an attempt to steal the Claíomh Solais was made by a team of British commandos. This was the first attempt, but it will not be the last. Our country has been ravaged and even though the tsunami is over and the earth has settled, this crisis is not over. This is not the beginning of the end. It is the end of the beginning."

"It could have been a lot worse. The intervention of the travellers and their supporters has protected our environment and our people from the effects of the global catastrophe. I don't know how long this respite will last and what will happen if their device should fail but for now, I am thankful for their help, and they have the thanks of a grateful nation."

"Tomorrow is a new day. As head of state, I am ordering that the current government is disbanded. Tomorrow, we will form a government of the people. We will give experts the power to plan for what is to come – experts in defence, agriculture, transport, medicine, housing and science. They will put together practical plans to get us through the immediate future."

"Fellow Irish men and women, despite what is to come, tonight we have reason to celebrate."

The statement ended and the audience, not knowing what to do next, applauded and then milled about. Politicians crowded together in the corners of the function room, trying to figure out if the President had the power to disband the government. It did not matter – what was left of the Supreme Court supported the President, as did the Armed Forces, Gardaí and just about anyone who was not a politician.

The President asked for Jack, Peter, some engineering and physics lecturers that had been evacuated from Dublin, and the travellers and McNamara family to accompany him to a private dining room. When the hotel staff left, the President asked them all to sit.

"Morrigan, what happens next?" the President asked.

Morrigan thought for a moment before replying.

"The Claíomh Solais was designed to give temporary respite while phase two of our plan was implemented. As you can appreciate, we haven't had much time to think about phase two, so this is not a considered response."

"It is clear that we need back-up devices, located strategically around the world in order to mitigate the ash cloud completely. Devices need to be activated simultaneously throughout the northern and southern hemispheres. This means we need thousands of devices and cooperation from every nation on the planet. It's the only way to ensure that life on the planet survives."

"We are on a countdown. We have a matter of days to implement phase two of our plan before nature is irrevocably damaged."

"Before you ask, we don't have blueprints for the Claíomh Solais and even if we did, the circuitry could not be duplicated by your engineers even before the folding, so there is no point in trying to recreate it now."

"We do, however, have another option. That option is to locate the other three devices left for us by our fleet commander, Anu. You know of her by other names, including Dana. I believe she is a mythological figure in Ireland."

"It is imperative that the Claíomh Solais is kept safe until we can locate the rest of the technology and replicate the Sword of Light."

The room was awed but President Brosnin quickly reassured Morrigan that the President, the Gardaí and the Army would do everything possible to secure Sliabh an Iarainn and the treasure it held.

"Who are you?" Jack Kelly asked, "and where are you from?"

"I suppose you can think of us as Irish. We are a crew that travelled here to help you deal with the aftermath of the folding," Semias answered.

"Your technology is way more advanced than anything we currently have available to us, but you look like you stepped out of a history book. Are you from the past or the future?" the President persevered.

Esras took over.

"We come from a place where time is fluid. To answer you truthfully, we are from both."

Hands and voices raised around the room, but Semias stayed them.

"When this is over, we will share everything with you but right now, it will raise more questions and distract us from our mission. We are humans, we possess no superpowers per say. Well, maybe Etain has superpowers – that has yet to be determined. We have the same hopes and desires as you do. Eventually, when our work is done, we will use our technology to return to where we came from."

At Semias's last comment, Uiscias turned to look at Saoirse.

The President asked Morfessa why Semias referred to the natural disaster as the folding.

Morfessa shrugged.

"I don't know. I guess we had to call it something. The earth folded, so the folding seemed good enough. It just took hold with us."

The leaders around the table nodded.

"There has to be more to it than this surely," Peter Clancy commented.

Etain answered him.

"Of course there's more, sir. Don't you know your history, or have you forgotten that the Tuatha Dé Danann had four treasures?"

The room reverberated with the naming of the Tuatha Dé Danann.

"Yes, you heard right – the travellers' boss is Anu, the titular head of the Tuatha Dé Danann. The Claíomh Solais is recharging on Sliabh an Iarainn, but there are three more devices – or treasures, as legend records."

Morrigan laughed.

"You know, your legends are quite accurate, considering."

"Mr President, phase two of our mission is to locate the remaining artefacts. With them, we can find a way forward, not only for Ireland but for all countries. Time is of the essence. We might need some support if you can help."

The room was on its feet. The President laughed and grabbed Morrigan's hand.

"What sort of team do you need? We can get you historians, physicists, linguists, cartographers – just say the word. By presidential order, all resources available are yours for the taking."

Morrigan nodded in acknowledgement.

"It's just as well you said that. News of our success will spread fast. The next attack we face will not be as easy to overcome. Every power in your world will be aware of the Claíomh Solais by now. Your enemies will find a way to reach Irish shores. We will need the treasures of the Tuatha Dé Danann to keep your people safe."

The President guided Morrigan away to meet some of the experts amassed in the room, while the gathered mass broke into small knots of conversation.

Morfessa looked around at his team and smiled. They were clean but dressed like scarecrows. He thought of the royal-blue uniforms that his team had worn aboard ship.

Morfessa spotted Jack Kelly standing alone in deep thought. He approached and cleared his throat.

"Could we start by getting my team some decent uniforms and kit? We wear royal blue, not green."

Jack Kelly laughed and shouted that five royal-blue uniforms, complete with motifs drawn from the Claíomh Solais, would be with them within hours.

"Actually, I need ten uniforms: one for me; one for the Goddess of War, Morrigan, and one for Esras, the soldier and doctor; for Brendan, the engineer; for Muireann, the geographer; for Uiscias and Saoirse, the physicists; one for Semias the ... Shit! I don't know ... honourable; one for Sadbh, the badass and one for the superhuman Etain."

Peter Clancy, in good humour, pushed forward.

"Since you've decided to design yourselves new uniforms, what are we supposed to call you?"

Morfessa turned and addressed the nine others who had been drawn together by fate.

"Some of us are of the Tuatha Dé Danann, some of us are Dubliners. We are now one tribe. Together, we are Na Fianna."